Bufflehead Sisters

Patricia J. DeLois

Patricia J. DeLois
2-19-08

Published by www.YouWriteOn.com
An Arts Council England site

Published in 2007 by YouWriteOn.com

First Edition

ISBN 978-0-9556500-9-3

British Library C.I.P.
A CIP catalogue record for this title is available from the British Library.

Published by YouWriteOn.com

This book is dedicated to my readers
and to my friends,
and especially to my friends who read.

When you've come to feel that you're the only child
Take good care of your brother.

Jackson Browne

Chapter 1

I was an only child. My mother suffered several miscarriages before me, and a few more after me. She was hospitalized three times in the first five years of my life, although at the time, no one told me why. I knew only that she was sick, and that the doctors were making her better, and that while she was gone, my grandmother would be taking care of me. I hated it. I missed my mother, and my grandmother was, in my view, a poor substitute.

For someone who had seven kids of her own, Gram didn't seem particularly fond of children. Most of what she said to me was either criticism or a direct order, except at meals, when, under the guise of cooking instructions, she boasted endlessly about the lightness of her yeast rolls, the richness of her cheesecake, the special ingredients in her mince pie. It was true she was an excellent cook, although her portions were stingy, and there was no pleasure in eating her food when she sat watching my every bite as if she begrudged every morsel wasted on a child who didn't know the difference between mashed and whipped potatoes.

At that time—this would have been in the early 60s—children were not allowed to visit the hospital, so in the evenings, while Dad was with Mom, I had to stay home with Gram. She would sit in front of the TV and knit, and I generally tried to stay out of her line of vision, lest she find some new fault of mine that needed correction. She told time by the hours of her favorite programs, and she usually sent me to bed before Dad got home. I knew he would come to my room to talk to me as soon as he got home, but in the hours that I lay awake waiting for him, I was lonely.

One night Gram forgot to send me to bed. I think she forgot about me altogether in her excitement over her favorite show of all, the Lawrence Welk Show, featuring, as she always referred to him, Mr. Lawrence Welk Himself.

I wanted to see Mr. Lawrence Welk Himself, but I didn't want to draw attention to the fact that I was still up, so I crept into the room and sat quietly on the couch. Gram was sitting in my father's chair, and she didn't seem aware of my presence.

The Lawrence Welk show was not something she watched passively, as she did her other programs; the Lawrence Welk Show was something she participated in, singing along with the vocalists,

tapping her feet in time to the dance numbers, and using a knitting needle to conduct the orchestra pieces along with
Mr. Lawrence Welk Himself. And when Mr. Lawrence Welk Himself introduced the Lennon Sisters, Gram dropped her knitting and applauded.

She didn't sing along with the Lennon Sisters but listened in rapt silence, closing her eyes to better appreciate the harmonies.

And the harmonies were exquisite. I fell immediately in love with the Lennon Sisters—they looked and sounded like angels. As the camera panned across them, I marveled at the family resemblance, how, in their matching dresses, they somehow looked all alike and yet distinctively different. They were the perfect embodiment of their voices, separate and unique but combining to form one perfect, resonant whole. And the youngest one was named Janet, just like me.

I wanted sisters.

If I had sisters, we could sing together like that. We could appear on The Lawrence Welk Show and meet Mr. Lawrence Welk Himself. Maybe we could even sing for Mr. Ed Sullivan.

Sisters would share their toys and their clothes with me. We would fix each other's hair, and paint each other's nails, and tell each other secrets. If there were a thunderstorm, we would huddle together so we wouldn't be afraid.

If I had sisters, my favorite sister would share my room with me, and the others would sleep in the guest room, and then it wouldn't be a guest room any more, and my grandmother couldn't come and stay with us. And we wouldn't need her to take care of us anyway, because my sisters and I would take care of each other.

*

A few nights later, as Dad was tucking me in, I asked him how long you had to pray for something before it came true.

He smoothed my hair against my pillow. "Prayers aren't the same as wishes, honey, they don't just come true. God answers all our prayers, one way or another. Do you mind if I ask what you're praying for?"

"Sisters," I told him, "like the Lennon Sisters. I want sisters more than anything else in the world."

He cleared his throat. "God doesn't always give us what we want, Janet."

"Why not?"

"Sometimes the things we want aren't part of His plan. We have to accept that He knows what's best for us."

"But if He made me, why would He make me want sisters if I can't have them?"

"He works in mysterious ways, sweetheart."

I continued to pray, but I saw no signs of any sisters, and I began to withdraw some of my demands. Okay, not three sisters, maybe only two, and it's okay if they don't sing, we can do other things together. Eventually my praying became begging, and all I wanted was one, just one sister.

And He sent me Sophie.

*

I didn't actually meet Sophie so much as I had her pointed out to me. It was the first week of kindergarten, and our teacher, Mrs. Weed, had distributed to each of us a picture of a drum, instructing us in her imperious voice to find our red crayons and color the drum red.

Mrs. Weed was a tight-lipped woman, as tall and rigid as a ship mast, and she sailed at a stately pace as she navigated her way around our little tables, peering down at our work. Just at the point where I was tiring of the color red, Mrs. Weed commanded us to put down our crayons and direct our attention to Miss Sophie Prescott.

"Sophie, would you stand up, please?"

Sophie was only slightly taller standing than she had been sitting. She wore denim overalls and a dirty pink blouse. Her hair was a nest of blonde curls that made me think of Goldilocks, and there was a smug look about her mouth that suggested she might have already helped herself to someone's porridge and found it just right.

"Here," announced Mrs. Weed, "is a student who failed to follow directions." She held up Sophie's drum, which was colored— rather sloppily, I noticed—red with purple trim and green drumsticks.

"You were asked to color the drum red," Mrs. Weed reminded us. "Not red and purple, not red and purple and green, but red. Here is a student who did not listen to the directions, and she will not succeed in school if she does not learn to listen and to follow directions."

I cringed at the thought of being unsuccessful in school, and I stole a glance at Sophie's face, expecting to see my own mortification reflected there. But Sophie looked entirely unperturbed as she gazed around the classroom with her hands in her pockets, like someone who had just stopped by to see what a kindergarten class looked like. Her neon blue eyes met mine and she smiled as if she recognized me, as if we were already friends. Mrs. Weed's lecture was having so little perceptible impact on her that I thought she must be deaf, or stupid.

"Boys and girls, don't make the same mistake that this student has made. Listen carefully to directions, and do as you are told." Mrs. Weed concluded her demonstration by tearing Sophie's paper in half and dropping it in the wastebasket. "You may sit down now, Sophie."

Later, at playtime, I was pushing the plastic shopping cart around the room when I saw Sophie sitting on the floor holding the Fred Flintstone telephone to her ear.

"What's your name?" she asked me.

"Janet."

She held the phone out to me. "It's for you," she said. "I think it's your father."

*

My father was a high school biology teacher, which was fine with me as long as he wasn't teaching in my high school. Sophie and I dreamed for years of being teenagers and going to high school, and I didn't want the experience ruined by a father on the faculty. I felt sorry for kids in that situation, an extreme example being Bobby Hillerman, whose mother taught English at our junior high and whose father was our high school principal. For seven crucial years Bobby could not escape his parents' supervision at home or at school, and if adults often commented on what a nice young man he was, well, really, what choice did he have?

It wasn't that Dad was an embarrassment to me—in most contexts he was perfectly presentable. He had dark intelligent eyes and a warm smile which revealed a lovely dimple to the left of his mouth. His hair was full, an attractive mixture of salt and pepper. But he was also tall and lanky, with knobby wrists and a large Adam's apple, and in his white lab coat and black-framed glasses he looked like a nerd.

10

As dearly as I loved him, I would have been totally humiliated to have him stand up in front of my classmates and talk about reproduction.

Dad supplemented his income by illustrating books for children, mostly nonfiction, although eventually he did some picture books, sometimes using Sophie and myself as models. He liked pen and ink and watercolors, and his preferred subjects were flora and fauna. He loved birds, and he kept several birdhouses and feeders to ensure that they would always be present in our yard. His hero was John James Audubon.

Abandoned at birth by his presumably unwed mother, Dad was placed with the Sisters of Mercy outside of Boston. The sisters christened him John Francis Regis, after the patron saint of illegitimate children, whose feast day happened to be the same day Dad arrived at the orphanage, June 16th. No one knew exactly when he'd been born, and so he was assigned that date as his birthday.

Raised by nuns and later educated by Jesuits, Dad believed he owed his life to the charity of the Catholic Church, and he became a lifelong doer of good deeds. He left Boston and settled in central Maine, where he volunteered twice a week at the soup kitchen, ran errands for the sick and the elderly, and donated regularly to the blood bank. Every Christmas he took me with him to deliver toys to the local orphanage.

Dad had nearly gone into the priesthood himself. He admired the brothers, and he felt he owed them a debt of gratitude, but all his prayers and meditations led to the same conclusion: he wanted a family of his own.

"And then I met your mother," he told me, "and I knew my prayers had been answered."

Dad told me all the time how special I was, and what a blessing, and I grew to understand that this was because his prayers were only partially answered. He and Mom had wanted a large family, but she had so many miscarriages, each more devastating than the last, that she finally lost heart and could not bear to try again. Despite her own Catholicism, she had her tubes tied. I was the only child she would have. My father urged adoption, but my mother believed she could never truly love a child that wasn't her own. Dad was surprised to discover that he'd married a woman who felt this way, but he counted his blessings and accepted her decision, or so he said. He loved my mother, and he didn't regret marrying her, but he couldn't help feeling that their love was slightly diminished by the boundaries she placed upon it.

My mother, on the other hand, felt their love was dissipated by my father's spreading it around to every hard luck case in town. She was constantly reminding him that charity begins at home; she resented the time he spent helping people who weren't even family.

If my mother bears any responsibility for what happened—and I'm not saying she does—it's only because of this: her definition of family was just too narrow.

Chapter 2

A few weeks into the kindergarten year, my mother asked me if I'd like to invite one of my school friends to come over and play on Saturday, and I chose Sophie. I got her phone number from her, and Mom called her house and spoke to Sophie's father, who took our address and agreed to drop Sophie off.

"Do you know who they are?" Mom said to Dad when she got off the phone. "It's Dr. Prescott and his wife Louise."

Dad shook his head to indicate that he still didn't know who they were, and Mom told me to go play in the study, which was what she did when she wanted to talk about people's marriages. It seemed unfair that I should always be excluded from these conversations, since I was expected to get married myself some day, but Mom said there were things I wouldn't understand. How could I, I wondered, if no one would ever tell me? Why did adults have to keep so many secrets, and when would I be old enough to know?

I retreated to the study. I left the door ajar, hoping to overhear whatever Mom knew about Sophie's family—and she seemed to know a lot—but she kept her voice low, and all I heard was that Louise had married one of her father's friends.

I thought about some of my father's friends—people he worked with, people with whom he served on church committees, fellow birdwatchers. They were probably all different ages, but to me they were adults and so, by definition, old. Some were fat, some were muscular, some were hairier than others, and they smelled like cigarettes, or cigars, or shoe polish. None of them seemed like anyone I would want to marry, and I could only conclude that Sophie's mother had been married off, like a princess, as part of some type of property arrangement.

This was in keeping with my idea of Sophie as an extraordinary person, different from my other friends. It wouldn't have surprised me to learn that she had a destiny, a fate all her own; perhaps she was royalty, and she didn't even know it.

*

When the doorbell rang on Saturday morning, Mom was surprised to find Sophie standing alone on our front steps, dressed in the same soiled blouse and overalls I recognized from school.

"I thought your Daddy would bring you in," Mom said. "Where is he?"

"He went to work," Sophie said. "Are you Janet's mother?"

"Yes," Mom said, "come in."

"Did you used to have Janet in your stomach?"

Mom ignored the question and turned to me. "Why don't you show your friend around the house?"

I took Sophie's hand and led her into the living room.

"Oh! You have a pin-ano," she breathed.

"A piano, you mean. Do you want to play it?"

"You *play* it?"

"Of course. That's what a piano's *for*. My mother's teaching me."

I climbed up on the bench and opened my lesson book. Sophie scrambled up beside me and watched in apparent rapture as I played a simple tune I had mastered, something about Dutch children and tulips.

When I was done, she asked me to play another one, and then another, and another. When I had played every song I knew twice and her enthusiasm had not waned at all, I reminded her that she still hadn't seen the rest of my house. She lagged behind me as I led her out of the living room, and I turned at the door to wait for her. She was walking slowly backwards, obviously reluctant to let the piano out of her sight. She stopped and looked over her shoulder at me, and then she ran back to the piano. She reached out with one small finger and hit one note on the keyboard, and then she laughed and ran back to me, and we resumed our tour.

We ended up in my room, where, at her insistence, I showed her everything I owned—my Barbies, my dollhouse, my crayons and colored pencils—and she had to touch every item, as if she needed proof of its substance. We played together until noon, when Mom called us downstairs for lunch.

We were in our seats at the kitchen table and Mom was serving up tomato soup with grilled cheese sandwiches when Dad came in from the back yard.

14

"You must be Sophie," he said. "I would shake your hand, but I've been cleaning up after the birds."

She gazed up at him as he washed and dried his hands at the kitchen sink. I suppose he must have been the tallest person she'd ever seen, even taller than Mrs. Weed. Her eyes grew wider—in fear, I thought—as he reached for her hand, but when he touched her she broke into a radiant smile.

"Are you John?" she asked.

The question seemed to amuse him. "Yes, I am, and I assume you've met my wife Helen?"

She nodded.

He released her hand and bent down to kiss me on the head.

"Are you girls having fun?"

"I like your pin-ano," Sophie said.

"She means the piano," I said.

"Ah," said Dad. "Marvelous."

Mom sat down with us. "Do you have a piano at your house, Sophie?"

"No." She shook her head. "We *used* to have a pin-ano," she added conversationally, "but Mama broke it."

"She broke it?"

Sophie nodded. "She hit it with the ax."

We all froze and looked at each other, but Sophie went on eating her soup.

"She hit it with the ax?" Mom repeated, and Sophie nodded again.

"She was mad at Daddy." She poked her finger into her sandwich and asked, "What's this?"

"It's grilled cheese," I told her. "We always have grilled cheese with tomato soup."

"This is tomatoes?"

"Haven't you ever had this before?"

She hadn't.

"What do you eat at home?" Mom asked.

"Cereal," Sophie said. "I can make cereal. I make it with *milk*."

"What else do you eat?" Mom prompted.

"Bananas, and apples, and raisins. And I can cook toast," she said proudly.

"I like toast," I told her.

"Do you cook it in the toaster?"

"Mom and Dad do."

Mom got up to make more sandwiches. "Do your parents cook, Sophie?"

"Sometimes Daddy makes my cereal and juice," she said. "Mrs. Albright cooks dinner."

"Oh, is that your housekeeper?"

"Yes. She cleans the house and does the wash, and she tells me to play in my room when Mama's resting because she's not a babysitter."

My parents exchanged a look.

"I play in my room, too," I said. "What do you play?"

She drew pictures, she said, and she painted, but not on the walls, she would never do that again. She sang and danced, and looked at books, and she talked to the people who lived in her head.

"And I have penguins," she said.

"In your room?" Dad asked.

"Not in my *room*." She looked at him as if he were being deliberately stupid. "You can't keep penguins in your room. You have to keep them in the bathtub."

Mom laughed. "Are you telling stories, dear?"

"Yes. Once there was a little penguin, and she got lost, and I found her. I take care of her, and then her brothers and sisters came, because their parents were mean to them, and they live with me, too." She glanced at Dad. "In my *bathtub*," she added pointedly. "I take care of them, and I teach them tricks. They're trick penguins, and they're going to be in my circus."

She went on to describe her circus, a grand production of which she was to be the star, a combination trapeze artist/lion tamer/ringmaster. She was currently designing costumes for the monkeys, and she'd been thinking that if she got rid of some of her bedroom furniture, she might have room for a few elephants. After all, she wouldn't need a bed if she could sleep on top of a pile of elephants.

When she finished her recitation we were all speechless.

"Well," Dad finally said, "it's good to have plans for the future. Is that what you're going to be when you grow up, a circus performer?"

16

"No." Sophie turned to Dad with her milk mustache and her electric blue eyes. "When I grow up, I'm going to be a giraffe."

*

Later, after Sophie had gone home, after I'd had my bath and put on my cowgirl pajamas, I was coming downstairs and I heard my parents' voices in the living room.

"—very peculiar people," Mom was saying.

I came into the room and saw her sitting in her chair under the floor lamp, taking down the hem of my favorite winter skirt, a red plaid wool with a black velvet waistband. She saw me and said, "This is the last year you're going to be able to wear this."

Dad set his book down next to his chair. "Ah, Janet, we were just talking about your enchanting little friend. And what a charming girl you must be to have made such a delightful friend. Did you enjoy your visit?"

I nodded, and he lifted me onto his lap.

"We'll have to invite her back, then," he said.

"Yes," said Mom, "but perhaps you have some other friends, too, that you'd like to bring home."

"I have other friends at school," I said, "but I like Sophie best."

"She's a pearl in a sea of oysters," Dad said.

"Can we take her to the duck pond?"

"Of course we can, sweetheart, that's a marvelous idea."

He seemed so pleased with me that I began to feel proud, as if I had, in fact, discovered a treasure, a thing of rare and exquisite beauty, a thing which I'd had the good taste to bring home as a gift for my family.

Chapter 3

Sophie came to our house often after that first visit, usually on Saturdays, but sometimes after school as well. She adored my father and his birds. She had less to say to my mother, but she appreciated Mom's cooking as no one had ever appreciated it before.

Mom could not abide a fussy eater, as she reminded me every time I questioned the ingredients in her casseroles, but even Mom was alarmed by Sophie's appetite.

"Don't they feed her?" she would say when Sophie was gone. "She eats like she was raised by wolves."

"Now, Helen—" Dad said, but Mom wanted answers.

"What kind of people raise their children like animals? For God's sake, John, look at her. Look at her clothes, look at her hair, and she won't keep shoes on her feet. Doesn't anyone *care* for her?"

But Mom was never one to complain about a situation when she could do something about it, and she began a campaign to civilize Sophie.

She started with lectures about the proper use of the fork. At first Sophie gave her the vacant stare she'd been practicing on Mrs. Weed, but she must have figured Mom's cooking was worth a trade-off, because she decided to conform to Mom's standards of behavior at the dinner table.

Soon Mom was bathing her and dressing her in clothes I'd outgrown. She washed her hair and made her sit still while she combed the snarls out of it. She gave Sophie a toothbrush to keep at our house, and she taught her how to use it. She conquered Sophie's barbarism on all fronts, except one. Even Mom could not keep shoes on Sophie's feet.

*

My mother was trained as a nurse, and she met my father while he was donating blood. He donated regularly and they saw each other often. He was shy and awkward, but she sensed an intelligence and a depth of emotion that most of her suitors lacked, and she loved it when he smiled and flashed that dimple at her. He began hanging around for a second cup of orange juice after he had donated, and he and Mom talked, but he did not ask her out.

"I was starting to think maybe he didn't like girls," she told me, "but I figured nothing ventured, nothing gained, and I finally asked him if he wanted to go out for coffee with me."

"Did you know he was going to be a priest?" I asked. I had always assumed that a priest made a great sacrifice when he promised never to marry. I hadn't known there were men who didn't like women, but if there were such men, I thought, the priesthood must be the perfect place for them.

"Oh, I knew he wasn't going to be a *Jesuit*," Mom said. "If they'd been Franciscans, I might have worried, but I knew he was no Jesuit."

*

My mother was the oldest of seven children, and while her mother was busy perfecting her pie crusts, Mom was largely responsible for taking care of her siblings, four sisters and two brothers. She fed them, she sewed for them, she tended their various ailments and injuries. She had little time for self-improvement, but she took piano lessons, which she then gave to each of the children in turn.

Mom played the piano the same way she did everything— competently, with no flourishes or embellishments. From the time I was five she gave me lessons twice a week, and I had to practice every day. I tried to lure Sophie into lessons, too, but she had no patience for practicing scales, and Mom had no patience for her. In the end, I managed to teach Sophie to hold up her end of a few simple duets, but mostly she preferred to listen, sometimes making up dances as I played.

My personal favorite was Bach, with his intricate themes and variations. Sophie was in awe of anything I could play, but she seemed especially fond of Mozart. My mother didn't take anyone seriously except Beethoven, and although she was generally pleased with my progress and my ability, I could never play the Moonlight Sonata to her satisfaction.

"Gently, Janet, gently," she would say. "This piece requires control." But there was a passion and a yearning in those minor chords that appealed to my sense of drama, and try as I might, I could not restrain myself.

"You're turning it into melodrama," Mom would say. "This isn't Tchaikovsky, dear, this is Beethoven. It should be understated."

And she would demonstrate, playing in such a controlled manner as to seem inhuman, but I had to admit, the effect was devastating, if not downright maddening. It never failed to move my father, who claimed that he decided to marry Mom the first time he heard her play it.

"She was so beautiful," he told me, "and I wanted to marry a woman who could play moonlight."

*

At school, Sophie continued to infuriate Mrs. Weed with her careless attitude and her disregard for authority. As the year went on Mrs. Weed became more openly hostile and more obviously determined to break Sophie, but no matter how often she used Sophie as a bad example, no matter how severely she punished her, Sophie never once expressed regret or remorse. She seemed to be constantly standing with her nose against the blackboard, or sitting with her head down on her desk. She was banished to the hallway, excluded from playtime, deprived of all the rewards and privileges that more obedient students enjoyed. None of it fazed her.

Then one day while Mrs. Weed was berating Sophie for her lack of attention, Sophie yawned. Mrs. Weed snapped and slapped her across the face. For a moment Sophie didn't respond, and we all held our breath. Then Sophie flung herself full force at Mrs. Weed, grabbed her by the arm, and bit her, hard enough to make Mrs. Weed scream. Mrs. Weed wrestled Sophie into her arms and carried her down the hall to the principal's office.

The rest of us looked at each other, speechless, until Linda Roberts started to cry, and Walter Thompson said he was going to sneak down to the office and find out what was going on.

He returned a few minutes later to report that the office door was closed, but he had distinctly heard Mrs. Weed yelling, calling Sophie a vicious little animal and a hateful little bitch. The school secretary was on the phone trying to get one or the other of Sophie's parents to come and pick her up, but so far, Walter said, there were no takers.

Neither Mrs. Weed nor Sophie returned to class that day. The school librarian came and read stories to us for the rest of the afternoon.

Sophie was suspended for a week for biting Mrs. Weed, and when she returned, her behavior was no different. She still embellished her pictures with extra colors, she still finished her workbook pages before Mrs. Weed was done giving instructions, she still drew pictures or stared out the window while Mrs. Weed was talking, but now Mrs. Weed ignored her. She seemed to have taken the position that Sophie didn't exist.

One day in late winter, Sophie suggested we dig our way to another country. Not China, she said—they would look for us there. We would dig a hole halfway to China, and then we would veer off toward Amsterdam.

"They have penguins there," she said.

There had recently been a thaw; most of the snow was gone but the ground had frozen again, and our project got off to a slow start. We were chipping away at the earth with our shovels when suddenly Sophie stopped. I looked up and followed her gaze to Walter Thompson. The see-saws had been removed for the winter, and Walter was leaning over the empty crossbar watching us.

"You're doing that wrong," he said. "What you need is some dynamite."

"Do you have any?" Sophie asked.

"I might."

He strolled over and circled us while we continued to work, but he was a boy, and he looked dirty and he smelled dirty, and I ignored him. He could have all the dynamite in the world, I thought, but there was no way we were taking him to Amsterdam with us.

Finally he stood still, and he stared at Sophie until she looked up at him again.

"You're a hateful little bitch," he said.

"So?" she retorted.

"You bit Mrs. Weed."

Sophie stood up, drawing herself to her full height, which was about level with Walter's shoulder. She narrowed her eyes threateningly.

"I could bite you, too," she said.

"I wouldn't be surprised if you did. Mrs. Weed says you're a vicious little animal."

"Maybe I am."

He nodded. "I think you are," he said, and then the corner of his mouth twitched and a grin spread slowly across his face.

Sophie grinned back.

"Watch this," he said, and he startled me by letting out an unearthly howl. He clapped his right hand over his left wrist and ran away from us, shouting, "Mrs. Weed, Mrs. Weed, Sophie bit me! She's a vicious little animal! She bit me!"

I gasped and turned to Sophie, prepared to offer myself as a witness for the defense, but to my surprise she was laughing.

"Sophie!" Mrs. Weed shouted, and Sophie collapsed onto her bottom, giggling helplessly.

I watched as Mrs. Weed bent over Walter and inspected his wrist. Then she examined his other wrist, and then she said, her clarion tone ringing across the playground, "Walter Thompson, you're a liar," and she sent him to the picnic table to sit with his head down for the rest of playtime.

It wasn't clear to me exactly what had transpired, but from that day on, Walter and Sophie were friends.

*

The best thing about playing with Sophie was that she always let me be the princess. I was Snow White, I was Cinderella, I was Sleeping Beauty, while Sophie played all the supporting roles. She was an earnest dwarf and a valiant prince, but the roles she relished most were the magicians—the fairy godmothers and the evil sorceresses. She didn't enjoy being wicked, and in fact she wasn't very good at it, always breaking character to assure me that she wasn't really going to kill me, just put me to sleep for a while. What she really loved was the business of mixing potions and casting spells, and she held up the game for long periods of time as she gathered ingredients and concocted potions and chanted over her cauldron, which was one of Dad's birdbaths.

When she wasn't poisoning me or otherwise plotting my demise, she gave me sincere advice on how to conduct myself. I must always be kind and patient and sweet and generous, because you never know when a wizard might be testing you, and good people attract good magic, making them less susceptible to bad magic, not that she herself would ever practice any bad magic, certainly not on me.

It was hard to tell sometimes when she was playing and when she was serious, because she had a habit of blurring the line between fantasy and reality, but she was serious about this. She believed in magic, and not just theoretically. She believed she *was* magic, and sometimes I believed it, too.

There were times when we looked at each other, as I imagined sisters did, knowing that we were both thinking the same thought. But there was more to it than that. She knew things without being told. She often announced a telephone call moments before the phone rang, and just as often she could tell you who it was and what they wanted. Once she described for Dad exactly where he was and what he was doing the first time he saw a cardinal.

"That's true," he said in amazement. "I remember that."

Sophie nodded. "I remember, too."

"How could you remember?" he asked. "That was twenty years before you were born."

Sophie shrugged. She couldn't explain it; she just knew what she knew.

*

One summer day as we were finishing our picnic at the beach, two seagulls landed nearby and eyed our food. Sophie tore off a piece of bread and held it out to them, but Dad said, "Seagulls aren't like the ducks at the pond, honey, they won't take it from your hand."

"Don't feed them," Mom said.

Sophie raised her arm to throw the bread, and Mom said again, "No, Sophie, don't," but a second later the bread was on the ground and the two birds were squabbling over it, and suddenly we were surrounded by seagulls. They filled the air above us and they covered the ground around us, and they kept coming, hundreds of them, it seemed, coming from miles around, gliding down to earth, landing silently and standing at eerie attention. That was the weirdest thing about them, not how many there were but how quietly they stood watching us. Years later, when I saw the Hitchcock movie The Birds, I would remember this.

"This is why you shouldn't feed them," Mom said. "Now they won't leave us alone."

But Sophie was delighted.

"They came to see me," she said, and she tore up the rest of her sandwich and threw it to them as if she were a queen tossing coins to the poor, bestowing gifts on her beloved subjects. Dad and I contributed the remainders of our lunch as well—mine had sand in it anyway—and when we had no more food to give them, the gulls stayed and continued to stare at us.

"You see?" Mom said. "Look what you've done. Now they won't go away."

"I'll just tell them," Sophie said. "They'll listen to me." She held up her empty hands and addressed the birds. "It's all gone," she told them. She waved her hands in a shooing motion. "Go on, now, fly away."

And they did. In one great rustle of wings, the gulls lifted themselves off the ground in unison and flew away, every last one of them.

Mom and Dad looked at each other with raised eyebrows. He shrugged.

"How did you do that?" I asked Sophie.

"I speak bird."

Mom shook her head. "You're a strange little girl."

"My Nana says I'm special," Sophie told her.

"Yes," Mom said, "that's what I meant."

Chapter 4

Just after we started first grade, Sophie's mother got mad at her Daddy again, and this time, Sophie said, "she broke the house."

She had picked up the fire poker and gone systematically through every room in the house, smashing mirrors, lamps, dishes, windows—whatever was breakable got broken.

At first it sounded pretty, Sophie said. The tinkle of glass from a faraway room was like music, like her Nana's wind chimes, and for a while she sat at the top of the stairs and listened, but as her mother got closer, the noise got scarier, and finally Sophie fled to her room, where she grabbed Bobo the stuffed elephant and crawled under her bed to hide.

"Bobo was scared," she told us, "but he couldn't cry because we had to be very quiet."

She stayed under her bed while her mother attacked her room, and she stayed there long after her mother had moved on, and even after the house had grown quiet, and eventually she fell asleep, resting her head on Bobo.

It was dark when she woke up and heard her Daddy calling to her. He was in her room with a flashlight, and after ascertaining that she wasn't hurt, he told her to stay where she was for a few more minutes. She heard glass crunching under his feet as he moved around her room.

"Where's Mama?" she asked.

"She's gone away for a while."

Sophie didn't know how long a while was, but she hoped it was long enough.

She listened as her father opened and closed her dresser drawers.

"What are you doing, Daddy?"

"I'm packing a suitcase for you," he said.

"Am I going away, too?" she asked, and that's when he told her she was going to stay at Janet's house for a while.

"And then I was happy," she told us, "because Bobo likes it here. Is a while a short time or a long time?"

"A while is an indeterminate amount of time," Dad said, "meaning we don't know how long it will be. We'll just have to wait and see."

"I hope it's a long time," Sophie said.

And so she came to live with us, and at last I had a sister.

*

"Janet's a bufflehead."

"Sophie's a yellow-bellied sapsucker."

This was our new favorite game: birds. We pored over my father's bird books as if we were shopping in a catalog, looking for the most resplendent feathers, the funniest-looking beaks, the most ridiculous names, and now we were goofing at the dinner table.

"Janet's a chachalacha." This one always made us laugh.

My father laughed with us, but Mom told us to stop giggling and eat our vegetables. "And stop calling each other names."

"Herman Nelson called me a cuckoo-baby," Sophie told her.

"Is that supposed to be funny?"

"No. He said my Mama is a cuckoo-bird, and that makes me a cuckoo-baby."

I noticed what she failed to mention: Herman said it loudest and most often, but he wasn't the only kid saying it.

"It sounds to me," Dad said, "like this Herman Nelson doesn't know what he's talking about."

Sophie gave a happy little bounce in her chair, an indication that she had suspected as much and was pleased to have Dad's confirmation.

"Herman Nelson is a tufted titmouse," she said.

*

That year, Sophie accompanied us on our annual trip to the orphanage when Dad delivered toys that had been donated through the church.

The orphanage was a large old house, a beautiful house, although not well kept up—the gray cabbage rose wallpaper was peeling in the hallway, and paint was flaking off the radiators, which hissed and groaned as they struggled to heat rooms with high ceilings. The entire place smelled like the cafeteria at school, like boiled vegetables. But I admired the wainscoting, and the French doors, and the rooms that could only be described as parlors. Sophie and I were left in one of these rooms, on a couch facing the Christmas tree, while Dad went into another room with Sister Albert.

The orphans' Christmas tree had no lights. It was green but spindly, with just enough branches to support a few strings of popcorn and cranberries, some candy canes, and several clumps of tinsel. Beneath the tree there were no presents, only the bare wooden floor on which someone had scattered some straw and set up a small manger scene.

There didn't seem to be any orphans about, and I was relieved. I usually stayed close to my father during these visits, because the orphans made me nervous. I don't know how old I was when Dad told me about his upbringing, but I was old enough to have formed an impression about orphans: they were associated with widows, people whose unfortunate status was defined by someone's death. A sad but simple fact. It surprised me to learn that an orphan's parents might still be alive. I knew how much my parents wanted me, and the notion that some of these children were unwanted made me tongue-tied around them. I pitied them.

So I was glad they weren't around, and glad Sophie was with me in case they showed up.

"I want to see something," she said, and she squirmed off the couch and knelt down to inspect the figures at the crèche. She picked up a piece of straw and poked at the manger.

"His diaper's painted on," she reported.

"You shouldn't be trying to look under Jesus's diaper," I told her.

"I just wanted to see. Hey, there's only two sheep here. Where's the other animals?"

She looked over her shoulder and addressed a group of five or six children who had clustered in the doorway to look at us. I hadn't noticed them.

"Don't you have any other animals?"

No one answered.

"There should be a cow, and a donkey, and a camel," she said. "What happened to them?"

One boy shuffled his feet, and a girl with curly brown hair wiped her nose on the sleeve of her flannel shirt. None of them spoke.

"Baby Jesus loves animals," Sophie said, and she reached into the pocket of her overalls and produced a plastic kangaroo, which she placed in the hay just to the left of the Virgin Mary. I had seen that kangaroo before—it belonged to the Noah's Ark set at school.

The curly-haired girl said, "I know where there's some horses."

"Baby Jesus loves horses," Sophie said.

The girl elbowed her way through the crowd and returned a minute later to give Sophie three horses—one grazing, one galloping, and one trying to buck a cowboy off its back.

Sophie arranged them around the manger, and then a blonde girl with chapped lips remembered where there were some circus animals, and within minutes all the orphans were scrambling around the house fetching animals and pictures of animals, and everything they found they presented to Sophie, who suddenly seemed to be co-hosting a Christmas party with Baby Jesus. I sat forgotten on the couch and watched in amazement as she laughed and chattered and made herself at home. By the time we left, all the orphans were Sophie's friends.

*

After we left the orphanage, Dad tucked us in the back seat and drove us around for a while to look at the Christmas lights.

"They're pretty," Sophie said, but she lacked her usual enthusiasm. Despite the rollicking good time she'd had at the orphanage, she was uncharacteristically pensive. She was so quiet that Dad asked if she was asleep.

"I'm not asleep," she said, "I'm thinking."

"What are you thinking about, sweetheart?"

"John, am I an orphan?"

"No, honey, an orphan is someone who has no parents."

"But one boy asked me if I was going to stay there. He said if my house was broken I could stay there. Then would I be an orphan?"

Dad glanced at her in the rearview mirror. "Do you think you'd like to stay there?"

"It's nice," she said. "There's lots of kids, and they all gave their toys to Baby Jesus. But you gave them some new toys, right, John? So they'll have a nice Christmas, right?"

"Yes, honey, but—Are you thinking you'd *like* to be an orphan?"

"Maybe, if I couldn't stay with you."

"Well, sweetheart, of course you *can* stay with us, but you know eventually you're going to go home with your parents. Isn't that what you want, Sophie?"

"I want to stay with you." She said it so softly it might have been a prayer, and I saw Dad glance in the rearview mirror again, but I thought he must not have heard her, because he never answered her.

*

I loved having a little sister. We were almost exactly the same age—I was born on January 28th, and she was born on February 2nd—but she wore my hand-me-downs, and she was easily persuaded to play my favorite games, and I'm sure at times I patronized her, caught up in my role as big sister. I initiated her into the routines of our household, and gave her advice on how to fit in. She seemed to irritate my mother frequently, and I must have told her a thousand times that they'd get along better if Sophie would just learn to keep her shoes on, but she wouldn't.

We went to school together every morning, and came home together every afternoon. We were the Bufflehead Sisters, and we were inseparable. After school I had to practice my piano, but then we played together until dinner time, we bathed and brushed our teeth together, and then one of my parents would read to us until bedtime.

It was usually Dad, which suited us fine. Mom would get bored and try to skip pages, thinking we wouldn't notice, and she read every story in the same disinterested monotone. Dad gave dramatic readings, using a different voice for each character. He gave us thundering giants, bellowing trolls, and simpering stepsisters. His tigers roared and his roosters crowed. His foxes were sly, his witches were wicked, and his big bad wolves were bad to the bone. We would curl up in our pajamas, one on each side of him, and lean against his chest, where we could feel the rhythm of the story in the rise and fall of his breath. I heard him tell Mom one day that he liked to keep Sophie on his left side, because his heartbeat calmed her down and put her to sleep.

As a result of Dad's nightly performances, Sophie and I were mad about books, and when we started learning to read, he took us to the library on Saturday mornings and let us choose our own. I still had a preference for the princesses and the mermaids, but Sophie read more broadly than I did, and she introduced new characters into our play. She was particularly fond of Tikki-Tikki-Tembo, and we hauled some old tires out of the garage and stacked them up to make a well, and then we took turns falling in and running to get the Old Man With the Ladder.

We had to wait until we were seven to get our own library cards, and we counted the days. Dad had promised that each of us, on our seventh birthday, would get a special trip to the library to sign our application forms and receive our cards. He kept his promise, and when it was Sophie's turn, he lied and said that she was his daughter, because parental permission was required for a children's card. While Sophie was checking out her books, I asked Dad if it wasn't wrong for him to lie about being Sophie's father, and that's when he taught me the phrase, "for all practical purposes."

At home that night, as Mom was clearing away the dinner dishes, she asked if anyone at school had done anything special for Sophie's birthday.

Sophie nodded. "Everybody sang Happy Birthday to Me, and Mrs. Tucker gave me a new box of crayons."

"That wasn't for your birthday," I told her. "She just gave you a new box of crayons because you ate yours."

"Just some of them. Anyway, I got some *new* crayons, and Walter gave me a piece of his Tootsie Roll, and Herman Nelson showed me his peanuts."

Oh, no, I thought.

"Light the candles," I urged my mother.

Sophie's cake was on display in the middle of the table, on my mother's crystal cake stand, a white cake with white frosting, her favorite, decorated with purple and green icing at her request.

"Don't you want us to sing to you?" I asked her. "Don't you want to make a wish?"

"I wish I could see Herman's peanuts again."

"Is there something special about Herman's peanuts?" Dad asked.

"No," she said, and she started to giggle. "They're really little. Not like Daddy's."

Mom had picked up the matches to light the cake, but now she put them down again. "Sophie, what exactly did Herman show you?"

"His *peanuts*. You know, those things that boys have?"

"She's talking about his penis," I said.

30

"Janet," my mother said, "I don't like you using those words."

Dad's dimple flashed as he tried to suppress a smile. "Would you rather she called them peanuts?"

Sophie turned to me. "Did I tell you it was soft and wiggly?"

"You touched it?" I asked.

A look of dread crossed Mom's face. "*Did* you?"

Sophie demonstrated with one finger. "I just poked it, like this."

"Oh, my God, stop right there," Mom said. She took several deep breaths and smoothed the tablecloth in front of her. It was Sophie's favorite tablecloth, in honor of her birthday, the yellow one with chickens on it.

Mom turned to me and asked, "Where you there when this happened?"

"No."

She turned back to Sophie. "Did that boy touch you?"

"No."

"Did you show him your private parts?"

"No, because it was *my* birthday, and anyway, he already saw mine yesterday because I forgot to wear underpants, so today I got to see his peanuts."

"Penis," I said.

"Enough," Mom said. "We're going to change the subject, but before we do—"

"They're just curious, Helen," Dad said.

Mom glared at him. "I don't ever want to hear that you girls are showing your private parts to other people, and you should not be looking at anyone else's, especially boys'. Do you know what private means? It means you keep it to yourself. Those parts are just for you and your husband. Nobody else."

"What about your doctor?" I asked.

"And sometimes your doctor," Mom amended. She reached for the matches, ready to light the candles and move on.

"What about Daddy?" Sophie asked.

"Yes, sometimes daddies."

"What about Nana?"

Mom sighed. "Close family members may see each other's bodies if there's a good reason for it, which, by the way, forgetting

31

your panties is not a good reason, Sophie, and I hope that's not going to happen again."

"Can I have my cake now?" Sophie asked, and Mom lit the candles and turned out the lights and we all sang Happy Birthday, and Sophie sang along with us. She made her wish and blew out the candles, standing on her chair to reach the cake.

Mom cut the cake and passed it around.

"I wished I could see Herman's peanuts again," Sophie informed her. "And anyway, if you didn't make me wear a dress, nobody would know if I had underpants or not."

"That subject is closed," Mom said. "You just make sure your private parts remain covered."

"It's not so important now," Dad said, "but as you get older you'll want to be more private about your body. You'll understand."

My father had explained this to me, and I was happy to be in a position to enlighten Sophie. I said, "Private parts are special because that's where you get babies from."

She looked at me blankly. "Babies come out of their mother's stomachs," she said. "Besides, you didn't see Herman's peanuts. There's no way he could have a baby in there."

"And now," Mom said, "we *will* change the subject."

Dad pushed his cake aside. He propped his elbows on the table and folded his hands in front of his mouth, the way he did when he was thinking, or praying.

"Perhaps Sophie and I should have a talk after dinner," he said.

I felt a sudden tension that stretched across the table between my parents. Sophie was busy lapping the frosting off her fork, but she was watching them, too.

In a low voice, Mom said, "John, don't you dare."

The tension increased. They seemed to be having some kind of a staring contest, a silent argument. I could hear Dad's cuckoo clock ticking in his study.

Finally I said, "I'll tell her."

"It's not your place," Mom said, and I wasn't sure if she was talking to me, or to Dad, or to both of us.

"Where's my place?" Dad asked. "What am I, a bystander? An observer?"

"She has parents."

Dad looked around, miming a search for Sophie's parents. He turned to Sophie and said, "Honey, if I may ask, what have your parents told you about your genitals?"

"My geninals?"

"Your private parts," I interpreted.

"Mama says don't touch yourself there."

"Anything else?" Dad asked.

"Nice girls don't play with themselves."

"That's true," Mom said.

"What have they told you about babies?" Dad asked.

"Mama says don't have them, they'll drive you crazy."

Mom and Dad exchanged a look.

"They're more trouble than they're worth," Sophie added.

Mom gasped. "Sophie, that's not true!"

Sophie shrugged, not really concerned.

Mom nodded at Dad. "Okay," she said, "talk to her."

*

One day in April I was practicing my piano, and Sophie was standing on her head on the couch listening to me. Suddenly she let out a squeal and tumbled off the couch. The phone rang, and she ran to the kitchen shouting, "That's Daddy!"

Mom answered the phone, and it was indeed Dr. Prescott. He said he was planning to take Sophie to her grandmother's for April vacation, and at the end of the week she would return home, and her mother would be there.

My heart sank. Mom had been reminding us periodically that this arrangement was only temporary, but I had liked to pretend otherwise, and except for that one wistful moment at Christmas time, Sophie never mentioned any thoughts she might have had about going home.

At dinner Mom broke the news to Dad, and although he tried to cover it up, I think he was just as crestfallen as I was.

"Well," he said, "that's—that's just marvelous, Sophie, are you excited?"

She nodded enthusiastically. "Daddy says I have a new room, and Mama won't break it this time because she's all better."

"That *is* good news," Dad said. "What do you think, Janet?"

33

"It's good news for Sophie. It's bad news for me. I'll miss her."

Sophie said, "But maybe I can still come to your house sometimes."

"Of course," Dad said. "Anytime."

"It's not the same," I said. "We can't really be sisters if we don't live in the same house."

"That was just pretend," Sophie said. "We can still pretend."

"But you won't be here," I pointed out.

"Pretend I am," she said.

Chapter 5

"Janet, what are you doing?"

Mom stood with her hands on her hips, squinting up into the oak tree at us.

"Nothing, Mom, just playing."

We were eight, and we still played together every Saturday. Sophie had been back at her parents' house for over a year, and as far I knew, things were going all right. Mom often asked her prying questions about how things were at home, but Sophie was vague and noncommittal.

"Come down from there, both of you. I want to know what you're doing with my sheets and blankets, and, oh my God, Janet, is that my good linen tablecloth?"

"We're building a nest," Sophie told her.

"Not with my linens, you're not," said Mom. "You get down out of that tree this minute and you bring me back my things. Now they'll all have to be washed."

We threw down the blankets, the sheets, and the tablecloth, and we carried down the rest.

"What's this?" Mom shrieked. "My hand mirror? My jewelry?"

"We're magpies," Sophie explained.

"I'll magpie you," my mother said. "Your father's going to hear about this."

She gathered everything into her arms and marched into the house.

"I think she means *your* father," Sophie said.

Indeed, she did. We got to the kitchen just in time to see her storm into Dad's study and throw everything on the floor. "You and your damn birds," she said. "Look at this." She slammed the door.

We could hear their voices but we couldn't make out the words, until we distinctly heard Mom say, "It's not funny, John."

Sophie and I sat at the kitchen table and waited.

"She's mad," I said.

Sophie nodded.

"What do you think she's going to do?" I asked.

She shrugged. "Probably just yell."

At last the study door opened and my father emerged. He strode past us without a glance, but then he stopped at the screen door and motioned for us to follow him.

"All right, Heckle and Jeckle, let's go."

He led us to the car, and as we climbed in I asked, "Where are we going?"

"I thought we'd go to the park and feed the ducks," he said. "Mom needs some time to herself. She's kind of upset. You girls know anything about that?"

"She's mad," Sophie said.

"I wonder why," Dad said.

"She's mad because we used her stuff," I said.

Dad nodded. "You used her stuff without asking. That would make anybody mad. Didn't you girls know that?"

"Yes," I said.

"But then how can we build our nest?" Sophie asked.

"Well, Sophie, if you had asked that question before you took Helen's things then she might have been willing to help you. Now she probably won't let you build a nest at all."

"But we want to live in the tree."

"Then I think the first thing you need to do is apologize, and if you do it very nicely and Helen forgives you, then we'll figure out what to do about building a new nest. Agreed?"

"Agreed," we said.

He shook his head. "Magpies," he said, and he smiled.

We stopped at Mr. Howard's bakery for some day-old bread, and Mr. Howard, who was a friend of my father's, threw in some stale doughnuts and gave Sophie and me each a cupcake for ourselves.

We fed the ducks, and on the way home we stopped and bought dinner at Mom's favorite Chinese take-out place. We brought it home and offered it to her along with our humblest apologies and our most sincere promises that we would never again take her things without asking. After one more lecture about respecting other people's property, Mom forgave us, and we all agreed that next Saturday we would put on our thinking caps and devise a better way to build a nest.

But by the next Saturday our plans were forgotten, because Sophie's mother got mad at her Daddy again, and this time she tried to break Sophie.

I think the whole second grade knew something was wrong when Sophie's mother showed up at school on Friday afternoon. There was still a half hour of school to go, and we were having a spelling bee when the door flew open and Mrs. Prescott stumbled in. Her voice was husky and her speech was slurred, but we all got the gist of her announcement, which was that she had important things to do and she needed Sophie at home. Mrs. Kirschner opened her mouth, perhaps to protest, but then she took a closer look at Mrs. Prescott and apparently thought better of it.

Mrs. Prescott was a tiny woman and usually appeared, when she appeared at all, as tidy and perfectly groomed as a porcelain figurine. Today her yellow hair was spilling copiously from its bun, her blood red lipstick had been applied heavily and inaccurately, and she had a clownish smear of blush across each cheek. The jacket of her blue linen suit was buttoned crooked. From where I stood I could smell the overpowering fragrance of White Shoulders, but it was masking another, more sinister odor.

Sophie made her way down the line of spellers, and when she came to me she grabbed my hand and said, "I'm still coming to your house tomorrow." I nodded stupidly. Until she said it, it didn't occur to me that anything might prevent her from coming to my house, tomorrow or any other day. Then she stood on her toes and kissed my cheek, and as she moved away from me I caught a glimpse of something I had never seen on Sophie's face before—it was fear. Sophie was scared of her mother.

I think Sophie's mother must have scared Mrs. Kirschner, too, because as soon as the door closed behind Sophie and Mrs. Prescott, Mrs. Kirschner went to her desk and scribbled a note, which she asked Elizabeth Harrington to deliver to the principal's office right away. Elizabeth returned a minute later with Principal Ross in tow, and Mrs. Kirschner put Elizabeth in charge of the spelling bee while she stepped out into the hall to confer in a low, urgent voice with Principal Ross.

*

I went home and spent the afternoon playing with paper dolls, and by dinnertime I had put the incident out of my mind.

The days were getting longer, and after dinner I took a walk around the back yard with Dad and helped him refill his bird feeders. I had my bath and came downstairs in my pajamas. Mom was in the kitchen having coffee with Mrs. Talbot, who was one of her biggest contacts on the gossip exchange. Mrs. Talbot worked in the admitting office at the hospital, and she knew the medical history of every family in town. I could tell by their hushed voices that they had moved beyond the discussion of gall bladders and blood clots and were on to the juicy stuff, the scandals. I wanted to know what they were saying, but Mom always discouraged me from hanging around when Mrs. Talbot was visiting, lest my presence inhibit her from telling all she knew. I usually heard it anyway when Mom repeated it to her other friends on the phone.

Dad was reading in his study, and I got my book and joined him.

It was just after eight o'clock when the phone rang, and Dad answered it.

"Yes, Ted, how are you?" He listened for a minute, and a look of alarm grew on his face. "My God, Ted, is anyone hurt?" He listened some more, and then he said, "Yes, of course. I'll be right there."

I followed him into the kitchen.

"That was Ted Prescott," he told Mom. "Something's happened over there and he needs us to take Sophie for the night."

"What is it?" Mom asked. "What happened?"

He glanced at me. "I don't know all the details, but I told Ted I was on my way."

"Can I come with you?" I asked.

"No, honey, you wait here. I'll bring Sophie back with me."

It was then that I remembered Mrs. Prescott's strange appearance at school that afternoon and the fear in Sophie's eyes.

"Did Sophie's mother do something to her?" I asked.

Dad turned and stared at me. Mom and Mrs. Talbot were looking at me, too, and I was suddenly very uncomfortable, but I wanted to know.

"Did she, Dad?"

"Don't worry, sweetheart, Sophie's going to be fine." He left.

Mom and Mrs. Talbot were still looking at me, and Mom was about to say something when the phone rang again.

"This could be news," she said, and she grabbed the phone.

"Mildred," she said, "what's going on over there?"

Mildred Farnsworth was the Prescott's next door neighbor and a member of my mother's bridge club. Mom nodded to Mrs. Talbot to indicate that information on this late breaking story was forthcoming.

"Oh my God," Mom said. "You're kidding...No...No...Oh my God..."

Mrs. Talbot was fairly twitching with anticipation.

"Hold on just a second, Mildred." Mom covered the mouthpiece with her hand and said, "Go to bed, Janet."

"Now?" I said. "But I want to know what happened to Sophie."

"Go on."

I started up the stairs, but I knew Mom wasn't going to check on me, so I took a position near the middle of the staircase, close enough to hear the conversation in the kitchen, but high enough that I could scurry to my room if Mom came toward the stairs.

I heard the breathless end of my mother's telephone conversation, and then I heard the whole story as she relayed it to Mrs. Talbot.

It seemed that Dr. Prescott, alerted by a call from the school, had gone home to find his wife loaded on drugs and alcohol and holding their daughter hostage with his antique Smith and Wesson revolver. Distraught over her husband's infidelities and depressed by her own chemical dependence, Louise Prescott was demanding satisfaction, and if she didn't get it she was going to leave this world and take her family with her.

Mildred Farnsworth was unloading groceries from the trunk of her car when she heard Louise's drunken ranting. This was nothing unusual, but today Mildred thought she detected a new note in the chorus, and her blood ran cold when she recognized it as the voice of little Sophie, pleading for her life. Mildred called the police, and hid behind her hedge until they arrived.

The police surrounded the house and used a bullhorn to try to reason with Louise. She would have none of it. This went on for a while, and an ambulance arrived to stand ready. Finally the police gained entrance to the house through the garage and followed the shrieks and screams to the basement, where they arrived just in time to hear Louise say, "Say goodbye to Daddy, because you're going to heaven, and Daddy's going to hell." And then she put the revolver to Sophie's head and pulled the trigger. The gun failed to fire, but one of the policemen instinctively shot a bullet into Louise's right shoulder, causing her to drop her weapon. Dr. Prescott rushed to her side to tend to her wound.

By this time the entire neighborhood was gathered on the sidewalk in front of the Prescott home, along with several reporters and a couple of television crews. Mildred was an expert at trading information, and she happened to possess a gift for being able to participate in one conversation while eavesdropping on another, and so by working the crowd, she was able to piece together the story, a story that would be on the eleven o'clock news tonight, and would, in fact, be on every newscast and in the papers for days to come.

Furthermore, Mrs. Farnsworth had learned that subsequent examination of the Smith and Wesson proved it to be fully loaded and in perfect working condition, and why it didn't go off and kill Sophie, as her mother had clearly intended it to do, was a mystery.

"He took better care of that gun than he did his wife," said Mildred, in what was to become an oft-quoted observation. "What were the chances that they would both malfunction so drastically on the same day?"

And so the media dubbed Sophie the Miracle Girl, and every story featured the image of the heroic policeman carrying Sophie out of the house, with a close-up of the Miracle Girl weeping on the shoulder of the man who shot her mother.

*

Dr. Prescott had given Sophie a sedative, and by the time Dad carried her into the house she was sleeping so soundly that Mom was able to give her a sponge bath and dress her in a nightgown without waking her up. We tucked her in and left a night light on in case she woke up and didn't know where she was. Mom tried again to send me to bed, but Dad said we needed to talk.

He made hot chocolate for me and served it to me in my special cup, a genuine bone china teacup with my birth flower, a carnation, painted on it. It had been a gift from Gram, but Mom said it was to be saved for when I was older. The fact that I was using it tonight confirmed my notion that I was mature enough to be sitting up after bedtime discussing serious matters with adults. Sipping from my teacup and replacing it delicately on its saucer, I could have been Mrs.

Talbot, or Mrs. Farnsworth, or any of the other ladies with whom my mother sat at this table talking about the world of adults.

"Janet," Dad began, "earlier you asked if Sophie's mother had done something to her. What made you think that?"

"She came to school today, Sophie's mother picked her up early from school, and I thought Sophie looked scared, like she was scared of her mother."

Mom asked, "Has Sophie ever told you before that her mother did anything to hurt her?"

I wanted to be the one asking the questions, but I didn't dare to push them, especially Mom. Any minute she might decide that I was too young to hear about these things, even when they happened to people my own age.

"Well," I said, "remember that time when Mrs. Weed slapped her? She said that sometimes her mother did that. But that was in kindergarten. I don't know if she still does it." Sophie had never mentioned it again, and I had not asked. It occurred to me now, from my new grown up perspective, that there might be a lot of things about her home life that Sophie didn't tell me, and I could see that I had been naïve to think that if she didn't complain, nothing was wrong. It had been childish of me to assume that because I kept no secrets from her, she kept none from me. It began to dawn on me that this was why the ladies gathered in their kitchens and bridge clubs, not to chat idly about the obvious, but to delve beneath the surface, to explore the mysteries of what otherwise went unspoken.

"Listen, honey," Dad said, "Sophie has had a very, very frightening experience. Her mother was—Well, her mother had—Her mother had some kind of an episode—"

"She went crazy," Mom clarified.

"She's a very sick person," Dad said, "and she didn't know what she was doing, Janet, and—" He looked at me helplessly, and I was alarmed to see how deeply shaken he was. He was near tears.

Mom finished for him. "She tried to shoot Sophie. Apparently she meant to kill her whole family, including herself. She's done a horrible thing, Janet, and she'll probably have to stay in the hospital for a long time before she's well again, if she ever is. Sophie's all right now, she's not hurt, but she's had a terrible, terrible experience, and it might take a while for her to recover from it. Do you understand?"

I nodded. "Is she going to live with us again?"

They looked at each other.

"It's too soon to say," Mom said.

*

It took a long time for me to get to sleep that night. By the soft glow of the night light I watched Sophie sleeping in the next bed, her cherubic face relaxed and untroubled. I tried to imagine the terror she must have felt during her ordeal, and I was haunted by a mental picture of a different outcome, the gun going off, Sophie's familiar face disappearing forever in an explosion of blood and bone and brains, Sophie gone. I remembered the kiss she gave me as she was leaving school that day, and I wondered if she knew then what her mother had planned for her.

I don't know how long I'd been asleep when I was jolted awake by the sound of Sophie's screams. I jumped out of bed, my heart pounding, and threw on the overhead light switch, half expecting to see Sophie's mother, back to finish the job, but there was only Sophie, thrashing around on her bed and shrieking as if she were on fire.

My parents burst into the room. Dad rushed directly to Sophie and scooped her up in his arms, but she continued flailing and screaming. Mom picked me up and carried me into the hall. She tried to position herself so that she could see what was going on and I couldn't, but I twisted and squirmed and struggled to see, and she finally gave up.

At last Sophie's screams stopped. She flung her arms around Dad's neck and clung to him, sobbing.

"I know," Dad said, "I know, honey, but you're all right now. You're here now, sweetheart, and no one's going to hurt you. Look," he said, "look around, Sophie, do you know where you are?"

She lifted her head and looked at him. She cupped his face in her tiny hands.

"I'm with you," she said.

"That's right," he said, "you're at Janet's house. Look, there's Janet, right there."

I waved to her.

"And there's Helen."

"And I can stay here?" she asked.

42

"Of course you can," Dad said, but I sensed my mother's hesitation, and I noticed she didn't respond.

"I don't want to go back there," Sophie said, and then she broke down sobbing again.

"It's all right, honey, it's okay," Dad crooned. He pulled the blanket off her bed and wrapped her up in it. "I'm going to take her downstairs to the rocking chair," he said. "Poor little magpie."

"Janet," Mom said, "why don't you come and sleep with me?"

So I slept with Mom in my parents' bed, and Sophie stayed the rest of the night in my father's arms.

*

The next morning my mother hid the newspapers and cooked a huge breakfast. She made pancakes, Sophie's favorite, but Sophie didn't eat them. She took only some juice and a slice of toast and didn't finish that.

After breakfast she curled up on the couch in Dad's study.

"It's a beautiful day, you should see all the birds in the yard," Dad said. "Can you hear them?"

But Sophie didn't care. She wouldn't go out, and she wouldn't allow him to open the curtains in the study so she could see them through the window. She refused all offers of entertainment, so Dad retreated to the kitchen and I sat in silence with her on the couch.

"You can go play if you want to," she said.

"Do you want me to go?"

She shook her head. I was afraid she was going to cry some more.

"I don't mind," I told her. "I'll sit with you. I don't have to do anything."

She was quiet for a while, and then she said, "Janet, if I was dead, would you come to my funeral?"

"Sure." I had never been to a funeral before.

"Do you think you'd cry?"

"Definitely. Sophie, if you were dead, I'd cry all the time. I wouldn't want to do anything any more, not go to the library, or feed the ducks, or go to the beach or anything, because it wouldn't be any fun without you. I wouldn't even want to go to high school, because you wouldn't be there. I would hate it."

"Maybe I'd be a ghost," she said. "Sometimes, when you die a really horrible death, your spirit doesn't go anywhere, it just stays on earth and haunts people. I guess if your own mother shot you in the head, that would be a pretty horrible death, wouldn't it?"

"God, Sophie, I don't see how it could get much more horrible than that."

"Would you be scared of me, if I was a ghost?"

"No. I'd be happy to see you."

"What if I was all bloody and stuff?"

"I'd get used to it."

"I could stay invisible," she said. "Then you wouldn't have to look at it. I think it would be fun to be a ghost. Maybe being dead isn't so bad."

"Maybe not," I said, "but being alive is still better. What if you had to go to hell?"

She pulled herself upright. Her face flushed with anger and her eyes blazed. "I'm *not* going to hell, Janet. If anyone's going to hell, it's my mother, not me."

I was a little taken aback, but I could see her point. "You're right," I said. "Your mother deserves to go to hell."

"I should have taken that gun away from her and shot *her* in the head, see how *she* likes it." And then she did start to cry again, but it was different this time. These were not the mournful sobs of last night, these were tears of anger, hard and bitter. She pounded her fists repeatedly into the couch cushions and her voice got louder. "I hate her! I hate her, I hate her, I hate her, I hate her, I hate her!"

"I don't blame you," I said. "I hate her, too."

Dad popped his head in the door. "Are you all right?"

"I hate my mother," Sophie told him, "and I hope she dies and goes to hell. And I hope she burns, and all her hair burns off and all her skin burns off, and I hope she never stops burning. And I hope the devil pokes her with a big pitchfork, and I hope it hurts."

Dad nodded. He came into the room and stood wiping his hands on a dish towel. "It's going to be very hard to forgive her."

"I'll never forgive her," Sophie said. "Never. And God won't forgive her either. She's going to hell."

Dad looked back and forth between us. "Do you want to know what I think?"

"What?" Sophie said.

"I think she's already in hell. I think it's true that people create their own hell, and the one your mother has created—well, it's particularly hellish. I understand how you feel, Sophie, but I think in time you'll find that it isn't really necessary to wish any more suffering on her."

"What about what she wished on me?" Sophie said. "She killed me."

"Well, no, honey, thank God she didn't."

"Yes, I was dead."

Dad crouched in front of her. "But, Sophie, you're not dead."

"Not *now*," she said, "but I was. Mama shot me, and I was dead. And there was a policeman there, and he got down in front of me, just like you are, and he was talking to me, but I couldn't hear him, because I was dead. And then he touched me, and I could feel his hand, and I could feel my arm where he was touching me, and then I wasn't dead any more."

Dad reached out his hand and let it hover over her arm. She directed it to the spot where the policeman had touched her.

"Just like that," she said. She looked at his hand on her arm, and then she raised her wide blue eyes to meet his soft brown ones.

"You're alive," he said, and she burst into tears.

"Oh, no, sweetheart, don't cry." He sat on the couch and held her. "Sophie, you've been given a gift."

She gave him a puzzled frown.

"You could have been killed, honey, but you weren't. The gun you heard was the policeman's. The gun that was aimed at you didn't go off, and you know what? There's nothing wrong with that gun, but when it was pointed at you, it wouldn't work. Now why do you suppose that is?"

"I did that," she said.

"*You* did?" This clearly wasn't the answer he was expecting. To him this was an act of God, a wondrous miracle, and I think he expected Sophie to be as awestruck as the rest of us. "How, Sophie? How could a little girl stop a gun from firing?"

"I said NO NO NO!"

"And you think that's what did it?"

"Yes, because I didn't want to die."

Dad turned his head and looked at me as if he needed to confirm that he'd heard correctly. I shrugged.

"Sophie," he said, "only God decides when people die. You don't get to say yes or no."

"I said no," she told him. "I decided."

It bothered him, I could tell, but he let it go and suggested that we visit the duck pond, and Sophie agreed to go.

*

When we got home, Mom told us that she had talked to Sophie's father, and the plan was for Sophie to spend one more night with us, and tomorrow her father would take her to her grandmother's house in Vermont, where she would spend the summer.

"What about school?" I said. "Can't she stay here until school is over?"

"There's less than two weeks left of school," said Mom. "Sophie gets to start her summer vacation early, and her grandmother gets to spend extra time with her."

"This is your father's mother?" Dad asked Sophie.

She nodded. "She's my Nana. She loves me."

"Well, then," said Mom, "that will be a nice place for you to go."

*

That night after Dad tucked us in and turned out the lights, Sophie asked me if she could sleep with me in my bed. I thought she probably wanted to talk, but she didn't. She brought her pillow and climbed into my bed, and she immediately curled up against me like a kitten and went to sleep.

I couldn't sleep, and after a while I crawled over the foot of the bed and wandered down the hall toward the bathroom. There was a light shining under my parents' door, and I went past the bathroom toward their room, where I could hear their voices, but I couldn't make out the words until Mom raised her voice.

"You think this was *Ted's* idea? *I* called *him*, John, and I told him we can't keep her."

I crept closer, and I heard Dad say, "Why would you do that, when we hadn't discussed it?"

"Because there's nothing to discuss, John, we can't keep her. We did it once, and that was enough. It's one thing if you want to give away all our money and do volunteer work all over town, it's another thing to bring other people's problems into our home."

"Is that what she is to you, Helen? Is that what you see when you look at her, someone else's problem?"

"She's not our child, John."

"I'm aware of that."

"Are you? Because sometimes I wonder. I see the way you look at her, and I think you believe that God has sent you another child. Well, He hasn't, and He isn't going to, and I think it's time you accepted that. This child belongs to them, for better or for worse, and we can't be responsible for her. She'll go to her grandmother's, she'll be fine."

"You're sure of that?"

"What do you want, John, do you want to sit up with her every night in the rocking chair? Do you think you can undo this?"

I didn't hear his response.

"And what about your own daughter?" Mom said. "Is this the kind of thing you want her exposed to?"

Again I missed his answer, except for the words he emphasized, "—a more compassionate person—" and then I didn't hear anything for a minute, until Dad said, "I'm going downstairs." I backed away from their door and was standing in front of the bathroom when he stepped into the hall.

He snapped at me. "Janet, what are you doing up?"

"I couldn't sleep."

He sighed and appeared to exhale some of his anger. He glanced down the hall toward my room. "Is she sleeping?"

I nodded.

"I can't sleep, either," he said. "Do you want to come downstairs for a while?"

So for the second night in a row I sat at the kitchen table drinking cocoa from my teacup. Dad made cinnamon toast.

"Janet, all this must be very upsetting to you."

It seemed to me that he was more upset than I was, and I tried to reassure him.

"Sophie's grandmother is nice to her," I told him. "She likes it there."

He hadn't even eaten any toast, and already he was tearing it to pieces for the birds. He nodded absently and said, "I'm sure she'll be fine, for as long as she's there."

"And after that?" I asked.

"I wish I knew."

"Her mother won't come back, though, will she, Dad? I mean, she won't come back and try to kill her again, will she?"

"God, no, honey, no one's going to let that happen. She's locked up, Janet, she can't get out. Is that what you're worried about?"

"Yeah."

"No, sweetheart, don't give it another thought. Whatever else happens, Sophie's going to live for a long time."

I didn't want to admit it, but it wasn't just Sophie I was worried about. What if her mother found her here and killed not just Sophie but me, too? Even worse, what if she killed everyone in the house *but* me? What if I woke up one day to find that Mrs. Prescott had destroyed not only my sister, but my entire family?

Chapter 6

The next day, after Sophie left, my father sat in the back yard all day watching his birds. At dinner he announced that he was going to call Uncle Bill.

"I have a job for him," he said.

Uncle Bill was the youngest of my mother's family, almost ten years her junior, and she disapproved of him because he was what she called a hippie protester, but sometimes in the summer he came to stay with us, bringing his backpack, his guitar, and his tool kit, and he earned his keep by helping Dad paint the house, or doing remodeling jobs. He and his brother, my Uncle Pete, had built Dad's study.

Uncle Bill was a carpenter by trade—"Just like Jesus," he said, and in fact he reminded me of pictures I had seen of Jesus. His complexion was darker than my mother's, a startling contrast to his eyes, which were the same light gray as hers. He wore a beard and a mustache, and his hair was longer than mine.

Like all of his siblings, he had taken piano lessons from Mom, but he preferred his guitar. My mother bemoaned his lack of what she called a classical mind, but he said give him a good simple folk song any day. He taught me protest songs, songs by Phil Ochs and Bob Dylan, and he talked openly about free love and drugs and politics. Mom was always admonishing him with, "Little pitchers have big ears," to which he invariably and inexplicably responded, "Good fences make good neighbors." He would wink at me as he said this, and long before I understood what they were talking about, I knew Uncle Bill was on my side.

*

After breakfast on the first day of his visit, Uncle Bill asked, "So, is this a big job?"

"You tell me," Dad said, and he led Uncle Bill out to the back yard. I tagged along, curious because Dad had not yet told any of us what the job was.

We went across the yard and stopped in front of the oak tree. Dad looked up into the branches, and Uncle Bill followed his gaze.

Dad said, "I have a couple of magpies who want to live in this tree."

Uncle Bill looked at Dad for a minute, smiling uncertainly. "Seriously?" he said. "You brought me here to build a birdhouse? I mean, don't get me wrong, man, I'll do it, but—"

"These aren't ordinary magpies, Bill." Dad put his hand flat on the top of my head. "These are human magpies, about this big."

"Oh, I see. *Magpies*." Uncle Bill nodded as if he'd come across this before. "You want a treehouse."

"Oh!" I said. "That would be so cool!"

"Do you think you can do it?" Dad asked.

Uncle Bill walked around the tree, studying it. He hoisted himself up and climbed around in the branches, jouncing the limbs to test their strength. He was standing right in our favorite spot when he said, "Right here would be good. We can put some supports under here, build a good-sized structure."

Back on the ground, he said, "Yeah, I think we can do it."

"How many rooms will it have?" I asked.

"I would go with one," he said. "One large room, sparsely furnished, and I'll tell you why, princess. Because—and John can correct me if I'm wrong—this particular species of magpie grows quite rapidly, and you don't want a house they're going to outgrow. You want to leave them some space, so that as they get bigger, they can still hang out in their treehouse. When they're teenagers, for example, they'll have a place to hide from their parents. They'll have a place to giggle over boys and write in their diaries and whatnot."

"In five more years we'll be teenagers," I told him.

"Well, there you are. And who, pray tell, is this other magpie?"

"Sophie," I said. "She's my sister."

*

The rest of the summer was taken up with plans and sketches, trips to the lumberyard and the hardware store, and an increasingly elaborate construction of platforms and ropes and pulleys and ladders, sawdust all over the yard, and the sounds of Uncle Bill hammering and sawing and singing. I was not allowed near the tree while he was working in it, but I was his special on-ground assistant, a job that consisted mostly of keeping him in fresh lemonade, and occasionally holding one end of the tape measure for him.

The final product was a rustic cabin with a shingled roof, high enough at its peak for Uncle Bill to stand up. It had windows cut out of the walls, as well as a front door, although there was no way to enter the front door without a ladder. Uncle Bill had put some footholds on the trunk of the tree, and the only way to get into the house was to climb the tree and come up through a hole in the floor. Uncle Bill said he put in the front door on principle, and that next summer he would build us a staircase and put in a doorbell.

But then we found out that Uncle Bill wouldn't be back next summer, because he was drafted.

"Don't worry," he said. "My status is 1-A-O, noncombatant. They can make me go, but they can't make me fight."

"Well, what's the point of drafting you if you're not going to fight?" I asked. "Isn't that why they have the draft, because they need more people to fight?"

"Oh, they do other things, besides fight," he assured me.

"Like what?"

"I have no idea," he said.

*

I was up early. Sophie had called the night before to say that she was home from her Nana's, and she was coming to visit today. I couldn't wait to show her the treehouse.

I was eating pancakes, too excited and distracted to follow the argument that Mom and Uncle Bill were having, something to do with Uncle Bill's reluctance to be a soldier.

"I just think it will be good for you," Mom said. "I think you need some discipline."

"You'd like to be a fly on the wall, wouldn't you?" he said. "You'd love to see Uncle Bill getting bossed around by William C. Westmoreland."

"I'd like to see you find some direction. You're twenty-three years old and all you've ever done is drift around like a bum. This is a chance to commit yourself to something greater. I hate to see you being half-assed about it."

Dad said to Uncle Bill, "I think it's a shame more people haven't taken your position."

And then the back door flew open and Sophie came in, all brown and gold from the sun, a little plumper than I remembered in a pair of pink shorts and a white peasant blouse.

I jumped out of my chair and hugged her, and planted a sticky, syrupy kiss on her cheek. She giggled, and then Dad scooped her up on his lap and kissed the syrup off her cheek, and she squealed and hugged him, and then he put her down and she ran to Mom and threw her arms around Mom's waist.

Mom patted Sophie's head and said, "I'm going to forgive your bare feet today and offer you some pancakes."

Sophie turned toward her usual seat, only to find Uncle Bill sitting in it. She stared at him, and he stared back.

"Sophie," Dad said, "this is Bill. He's Janet's uncle."

She continued to stare, and she reached out with one finger and touched his beard.

"You're Janet's, too?" she said.

He cocked his head. "I'm her uncle. And you must be—is it possible? Could it be, I'm finally meeting the amazing, the incredible, the marvelous, magnificent Sophie that I've been hearing about all summer long?"

"*I'm* Sophie," she said.

He shook her hand. "It's an honor to meet you. Janet tells me you're sisters."

"Sometimes," she said. "And sometimes we're brothers."

"You don't say," he said. "When are you brothers?"

"When we play Tikki-Tikki-Tembo. You have to have a brother, and your brother falls in the well, and then *you* fall in the well and your brother has to run and get the Old Man With the Ladder to come and fish you out."

"Sounds like a good time," he said.

She nodded. "It's fun."

He pulled out the chair next to him and urged her to sit down. "Here, sit right here next to me and tell us what spectacular things you've been doing all summer while we've been pining away for you."

She picked strawberries, she said, and she helped make jam and pies and strawberry shortcake. She ate ice cream and watermelon and went swimming at the lake. She visited friends of Nana's who lived on a farm, and she milked a goat. There were numerous picnics, and on the 4th of July there were fireworks.

"And we went to the library, and I got a library card, and now I have two library cards. And look, Nana gave me this."

I hadn't noticed the chain around her neck, but now she pulled on it and from inside her blouse she produced a ring, a small square emerald in a gold setting.

Mom came over and examined it. "That's lovely, dear. You'll have to be very careful not to lose it."

"Was it your Nana's ring?" Dad asked.

Sophie nodded. "She was going to give it to me when I got older, but she decided to give it to me now. I guess in case Mama kills me. And guess what else? Daddy gave me a kitten."

"Really?" I said. "A real live kitten?"

I had always wanted a kitten, but my mother didn't like cats—she thought they were sneaky—and Dad said we couldn't have one anyway because of the birds.

"Is it a boy cat or a girl cat?" I asked.

"Daddy says it's a boy."

"Just what that household needs," Mom muttered. "Another tomcat." She set a plate of pancakes in front of Sophie. "There you are, dear."

"So, Sophie," said Uncle Bill, "I hear you got a kitten."

She put down the syrup and stared at him in disbelief. "I just *said*. I just *said* I got a kitten."

"Oh." Uncle Bill scratched his head. "Maybe that's where I heard it."

"I just *said* Daddy gave me a kitten. His name is Sid."

"Why did you name him that?" Mom asked.

"I didn't," she said. "That's his name, he told me. Sid Arthur."

Uncle Bill's mouth dropped open, but Sophie didn't notice. She had tipped her head back and was trying to lick syrup off her chin.

"Use your napkin," Mom said.

"Sid Arthur?" Uncle Bill said. "Sophie, is your cat's name Siddhartha?"

Her face lit up. "Do you know my cat?"

"No." Uncle Bill looked at Dad as if for help.

"Siddhartha was the name of the man who became the Great Buddha," Dad said. "He was a wealthy young man who gave up everything to seek enlightenment, and he found it. Did you know that, Sophie?"

She nodded vaguely. "I call him Sid. He has black fur, and his eyes are green like Janet's. When I pet him, he purrs, like this." She made a noise in her throat that sounded like a growl. "And his tongue is scratchy when he licks me."

"Does he eat birds?" I asked.

"No, he's too little. Can he come to your house if he doesn't eat any birds?"

"No cats," Mom said. "I hate them."

"And sooner or later," Dad said, "he *will* go after birds."

"Tell him it's a sin to kill a mockingbird," Uncle Bill advised.

"Is it?" I asked.

"It is when people do it," said Dad, "but I don't know that a cat can commit a sin."

"Oh, now we're talking," said Uncle Bill. "This is exactly the kind of theological discussion I like to engage in. Does a cat have a soul? Can a cat commit a sin? If a cat can't commit a sin, does that mean all cats go to heaven? Helen, what will you do if you get to heaven and it's full of cats?"

"I have a question," Sophie said. "Is Buddha a false god?"

They all looked at her, and they all opened their mouths, but nobody answered her.

Finally Dad said, "Buddha was a holy man, like Jesus."

"But he's not a Christian god, dear," said Mom, "and as a Christian, you shouldn't worship him."

"But at the same time," Uncle Bill said, "you shouldn't kill Buddhists. I, for one, will not be killing any Buddhists."

"Why not?" Mom said. "They set themselves on fire anyway."

"Then they don't need me, do they?"

"What's adultery?" Sophie asked.

Another silence. Again it was Dad who spoke first. "Are you studying your commandments, Sophie?"

"Nana sent me to catechism classes."

"And what did they say adultery was?"

"They said it was pretending to be something you're not."

Uncle Bill hooted.

"But we do that all the time," I said, alarmed, thinking of all the confessions we'd have to make if one of our favorite pastimes turned out to be a sin.

"I don't think that's quite what they meant," Dad said.

"It's not really something you girls need to worry about just yet," said Mom.

"Yeah," Uncle Bill agreed. "Adultery is for adults."

Sophie was watching Dad. "But what does it mean?" she asked again.

"When two people get married," he said, "they promise to love each other forever. If one of them breaks that promise and loves someone else, that's adultery. In terms of pretending, you might say that it's pretending you're not married when you are, or pretending to be married to someone who is not, in fact, your husband or wife, because either you or the other person already *has* a husband or wife. Do you see?"

She nodded. "Do I have to honor my father *and* my mother?"

I saw Dad wince, and he appeared somehow to collapse a little, as if something inside him had given way.

Uncle Bill said, "There may be special dispensations for people in your situation, munchkin."

"No," Dad said, "there are no special dispensations. You have to find a way to do it, Sophie, even if it takes a whole lifetime. Just remember, sweetheart, that God doesn't give you such a difficult task without also giving you the strength to do it. Forgiveness is His greatest blessing. Sometimes it's hard, honey, but give yourself time."

Sophie thought about this, and when she spoke again, her voice was small and tearful. "Maybe God will forgive me for not being able to forgive my mother."

"Maybe," Dad said, "but how could you ask Him if you hadn't tried your hardest?"

She sighed heavily, as if she were already weary of trying.

Uncle Bill turned to Dad.

"Jesus Christ, John, she's just a kid. Cut her some slack, man."

Dad looked surprised. "I don't mean to be harsh, but there are no exceptions to the commandments. As you yourself have pointed out, Bill."

"I'm talking about grown people killing each other for no reason. She's what, eight? After what happened to her, you're saying the burden is on *her*, to forgive something that's unforgivable?"

"I'm saying she won't find peace until she does," Dad said. "In the eyes of God, nothing is unforgivable."

*

After breakfast we took Sophie out to the back yard. When she saw the treehouse, she gasped and trembled with delight.

"Is that a birdhouse?" she asked.

"It's a treehouse," Dad said.

"Uncle Bill built it," I told her.

She gazed up at Uncle Bill. "Is that where you *live*?"

He laughed. "No. I heard there were a couple of magpies in the area who wanted to live in that tree. It's for them."

She seized my hand. "Janet, we can live there!"

"Just pretend," I cautioned her. "Just sometimes."

"Oh." She frowned. "Well, that's okay. I have to go home sometimes anyway, to play with my kitten."

"Come on," I said, and I led her up to the treehouse. She ran from window to window, leaning out each one to admire the view and exclaiming over the smell of fresh wood and summer leaves.

"This is the best house in the world," she said. "We can play Robin Hood, or Tarzan, or Swiss Family Robinson."

She went to the front door and waved to Uncle Bill.

"Hey," she yelled, "can we have a rope?"

"A rope?" he repeated.

"Yeah, a Tarzan rope, so we can swing down from here."

"What are you, one of the Flying Wallendas? No, you can't have a rope."

She pouted. "I thought you were *nice*."

"I'm not," he told her. "I'm sorry if I gave you that impression."

She crossed her arms and turned from the doorway in a huff. If there had actually been a door, I'm sure she would have slammed it.

I said, "Maybe when we're bigger he'll give us a rope. Maybe when he gets back from Vietnam."

"Vietnam?"

"He's been drafted," I told her. "He's going to Vietnam."

"*Him*?" She went back to the door and peered down at him. "What do they want *him* for?"

"I don't know." I looked out the window at him, and I could see what she meant. From this vantage point he looked small and scruffy, standing there in cut-off jeans and a stained tee shirt, scratching his beard. He didn't look like someone who would be useful in a war.

"Anyway," I said, "he's not going to fight."

Uncle Bill saw us watching him, and he called up to Sophie, "What do you want now, a fire pole?"

She didn't answer. She came and huddled next to me on the floor and said, "We have to stop him."

*

She spent the next few days trying to talk him into burning his draft card, and when that failed, she offered to run away to Canada with him.

"It's nice there," she said. "They have the Northern Lights all the time, plus they even have a queen."

"You make a strong argument, peanut, but I couldn't take you away from Janet."

"Janet can come, too," she said.

"I would," I said, "but I don't think Mom will let me."

"Whoa, hold on," said Uncle Bill. "I can't be trying to cross the border with an entourage of little girls. They'd think I was something worse than a draft dodger. No, ladies, the long and the short of it is that Uncle Bill's ass belongs to Uncle Sam."

"Don't go," Sophie said, punching his arm for emphasis.

But he went anyway, and I don't think she ever forgave him for it.

Chapter 7

After Sophie's mother was committed, the Prescotts'
housekeeper quit her job—"Jumped ship," as my mother put it. She
had threatened to quit after the broken glass incident, and rumor had it
that Dr. Prescott had given her a substantial raise to persuade her to
stay. Now she was gone, and no amount of money would bring her
back.

So Dr. Prescott hired what turned out to be a series of nannies,
none of whom lasted more than a few weeks. Sophie could be very
difficult when she wanted to be, and she saw no reason to put up with
strange women coming into her house and telling her what to do. She
refused all of their requests, no matter how reasonable or how well
phrased. She wouldn't get dressed for school, wouldn't go to bed,
wouldn't eat, wouldn't bathe, wouldn't pick up her clothes or her toys
or her books. She sat cross-legged in the middle of her room singing
some variation of We Shall Overcome, and when they tried to pick her
up, she went limp.

If a few days of this didn't drive them away, she resorted to
such guerrilla tactics as throwing tantrums, peeing her pants, and
stealing things out of their pocketbooks.

The last nanny was tough. She was strong and she was mean,
and she pitted her will against Sophie's and usually won through sheer
brute force. So Sophie got up early one morning and filled a laundry
bag with some clothes, some carrot sticks, a half dozen cans of cat
food, a can opener, and Sid, and she walked to Route 1 and stuck her
thumb out.

The nice lady who picked her up reminded her of her Nana,
inspiring her to say that she was on her way to San Francisco to live
with her grandmother. Sophie's house had burned down, she claimed,
and her parents died in the fire, and now she was going to San
Francisco to live with her Nana, who was too poor to come to the
funeral or to send Sophie a bus ticket.

She thought her story was going well, but her new friend
betrayed her, and instead of helping Sophie on her way, the lady drove
to the police station and turned her in. Convinced that she had been
unfairly arrested, Sophie refused to cooperate with the police. She
wouldn't tell them her name, and when they persisted in questioning
her she spit on the floor and called them pigs. They laughed at her,

which made her even angrier. They threatened to jail her for truancy, and she said, "Go ahead." They threatened to take her cat away from her, and she told them that Sid would scratch their eyes out, and if he didn't, she would.

Finally someone recognized her as the Miracle Girl and called her father.

Dr. Prescott was not pleased at being asked to retrieve his nine-year-old daughter from the police station. The nanny believed she could turn Sophie around, but Dr. Prescott doubted it. He dismissed the nanny, and he told Sophie that her behavior was as bad as her mother's and he was just going to have to send her to boarding school. Sophie begged for another chance. She didn't need a babysitter, she said, she could take care of herself. She could get herself to school and back, she wouldn't run away; she could be good, she would prove it.

So the last nanny was not replaced, and Dr. Prescott decided to forgo the housekeeper as well, leaving the domestic chores to whichever of his girlfriends was inclined to perform them. Sophie found that as long as she stayed out of his line of vision and no one complained about her, she could do what she wanted. He occasionally gave her a wad of cash, and even though she always had a very haphazard way of managing money—she never counted it, it was crumpled up in a dozen different pockets, or used as bookmarks, or given away to people on the street—she managed to feed herself and Sid, although in fairness to my mother it must be said that Sophie's diet was frequently and considerably supplemented by meals at our house.

*

If Dr. Prescott had been discreet about his lovers in the past, and he hadn't, he now made no attempt to hide them. He brought them into his house—sometimes two or three in a week, according to his neighbor Mrs. Farnsworth—and Mrs. Talbot reported that every one of them was small and blonde, and young. They were nurses, patients, other doctors' wives. They were pharmacists, physical therapists, switchboard operators, and housekeepers, and those were just the ones he met at the hospital, Mrs. Talbot said—that didn't even include any cocktail waitresses, cashiers and bank tellers he might be seducing in his off hours. He made no move to end his marriage to Louise, and the bridge club agreed that his official status as a married man served to keep his women at a distance, lest they get any ideas about settling down.

I had a chance to hear the bridge club's opinions one Wednesday afternoon when I was home sick from school. I was settled on the couch in Dad's study with a box of tissues, a cup of orange juice, a blanket, and a copy of Alice in Wonderland, which Sophie had recommended as the best book to read when you felt feverish.

They talked quietly at first, and the murmur of their voices and the shuffling of the cards were soothing sounds that lulled me nearly to sleep, but then I heard Dr. Prescott's name mentioned, and I roused myself and paid attention.

Lucille Parker was saying that her niece was friends with Carol Kincaid, who was one of Dr. Prescott's current girlfriends. Lucille's niece was quite properly concerned that her friend was dating a married man, but Carol claimed that Mrs. Prescott didn't count as a wife because she'd been permanently removed; she would never be released from the hospital. She would stay locked up for as long as Dr. Prescott was willing to pay the bills, and since he now had control of his wife's money, he could afford to keep her locked up for a long time. So, according to what Carol told Lucille's niece, Dr. Prescott had all the advantages of being married to a wealthy woman, and none of the disadvantages.

"Imagine," Lucille said, "he's using her own money to keep her locked away."

"I heard it's like a country club there," said Mrs. Farnsworth. "She's probably hobnobbing with some Kennedys."

"At least it's not costing the taxpayers," Mom said. "They could have put her in jail for the rest of her life. It was bad enough the way she neglected that child, but to put a gun to her head—They should lock her up and throw away the key."

"I think he drove her to it," said Ruth Doyle, "the way he carries on. Not that that's an excuse, but I can see how it could happen. A woman can be driven to extremes."

"Still," said Mrs. Farnsworth, "it didn't help to sit in the house and drink all day."

There was a murmur around the table. Mrs. Farnsworth spoke with the authority of having lived next door to the Prescotts for many

60

years. "I could count on one hand the number of times she's left that house since that little girl was born."

"Well, I wouldn't show my face, either," Mom said, "if I allowed some man to treat me so shabbily. Running around with all those young girls. I'd pack his bags and kick him out of that house so fast his head would spin."

"They say the wife is always the last to know," Lucille said.

"She had to have known," said Mrs. Farnsworth. "He didn't come home for days at a time."

"Maybe she trusted him," said Ruth Doyle. "Maybe he said he had to work extra shifts at the hospital, and maybe she had no reason to doubt him."

Ruth Doyle had recently reconciled with her husband after he had an affair with their son's second grade teacher. I had heard Mom talking about it on the phone, and she'd said that Ruth Doyle was a fool.

"Well," Mom said, "thank God I don't have to worry about that. I know John would never think of breaking his marriage vows."

"Don't be so sure," Ruth Doyle said.

"I think I know my husband," Mom snapped. "He was in training for the priesthood, and I can assure you he has that part of himself under control." And then she made a tsk-tsk sound and said, "For God's sake, Ruth, pay attention. You just trumped my ace."

*

I asked Sophie if she knew Carol Kincaid, and she said she wasn't sure. She thought there was a Karen, but it might be a Carol, or there might be one of each. She was quite concerned about the ladies her father brought home, because sometimes they ranted and shrieked as her mother had done, and always they made strange noises in the night.

"I think Daddy's mean to them," she told me. "I think he hurts them."

One night at dinner Mom asked Sophie how things were going at home, and Sophie put her fork down and looked guiltily around the table, wringing her napkin in both hands.

"What's wrong, dear?"

Sophie fastened her blue eyes on me, and I nodded encouragement. I knew what was bothering her, and I had been urging her to talk to my parents about it.

She hid her mouth behind her napkin and said, "I think Daddy's doing something bad."

Mom was all ears. "What is he doing?"

"He brings these ladies home," Sophie said, "and he *does* something to them."

My parents exchanged a look, and Dad asked, with obvious trepidation, "What do you think he does, honey?"

Sophie lowered her voice to a whisper. "I think he kills them," she said. "He takes them to his room, and they make these noises, like this." She let out a series of moans punctuated by sudden sharp cries, as if she were suffering some relentless and diabolical torture, and although she had told me about this before, I found it quite alarming, and I saw by my parents' expressions that they did, too.

"And then, in the morning, they're *gone*," Sophie concluded.

Mom cleared her throat. "Don't they ever come back?"

"I don't know. Sometimes I think they do, but sometimes there's all different ones. I don't know."

Dad rested his hand on her forearm. "Sweetheart, he's not killing them, I promise you."

"But he hurts them. They make these noises, like this—"

"No, honey." He cut her off before she could demonstrate further. "They're not hurt, Sophie, they're making love. It's something grownups do."

"*You* don't," she said, and his hand jumped off her arm as if it had been shocked.

He said, "Remember, we talked about this? About how grownups make love, and how they make babies?"

She glared at him. "You didn't tell me what it *sounds* like. And if that's what they're doing, then how come there's no babies?"

Mom stepped in. "What grown people do in private is no one's business, and certainly not yours. It doesn't concern you, dear, and it's very rude of you to be listening."

"I wasn't *listening*," Sophie said. "I *heard*."

"Well, you should try not to hear any more. What your Daddy does with his girlfriends is a private and personal thing, and it's something nice people don't talk about. Finish your dinner, dear. No one is being killed, and you have nothing to worry about. And by the way, Sophie, what's this I hear about you spitting on the floor at the police station? That doesn't sound like something a nice girl would do, now, does it?"

Sophie crossed her arms over her chest and declared that she didn't care, she was arrested for no reason, just like Huey Newton.

"Are you a Black Panther?" Dad asked.

"I think I'm a flower child."

"How can you tell?"

"Well, I want to stop the war," she said. "I think people should love each other. And I think I'd like to drop acid."

"Sophie, I don't think you know what that means," said my mother.

"Yes, I do. You take LSD and it expands your mind. You can smell colors and taste sounds. I think I'd like that."

"You can also freak out and jump out a window," Mom said. "I don't think you'd like *that*. Drugs are very dangerous, Sophie, hasn't your father talked to you about this?"

Sophie nodded. "He says don't do it."

"Well, he *is* a doctor," Mom said.

"But Dr. Leary is a doctor, too, and he says it's all right."

My parents stared at her.

"Where exactly are you getting this information?" Mom asked. "How do you know so much about drugs, and Dr. Leary, and Black Panthers?"

"I can *read*," Sophie said in a tone that suggested Mom had insulted her intelligence. "John's got Time magazine right there in his study."

"Well, perhaps you're too young to be reading it, if it's given you the impression that it's a good idea to take drugs." Mom gave Dad a pointed look, and then to me she said, "Do you read it, too?"

"Sometimes."

"And what have you learned about drugs?"

"They can damage your chromosomes."

She pointed her finger at me. "You just keep that in mind," she said. "Do you hear that, Sophie? Do you know what it means to have damaged chromosomes?"

"It means you might have mutant babies," Sophie said.

"Well, is that what you want?"

Sophie shook her head. "I'm not going to have babies. I'm going to adopt orphans."

"How noble." Mom shot Dad a look, as if she suspected him of putting Sophie up to this.

"How many children are you planning to adopt?" Dad asked.

"Nine." She appeared to be trying out this number, listening to it with a critical ear. "That sounds about right."

"That's a lot of children," Mom said. "Do you have any idea how much responsibility that is?"

Sophie nodded. "You have to love them. My Nana says that children need love."

"Well, they need a lot more than that. They need food and clothes and trips to the dentist. And they need shots, and medicine when they're sick, and you have to be up at all hours of the night with them. You have to clean up after them, and do their laundry and cook their meals and teach them how to behave. You do everything for them, and then they won't do one simple thing you ask them to do, like keeping their shoes on their feet." She tapped her finger on the table in front of Sophie's plate. "What do you think of that?"

Sophie smiled indulgently. "I won't make them wear shoes."

"No, of course not. You'll just let them run wild and free, because that's what hippie flower children do." She glared at my father. "What are you smiling at?"

"I was just thinking of Bill," he said.

"That's all we need," Mom said, "is for Bill to be here contributing his half-assed ideas."

*

Uncle Bill had finished his basic training and gone to Vietnam in January. He was working as an orderly in a hospital near Saigon. It kept him humble, he said, and it kept him too busy to think, for which he was grateful. His letters to me were mostly cheerful and chatty, although later on he would tell me that he felt like a fool in a fairy tale, someone who wasted his wish by not detailing it enough. It wasn't enough to have said that he didn't want to kill anyone; he should have also stipulated that he didn't want to watch anybody die.

Sophie was still mad at him.

"I'm writing to Uncle Bill," I would say. "Is there anything you want me to tell him?"

"Tell him I hope he's having fun with his army buddies." Or, "Ask him if he can see the Northern Lights from there."

I passed these messages along, and Uncle Bill retaliated by calling her names. Not bad names, just names that weren't hers. Trixie, Josephine, Nefertiti. Sybil.

"Tell your friend Tallulah I saw a monkey that looked just like her," he wrote.

"Tell him I'm going to find someone else to go to Canada with."

"Sophie, I don't know why you're so mad at him. He works in a hospital, it's not like he's going around killing people."

"He's helping them with their war."

"He's helping people who are hurt," I said. "There'd be more people dead if it weren't for him."

"Janet," she said, "what if somebody kills *him*?"

I felt a sudden chill. "Do you *know* something?"

"No," she said. "No, it's not that. I *don't* know. But it could happen, and then wouldn't you wish he'd gone to Canada, or even to jail?"

"Dad says they're not supposed to bomb hospitals."

"They're not supposed to kill babies, either, Janet, but everyone knows they do. It's a *war*, they're killing everybody."

"Well, but, Sophie, if you think he's going to get killed, then shouldn't you be nice to him and stop being so mad at him?"

"If he gets killed, I'll be even more mad at him," she said. "And you can tell him I said so."

Chapter 8

Sophie spent most of every summer with her Nana, until the summer we were eleven, when her father agreed to let her spend just one month at her grandmother's and then she could come home. She wrote me letters from Vermont saying that she was having a nice time but she couldn't wait to get home so we could be together for days on end with no school and nothing to do but read. She was borrowing from the adult section of the library, and she advised me to drop Nancy Drew and take up Miss Marple, which I did, with great pleasure.

And when she came home, we did, in fact, beat a steady path from the library to the treehouse, taking breaks from our reading occasionally to accompany Dad to the beach or the duck pond.

One night at dinner Dad asked, as he often did, what we were reading.

"Little Birds," Sophie said. "It's by somebody with a funny name."

There was an odd silence, and I looked up to see both my parents' forks stopped in midair.

"Anais Nin?" Dad asked.

"That's it." Sophie nodded. "You know what, though? It's not really about birds at all."

My mother asked, "Where did you get this book?"

"It was on Daddy's bookshelf. I thought it was about birds."

"You're always welcome to borrow my bird books," Dad said.

"Sophie, does your father know you're reading this book?" Mom asked.

Sophie shrugged.

"I'm just wondering," Mom said, "if perhaps the book is a little too...*adult* for you."

"Maybe," Sophie agreed, "because some of it I didn't get at all. Like, there's this one part—"

Mom put her hand on top of Sophie's and patted it. "Maybe you should read it again when you're older, dear, and we'll talk about it then."

Sophie caught my eye across the table and smirked. I knew the part she was talking about; we had pored over the book together, and we agreed that it was deeply disturbing. Parts of it were downright bizarre, while other parts caused acute pangs of indefinable longing.

"See? This is what happens," Sophie had whispered to me in the treehouse. "These people just can't stop themselves. It's like being under a spell."

Dad cleared his throat. "Is there something about this book that's bothering you, Sophie?"

Mom scowled at him. "John, we're not going to talk about the book now. That subject is closed."

"It's okay," Sophie told him. She patted his hand. "We can talk about it when I'm older."

He blushed, suddenly and very deeply.

"I don't appreciate your sarcasm, young lady," said my mother, "and I don't have to put up with it."

"Sorry," Sophie murmured, but I think she was talking to Dad.

There was a silence that went on too long.

"I'm reading Oliver Twist," I offered.

"How marvelous," Dad said. "Tell us all about it."

*

When dinner was over my mother dismissed us.

"Why don't you girls go outside? Dad and I need to talk."

"Don't go too far," Dad said. "I'm going to need some models to turn cartwheels for me."

Outside, Sophie headed for the treehouse, but I dragged her back to where we could crouch under the kitchen window and listen.

"…not your responsibility, John. She's got family, let them deal with it."

"Helen, if they have questions—"

"If Janet has questions, she can ask. But Janet isn't asking, because Janet isn't reading pornography."

"Obviously the subject is going to come up, one way or another, and I'd like to know what their concerns are. I don't want them to be confused about it, or frightened by it."

"And you think I do."

"I didn't say that."

"Why not? Go ahead and say it, John, you don't want them to be *repressed*. You want them to be free and uninhibited and *healthy*."

"We were raised with guilt and shame, Helen, and what good did it do us?"

"It kept us *decent*," she said. "We don't have pornography laying around the house for our daughter to read. We don't have a parade of lovers in and out of our house."

If Dad made any response to this, we didn't hear it.

Then Mom said, "I think Janet should be spending more time with her other friends."

Sophie and I looked at each other and held our breath.

"We can't choose her friends for her," Dad said.

"Maybe not, but we can encourage some friendships more than others. I'd like to see her spend more time with normal children from normal families."

I heard Sophie take a sharp breath, and I thought maybe we'd heard too much. I tried to pull her away, but she shook me off.

"My God, Helen, how can you say that to me?"

"Don't be ridiculous, John, I'm not talking about *you*. At least you had some discipline in your life."

"That's because I was fortunate enough to be raised by decent Christian women who weren't afraid to care for other people's children."

"And what's *that* supposed to mean?"

"I may not know as much about normal families as you do, Helen, but this is my house and I won't have that child turned out of it. She should be spending *more* time here, not less, and if she has questions, then by God I'll try to answer them."

We heard his chair scrape the floor as he stood up, and we ran away from the house, into the yard to practice our cartwheels. Dad emerged a few minutes later with his sketchpad, and we put on a show of gymnastics for him. I wasn't as agile as Sophie, nor did I have her stamina. I could turn a lot of cartwheels, but she could turn more, and when at last Dad had what he needed, we threw ourselves down on the grass to rest. I was on my back, looking at the clouds; Sophie lay on her belly, playing with a blade of grass and some ants. Dad continued to sketch.

"Sophie," Dad said, "did you have questions about the book you're reading?"

"Well…" She glanced at me, and I could see that, knowing he had fought for the right to answer her questions, she now felt obliged to ask some.

"How old do you have to be to make love?"

If this question surprised him, he didn't show it, although he seemed a bit confused; in considering his answer, he looked at me for a moment as if I had asked the question.

"There's no particular age," he said. "Most people are physically ready long before they're emotionally ready. It's not enough to have a physical desire for someone. You should wait until you also have a deep emotional bond. That takes time, and maturity."

"You don't believe in free love, do you?" Sophie asked.

"I do not. When God tells us to love our neighbor, He's not advocating free love. Physical love is one of His gifts, and it shouldn't be squandered for the sake of pleasure."

"Do you think pleasure is a sin?"

"No, honey, not at all, but it shouldn't be your primary consideration in deciding to make love. You have to have love, and trust, and commitment. You have to be willing to accept any children that result from your lovemaking. You girls have plenty of time, this isn't something you need to worry about now." He peered at her over the top of his glasses. "You're not planning to make love soon, are you?"

"I think I could do it," she said, "but all the boys I know are too stupid. I bet they don't even know how to kiss."

"They will, soon enough," he said. He leaned over and cupped her chin in his hand. "Promise me, sweetheart, that you'll wait for someone special. Promise you won't give yourself to just anyone."

"Okay," she said, "but I hope I don't have to wait till I'm *old*."

*

After that, Sophie amused herself by randomly lying about the books she was reading. Usually she would tell the truth, but every once in a while, in response to Dad's question, she would cast a mischievous glance at my mother and say that she was reading Portnoy's Complaint, or Tropic of Cancer. The day she said she was reading Lolita, Mom told Dad to for God's sake stop asking, but he never did.

*

At the end of that summer, Uncle Bill came back to us.

There were several months during his tour when I received no letters from him, and although he'd been back in the States for nearly a year, he had not been to our house. I saw him at Aunt Louise's house at Thanksgiving, and again at Gram's for Christmas, and I was disturbed by the change in him. He was subdued, almost eerily quiet, and distant. His gray eyes had lost their twinkle, had lost, in fact, almost all signs of life, and he seemed unable to give his full attention to any of us for any length of time.

At Easter he didn't show up at all, and my mother and her sisters squabbled over what should be done with him. Some said college, some said marriage, some re-enlistment, and some advocated a combination of the above. Aunt Cathy said flatly that he should get off his ass and get a job.

It was early September when he came to stay with us, and Sophie refused to come see him.

"Still mad at me, huh?" he said. "Damn, that little girl can hold a grudge."

He seemed a little more alert than he had been at the family gatherings, but he still didn't say much, and he didn't take on any chores. He seemed content to sit in the back yard for hours at a time, smoking cigarettes and staring into space. He claimed to be watching the birds, but he sat out there even after dark, when he smoked sweet smelling cigarettes that he rolled himself. The smoke drifted through my open window, and I had my suspicions, but I wasn't sure until I heard my mother accuse him of smoking marijuana.

I had gotten up from bed to use the bathroom, and when I heard their voices coming from the living room, I crept to the top of the stairs to listen.

"Maybe you should have stayed in the army," Mom said, "if you're just going to waste your life."

"I'd rather waste it myself than let the army waste it for me," he said, "although God knows they've got it down to a science."

"We have a child in the house, Bill, and we don't want drugs around."

"I thought I was being very discreet."

Dad said, "No one's questioning your discretion, Bill. But you understand, we can't condone the use of illegal drugs."

"You're not really trying," Uncle Bill said. "I think if you tried a little harder, if you really applied yourselves, you could condone it. After all, Uncle Bill's just trying to get through the night. Uncle Bill just needs to get some sleep."

"Those drugs are addictive," Mom said.

"It's just a little weed, Helen, it's not morphine. It's not heroin, for God's sake. It's just a little weed, to take the edge off. Is that so much to ask?"

"So," Mom said, "you think drugs are a good way to escape your problems?"

"It's been my experience that drugs are a *great* way to escape your problems. Sex and alcohol are good, too. In fact, you know what? I'm going out. I'll see you later."

"William," Mom said in her most dangerous tone, "I'm not done talking to you."

Uncle Bill was at the front door so fast that I didn't have time to hide. He saw me at the top of the stairs and saluted me.

"Don't wait up," he called to my parents, and then he was gone, his VW bug sputtering away down the street.

*

I woke up when he pulled into the driveway. I looked at my clock; it was 2:40. The car door slammed, and a minute later I heard Uncle Bill groan as he lowered himself into a lawn chair in the back yard. I crawled to the foot of my bed and peered out the window. A match flared, and then I smelled that sweetish smoke. I knew now that Uncle Bill was getting stoned. I hoped Mom wouldn't find out.

I held my breath as the screen door opened and shut, but it wasn't Mom; it was Dad. He took the seat next to Uncle Bill. They didn't speak, and for a few minutes I heard nothing but crickets and the occasional whoosh of air as Uncle Bill exhaled smoke.

Finally Uncle Bill said, "I'm a bad influence, I guess. Maybe I should go."

"Go where?" Dad asked.

"I don't know. That's just it, John, I don't know where I'm supposed to be. I don't know what I'm supposed to do. There's so much shit in my head, I'm no good for anything any more."

"Maybe you just need some time, Bill. You don't have to make any decisions right now. Stay here. Take all the time you need."

"Don't let Helen hear you say that."

"Come on, Bill, you know Helen. She wants you right here where she can keep an eye on you."

"She wants me right here under her thumb, you mean."

"And I want you here, too, and I know Janet wants you here."

"I hope she doesn't spook too easy."

"She doesn't." I liked the certainty with which Dad said this. I didn't know whether I spooked easily or not, but I wanted to be someone who didn't, and I took Dad's statement as a vote of confidence.

"I don't know," Uncle Bill said. "She must have noticed that Uncle Bill's not the same. He's not much fun. He's pretty fucked up, if the truth be told."

There was a silence, and then Dad said, "You should be proud of what you've done, Bill. Not everyone has the character to perform the kind of service you did."

I saw Uncle Bill shake his head. "I don't feel proud. I feel sick. I feel ashamed—of myself, of my country, of the whole human race, if you want to know the truth. What's going on over there, John, it's insane. You can't imagine."

I steeled myself to hear Uncle Bill describe some of the horrors of war, but whatever he was remembering, he kept it to himself.

"I spent a year of my life in hell," he said, "and I have to feel *lucky* because I got out alive. Okay, I was lucky. But I sure as hell didn't do anything to be proud of, believe me. All I did was witness other people's suffering, and the truth is, I couldn't wait to get out of there and let them suffer without me. There's nothing noble about that."

"Sometimes other people's suffering can be harder to bear than your own. Don't be so hard on yourself, Bill. I wish there were more people like you, people who refused to carry arms and insisted on doing something helpful instead."

"If everybody refused to carry arms, then no one would need my help. What a world *that* would be. I don't know. I tried to be useful, but any good I did was just a drop in the bucket, John, a drop in the fucking bucket. And it's still going on—and on and on, with no end in sight, and it's all so fucking *pointless*. God, I don't want to go back there, but I can't quite turn my back on it. I don't know how to be useful, and I don't know if it even matters. I'm not sure I have it in me to try any more." He sighed. "Uncle Bill doesn't know what to do with himself."

"Well," Dad said, "now that you mention it—"

"What? Is there something you need done? Jesus Christ, John, why didn't you say so?" Uncle Bill stood up. "You see? You see what an asshole I am? I'm sitting here feeling sorry for myself, and you've got something that needs to be done. Is it a big job?"

"No," Dad said. "It's nothing, really, Bill. I was just going to say that if you feel like building something, I could use some new birdhouses."

*

I reported this conversation to Sophie as proof that the army had not made a warmonger out of Uncle Bill.

"You should come see him," I said. "You could cheer him up."

"I'm not the damn USO," she said. "Tell him to call Bob Hope, if he needs cheering up."

She finally agreed to come, but when she stepped into the back yard and saw him, she stopped dead in her tracks.

"*You*," she said.

"Hey, Esmerelda," he said. "How are you, peanut?"

"I don't want to see you," she said, and she sprinted across the yard and climbed up into the treehouse.

"Sophie!" Mom shouted after her. "You're being very rude!"

"It's all right, leave her alone," Uncle Bill said.

"She knew you were here," I told him. "She knew she was going to see you."

"I spooked her," he said.

"What do you mean?"

"There's a lot of ugly stuff in my head, princess. Some people are more sensitive to it than others."

"Well, that's just ridiculous," Mom said. "Sophie! Come down from there right now!"

Dad started to get up. "I'll talk to her."

"Leave her alone," Uncle Bill repeated. "It's not her fault. Hell, sometimes I spook myself."

I started across the yard to join Sophie, but Mom stopped me.

"No," she said. "If she wants to be rude and antisocial, she can sit up there all by herself. Maybe by dinnertime she'll be ready to come down and act like a decent person."

But Sophie didn't come down for dinner, nor for hours afterward.

"She'll have to come down sometime," Uncle Bill said, and Mom went to check the china cabinet. She hadn't forgotten the time a couple years ago when Sophie took her soup tureen up to the treehouse to use as a chamber pot.

All the dishes were in their proper places, but still Sophie didn't come down, and finally, just before dark, Mom sent Uncle Bill out to bring her in.

"You thought it was such a good idea to humor her. 'Oh, leave her alone,' you said, 'she can't stay up there forever.' Well, now you see how she is. You get her down from there before dark, or I will personally go up there and *throw* her down."

So Uncle Bill went, and I went with him.

He strolled to the foot of the tree.

"Hey, Rapunzel," he called up to her. "How long you gonna stay up there?"

She didn't answer.

"You on a hunger strike?"

Nothing.

"Ma'am, I must inform you that I have orders from the high commander to remove you from this tree, and I am authorized to use such force as may be necessary to accomplish this mission. Don't make me come up there."

She did not appear, but from inside the treehouse her voice came.

"I don't *want* you up here."

"Okay, then, now we're getting somewhere. If you don't want me up there, then you will kindly get your butt down here."

He watched the treehouse expectantly. He cocked his head, as if listening for something.

"Hey," he said, "I put that treehouse up there, and I can damn well take it down."

She poked her head out the window.

"What are you going to do?" she sneered. "Throw a hand grenade up here?"

"Shit," he said. "What the hell are you so pissed off about?"

"I told you not to go."

"I came back, didn't I?"

"And now you feel bad all the time."

He stared up at her for a minute. "And you're mad at me for that?"

"Yes. And you have nightmares."

"Damn," he said, "have mercy, girl. You've got a hard heart, you know that?"

She disappeared back into the treehouse. Uncle Bill sighed and sat down with his back against the tree. I sat down facing him, and we looked at each other.

"Does she get mad at you when you have nightmares?" he asked.

"No, but she usually knows when I've had one. She picks up bad vibes."

"Well, I guess Uncle Bill's got plenty of those. What about you, princess, do my vibes bother you?"

"No," I said. "I wish you weren't so sad, but I don't think you did anything wrong. I'm not mad at you."

He smiled. "You're a lot like your father, aren't you?"

I shrugged.

"That's good," he said. "You're a nice kid."

We sat quietly for a few minutes, and then we noticed it was getting dark. Uncle Bill heaved himself to his feet to address Sophie again.

"Hey, Goldilocks, listen: you were right, okay? I shouldn't have gone."

She reappeared in the window and scowled at him. "I *told* you."

"I know you did, and you were right, okay?"

"You didn't listen to me."

"I know. I'm sorry."

There was a pause while she appeared to consider his apology.

"You called me Tallulah," she reminded him.

"Come on, Sophie, I was just teasing, you know that."

She leaned further out the window. "Janet says you never play your guitar any more. How come you don't?"

He looked at me with something like surprise, as if he'd forgotten that he had a guitar.

"Did you want me to play?" he asked me.

I nodded.

He looked up at Sophie. "If I play my guitar, will you come down from that damn tree?"

"Will you play the song about the little boxes?"

He bowed. "If it pleases Her Majesty."

"And you have to play a song for Janet, too. Even if it's the longest song she can think of."

"Of course," he said. "Any song she wants."

I chose The Boxer because it was the longest song I could think of, and because I loved it, and because I knew Uncle Bill loved it, too.

*

He stayed with us for a while, and he built so many birdhouses that Dad had to start giving them away. At first he worked in thoughtful silence, but more and more I would hear him whistling or singing, and one day he asked me, "What do you think about furniture?"

"Furniture?"

"Yeah, you know, tables, chairs, coffee tables and whatnot. People need furniture, right?"

"Sure," I said. "Otherwise we'd be eating off the floor."

"My point exactly. Furniture is the cornerstone of civilization, wouldn't you say? It's what separates us from other animals."

"If you say so, Uncle Bill. So, does this mean you're going to stop building birdhouses and start making furniture?"

"I'm considering it. What do you think, princess?"

"I think we have enough birdhouses. I think what the world really needs is more furniture."

He clapped his hands. "All right, then."

He took a job with a cabinetmaker in Portland, about an hour away from us. He came to dinner once in a while, and he seemed very nearly himself again.

"You think you're fooling everybody," Sophie said to him one Sunday at dinner, "but you're not fooling me. You still have nightmares."

"What are you, the dream police?"

She twirled her fork in her mashed potatoes and said nothing.

"Do you, Uncle Bill?" I asked.

"Yes," he said, "if you must know."

"I *do* know," Sophie said.

He gave her a long look. "Who monitors *your* dreams?" he asked her. "How frequent are *your* nightmares?"

She said, "I'm not dreaming about the Nam."

"No," he said, "I don't suppose you are."

Mom said, "I'm sure no one wants to talk about their nightmares at the dinner table."

"I know *I* don't." Uncle Bill pointed his fork at Sophie. "And my advice to you, cookie, is not to go messing around in Uncle Bill's head, because I guarantee, little girl, you won't like what you find."

"I already don't," she said. "You drive me crazy."

"Don't take it personally, dear," said Mom. "He does that to a lot of us."

Chapter 9

For her twelfth birthday, Sophie received a Ouija board from one of her father's girlfriends. Not to be outdone, a rival girlfriend presented her with a pack of tarot cards. Sophie was unmoved by these gifts, as she felt these women had missed the point: Sophie was psychic, she didn't need boards or cards to read people.

But then she took a second look at the cards. She liked the pictures, and she started carrying them around with her, constantly studying one picture or another. Other girls at school asked her if she could read them, and it seemed that she could.

She became an essential guest at pajama parties, so much so that the parties at which she did not appear were deemed failures. It was risky business for those hostesses who were only pretending to like her so she would provide an evening of entertainment, because she detested insincerity, and she might decide at the last minute that she didn't feel like spending the night with a bunch of phonies.

I was always invited, too, sometimes because the hostess genuinely liked me, but sometimes just as a lure to get Sophie to come. I greatly preferred the parties she chose to attend, because people liked her while she was there, sitting in a corner all night reading cards for one girl after another while everyone else played Truth or Dare. When Sophie failed to appear, she was the topic of much gossip and speculation, and I was in the uncomfortable position of being the authority on the subject. The attention was flattering, but it was outweighed by the pressure to be disloyal to Sophie. A few times I caught myself doing it, trading inside information about Sophie for a few minutes of popularity. I wasn't gossiping, I told myself, I was merely filling in the facts, setting the record straight. It wasn't like Sophie had any secrets.

"Who does she like?" they would ask, but Sophie had no use for romance at that age. Or, I should say, she had no romantic interests in the conventional sense, because she fell in love all the time, but the objects of her desire were either fictitious or dead. Robin Hood, Merlin the Wizard, Gandhi, the Artful Dodger, Martin Luther King—these were the people she imagined herself with, but I could never explain that to the pajama party crowd, and they wouldn't have believed me anyway. They were convinced that her lack of interest in boys was just an act devised to hide the fact that she wanted the same boys they did, and they reasoned that since she was competing secretly, she must have a secret weapon, and it must be connected to her psychic powers and her black cat and her tarot cards. And they would convince themselves, at least for the duration of the party, that Sophie was a witch.

*

The night Sophie blew off Rachel Harrison's party was the worst.

Rachel was the most popular girl in the sixth grade, and the party she had for her twelfth birthday was meant to be the biggest event of the year. Fifteen girls were invited for an afternoon of horseback riding, followed by dinner at a fancy Italian restaurant, after which we would return to the Harrison's for cake and a pajama party.

Throughout the week before the party, Rachel, who had never given her the time of day before, was suddenly talking to Sophie every day, reminding her that we were all counting on her to come to the party and bring her tarot cards. She made it clear that she didn't care if Sophie skipped the other activities of the day, but Rachel had promised her friends that Sophie would read their cards, and Sophie couldn't let all those people down.

In fact, Sophie could let all those people down, and she said so. She declined the invitation up front, but Rachel was accustomed to getting her way, and on the day of the party she appeared confident, almost right up until bedtime, that Sophie was going to show up.

When we were all in our sleeping bags and the lights were out, Rachel started talking about Sophie and her powers. She repeated the story of the Miracle Girl, and she stated that it was not luck or God that had prevented the gun from firing, but witchcraft. Sophie used her powers to save herself, Rachel said, and she claimed to have heard this directly from Sophie. I knew this was untrue. Sophie never talked about that night; Rachel heard it from me—not that it was witchcraft, but that Sophie believed she had saved herself—and my face burned with shame when I realized how cheaply I had sold out my best friend, for nothing more than the thrill of trading confidences with someone as popular as Rachel, confidences she would use to her own ends the minute she had an audience.

I huddled miserably in my sleeping bag and listened as Rachel went on to say that what Sophie *didn't* tell people was that she had *made* her mother crazy. Angry over some trivial matter—perhaps her mother's refusal to buy her a new Barbie doll—Sophie had put a curse on Mrs. Prescott. Rachel described Sophie as so cold-hearted that you might never know you'd been cursed; she did it silently, without even changing the expression on her face, those unearthly blue eyes cool and steady, giving away nothing.

"She gets those eyes from her father," Rachel said. "He's the devil." Dr. Prescott put spells on people, too, she said, that's why women couldn't resist him. That's why they were willing to betray their husbands and their families, willing to degrade themselves in any way Dr. Prescott wanted them to, because he possessed the same evil powers he had passed on to Sophie.

And still I said nothing. It was Rachel's party, these were her friends, and I was nobody; I was just a contact, useful only because I knew the Miracle Girl, and now less than useless because I had failed to make her appear.

I pretended to be asleep, and Rachel continued to talk about the Prescotts. Mrs. Prescott had not attacked Sophie because she was crazy, Rachel said; on the contrary, her attempt on Sophie's life was her last act of sanity as she tried to eliminate the evil she had brought into the world. But Sophie had thwarted her, and now she was locked up forever in an insane asylum, howling and drooling and ranting that she should have killed Sophie at birth, and here was Sophie, loose in the world and free to unleash her horrendous powers on anyone who displeased her.

"And people feel sorry for her," Rachel said, "because they think she's this poor abused child, when really, she's mean and twisted and evil, and she puts curses on people all the time. Remember, Alison, how you cut in front of her in the lunch line, and she said it was okay, but then a week later you got all those zits, right before the dance?"

Later on, in high school, when we studied the Salem witch trials, I would remember this party, and how half a dozen girls, one after another, suddenly connected Sophie to some misery in their lives. Failed diets, pad perms, unrequited love, as if Sophie could not only see bad news in their cards but could invent it out of pure spite and make it come true. Only one girl, Vanessa St. Pierre, spoke up on

Sophie's behalf, saying that Sophie didn't have a mean bone in her body.

And I knew this was also untrue.

*

The following Monday during lunch break, Sophie and I were crouched in the school yard shooting marbles with Walter when Alison Glickman approached us. Alison was a giggly, stupid girl with a face like a horse, and as far as I could tell, she was only popular because her family had a pool, and because she did everything Rachel Harrison told her to do.

"Um…Sophie?"

Sophie looked up. Alison giggled and shuffled her feet in the dirt.

"What do you want?" Walter said. "We're busy."

"Um…" Alison glanced over her shoulder. "Sophie, is it true that, um…you're a witch?"

She glanced over her shoulder again, and I followed Sophie's gaze as she peered around Alison's legs to see Rachel and a group of her friends clustered around the water fountain, watching.

"What are you, an idiot?" Walter said, but Sophie held out her hand to quiet him.

"It's okay," she said. "She's just asking a question."

Sophie stood up, and Alison took a step backwards. Sophie lifted one finger and pointed it at Alison.

"Don't move," she whispered, and Alison went rigid. Her eyes, bulging with fear, were locked on Sophie's.

Sophie wiggled her fingers and moved her arm in a circle, murmuring something under her breath. From where I was sitting, it sounded like "Tikki-Tikki-Tembo."

"What was it you wanted to know?" Sophie asked.

Alison blinked several times and swallowed hard.

"It's okay, you can ask." Sophie's voice was soft and seductive, and her eyes never left Alison's.

I looked over at Rachel and saw that she and her friends were leaning forward, watching anxiously. They appeared poised to move, whether to come to Alison's aid or to flee in the other direction, I couldn't tell.

"Is it true?" Alison was almost whispering herself. "Are you a witch?"

"Yes." Sophie nodded solemnly, as if to confirm that Alison had heard correctly, and then she smiled her sweetest smile.

Alison emitted a high pitched squeak and almost fell over herself as she turned and ran back to her friends, who also turned and ran.

"What was that all about?" Walter asked.

"Rachel's mad because Sophie didn't go to her party," I told him.

He looked up at Sophie. "So now you're a witch?"

She nodded.

"Oh, brother," he said, "that's all we need, is for you to start thinking you're a witch."

"How do you know I'm not?" she asked.

"For one thing, I've been winning all your marbles. So, did you put a spell on her?"

"I cursed her," Sophie said.

"What kind of a curse?" I asked.

She smiled. "Rachel Harrison is the best friend she'll ever have."

*

By the time we entered seventh grade, Rachel and her friends had stopped talking behind Sophie's back and started taunting her to her face. They pretended to believe she was a witch, they pretended to be afraid of her, they begged her not to turn them into frogs or toads or whatever. They asked her what made her so evil, and they feigned concern that she might be turning into the next Donna Skidgel.

Donna Skidgel was the scariest girl in school. Held back twice in the earlier grades, she was now killing time in the eighth grade until her sixteenth birthday, when she could quit school without being harassed by truant officers.

So while we were in the seventh grade, when breasts and periods were still new to us, Donna was already a fully developed teenager, and she would have been pretty if she'd had proper dental care and a better wardrobe, if she'd come from better circumstances. Her mother was dead, and Donna was responsible for the care and feeding of her father and two older brothers, none of whom had ever held a steady job. Donna was angry all the time; she had a quick temper and a foul mouth, and there was no one she could not or would not beat up if the spirit moved her. Even the teachers took pains not to provoke her.

So when Donna got off the bus one morning and headed toward us, I was nervous. When it became clear that our little patch of the school yard was, in fact, her destination, I was terrified to the point where I could not speak, I could only nudge Walter and nod in the direction of our impending doom.

"What the fuck?" Walter said softly, and I think he would have flattened himself against the building if I had not already scuttled behind him for protection. Only Sophie showed no fear, watching Donna's approach with mild curiosity, and it was Sophie for whom Donna had come.

"Are you the girl who reads cards?" Donna asked. She had a sallow complexion and greasy hair, and she wore a skirt and blouse that she'd clearly outgrown. She smelled yeasty.

"Yes, I read cards," Sophie said.

"Is it free?"

Sophie nodded.

"Can you do it now?"

"Sure," Sophie said.

Donna glanced at us.

"We were just leaving," Walter said.

"No," Donna said, "we'll go out back. I want to have a cigarette for this."

I didn't want to accompany them, but I didn't want Sophie to be alone with Donna, either. Sophie wouldn't lie about what the cards said, and what if Donna didn't like what she heard?

"Will you be okay, Sophie?" I asked.

"I'm fine," she said absently, already digging in her purse for her cards. "I'll see you later."

*

The three of us were together again at lunch time, and Walter asked, "So, what's in Donna's future? Jail time?"

"Don't," Sophie said. "Don't make fun of her, Walter, you have no idea what her life is like."

"So tell me," he said.

She shook her head, indicating that it was against her better judgment. "She's in a bad situation, and no one will help her. Her brothers rape her."

"Did she tell you that?" I asked.

"No," she said. "I just know. One brother is nicer than the other, she doesn't mind him so much, but the other one is mean, he hurts her."

"That's disgusting," Walter said. "You're a sick person."

"Me?"

"You don't *know*," he said. "You're just imagining things. You have a sick mind."

"I couldn't have imagined a thing like that in a million years," she said. "See, this is why I shouldn't tell you anything. You never take things seriously."

"What did her cards say?" I asked.

"She has to do something," Sophie said. "Things aren't going to change unless she does something to change them."

"What do you think she'll do?"

She shrugged. "If I were her, I would run away."

But Donna wasn't Sophie, and she didn't run away. Instead, two days after Sophie read her cards, Donna stabbed her older brother seven times with a steak knife. She didn't kill him, but she did enough damage to send him to the hospital.

The next day it was all over school that Donna had finally cracked and gone on a murderous rampage, and rumors varied wildly about the size of the weapon, the extent the injuries, and even the number of victims. The one fact consistent in every story was that Sophie had recently been seen reading Donna's cards, presumably advising her on a course of action, possibly casting a spell. The principal's office issued a proclamation forbidding the use of tarot cards, Ouija boards and other instruments of the occult on school property, and Sophie was specifically warned that if any teacher caught so much as a glimpse of her tarot cards, they would be confiscated, and Sophie would be punished severely. Sophie told us that she wasn't worried because she was pretty sure she knew her First

Amendment rights. And as it turned out, the faculty's attempts at intimidation were pretty lame compared to the student body's.

*

She was reaching into her locker one day when the door suddenly slammed shut, almost catching her hand. She looked around and found herself surrounded: Rachel Harrison, Alison Glickman, and Katie Foster.

"*You* did it," Rachel said.

Sophie spun the combination on her locker again. "I didn't do anything. I'm just trying to get my math book."

"We saw you with Donna Skidgel," said Katie. "You made her do it."

"You hexed her," Alison said.

Sophie retrieved her math book and shut her locker. She turned to face them. "If you really believed that, you wouldn't be bothering me."

"We know what you are," Rachel said, "and we're not scared of you because we're better than you."

"So, then, what do you want?" Sophie asked.

"We want you to know we're watching you," Rachel said.

"And you're going to pay for what you've done," added Katie. "You'll be sorry."

"Yeah," Alison said. "You're going to get what you deserve."

Sophie nodded. "So will you."

She tried to push past them to go to class, but one of them shoved her and she fell back against her locker, and then Alison grabbed her arm and twisted it, and Rachel caught a fistful of her hair and hissed into her ear, "Just remember we're watching you, witch."

Sophie didn't tell us about this until the next day, when someone left a dead sparrow in her locker.

"They've got your combination," Walter said. "They can get in whenever they want to."

"I think we should tell the principal," I said.

They looked at me blankly, and then went on as if I hadn't spoken.

"You can move your stuff into my locker," Walter said. "But we should leave something for them. A snake or something."

"No more dead animals," Sophie said.

"I meant a live one."

"No."

"Okay, how about this? We'll put in an alarm system, so when they open the door it will go off, or, no, when they open the door it will give them a shock. They do that with rats, don't they? How about it, Sophie? It can be our science fair project."

"No, Walter."

"Maybe just a mild shock," I said.

"Well, we'll think of something," Walter said.

But Sophie didn't want to think of something. She wanted only peace. She moved her stuff into Walter's locker and resolved not to go near her old locker again.

*

I heard my mother tell Mrs. Talbot what she heard at her bridge club about the Skidgel case.

According to Ruth Doyle, whose sister-in-law worked at the Department of Human Services, Donna was not cooperative with investigators. She refused to say anything more than that her brother was "bothering" her, but while the brother insisted that Donna attacked him in the living room for no reason, the evidence indicated that he had been stabbed in Donna's bed. He tried to change his story, saying that he had followed Donna to her room after the initial stabbing and fallen onto her bed, where she stabbed him some more. No one believed him, but without Donna's testimony he could not be prosecuted; no one was inclined to prosecute Donna, either, and so the matter was resolved by a judge ordering the brother out of the house.

I wondered if Ruth Doyle's sister-in-law knew that this left Donna to be raped only by the nicer of her two brothers. In any case, Donna herself seemed to find this a tolerable situation. She returned to school, and although the general consensus was that she was now scarier than ever, my own impression was that she was somewhat calmer, slightly less volatile. Or maybe I just felt less fear because, as a friend of Sophie's, I had been elevated, if not to the status of a friend, at least into that narrow category of people toward whom Donna bore no ill will.

Donna clearly credited Sophie with the improvements in her life, and she began to invite Sophie out behind the school every morning for a cigarette before homeroom. Alison Glickman asked me if I wasn't jealous that Sophie had found a new girlfriend, and she advised me that I ought to dump Sophie anyway, because I couldn't be Sophie's friend and Rachel's friend, too. I had no intention of dumping Sophie, I told her, and from then on I was *persona non grata* to Rachel's inner circle, although some of the more peripheral members of her clique would talk to me if Rachel wasn't around.

*

Sophie didn't use her locker any more, but she still had to pass by it every day, and when her enemies realized she wouldn't receive any messages they left inside her locker they began to leave them on the outside. In thick black marker someone drew upside down pentagrams, and hearts with the initials "S.P.+D.S." inside them. They wrote "witch" and "queer" and "slut." Sophie was called to the principal's office to account for the disgraceful state of her locker, and she was told that unless she identified the responsible party, she would have to stay after school and clean it herself.

At three o'clock she went to the janitor's office and asked Mr. Rollins for cleaning supplies. Mr. Rollins not only fetched the supplies for her, he accompanied her to her locker and insisted on cleaning it himself.

"Why should you have to clean it?" he said. "You didn't do it."

"You didn't, either," Sophie said. "Did you?"

He laughed. "No, I didn't, but I'm on the clock. If I clean it up, at least I'm getting paid for it. How much are they paying you?"

"Nothing," she said. "I'm being punished because I wouldn't tell them who did it."

"Do you know who did it?"

"Someone who doesn't like me."

"That must narrow it down, doesn't it?"

"Somewhat," she said, "but even if I know who it is, it's just my word against theirs. There weren't any witnesses."

"Well, maybe next time someone will be watching."

And the next time, Mr. Rollins was watching. He caught Alison Glickman red-handed, and there was no question of its being his word against hers. She was busted, and she had to serve a week of detention plus clean off Sophie's locker with no help from Mr. Rollins, who confided to Sophie that he had watered down the cleaning solution a bit so that Alison would have to work longer and scrub harder to undo her hateful deed.

Sophie figured that would be the end of it, and she moved back into her locker.

"Thank God," Walter said. "What a slob."

But it wasn't over, because a couple weeks later Walter and I were standing behind her, waiting for her to get something out of her locker, when suddenly she gasped and dropped her books on the floor.

"What's wrong?" I asked.

She didn't answer, but reached into her locker and took out a piece of paper, which she held in both trembling hands.

"What is it?" I asked.

She still didn't answer, and Walter and I huddled up behind her to look over her shoulder.

"Jesus Christ," Walter said.

It was a picture of a man being shot in the head, the famous photograph of the execution of a Viet Cong prisoner. It was a shocking enough picture as it was, but someone had labeled the victim and the assassin, respectively, "Sophie," and "Sophie's mother."

"Jesus Christ," Walter said again. "What a sick fuckin' thing to do."

Sophie remained motionless, her eyes glued to the picture, and finally Walter tore it from her hands.

"Stop looking at it." He ripped it to pieces and scattered it on the floor. "You want to make yourself sick? That's just what they want, Sophie, they want to see you upset and crying. Don't give them the satisfaction. Forget about this."

She stood with both hands covering her mouth, and I wasn't sure whether she was going to cry, or vomit, or both.

Walter took her by the shoulders and got in her face like a drill sergeant. "This didn't happen, you understand? Don't cry, Sophie, stop it. You're tougher than they are. You're a vicious little animal, remember? They're snakes, and you're a fuckin' mongoose, okay? Remember that."

I crouched down and gathered up her books and the papers that had spilled out of them. If Walter wanted to pretend this hadn't happened, I was happy to oblige.

"Here," I said, "here's your books, Sophie, what do you need?"

She looked at me without comprehension.

"What's your next class?" I asked. "Come on, you're going to be late."

"Science." She pulled a thick book out of her locker. "This one."

"And what's after that?"

"After that I have gym." She glanced at Walter. "Rachel's in my gym class."

"Good," he said. "Then she can see how cool you are. Act like nothing happened, don't let on that you ever saw anything."

"Okay," she said, "I just hope nothing happens in gym class."

Nothing happened in gym class that day except a lot of whispering and giggling among Rachel and her friends, but the following week someone stole Sophie's gym suit and towel while she was in the shower, leaving her naked and stranded.

Sophie's friend Gina was also in the class, and she told me she hadn't known what Rachel and her minions were up to until it backfired. Rachel had underestimated Sophie, or, rather, she had overestimated Sophie's modesty, because instead of cringing and crying and bleating for help from the shower, Sophie walked into the locker room wringing out her hair, as casually, Gina said, as if she were completely dressed.

Which, of course, she wasn't. Her nipples standing out from her small breasts, her tiny patch of pubic hair sparkling, her whole body sleek and glistening, Sophie walked right up to Rachel, "as close as I am to you," Gina said, and politely asked if Rachel had an extra towel.

The look on Rachel's face, Gina reported, was priceless, but then, just as Gina stepped forward to lend Sophie her own towel, Miss Whitcomb came in, and the look on *her* face was even more priceless. She blushed and stammered and finally demanded to know what was going on, and Sophie turned to her and calmly explained that she'd lost her towel, and Miss Whitcomb ordered her to report to her office as soon as she had some clothes on.

In her office, Miss Whitcomb gave Sophie a faltering talking to, telling her that she was a lovely girl, and it was good that she wasn't ashamed of her body, but the prolonged exhibition of her dripping wet nudity might be misconstrued by the other girls, might be seen as being deliberately provocative, and besides, she might catch cold, and so would she please, in the future, cover herself on her way to and from the shower?

A week later, after they'd taken her towel again, Sophie remarked to Walter and me that she didn't understand why a bunch of girls wanted to see her naked, when she just had all the same body parts they had.

"Maybe they wanted to see if you're a natural blonde," Walter said. "I wouldn't mind seeing for myself."

She smacked his arm. "Don't be stupid, Walter, you've known me practically my whole life. This is the same color my hair was when I didn't even have any other hair."

"I think the object was to embarrass you," I told her. "Most girls would be embarrassed."

"*Nice* girls," Walter said.

"Not me, though," Sophie said. "They wanted to get me in trouble with Miss Whitcomb, too, but this time it didn't work because Gina was watching them, and she brought me *two* towels. And now they won't be able to do it any more, because I'm going to put my towel in a plastic bag and bring it into the shower with me every time."

"That's a good idea," I said.

"That's smart, huh? And you know what else? I've started practicing magic."

"*Really* smart," Walter said.

"What kind of magic?" I asked. "What are you doing?"

"I'm making myself stronger so they can't hurt me any more."

Walter and I looked at each other.

"So," he said, "we're not talking about card tricks and pulling rabbits out of hats."

"No," she said, "not that kind of magic."

I said, "I think what we're talking about is witchcraft."

"Yes," Sophie said. "I think it's working, too. I feel stronger already."

*

90

I worried about this. Messing around with black magic was a dangerous thing. As I understood the spirit world, it was inhabited by many good souls—your ancestors, your guardian angels and such—but there were also bad spirits, even demons, who lurked around waiting for a sign of weakness, a lapse of faith, and then they would rush in and set up housekeeping in your soul, feeding you evil thoughts and using your body for their own wicked purposes.

Walter didn't take it seriously at all, and told me I was silly for even giving it a second thought.

"It's just her latest thing," he said. "If you're really worried about her, find her something new to play with. Buy her a yo-yo, she'll forget all about this."

But she was acting strange in other ways, too, like stealing things from her mother, although her mother had been gone for four years and could arguably be said to have given up her claim to whatever she'd left behind. Still, there was something furtive about the way Sophie went through her belongings and selected items to stash in her room. She showed them to me as if they were relics, and they did seem like rare artifacts, mostly old and useless things—a hat pin, a powder puff, tubes of used lipstick like crayon stubs, tiny little lace-edged hankies. And then there were the things she openly appropriated, which she did use—a scarf she sometimes tied in her hair, a black velvet ribbon she wore as a choker, a string of pearls, a red silk camisole.

One night she came to our dinner table wearing the camisole with her jeans.

"I don't mean to embarrass you, dear," said Mom, "but you're wearing your underwear."

"It's my mother's," Sophie said, not embarrassed at all.

"Yes, but the point is, dear, it's underwear. We don't come to the dinner table in our underwear. Why don't you run upstairs and see if you can't find a shirt to wear."

Sophie went upstairs.

"Honestly," Mom said, "that girl has no common sense at all."

"I wouldn't have known the difference," Dad said.

"No, you wouldn't." Mom gave him a look that suggested his own common sense wasn't much greater than Sophie's. Then she looked at me, and I knew exactly what she was thinking.

"I would know the difference, Mom."

"I should hope so."

Sophie reappeared wearing one of my father's white dress shirts. The sleeves were rolled up about forty times, the shoulder seams fell halfway to her elbows, the hem came to her knees. She looked adorable.

"Is that one of John's clean shirts?" Mom asked.

"No, this one was in the hamper."

"That's a shirt he's *worn*?"

"Yes." Sophie pulled the collar up around her face. "It smells like him."

"Take it off," Mom said. "Immediately. Janet, take her upstairs and find her a decent shirt to wear."

She had clothes of her own in my closet, but she ended up putting on one of my sweatshirts. And I saw her put it on, but I didn't see what she did with my father's shirt. I assumed she put it back in the hamper, but the next day at school she was wearing it. She told me she had slept in it.

"Why?" I asked.

"It will help my magic," she said, and I insisted that she explain to me exactly what this magic entailed.

"Come to my house after school," she said. "I'll show you."

*

I had been to Sophie's house before, and it always looked the same, like a recently-vacated hotel room. There were a few personal effects in sight—a piece of mail, a stray article of clothing—but they looked forgotten, and the furniture appeared unused. The rooms seemed deserted in an almost ghostly way.

And then, in contrast, there was Sophie's room, which was a wild disarray of clothes, books, magazines and album covers. The air was heavy with incense and the jasmine perfume she sometimes wore. She led me to an old toy chest at the foot of her bed, and on top of it were several candles of different colors, an ashtray, and an assortment of plants, feathers, rocks and sticks, a string of pink rosary beads, and a bowl of water, from which Sid was drinking.

"This is my altar," she said. She scooped Sid into her arms, and he settled on her lap as she sat cross-legged on the floor. I sat down next to her.

"First I have to show you this," she said, and she shuffled through her tarot deck until she found the card she wanted. She handed it to me, saying, "Do you know what this is?"

I read off the card. "The Magician."

"The Magician," she said. "Do you know what he does?"

"Magic?"

"He can *make things happen*, Janet." Her blue eyes were burning into mine, trying to make me see. She explained how the Magician used the elements of nature, directing them with the force of his will, focusing his energy toward the manifestation of his desires.

"With the *force of his will*, Janet."

I said, "You really believe in this stuff, don't you?"

"It's real," she whispered. "I can do it."

"What have you done?"

"So far I've just been building up my strength, but I have power, Janet. I can feel it."

I thought of Walter, and I pictured him rolling his eyes.

She told me about all the objects on the altar, where they came from and how they connected her with the elements, and how she surrounded herself with positive energy to build up her power.

"What about the rosary beads?" I asked.

"Nana gave me those. And I always wear the ring she gave me, and I always have Sid here. You're supposed to be naked, but now I wear John's shirt, because that's powerful, too."

"I don't think Dad would want you using his shirt to do witchcraft."

"But, see, this is all good. I'm not doing anything evil, Janet. Look, there's no black candles. This is just a way to focus my energy. With enough willpower, you can do anything."

"Within reason."

"You just have to believe that it's possible."

*

That night I crept into Dad's study while he was grading test papers. I sat quietly on the couch and waited. For a few minutes there was only the sound of his pen slashing the wrong answers. Finally he got to the end of a test, scribbled a grade at the top, and turned his attention to me.

"Something on your mind, Janet?"

"Is witchcraft a sin?"

"Witchcraft?"

"Yeah."

He took his glasses off and peered at me. "Well, honey, my understanding of witchcraft is that it's an attempt to usurp God's power, to claim it and use it as your own. In that case, I'd have to say yes, it's a sin of pride."

"What if someone is just using it try to make themselves stronger, so they can turn the other cheek?"

"Janet, who are we talking about?"

"Sophie."

"What is she doing?"

"Some kids at school are being really mean to her, Dad, and she's using magic to make herself stronger so they won't hurt her any more. So, that's not really a sin, is it, if that's all she's asking for?"

"It depends," he said. "Who is she asking?"

I didn't know.

"Honey, it's very common for girls your age to be interested in these things. Some people believe that adolescents are particularly sensitive to the paranormal and the occult, and that they may even possess powers that they might not have at any other time in their lives. Someone like Sophie, who tends to be psychic to begin with, might be particularly inclined to experiment. I'm not saying this is something to be taken lightly, but as long as she's not conjuring demons, she probably isn't doing any harm. If she's having a hard time at school, it may just make her feel better."

"So you think it's okay?"

"I think it's perfectly normal," he said. "But I also think Sophie spends too much time alone."

94

Chapter 10

"Sophie, don't be a baby."

She was sitting across from me in the cafeteria, and she was getting more stubborn by the minute, digging in her heels the way she did, while I was getting more and more desperate.

Mary Ann Kimball was having a make-out party, and she told me she could get Jack McCarthy to be my date, but only if I could get Sophie to go with his friend Jason.

"Sophie, we're probably the only two girls in the eighth grade who have never been to a make-out party. Don't blow this for me."

"I'm not kissing Jason."

"You don't have to kiss him, you just have to go with him. Come on, Sophie, I would do it for you."

She gave me her blank stare, and I was given to understand that she would never ask me to do anything remotely like this.

"Come on," I said. "If you don't go, I can't go."

"So what? It's just a make-out party. You want some stupid boy sticking his tongue in your mouth and trying to feel you up?"

That was exactly what I wanted. "If it's Jack McCarthy, I wouldn't mind."

"Jack McCarthy isn't even nice," she said. "He pees on the sixth graders in the shower."

"How do *you* know what he does in the shower?"

"Walter told me. And Walter also told me that Jack was telling all the boys that Gina Gleason let him touch her pussy, and Gina told me they only went to second base. You want him coming to school on Monday telling lies about you?"

"You sound like my mother." Even as I said this, I knew it was not going to win her over. She went dangerously quiet.

"Sophie, please. You don't have to do anything except show up. You don't have to make out with anybody if you don't want to."

"I don't have to do anything, period. I'm not going."

"Well, that's fine for you. That's fine, if you want to be a social retard, but I don't see why you have to ruin it for me. This is what normal kids do, Sophie, they go to parties and they make out, and Jack McCarthy is the cutest boy in school, and I have a chance to kiss him."

"Maybe your mother was right, maybe you should have spent more time with normal children from normal families. Then you'd fit in better with all your normal friends."

I knew she was hurt, but I didn't care.

"I don't care. I'm tired of not being invited places because of you. I'm tired of you always having to be different. I'm tired of sticking up for you all the time."

Her eyes widened as she took this in, but otherwise her expression didn't change.

"All right, then." She nodded and began to gather up her books, keeping her eyes away from mine. "You don't have to stick up for me any more, Janet. The next time your normal friends start talking about me, you can just join right in, just like a normal person."

I could tell exactly how offended she was by how high she held her head as she walked away.

*

So Jack went to the party with Mindy Travis, and I spent a miserable weekend at home.

"What's Sophie doing?" Dad asked as I sulked around the house on Saturday afternoon.

"Who cares? Sophie's a baby."

"Why do you say that?"

"Because she is." I found his concern irritating, partly because I suspected he was more concerned about Sophie than he was about me. "She can't ever just act like a normal person."

He laughed, and when I looked at him askance, he said, "Well, she's never been a normal person, Janet, and really, isn't that one of the reasons you love her? *Rara avis*?"

"I'm sick of her."

"Why, sweetheart? What's she done?"

"You wouldn't understand."

I went to my room and slammed the door, and wept huge tears of self-pity because no one understood.

*

I didn't see Sophie Monday morning before school—out back smoking cigarettes with Gina Gleason, I figured—but I did see Mindy Travis.

"You are so lucky you didn't go to that party with Jack," she told me. "What a creep."

"Really?"

"Oh, my God, Janet, you know what he said to me? He told me that he was supposed to go with you because his friend wanted to bang Sophie—exact words—but he was glad he ended up with me because I've got bigger tits than you—which isn't even true—and he didn't understand why I didn't take that as a compliment. Can you believe that?"

Before I could respond, she held up her hand to stop me. There was more.

"And then, when I wouldn't kiss him, he said he didn't really care about kissing anyway, he just wanted to squeeze my melons—exact words. And *then*, to top it all off, he's talking to his friend, right in front of the friend's date, about how the friend wants to bang Sophie, and he says, 'I don't know what you like about that little bitch. I'd like to shove my dick right into her prissy little mouth.' Exact words, Janet, I swear to God. Practically everybody at the party heard him. What a creep."

"Wow," I said. "I guess it's probably true about him peeing on the sixth graders in the shower, too."

"Ugh, that's disgusting. He must just be *too* cute, if he gets away with shit like that."

I made a mental note to ask Walter how far Jack claimed to have gone with Mindy.

*

Sophie stayed mad at me for a while. She avoided me, spending more of her time with Gina Gleason, smoking cigarettes and using bad words. When she and Gina pierced each other's ears, I thought I had lost her for good. I humbled myself to the extreme, and finally convinced her that I'd learned my lesson about normal people. I told her about my conversation with Mindy, but I left out the things Jack had said about her, and so I wondered who told her when, one day at the lunch table, she turned to Walter and asked him if he thought she had a prissy little mouth.

He looked puzzled. "I don't think 'prissy' is a word I associate with you. Why? Is that some kind of girl thing you're supposed to have?"

"It's a yes or no question," she said.

"I don't know what it *means*."

"It means do you think I have the kind of prissy little mouth you'd like to shove your dick into? Yes or no?"

His mouth dropped open, and when he tried to work it to say something, he could not. He looked at me as if for help.

"He's taking the fifth," I said. "He doesn't want to incriminate himself."

"Jesus Christ," he finally said. "This is a trick question, right?"

"Just tell me the truth," she said.

"Okay, yes. If that's what a prissy mouth is, then you have one, okay? Is that the answer you want? Does that make you happy?"

"Do you think other boys think that, too?"

He looked at her for a long moment. "I'm sure they do."

"How many?"

He blinked several times. "All of them, okay? Even the queers, Sophie, okay? You have a pretty little mouth, and every guy in the world wants to fuck it."

"Not pretty," she said, "prissy."

He looked at me. "Why are we having this conversation?"

"You should have taken the fifth," I told him.

"Because I got a note," Sophie said. "Somebody passed me a note, and it said, 'I hope you like to give head because I'm going to shove my dick right in your prissy little mouth.'"

"Oh, my God," I said. "Exact words."

"Yes," she said, "and I was just wondering if there were a lot of people who felt that way, because I was going to do something to protect myself, and I didn't know if I should do something big or something small."

"Do it big," Walter said.

"What is it you're going to do?" I asked.

"It's a spell," she said, and when she saw the look on my face she added, "Just to protect me, Janet, I'm not doing any evil."

"Why not?" Walter said. "Strike the fuckers down, that's what I say. Burn the whole fuckin' school down, and all the assholes with it. If you've got the power, sister, I say twitch your little nose and do it."

"Sophie, I think I know who it is." I told her what Mindy had told me. "Who passed you the note?"

"I don't know. It was on my desk in geography class. It was passed around a lot, I know that, but I couldn't tell where it came from."

"It must have been Jack," I said.

"Or someone who heard him say it," Walter said. "The guy repeats himself a lot. He might have said it to a lot of people, and a lot of them probably thought it was a good idea."

"*You* did," Sophie pointed out.

"That was a trick question," he said. "It's one thing if you're offering, it's another thing if some asshole is threatening you. Cast your little spell if you want to, but it wouldn't hurt to start carrying around a baseball bat."

*

The second note was even more disgusting than the first, but it didn't pass through as many hands, and Sophie was able to pick up a trail.

"It's not Jack," she told me, and I was oddly relieved. I was over him completely, but it was still gratifying to know that he wasn't the nastiest boy in school.

The third note was longer and promised Sophie that one day in the near future she could expect to be gang raped. The sender went into horrific detail describing the condition in which Sophie's body would be found when he and his friends were done with it.

"Aren't you scared?" I asked. "If I got a note like that, I'd be terrified."

"I know who it is," she said. "They're not going to do anything."

"Who is it?"

"Don't worry, Janet, nothing's going to happen."

The notes continued, but otherwise, nothing did happen.

*

That year at Thanksgiving, Uncle Bill brought home his new girlfriend. Her name was Rebecca—not Becky, she insisted, but Rebecca. She was a thin, brittle-looking girl, pale skin, wide brown eyes, and a braid of auburn hair so thick it was almost as big around as she was. She looked like a stick figure in the bulky hand-knit sweaters that she wore, and she smelled like sandalwood. She ate no meat or white sugar, and she never went anywhere without a supply of her own herbal tea, which she had specially blended to purify her body. She urged all of us to try it, but Mom said pointedly that when she felt the need for purification, she usually just took a bath, and Sophie claimed that she was pure already.

Sophie disliked Rebecca, and behind her back she called her Becky Oatmeal.

"But she's kind of a flower child," I said. "I would think you'd like her."

"She's a phony, Janet. She likes to pretend she's unconventional, but it's just an act. Underneath, she really just wants the same thing every other white bourgeois chick wants."

"What's that?"

"She wants to get married, Janet."

"Do you think Uncle Bill will marry her?"

She gave me a sly look. "Would you marry Jack McCarthy?"

"No," I said. "He's gross."

"You were going to let him feel you up. I'm just saying, people do stupid things when they're in love."

*

Two weeks before Christmas Rachel Harrison was out shopping with her friends when she slipped on a patch of ice and fell off the curb into the path of a truck. The driver of the truck had not been going fast—in fact, he was braking to make the turn into the parking lot where he was delivering a load of Christmas trees—but he could not stop, and Rachel was killed under his wheels.

We didn't have grief counselors or social workers to instruct us on how to cope with the untimely death of a peer, but the school authorities did recognize it as a tragedy, and we were given time off from school to attend Rachel's funeral.

Almost the entire student body was there, not, I dare say, because Rachel was so well-liked, but because her death was such a jolt to us. Most of us had never been to a funeral before, and for a lot of us it was our first real confrontation with death, our first chance to observe, at some distance, something that would inevitably strike closer to home, something that could, we now knew, strike any one of us at any moment.

Sophie did not attend the funeral, and she had nothing at all to say about Rachel's death. When my mother mentioned at dinner one night that the Harrisons were taking it hard, my father tried to solicit Sophie's feelings on the subject, but she just shrugged.

"I don't want to speak ill of the dead," she said.

"No one's asking you to, sweetheart," but he clearly wanted her to say something.

She looked at me for a minute, and then she said, "It won't be the same without her."

*

At school, I saw the way Rachel's friends looked at Sophie, with a mixture of fear and hatred, and I saw the deliberately blank look Sophie gave them in return.

"The notes have stopped, haven't they?" I asked her.

She nodded.

"It was Rachel, wasn't it?"

"Yes," she whispered.

"God damn," Walter said. "You did this?"

"I didn't do it," she said. "It just happened."

"You did something," I said.

"I just sent it back to her, that's all. She was sending out all that evil, and it wasn't enough just to protect myself. I had to make sure it didn't bounce off me and hit some innocent bystander. I had to make sure it went back to its source."

We were quiet for a minute.

"The Christmas trees were a nice touch," Walter said.

"I didn't do it, Walter. All I wanted was for her to leave me alone."

"Well, you got your wish, didn't you? She won't be bothering you any more. No one's going to fuck with you now."

"That's all I ever wanted," she said. "I just wanted them to leave me alone."

*

And they did leave her alone. In fact, she was treated with the same mixture of fear and respect we used to show Donna Skidgel, back when Donna was the scariest girl in school.

It was around this time that Sophie started wearing her mother's clothes to school. Not just the occasional scarf or bracelet, but the entire wardrobe. A black velvet cocktail dress. Red crepe hostess pajamas. A silk kimono, the color of lilacs, with matching mules. A pink satin bed jacket, which she wore with a pair of white sailor pants. Pearls, gloves, linen suits with pillbox hats.

The first time she wore the mink jacket, she was paged over the intercom and instructed to report to the principal's office. Everyone gleefully assumed she was in trouble, but she reported that she and Mr. Hannon had enjoyed a perfectly polite conversation, in which they agreed to disagree about what constituted appropriate clothing for an eighth grader. Nothing in the school dress code prohibited mink, so Mr. Hannon was forced to appeal to Sophie's reason, an unfortunate task for a man in his position, and a complete waste of time. Sophie had long ago conceded the necessity of wearing shoes to school, a concession she regretted five days a week throughout the school year; she was determined not to give another inch.

My mother almost dropped dead when she saw Sophie in her mother's mink, and when we sat down to dinner, she asked if Sophie's father knew she was wearing it.

"He knows," Sophie said.

"And it's all right with him?"

"He said he didn't think Mama would like it."

"I see. And what did you say?"

"I said, 'What's she going to do, Daddy, shoot me?'" She laughed, no doubt remembering the look on her father's face.

I laughed, too.

"That's not funny," Mom said sharply, but the more I tried to sober up, the funnier it seemed, and I couldn't control myself. My laughter set Sophie off, and hers set me off, and it was several minutes before we gasped and got the last of our giggles under control.

102

Dad fixed Sophie with a stern look. "It's good to have a sense of humor, honey, but it's not good to hide behind it."

"Well, so what?" She stopped smiling and mashed her peas with her fork. "They're just clothes, it's not like she's using them."

"You shouldn't try to look older than you are," Mom said. "That's just asking for trouble."

"Sophie," Dad said, "how *is* your mother?"

She shot him a forbidding look and didn't answer.

"John's asking you a question," Mom said.

"I don't know," she said. "I suppose she's as mental as ever."

"Is she still in the hospital?"

"I guess." She shrugged, as if she didn't know and didn't care.

"Is it a nice place?"

She tried to give him the blank stare, but she was too angry to pull it off. It never worked on him, anyway.

"They've got nice stationery," she said. "I'm sure it's a nice place. I'm sure it's nicer than she deserves."

"What do you think she deserves?" he asked.

"Well, if it were up to me, she'd be chained to a wall in a dungeon with rats chewing on her toes."

Dad said nothing. Mom caught his eye and said, "I guess we're not making much progress in the forgiveness department."

He shook his head.

"I don't see why we can't just forget about it," Sophie said.

"A wound doesn't heal properly if it hasn't been cleansed," Dad said.

She rolled her eyes. "You're worried about my soul, right? What do you want me to do, John, go to confession and say that I hate my mother? That won't change anything."

"Maybe not, but it's a good place to start."

She glared at him. "Is that what worked for you? Have *you* forgiven my mother?"

"It's not my forgiveness that she needs," he said. "But if it were, I would try to imagine how desperate she must have felt to have done something so rash, and how she must suffer now, knowing she can never undo it. I would try to imagine how tortured her soul must be, and I would try to have some compassion."

"Well, I guess that's the difference between you and me."

"Honey—"

"She tried to *kill* me, John, in case you've forgotten."

"She *is* killing you, honey, this bitterness is eating away at you."

"I was fine. I was fine until you brought it up. I don't have anything to feel bad about. *She* tried to kill *me*."

"And I'm asking you, are you going to let her do it?"

"Fuck you, John."

My mother gasped. "Sophie!"

But Sophie was on her feet, saying it again, and she repeated it several times as she gathered up her mink and ran from the house.

Mom sat with her mouth hanging open. Dad looked at me, his lips pursed.

"She doesn't like to talk about her mother," I said uselessly.

"So I see," he said. "I'm sorry you had to hear that."

Mom recovered herself. "You're not going to let her talk to you like that, are you?"

"I'm not going to wash her mouth out with soap, Helen, if that's what you mean. My biggest concern right now is not her vocabulary."

"How about some concern for your family?" she said. "We have a decent family, and there's no reason why we should be subjected to scenes like this at our dinner table." She turned to me. "You know, don't you, that if you ever spoke to either one of us like that, I would slap your face off."

"I know, Mom. She's just upset, because of her mother and all."

"It's too much," Dad said. "It's too much for one little girl to handle all by herself."

Mom pointed her fork at him. "This is what happens, John, when you butt into things that are none of your business."

"Whose business is it?"

"Her family," Mom said. "Her teachers. Maybe Catholic school would be good for her."

"What about her friends?" I said. "Isn't it their business, too?"

"Her friends should probably speak to her about the kind of language she's using. Beyond that, I don't know that you can really help her with the larger problems."

"I would if I could," I said.

"You're a good friend," Dad said. "She's very attached to you, Janet, and that's exactly what she needs, that feeling of attachment. She needs to feel like she belongs to somebody."

"Well, she doesn't belong to us," Mom said, "and I don't think it helps her to pretend she does."

*

I called Sophie later that night. She let it ring a long time, and when she finally answered I could tell she'd been crying. When I asked what she was doing, she said she was just sitting in the dark holding her cat.

"I can't believe you said that to Dad," I said.

"Oh, shit, Janet, is he mad at me?"

"He doesn't seem to be. I think he's worried about you, Sophie."

"Does he think I'm going to be mental like my mother?"

"I don't think that's it. He grew up without a mother or a father, and he knows what it's like. And look at him, Sophie, he turned out all right."

"I'm not like him, Janet. He's always such a good person, and I'm not that good."

"He's nice," I agreed, "but he's kind of boring. Sometimes I wonder if he was ever tempted to do something bad, I mean even once, ever, in his whole life."

"Oh, I know." She was sounding more like herself. "It kills me when he talks about kissing your mother in the pantry like it was the most scandalous thing on earth. He should see what my father does with his girlfriends. Last night it was the Coyote."

Sophie had recently given her father's girlfriends descriptive names inspired by the noises they made when he was fucking them: Coyote, Sea Lion in Distress, Badger Caught in a Bear Trap. Only one was articulate enough to receive a humanesque name—the Cheerleader, so called for the enthusiastic manner in which she shouted encouraging directives.

We talked for a while, and before we hung up, she said, "I guess I'll have to apologize to John. There's a lot of people I should be telling to go fuck themselves, but he isn't one of them."

"That's exactly what you should tell him," I said, "but you're going to have to apologize to Mom before you can get to Dad."

Not only did she have to apologize to Mom, she had to endure a forty-five minute series of lectures, including How To Be a Gracious Guest in Someone Else's Home and Why It Is Dangerous For a Young Girl To Dress Older Than Her Age. She must have thought the worst was over when she was finally admitted to Dad's study, but apparently there was more to come.

Dad accepted her apology and then said, "Janet, would you excuse us for a few minutes?"

They were in the study with the door closed for a long time.

"If you're going to hang around the kitchen," Mom said, "you might as well help with dinner. Why don't you make a salad?"

As I sliced up a tomato, I asked, "What do you think they're talking about?"

"I suppose they're talking about their lousy childhoods," she said. "Two motherless children."

It was odd to realize that they had this in common, something other than me. Odder still that I had never realized it before, or at least, had never considered it as something that might bind them to each other. I had offered Dad as someone who might be useful to her, like a guidance counselor. I hadn't meant for her to supplement my friendship with his. They had always been friends, and it had never bothered me before, but then, they had never excluded me from their conversation before. Sophie and I kept secrets from my father; they weren't supposed to keep secrets from me.

It's probably nothing, I thought, probably he's just reassuring her that she's not going to be mental like her mother.

"Mom, do you think Sophie's mother is really crazy?"

"Of course she is, Janet, do you think sane people try to kill their own children?"

"Do you think Sophie would be more normal if she had a regular mother?"

"I would think so, dear, but that's something we'll never know." She paused in her potato peeling. "Janet, I hope she's not holding you back, socially."

I felt my face redden. "What do you mean?"

"I mean, are there people who don't want to be friends with you because of her?"

106

"A few. But they're not people I really care about anyway."

There was a long pause, and then she asked, "Does she do things with boys?"

"What boys?" I asked, and then I realized what she was asking. "No, Mom, she doesn't even like any boys except Walter, and he's just a friend."

"I hope you're right, because I hear about these make-out parties, Janet, and I don't want to hear that you girls are involved in anything like that."

"We're not," I sighed.

Finally Sophie emerged from the study. She was wearing my father's gray cardigan and clutching what looked like a very used handkerchief. Her face was pale and her eyes were red and puffy. She had the drained look of a person who's been recently bereaved.

"Are you all right?" I asked her.

"I'm not sure." She shook her head. "He seems so nice, but—"

"Sophie, I think you'd better wash up for dinner," Mom said, and Sophie closed her mouth and went obediently, zombie-like, down the hall and up the stairs.

Dad came out of the study, and the front of his shirt was soaked with tears.

"God, Dad, what'd you do to her? She's a wreck."

"Is she going to eat something?" he asked.

"We're all going to eat something," Mom said, and she turned from the stove and looked at him. "I hope you're going to change your shirt before dinner, John."

*

"He tricked me," Sophie told me later on the phone. "I thought if I apologized for saying fuck you, then he would say he was sorry for asking all those questions about my mother. But he still wanted to talk about my mother."

"What did he say?"

"He made me cry, Janet, you know I hate that."

I understood this to mean that she didn't want to discuss it, lest it make her cry again.

"I'm going to the soup kitchen with him Thursday night," she said. "Do you want to come?"

"What for?"

"To help those less fortunate than ourselves."

"Oh, brother. Do we have to?"

"He talked me into it," she said. "You can come if you want to."

I didn't particularly want to, but I didn't like the idea of Dad and Sophie going off and doing things without me, so I said I'd go.

*

The food looked and smelled just like what was served in the school cafeteria: bland-looking chicken legs with mashed potatoes and limp green beans. It didn't smell appetizing to me, but then, as Dad pointed out, I wasn't hungry.

I tried to feel charitable as I doled out scoops of grayish-white potatoes. I was feeding the hungry, I told myself, but in truth, the hungry were a little too edgy for me. Many of them seemed unclean, and even the women had scars and tattoos and sometimes fresh bruises, and they mumbled to themselves and said things that made no sense to me. There was one man who was so exceptionally clean and well-dressed that at first I took him to be some kind of social worker, but when we were face to face I saw a strange light in his eyes, and he quoted e.e. cummings to me as if it were ordinary conversation. I smiled and nodded and gave him his potatoes, but inside I was cringing.

Sophie knew him. She was dishing out green beans beside me, standing on a crate so she could reach across the serving counter, and she greeted this man by name.

He frowned. "Do I have overdue books?"

"Your books aren't even checked out," she said. "You never have overdue books."

"I don't owe anybody," he said, "and nobody owes me."

"Damn right," Sophie said.

He smiled and moved on.

Dad happened to be walking by with a stack of clean plates. "Sophie, do you know that man?"

"That's Leon," she said. "He's always at the library. He's turned me on to some great books."

"I see." He delivered the plates and went back to the kitchen.

"I've told you about Leon," she said to me.

"Yeah, but you didn't tell me he was crazy."

"He's my friend, Janet."

She had other friends there, too, people she'd met at bus stops and park benches all around town. To me they looked like losers, but Sophie knew them as musicians, grandmothers, war veterans, and poets. She had such a great time that she decided to volunteer every Thursday, and she did, for quite a few years. I decided that this was one thing she and Dad could do without me.

Chapter 11

There were four junior highs but only one high school, so we were all thrown together our freshman year, and Sophie became a celebrity all over again as people who had heard of the Miracle Girl finally saw her in the flesh. She hated it. After the first two days of school she refused to eat in the cafeteria because everywhere she looked she saw people staring at her.

And the teachers were no better than the students. There were the raised eyebrows when they came to her name on the class list, the looks that lasted a beat too long when they took attendance, clusters of teachers who stopped talking as she approached them in the halls. Mr. Nelson, her world history teacher, took her aside after class one day to let her know that he was available if she ever wanted to talk.

"I understand," he told her. "I have a history of mental illness in my family, too."

So high school was not at all as we had imagined it. We didn't play field hockey in plaid skirts, we weren't cheerleaders or members of the student council, we didn't wear lipstick or sweater sets. Sophie didn't even wear her mother's clothes any more, except for the occasional silk blouse under her overalls.

But it wasn't a complete disappointment. I couldn't play the piano for the orchestra—I wouldn't be allowed to audition until sophomore year—but I played the flute, which I had taken up in the sixth grade, and I joined the marching band, where I developed a crush on a trumpet player named Brian. Sophie didn't join anything—unless you count a group of stoners who met in the back parking lot during lunch—but she fell in love, too, with Hector Pappaconstantine, a quiet, beautiful boy with dark curls and soulful brown eyes.

"Just like Cat Stevens," she sighed. She loved Cat Stevens.

Hector ran track, and he sat beside her in her world history class, where they made eyes at each other for several weeks before he finally asked her out. They planned to go to a movie, but when Saturday night came, they decided to skip the movie and go right for the pizza instead, which gave them a chance to talk. He had read Alan Watts. He was into Zen; it made him a better runner. He was fascinated by Sophie's psychic abilities and asked if she had ever tried astral projection, and in the hours that they spent talking, he never once mentioned anything he might have heard about her or her crazy mother. He held her hand as he walked her home, and he kissed her once, very sweetly, as he said good night.

So they started dating, and soon they were meeting every day after track practice, spending idyllic autumn afternoons making out in the woods. But it started getting dark earlier, and cold, and one afternoon while her father was at work, she brought Hector into her house, and into her bed.

It was the first time for both of them, but, as Sophie pointed out, it was a natural enough thing and required only that you act on your impulses, something she was good at. As for Hector, Sophie joked that he started out as a sprinter but was learning to pace himself for cross country.

"He's training for the marathon," she said. Again, his Zen training served him well. He and Sophie spent hours practicing and experimenting, and she declared she could not imagine why so many married couples complained of boredom. Still, she secretly borrowed her father's illustrated Kama Sutra, just in case, unlikely as it seemed, she and Hector should ever run out of ideas of their own.

Our school didn't have any formal designation for Class Couple, but if we had, Hector and Sophie would have been it. They looked good together, and they were obviously in love. They appeared together holding hands at football games and school dances, they spent every lunch period together—Sophie didn't mind being seen in the cafeteria with Hector—and they met between classes to make out in the halls.

Hector took her home to meet his family, and I think she fell for them almost as hard as she'd fallen for Hector. They were a large and noisy crowd, and they praised Hector lavishly for bringing home such a lovely girl. They teased her about being so small, and made it their mission to fatten her up. Far from being appalled by Sophie's appetite, they were impressed and inspired by it. They loved to feed her. Mrs. Pappaconstantine taught her how to make moussaka, and for many years that was the only thing Sophie could cook.

After dinner Hector would take her home on his bike, and people who had been used to seeing Hector running through town now became accustomed to the sight of Hector pedaling his bike with Sophie perched prettily on the crossbar.

It did not escape his parents' notice that Hector was taking an inordinate amount of time to deliver Sophie to her house, and when he fell asleep in Sophie's bed one night and did not come home at all, his father gave him some condoms and told him that if he was man enough to lay with a woman, he was man enough to be responsible about it. Sophie was a sweet girl, he said, and no one, least of all Mr. and Mrs. Pappaconstantine, wanted to see her get into trouble.

Although she was almost fifteen, Sophie still didn't have regular periods, and she was convinced she couldn't get pregnant. Fortunately, Hector was not convinced, and insisted on using the condoms. Sophie usually humored him, but occasionally she felt insulted by his lack of faith in her, and she stubbornly held out for what she called "all natural."

"How can you take that chance?" I asked her, but that was the point, she said, she wasn't taking a chance. She *knew*.

*

"Sophie, we hear you have a boyfriend," Dad said to her one night when she came for dinner.

She smiled dreamily. "Hector," she sighed.

"You need to be careful," Mom said. "It's dangerous to get too serious about one boy at your age."

"Dangerous?" Sophie leaned forward, intrigued.

"If you spend too much time with one boy, you might get carried away. Boys that age have only one thing on their minds, and they might pressure you into doing things you're not ready for. You might end up going further than you intend to."

Sophie stamped patterns in her mashed potatoes with her fork.

"How far do I intend to go?" she asked.

"I beg your pardon?"

"What if I want to go all the way? Then how could I go further than I intended to?"

"Well, that would be a mistake, dear. You want to save your virginity for your husband."

"I do?" Sophie pretended to think about this. "Did you save yours for your husband?"

Mom flushed. "That is an impertinent question, young lady. That is none of your business."

"They why is it your business whether I'm a virgin?"

112

Dad and I froze, but Mom didn't miss a beat. "Because if John has his way, I'll be the one raising your bastard child."

"That's enough," Dad said.

Sophie crossed her arms and raised one eyebrow at Mom.

"That's a nice thing to say," she remarked, "especially in front of your bastard husband."

Mom went white. "How dare you speak to me that way, you ungrateful little—"

"Stop!" Dad shouted, slapping the table with the flat of his hand. "Both of you, stop it right now."

"I don't have to tolerate this," Mom said.

"Listen," he said, "I think we can all agree that what Sophie decides to do with her virginity is her own business. But, Sophie, do you understand that Helen is offering you guidance? She's not trying to tell you what to do—correct me if I'm wrong, Helen—she's just trying to give you some perspective. We're talking about a most precious gift, sweetheart. You can only give it once, and you want to be sure you give it someone worthy of it."

Sophie glanced at me.

"Okay," she said, playing along. "How do I know when someone's worthy?"

"When he marries you," Mom said. "*Then* he's worthy."

"What if I don't want to get married?"

Dad said, "Honey, of course you'll want a family."

"I don't want to get married," she said stubbornly. "All my children are going to be bastards."

Mom opened her mouth but Dad overrode her.

"The point *is*," he said, "that in any event you want to save your virginity for somebody special, and not just give it away to the first boy who wants it."

She shrugged. "I think virginity is overrated. Anyway, I think this is what's called a moot discussion. Let's talk about *your* virginity, Janet. What are you planning to do with yours?"

"I was thinking of auctioning it off."

Sophie laughed.

"Oh, great," Mom said. "Now you're going to be a smartass, too." She turned to Dad. "Do you see? Whose influence is that? Does she get that from us? I don't think so."

"Maybe from your side of the family," he said.

Sophie nodded. "It's that Bill," she said. "I think he puts ideas in our heads."

*

Uncle Bill was living with Rebecca, along with three other adults and two children who shared a communal type farm house in upstate New York. He had left his job with the cabinetmaker and was once again freelancing as a carpenter.

"I suppose these people are all a bunch of potheads," said Mom, and Uncle Bill told her that not only did they all smoke it, but one of the guys also grew it and sold it, so there was always plenty for everyone.

"Not only that," he said, "but we all believe in free love, too," although this, he confessed to me, was said only for effect, and was not entirely true. Rebecca, he regretted to say, believed in no such thing.

*

The upperclassmen on the track team always invited Hector to their parties, and Sophie spent nearly every weekend with Hector and his friends, especially his best friend Ray Dostie. Ray and his girlfriend Charlene were juniors, and they were able to procure alcohol, and although Hector drank very little himself, he didn't mind if Sophie did a few shots of whatever was going around.

"He thinks if I'm drunk I won't notice the way he and Charlene are looking at each other," she told me.

"You think he's looking at Charlene?"

"He likes her tits."

"They're pretty big," I said. "Maybe he just can't avoid looking at them."

"She wants to make it with him, too, I know she does."

"Sophie, he doesn't want Charlene. He's crazy about you."

*

One Saturday night toward the end of May, Ray Dostie threw a huge party at his house, his parents having gone to Iowa to attend a cousin's college graduation. The track team had won their last meet, they were no longer in training, and they were planning to cut loose and have the blowout party of the year. Sophie insisted that I go with her, because she knew for a fact that Brian the trumpet player would be there, and she knew that our time to get together had come.

"You think so?" I said.

"Janet, I *know*. I saw him in the library this morning, and I asked him if he was going, and he said he wouldn't miss it. And I put my hand on his heart—*right on his heart*, Janet—and I could feel it in his heart that he wanted to see you there. So, I'm taking you to that party, bufflehead. Wear your lucky underpants."

"I don't have lucky underpants, Sophie."

"Well, pick out some good ones, because they're about to become your lucky ones."

She took me shopping on Saturday afternoon and picked out a green silk blouse for me, emerald like the color of her grandmother's ring. It was a bolder color than I usually wore, but I liked the way it made my eyes look greener, and it seemed to lend some luster to my usually dull brown hair.

"You look beautiful," Sophie said. "Plus, it's a touch-me blouse. Doesn't it feel great? He's going to be dying to touch it, and once he does, he won't be able to stop."

"I don't know if *I* can stop," I said. "I'll look like a feeb if I show up and I can't stop touching myself."

"There's nothing wrong with touching yourself," she said. "It just shows him how touchable you are."

*

It was a great party. Ray managed to blend people from every faction of the school into one large, friendly group, straights and freaks and everyone in between. I remember at one point I could feel the floor shaking and the house rocking with exuberance as everyone danced to the Rolling Stones, and it struck me that we were young and we were doing exactly what we should be doing, all of us. This was the high school experience that Sophie and I had longed for, and at the precise moment that I realized this, Sophie appeared beside me, dancing wildly, her nearly sheer leopard print shirt sliding up to expose her belly as she swung her arms over her head. She saw that I was dancing with Brian, and she stopped jumping up and down long enough to reach out and hug me, and then she danced away, laughing and blowing kisses.

I saw her one more time that night, when I went to say goodbye to her. She was smoking a joint with Walter, and when she saw me she hugged me again.

"You're leaving with him, aren't you?" she said.

"Yes," I said, and she squealed.

"Has he touched your blouse yet?"

"Sophie, he's been touching it all night. My arm, my shoulder, my back. I think this is going to be my lucky blouse."

"Well, here, invite him in." She unbuttoned my top button, hushing my protests. "It's just one button, Janet, don't be a baby."

"She's right," Walter said. "It's nice like that, with the collar open. It makes you look sophisticated."

"Okay," I said. I was anxious to go. "I'll talk to you tomorrow."

"Yes, you will," she said. "And you'll tell me everything."

*

I told myself, as Brian and I left the party, that it was silly to feel so nervous. Brian was easy to be with, that's what I liked about him in the first place. He loved music, he read books, we were in complete agreement as to which members of the band were the worst pains in the ass. We had a lot to talk about, and as he walked me home, I relaxed and enjoyed his company. When we reached my house we stood and talked a while longer, and then I offered to show him the treehouse.

The leaves weren't full yet, and there was just enough moonlight for us to find our way into the tree. Inside the treehouse it was cool and dark, and we sat close together and continued to talk quietly, and then he kissed me, slowly, experimentally. His mouth tasted slightly of beer, and although I hadn't learned to like beer, I had the absurd notion that I was enjoying a cool one on a warm night.

The first kiss went pretty well, and we tried a few more. He had one arm around me, and his other hand touched my blouse at the collar, and then moved to my neck, my face, my hair.

And then he leaned back and looked at me, and he said, "I bet you don't even know how pretty you are."

116

I shook my head. "I'm not. I always wanted to be pretty like Sophie."

"No," he said. "Sophie's cute, but she's flaky as hell. If I were going to go out with someone, I'd want somebody more down to earth. I'd want somebody like you."

I didn't know what to say. Was he asking?

"Janet, if I asked you to go out with me, what would you say?"

I laughed. "I don't know. I guess I might say yes, if you were really asking."

"Okay, I'm asking. Will you go out with me?"

On an impulse I reached out and put my hand over his heart, to see if I could feel what Sophie felt. What I felt was how real he was, and how alive. I felt a warmth that seemed to grow under my touch.

"Yes," I said.

*

Early the next morning, my father was visiting his bird feeders when he sensed that he was being watched. He looked up at the treehouse and was startled to see Sophie's face in the window. It was an unusual place for her to be at 6:30 on a Sunday morning, but Sophie was an unusual girl, and her presence there did not disturb him as much as her strange silence. It seemed to him there was something wary about her gaze. He felt as if he had inadvertently treed some small and skittish animal, and he wanted to lure her down without scaring her away.

He said, "Good morning, Sophie."

He didn't hear her reply, but she moved away from the window and appeared in the doorway. She seemed bleary and rumpled, and it was obvious that she'd spent the night up there and slept badly, if she'd slept at all.

"Do you want to come in the house?" he asked. "You must be cold up there."

She cast a glance at the house and shook her head.

"How about some breakfast?"

"No, thank you." Her voice was croaky, and Dad thought she might be shivering.

"Is there something I can get you? A pillow? Some blankets?"

She hesitated. "I could use your bathroom."

117

"Well, of course, honey, come on in."

She climbed down the tree with uncharacteristic caution, and when she reached the ground and turned toward him, he was alarmed by her appearance. She was pale and shaky, her eyes were red, the lids swollen. Her thin shirt was on inside out, and her jeans were sagging around her hips as if she'd lost weight overnight.

"Sweetheart, are you all right?" He started to put his arm around her, to guide her into the house, but she flinched and shied away from him.

She was in the bathroom for nearly an hour with the shower running, and when she came out it was obvious she'd been crying. Dad hadn't wanted to wake me looking for clean clothes for her, so he'd given her his bathrobe to wear, and she took it but she refused to surrender her own clothes to be washed. He found them later stuffed in the kitchen garbage can.

When I came downstairs Dad was in the living room reading the paper. He asked me how my night was, and I told him that I was going out with Brian.

"Brian the trumpet player? How marvelous."

"Sophie told me it was going to happen," I said. "I can't wait to tell her."

"Janet." He leaned toward me with a look of concern, and that's when he told me how he'd found her in the yard, how bad she looked and how strangely she behaved.

"She's in the study now," he said. "She won't tell me what's wrong."

I went to the study door and knocked.

"Sophie?"

I opened the door and went in. The curtains were closed, and Sophie was curled up into a tiny ball in the corner of the couch, almost lost in the folds of my father's robe.

I perched on the couch near her. "What happened? You were having such a good time when I left."

"It was a great party," she said sadly.

"Yes, it was. What happened?"

"Hey," she said. She sat up and wiped her tears on Dad's robe. "You left with Brian. Oh, Janet, tell me what happened."

"Sophie, don't you want to tell me—"

"No," she said. "Yours is better. I want to hear yours."

So I told her everything. "I could have gone on kissing him forever."

"That's so sweet." She tried to smile, but the smile dissolved in a fresh flood of tears.

"Sophie, what happened? Did you and Hector have a fight?"

She shook her head, too emotional to speak. She pulled the robe over her head and disappeared into it like a turtle.

"But you love each other," I said. "You'll work it out."

There was a vigorous thrashing under the robe; I took it to be her head shaking in denial.

"Sophie." I tugged gently on the blue velour. "Come on, don't be so dramatic."

There was a sharp knock at the door and my mother poked her head in.

"It's time to get ready for church, girls." She had almost shut the door again when she did a double take. Her eyes narrowed in disapproval. "Sophie, where are your clothes?"

Sophie's voice was muffled. "I have some up in Janet's room."

"Well, go put them on, please. What do you have for shoes?"

Sophie's head emerged from the bathrobe. "I don't have any."

"You came here without shoes? How many times do I have to tell you that in this house—"

"I lost them," Sophie said. "I had shoes, but I lost them."

"That's because you don't keep them on your feet." Mom turned away, and her heels clicked angrily down the hall as she went to report to my father.

"John," she called. "She has no shoes. How can she go to Mass without shoes?"

I followed her into the living room. "If Sophie can't go to church, can I stay home with her?"

"You may not," Mom said. "In this house, we go to church on Sunday."

"On the other hand," Dad said, "you're certainly old enough to make that decision for yourself."

"John, what did I just say?"

"Helen, she's been to church every Sunday of her life. Let her make up her own mind."

So Mom went to church mad, and I stayed home and heard Sophie's confession.

It was a great party, tons of people, I knew that. Walter had some kickass weed, and some guy named Jeff had a bottle of Southern Comfort.

"Janis Joplin used to drink Southern Comfort," she told me, "so I pretended I was her." With a hit of acid she could have completed the transformation, she was sure, but there didn't seem to be any acid around.

Still, it was a great party, and when it was over, when everyone had either passed out or gone home, Sophie and Hector and Ray and Charlene gathered in the basement rec room, where the Dosties had a piece of furniture known as The Pit, a nine-piece sectional sofa arranged as an enormous day bed. Ray had some hash—"guaranteed to make you horny," he said, winking at Sophie—and the four of them sprawled out on the couch and smoked a bowl.

The lights were low, and the hash made everyone spacey, and they soon ran out of conversation. Ray and Charlene began to make out on one side of The Pit while Hector and Sophie made out on the other side. She couldn't say how long this went on—it seemed like hours—and on top of the Southern Comfort and the dope, Hector's kisses were making her dizzy.

Eventually he began to undress her. She was used to more privacy, but she didn't want to stop and she was too wasted to move, and besides, Ray and Charlene obviously didn't care. They were already naked themselves. So she stayed where she was and gave herself up to Hector.

And that was fine, she could live with that. Hector was her boyfriend and she wasn't ashamed of anything they did together. And in fact, she said, it was an incredible experience, because at one point all four of them found the same rhythm, and it was like something cosmic, as if they had all merged into a single being, and Sophie felt her own joy combined with and multiplied by theirs—bliss to the power of four.

"It was very Zen," she said.

But then suddenly, abruptly, Hector stopped and withdrew from her, leaving her crazed and burning. She could hear his voice, but she couldn't make sense of the words, and he seemed to be talking to someone else anyway.

She reached for him, begging him to come back to her, and he did, he was with her again, and she almost sobbed with relief. They were moving together again, and his voice was in her ear, low and sexy, and now he *was* talking to her, he was asking her if she would do something for him, and she said yes, oh, yes, Hector, anything. And then he said something she didn't understand, something about Ray, and the next thing she knew Hector was moving away from her again, trailing his fingers through her hair, saying it's okay, don't worry, it's all right. And then Ray was looming over her, and Hector was turning away, into Charlene's open arms.

Sophie shook her head, trying to clear it, and she tried to sit up, but Ray's hands were on her shoulders, pushing her back down, not roughly, but firmly.

"It's okay," he said. "I'm going to take care of you," and she finally understood that she had been traded.

"Oh, no," I said. "Oh, no, Sophie, please tell me you didn't."

"I had to," she whispered. Because if you tell someone you would do anything for them, and then they ask you to prove it, you have to. There was nothing else for her to do but to close her eyes and hope it would be over quickly.

It wasn't. Ray had spent himself with Charlene, and he was in no hurry to be done with Sophie. He told her as he mounted her that he'd been waiting a long time for this, and he predicted that it was going to be good.

He was bigger than Hector, and he smelled of sex with Charlene. She wished he wouldn't talk, but he did, constantly, murmuring appreciatively, whispering things he knew about her, things he could only have heard from Hector, and she realized that they had planned this, Hector and Ray, and maybe Charlene, too. Charlene had always wanted Hector.

And now, beside her on The Pit, Charlene was cooing and moaning as Hector made love to her, and Sophie felt robbed. She wondered what happened to that cosmic bliss they had all shared just a few minutes ago.

An involuntary groan was forced from her throat as Ray ground himself deeper into her, and he seemed to take this as encouragement. His breath was steaming in her ear—he was still talking, telling her how good it was, telling her how much she liked it, describing in crude and graphic terms how specific parts of her body were responding to him, and she was shocked to discover that what he said was true, that while her mind had been on Hector and Charlene, her body was responding to Ray's with horrifying enthusiasm.

How could that be? She didn't want it, she wasn't enjoying it, but she couldn't deny that, to anyone watching—to those who *were* watching—it would certainly appear that she was displaying all the signs of orgasmic pleasure. So, was it all in her head, the difference between Hector and Ray? If sex was just sex, then what was the difference between giving herself and being taken?

"It fucked up my head really bad," she told me, and when it was finally over, she pushed Ray off of her, grabbed the clothes she hoped were hers, and stumbled up the stairs. She found the bathroom and puked several times, crouching naked in front of the toilet with Ray's slime dripping out of her. She was dying to take a shower, but she couldn't stay in that house another minute, and despite her trembling she managed to pull on the clothes she had—her shirt and Hector's jeans—and walk out the back door of Ray's house. And then she walked four and a half miles to my house, stopping only once, in the middle of the bridge, where she took off the charm bracelet Hector had given her for Christmas and threw it in the river.

*

When my parents got home from church I was playing Cat Stevens on the piano, and Sophie was curled up in my father's chair, resting her head on the padded arm. She was still wearing his robe, and that was the first thing my mother noticed.

"Sophie, I thought I told you to get dressed."

"You did," Sophie said. "I forgot."

Mom handed her coat to Dad and planted her fists on her hips. "Well, I think now it's time for you to get dressed and go home."

"No, it isn't," Dad called from the hallway. "Sophie's going to eat some pancakes, aren't you, Sophie? You must be hungry."

"John—"

"I'm starving," Sophie said. She climbed out of the chair and gathered up the excess length of Dad's robe. "I'm going to get dressed right now."

122

She skirted my mother, and I heard her bare feet scampering up the stairs.

I shuffled my sheet music to avoid my mother's eye.

"John, are you getting some perverse thrill out of undermining everything I say today?"

"I'm sorry, but there's something about going to church that makes me want to be charitable. Come on, Helen, we can spare a meal for a hungry child. She seems to have had a rough night."

"Well, whose fault is that?"

Their voices moved down the hall toward the kitchen.

"And now," I said to the empty room, "a little pancake music." I played the Maple Leaf Rag, one of my father's favorites.

*

A while later, as we sat down to eat, Dad said, "Janet, have you told your mother your news?"

"Mom, Brian asked me to go out with him."

"Well, it's about time," she said. "Your father was slow like that."

"It was a big decision," Dad said. "I wasn't really supposed to be dating, you know." He cut his pancakes into precise pieces, wielding his butter knife like a scalpel. "So, Janet, tell us about this momentous event. Was it very romantic?"

I gave them the edited-for-parents version of the evening, being sure to include Brian's professed belief that I was pretty.

"I like him already," Dad said. "He has excellent taste."

"He's liked her for a long time," Sophie said, "but he's shy. They make a really cute couple."

"And is this trumpet-playing Brian a friend of yours, too, Sophie?" Dad asked.

"Well, I don't know him as well as *Janet* does—" she smirked at me—"but I know him. He's nice."

Dad nodded approvingly. "I'll look forward to meeting him."

Mom cleared her throat. "Speaking of things that happened last night, Sophie, I understand you slept in the treehouse."

"Yes."

"Why didn't you ring the doorbell?"

I was surprised that Mom would bring this up. It was a sore point between my parents—Dad thought Sophie should have a key to our house, but Mom would not allow it.

"I didn't want to wake everybody up," Sophie said. "It was late."

"How late? How late was it?"

Sophie stopped eating and looked at my mother. I watched her face compose itself into the mask of blank indifference, the face she wore for the teachers at school.

"I don't know how late," she said.

"Two o'clock? Three o'clock? Four?"

"I really don't know."

"Had you been drinking?"

Dad put down his fork. "Helen—"

"I'm not accusing, John, I'm just asking."

"Yes," Sophie said.

"And did you take any drugs?"

"I smoked some dope."

"And did you have intercourse?"

Dad blushed and sputtered, "For God's sake, Helen, what a question. Let her eat her breakfast."

"I want to know what's going on. I want to know what we're dealing with here." She turned back to Sophie. "Was Hector with you in the treehouse?"

"No," Sophie said, "he absolutely was not."

Mom cut through her stack of pancakes and stabbed them with her fork. "Who gave you permission to sleep in our treehouse?"

There was a stunned silence from all three of us. A look of hurt surprise broke through Sophie's mask, and for a second she lost her breath, as if it had been knocked out of her.

"She has my permission," Dad said. "What are you trying to do, Helen?"

"I want to know when someone is sleeping in my yard," she said. "Do you want her alone in the treehouse all night when no one knows where she is? She's someone's child, John, she's not one of your birds that can flutter in and out of here at will. She has to answer to someone, and while she's under my roof she can answer to me. Is that too much to ask?"

He glanced at me and Sophie. "Maybe this is something we should discuss later, Helen."

"I want to know what's going on. I don't like waking up to find that someone's slept in my yard, used all my hot water, and is lounging around my house in my husband's bathrobe. I want an explanation, John, I think I'm owed at least that."

It was quiet except for the gentle scrape of Sophie's fork on her plate as she pushed her food around.

"I had a fight with Hector," she said softly. "We were at a party and we had a fight and I left, and I was walking home, but your house was closer, and I didn't think anybody would mind if I stayed in the treehouse." She took a deep breath. "I'm sorry about the hot water."

Mom said, "I just wish you had rung the doorbell, dear. I'd much rather have you sleeping in the house where it's safe."

"She's right," Dad said. "You could have called from the party, and I would have come to pick you up. You shouldn't be walking around alone at night."

"Yeah, I know," Sophie said. "Something bad might happen to me." A bitter laugh escaped her. "We can't have that."

"Certainly not," Dad said. He pinned her with a direct, penetrating look in the eyes, and she looked away, down at her plate.

"And one more thing," said Mom. "I have to say that I don't approve of your drinking and using drugs. If it continues I'll have to ask you not to come here any more. Do you understand that?"

"Yes," Sophie said.

"And Sophie," Mom added, "I hope you're being careful." She gave her the you-know-what-I'm-talking-about look.

Sophie opened her mouth and then shut it. The telephone rang, and she closed her eyes and said, "Please, tell him I don't want to talk to him. Tell him to leave me alone."

Dad answered the phone. "Yes, Hector, she is here, but she says she doesn't want to talk to you right now. Maybe the best thing to do would be to leave her alone for a while…Yes, I'll tell her. Goodbye, Hector."

He resumed his seat. "He really needs to talk to you," he reported. "It's important. He wants you to call him."

"Yeah, well…" Sophie pushed her pancakes around some more. "I don't care any more what he wants. He's used up all his wishes."

*

The next day Sophie showed up at school wearing a lace tablecloth as a shawl, and for the rest of the school year she wore it every day, keeping it wrapped tightly around her shoulders, huddling constantly as if she were cold, even though it was practically summer.

"And you wonder why people think you're strange," Walter said, but she was beyond that.

She chose to serve detention every afternoon rather than attend the history class she shared with Hector, and when Mr. Nelson tracked her down and begged her to return to class, she played the history-of-mental-illness-in-the-family card and persuaded him to require her attendance only on the day of the final, with the provision that on that day she would not sit in her usual seat, but in the back corner of the room, the back corner being her preferred spot in all her classes now.

There were only a few weeks left of school, but that was long enough for rumors to spread about the reasons for Hector and Sophie's breakup. The most popular story was that Sophie had gone insane and tried to stab Hector when she caught him talking to another girl, but that didn't stop a number of girls from trying to scoop him up on the rebound. They flocked to him like widows to a widower, but Hector was convinced that he could win Sophie back if only he could get her to talk to him.

She would not. When people asked her what happened, she answered shortly that they'd had a fight, but in fact they never did, because Sophie refused to be in the same room with him, refused to answer her telephone when he called, refused to respond to messages delivered by his friends. Hector begged me to talk to her on his behalf, to persuade her to give him another chance, but I told him her mind was made up, and I wouldn't change it even if I could.

Finally, in what was clearly a desperate move, he sent Charlene to corner Sophie in the girls' bathroom and convince her to talk to him. Sophie locked herself in a stall and repeatedly flushed the toilet in an effort to drown out Charlene's voice, but Charlene just spoke louder.

"He wants to talk to you," Charlene shouted. "He's worried about you."

Sophie didn't answer.

"Come on, Sophie, he just wants to talk to you. He loves you."

126

Sophie flushed again.

"You're acting like a baby."

A brief pause, and then Sophie said, "Is that coming from him or from you?"

"That's coming from me," Charlene said. "Look, I never did anything like that before, either, but you're making too big a deal of it."

"But you knew it was going to happen, didn't you?" Sophie came out of the stall and confronted Charlene. "You were in on it the whole time, weren't you?"

Charlene looked surprised. "Weren't *you*?"

"No."

"Hector was supposed to talk to you about it."

"When?"

"Weeks ago. Right after Ray found out his parents were going away."

Sophie dropped back against the wall and clutched her shawl tighter around her shoulders. "He never said a word."

"Well, anyway, you didn't seem to mind so much. You seemed to be having a good enough time."

"I know," Sophie said. "I know how it seemed. It was weird."

"Yeah, well, you're going to have to talk to him sooner or later, you might as well stop playing these silly games. The poor guy's a wreck. Why don't you just let him say he's sorry and get on with it?"

"No." Sophie headed for the door.

"Well, what am I supposed to tell him?" Charlene asked.

"Tell him to find someone new."

And as the door swung shut behind her, she heard Charlene say, "I've been telling him that all year."

*

"So, is anyone going to tell me what happened?" Walter asked.

We were on our lunch break, standing at the edge of the woods behind the school. Walter and Sophie were passing a joint back and forth.

She leaned back against a tree and stared into the woods, pulling her shawl closer around her shoulders.

"Anyone?" he said. "Janet?"

I kicked at a rock embedded in the forest floor. "Her lucky underpants didn't work."

"Oh." He studied Sophie's profile. "I guess the problem with lucky underpants is that they're only lucky until you take them off."

She glanced at him as she passed him the joint, then she looked away again.

"He traded me," she said, "for something bigger and better equipped."

Walter squinted through the smoke. "What do you mean, he traded you?"

"He traded me for Charlene."

"Charlene? That cow?" He made a face. "What do you mean, he *traded* you? You mean like a baseball card?"

"Walter, you're a guy," she said. "Do you think my tits are too small?"

"Are you kidding? You've got great tits," he told her. "They may even be perfect, but of course it's hard to say for sure without conducting a more thorough inspection. If you would just allow me—"

"I'll drop them off at the lab," she said.

He stubbed the roach out on the bottom of his shoe and tucked it into his cigarette pack. He lit a cigarette for Sophie, and one for himself.

"So, just to make sure I understand this, when you say Hector *traded* you, do you mean, like, for sex?"

She pulled her shawl tighter and refused to look at him. He gave me a questioning look, and I nodded.

"So, Hector and Charlene, and—?"

She covered her face with her hands. He looked at me again, and again I nodded.

"Jesus Christ, Sophie, you went along with this?"

"I didn't *want* to."

"But you did it anyway?"

"Hector wanted me to," she whispered.

"That's *it*?" Walter exploded. "*That's* your reason, that Hector *wanted* you to? What the fuck's wrong with you?"

"Walter—" I said.

"Well, what is she, a fuckin' slave? He fuckin' *traded* her?" He pulled her hands away from her face. "You let him do that to you? You think you have to do everything Hector wants you to do? Jesus

Christ, Sophie, if you did everything *I* wanted you to do—" He stopped.

"What?" she asked.

"Well, you never would have been with Hector in the first place. The guy's a fuckin' moron, and you're a moron for going along with it. You can do better than that. Jesus Christ."

"He wants her back," I said.

"Fuck him," he said. "Sophie, if you go back to him, I swear I'll kill you."

"I can't go back to him," she said. "I can't even look at him."

"He's a fuckin' asshole," he said, "and that goes for his friend Ray, too."

"And Charlene," I added.

"Jesus Christ, that fuckin' bimbo."

"Charlene told me I was making too big a deal out of it," Sophie said, and she told Walter about the conversation in the girls' room.

"That fuckin' bitch," he said. "I bet she's lying, too, I bet that's *not* the first time she's done something like that. Fuckin' bimbo."

"No," Sophie said. "She was telling the truth." She looked at us as if she'd just thought of something. She began to pace between the trees, and I could see the wheels turning in her head.

"I've been looking at this all wrong," she said. "This is a *good* thing. In fact, Janet, I bet your father would call this a blessing."

"I don't think so," I said.

"Some fuckin' blessing," Walter said.

"Yes, because now I know the truth. I thought Hector loved me, but now I know the truth."

Walter and I looked at each other.

"I guess that's what you'd call looking on the bright side," he said.

"So all I have to do," Sophie said, "is just never fall in love again." She looked pleased with herself, as if she'd just solved a riddle. Her shawl slipped off one shoulder.

"Well," I said, "just don't fall in love with Hector again."

"Don't fall in love with Ray, either," Walter advised. "Or Charlene, for that matter."

"Not with anyone," she said. "Then I'll always know I'm not being used."

Walter rolled his eyes.

"But Sophie," I said, "what if—"

"Forget it," Walter said. "Don't try to reason with her."

"No," I said, "but, Sophie, what if there's someone who really truly loves you?"

"I won't let them," she said.

Chapter 12

During the summer that followed, Sophie became a slut.

She became a serious user of drugs and alcohol, going to parties several nights a week, and each night she left with a different guy. It didn't seem to matter who it was; she would do anybody, anywhere. By the beginning of our sophomore year she had been with more than two dozen boys, in the woods, on the golf course, on headstones in the cemetery, in the dugout at the Little League field, in cars, in hammocks, on picnic tables.

Another girl might not have been able to get away with this, but Sophie was the Miracle Girl, and her behavior was seen as an extension, indeed as a bonus, of her pre-existing eccentricities. She had always been strange, but now she was strange and alluring, and the phrase Miracle Girl took on new meaning as stories of her sexual prowess became legend.

You would think that there would be little status to be gained by fucking her, since it was so easily done, but that was not the case. I don't know exactly what distinguished her from the other girls they could have had, and did have, but the prevailing attitude among the guys from school was that screwing Sophie was a rite of passage. It made you a man, and not just any man, but a Playboy kind of man, a sophisticated man of particular tastes. It was a status symbol, like owning a certain kind of car or the right stereo equipment.

And the truly elite were those who could say they'd had her more than once, because while she would try anyone once, there were very few to whom she would return for more, and none who touched her heart.

Not that any of them were interested in her heart. Nailing Sophie was a competitive sport, like fox hunting. They might all join in the chase, they might all take their shots at her, but in the end no one could say he'd bagged her, because no one could pin her down for longer than it took to rut in the bushes with her.

"What's wrong with you?" I asked her on the phone one night. "What are you doing?"

"I'm just having fun. What's wrong with that?"

"It just seems like that's all you care about any more, is partying and—" I broke off, unsure how to put it, unable to come up with a polite term.

"I'm having *fun*," she repeated, but I was unconvinced and she knew it. "Janet, don't make such a big deal out of it. It's just something to do so I don't have to think about anything."

"Like what?"

"Like anything. Like why was I born? Like why did my parents even have me if they didn't want me? She could have had an abortion. Hell, Daddy could have done it. He's done it for his girlfriends."

"He has? How do you know that?"

"I just know." She sounded miserable.

"Well, then, they must have wanted you."

"Maybe they wanted a baby," she said, "but they didn't know it was going to be *me*. If they'd known, then my mother could have killed me before I was even born. It would have saved everybody a lot of trouble."

I didn't know what to say.

"Maybe that's all it was," she said, "maybe it was just sort of a late term abortion. It was just eight years too late."

"Dad thinks maybe your parents just have too many problems of their own."

"See?" she said. "I'm not even one of their problems."

*

Uncle Bill came to stay with us that summer, to help Dad paint the house. Rebecca was not with him.

"She wants to have children," he told us. "Fine, I say, bring 'em on, let's have some kids. But no, we have to get married first. Sure, I say, why not? Let's get married. But that's not enough. I have to make more money, we have to buy a house."

"Well, of course," Mom said. "If she's going to have children, she wants a secure and stable environment."

Uncle Bill sighed. "I think what she really wants is a completely different guy."

*

We planned a barbeque for the 4th of July, and we invited Sophie to join us.

It was late afternoon when she shimmered into the back yard, all bronze and gold in a pink halter-top sundress and a dozen gold bracelets glittering on one arm. Her fingers and toes sparkled with frosted pink nail polish.

"Oh, my," said Uncle Bill, "look at you. You look like a tropical sunset."

She flashed him a dazzling smile. "You think so?"

"Oh, yeah, honey. Add a little rum to that and you've got paradise."

"Watch yourself, Bill," said my mother as she passed by with a plate of chicken.

Sophie watched Mom go by and then sidled up to Uncle Bill. "So, how are things at Sunnybrook Farm?"

"I'm here alone," Uncle Bill said. "What does that tell you?"

"You're taking a vacation?"

"She's sick of me," he said. "She's had it up to here. Uncle Bill's charm has worn off."

Sophie purred. "I find that hard to believe."

"I smoke too much dope," he said. "I have no ambition. Do you find *that* hard to believe?"

Sophie crinkled her nose. "She's not much fun, is she?"

I didn't think Mom could hear them, but she turned around and said, "Relationships are serious things, dear, they're not meant to be fun."

"Still," Uncle Bill said, "it wouldn't hurt to have a sense of humor. Hey, Trixie, you'll appreciate this: she wants to get married and move to Ohio. She wants me to take a job with her father. You know what her father does?"

"What?"

"He sells *shoes*."

Sophie screamed.

"My sentiments exactly," he said.

"Sophie," Mom said, "why don't you and Janet go into the kitchen and make some lemonade?"

Sophie squeezed the lemons while I measured the sugar.

"I'd forgotten how cute Bill is," she said with a wicked smile.

"Oh, no, Sophie, you wouldn't. Would you?"

Her smile grew broader.

"No, Sophie, don't."

"Why not?"

"Well, he might be getting married, for one thing, and he's way too old, Sophie, he's twice our age. And he's my *uncle*. He's practically *your* uncle, too, it would be like incest or something. And if Mom ever found out, she'd kill you both. Just forget it, okay?"

She shrugged. "It was just a thought." She strained the juice into the pitcher. "He's got a nice ass, though."

"I'm serious, Sophie, if you seduce Uncle Bill, I'll be really mad at you."

"Okay, all right, don't worry about it. I'll be good."

*

When the chicken was cooked and the potato salad had been passed around, Dad remarked that we hadn't seen much of Sophie this summer.

"I've been pretty busy," she said.

"Are you staying out of trouble?" Mom asked.

Uncle Bill laughed. "That's the wrong question. It's not whether she's staying out of trouble, but what kind of trouble is she getting into? Let me guess. Shoplifting?"

Sophie smiled and shook her head.

"No," he said, "too mundane. Wait, I've got it: stealing cars."

She clapped her hand over her mouth to stifle a squeal. In fact she had told me that sometimes when one of her father's girlfriends was spending the night, Sophie would borrow her car keys and go for a drive.

"Let's do it," she said to Uncle Bill. "You and me, right now, let's steal a car and get out of here. It'll be fun."

"We'll rob banks," he said. "We'll be Bonnie and Clyde."

"Except we won't kill anyone," she said.

"And no one will kill us," he added.

"Bonnie and Clyde." Mom gave a snort of derision. "More like Abbott and Costello."

"More like Lolita and Humbert," I said, giving Sophie a pointed look.

"That could be fun, too," she said, and then she gave a little yelp as I kicked her under the table.

"Heckle and Jeckle," said Dad.

134

"Tweedledee and Tweedledum," said Mom.

"Masters and Johnson." That was Sophie. I kicked her again, and she kicked me back.

"Simon and Garfunkel," said Uncle Bill. "So, Sophie, who's the lucky guy? You got a boyfriend?"

"No boyfriend," she said. "I'm freelancing."

"What exactly does that mean?" asked Mom.

"It means I do what I want. It means if I like somebody, I can go with him, and if I like somebody else, I can go with him, too." She turned her big blue eyes on Uncle Bill. "It means I'm completely available."

"I hope you're not spreading yourself too thin," Mom said, and then, when Sophie laughed, "What's so funny?"

"Aren't you the one who told me it was dangerous to get too serious about one boy? Well, now I'm not serious about any of them. Janet's the one who's in danger now."

"No, I'm not," I said. "I can handle Brian."

"Talk about your lucky guy," said Uncle Bill. "I bet he's eating out of your hand."

"He's crazy about her," Sophie said.

"As he should be." Uncle Bill nodded his approval. "Do you ever double date?"

Sophie and I exchanged a look—she didn't exactly "date"—and then she looked directly into Uncle Bill's eyes and said, "What did you have in mind?"

He blushed. "I mean Janet and Brian, and you and some boy your own age, Missy."

"I've been thinking," she said, "that maybe I shouldn't limit myself to boys my own age."

"Oh, yes, you should," Mom said. "You just put that thought right out of your head, young lady. John, tell her."

Dad cleared his throat. "An older man would be taking advantage of you, sweetheart. That's why there are laws to protect you."

"But Helen says that boys my age only want one thing, so what's the difference?"

"Boys your age want it," Mom said, "but they don't really expect to get it. High school boys are less sophisticated, they can't manipulate you the way an older man could."

"I'd hate to discriminate against somebody because of their *age*," Sophie said. "What if there's someone who's perfect for me but I never gave him a chance because he happened to be a little older than me? How old is too old?"

"As long as you're in high school, you should be dating high school boys," Mom said.

Sophie sighed. "High school boys are so stupid."

Mom laughed. "Most men are stupid, dear, you'll get used to that. That's why it's important to be selective, and to hold out for one who *isn't* so stupid, one who doesn't keep his brains in his pants."

Dad and Uncle Bill looked at each other.

"I guess I'll take that as a compliment," Dad said.

"Well, certainly, dear." Mom patted his hand. "I wouldn't have married you if I thought you were only interested in sex, and I certainly wouldn't stay with you if I thought you wanted to fool around with young girls."

"Well, there's not much chance of that," Dad said. "Even if I were interested in them, I don't think they'd be interested in me. I'm not very cool."

"You're not cool at all, Dad," I told him. "No offense, but you're kind of a nerd."

"I don't mind," he said.

"None of these high school girls have crushes on you?" asked Uncle Bill.

Dad shrugged. "Not that I'm aware of. They go for the younger guys in the English department."

"I don't think you're a nerd," Sophie said. "I think you're very nice."

Something about the sincerity of her tone made us all turn to look at her, and she looked back at us, surprised by the attention.

"I do," she said. "I think he's the nicest grownup I've ever met. I even think he's kind of attractive, but maybe that's just because I know how nice he is."

When everyone continued to stare at her without saying anything, she asked, "What's wrong with that?"

"Are you saying you have a crush on my husband?" Mom asked.

"No," Sophie said, "I'm not saying that at all. I'm just saying that I think he's nice, and I think if there was some girl in his class,

136

and maybe people didn't like her very much and no one was ever nice to her, then maybe she'd have a crush on him, because he's so nice. That's all."

Her bracelets jingled as she brushed a stray curl off her forehead. She looked to me to say something.

"In that case," I said, "you've got nothing to worry about, Mom. Sophie doesn't usually go for nice guys."

*

One night she was driving some woman's car when a policeman signaled her to pull over. She toyed with the idea of outrunning him, she told me, but she wasn't that good with the stick shift yet, and she was just stoned enough to be mesmerized by the flashing blue lights, so she stopped.

The cop asked to see her license, and she was forced to admit that she didn't have one. He asked whose car she was driving, and she explained that she didn't exactly know, she had found it in her driveway. He asked for her name, and she clammed up.

As he crouched down to speak to her at eye level, she had a strange sense of déjà vu, and in the middle of his speech about how much trouble she was in, she interrupted.

"I know you. You shot my mother."

That shut him up. He blinked several times and then peered at her.

"You should have killed her," she added.

"You're that little girl," he said. "Sophie, right? The Miracle Girl?"

She nodded.

"I'll be damned," he said. "How are you?"

"I'm fine. How are you?"

"Good," he said, "real good. How old are you now?"

"Fifteen."

"No kidding." He was smiling and nodding, but then he stopped and frowned at her. "I hate to see you like this, getting into trouble. You really aren't supposed to be driving this car, are you?"

"Not really."

"What are you doing, turning into a juvenile delinquent?"

She shrugged.

"Don't," he said. "Don't do this. I've seen it happen too many times. Don't let one bad experience ruin your whole life."

"It's a little late for that."

"No, it isn't, don't say that. It's never too late. Listen to me, I know it's hard. Sometimes people with these types of family problems, they have to work twice as hard to stay on track, but it's worth it in the long run, believe me. Don't throw your life away. Do your homework, get good grades, stay out of trouble. Okay?"

"What do you care?"

"I'm serious, I don't want to see you mess up your life."

But Sophie's concerns were more immediate.

"Are you going to arrest me?" she asked.

"No," he said, "not this time. Here's what I'm going to do: I'm going to follow you while you drive this car back to wherever you found it. I'm going to make sure that you get home, which is where you belong. I'm going to see you safely into your house, and then I'm going to drive away and pretend this never happened, but I want you to start doing things by the book. Get your permit, if you want to drive, and get a licensed driver to teach you, and don't ever, ever take someone's car without their permission, you got that?"

"Yes."

"And let me be clear about this: if I ever catch you doing something like this again, I will bust you, I guarantee it. Do you want to end up doing time in the Youth Center?"

"I'm guessing the answer you want is no."

"Damn right," he said. "Your mother, she's still locked up, right?"

"Yes."

"Don't let it happen to you. Drugs and alcohol, don't kid yourself, that's how people ruin their lives. That and grand theft auto. Let's go now, honey, it's time for you to go home."

*

On a muggy night in August, Uncle Bill instructed me to pack up the cooler, because he was taking us all to the drive-in.

"What's playing?" I asked.

"Oh, you're going to love it, princess. A disaster double feature. The Poseidon Adventure and The Towering Inferno. Ooooh," he cooed in his Merv Griffin voice. "Irwin Allen. *Master* of realism."

"I'll pass," Mom said.

"Are you kidding? How can you pass up an opportunity like this?" He opened his arms and sang to her in a hideous falsetto, "There's got to be a morning a-after."

Mom waved her hand at him as if she were brushing off a bug. "You're insane if you think I'm going to spend four hours cooped up in a car with you."

"I'll go," I said.

"Great. How about you, John? Come on, it'll be inspirational. Disasters bring out the best in people."

"All right," Dad said.

"All right, then. Surf's up. Hey what's your friend doing tonight?" Uncle Bill asked me.

"He has to work."

"Not your *boyfriend*. I'm talking about your girlfriend. Sexy Sadie. What's she up to?"

Sophie had heard that Ray and Charlene were fighting, and she was going to a party where Ray was supposed to be.

"I'm going to fuck him," she told me, "and this time I'm going to enjoy it."

"She has plans," I told Uncle Bill.

*

The first feature was The Poseidon Adventure. I sat up front with Dad while Uncle Bill sprawled across the back seat drinking beer. When the ship turned upside down and Gene Hackman was urging everyone to climb the Christmas tree, Uncle Bill tapped me on the head and said, "It's the old you-can't-climb-the-Christmas-tree-in-that-dress-you'd-better-take-it-off routine. Oldest trick in the book, don't fall for it. Notice that no one's telling Shelley Winters to take *her* dress off. A word to the wise, princess."

"Thanks, Uncle Bill."

"God damn it." He slapped at a mosquito. "If we can put a man on the moon, why can't we make a car with screen windows?"

He kept up a running commentary throughout the movie, including his views on filmmakers who kill Roddy McDowall off early in the picture. "That's just a waste of talent. Why hire a star of that caliber if you're just going to waste him?" He wanted to take bets on which characters would survive.

"That's not fair," I said. "You've seen it before."

"Yeah, but I'm hoping this time it will turn out different."

We swapped seats for The Towering Inferno, and I got bored and dozed to the sound of fire engines. I drifted in and out of sleep, and at one point I woke up to hear Dad and Uncle Bill talking.

"Hell, what do I know about girls?" Uncle Bill was saying.

Dad sighed. "They're lovely, though, aren't they?"

"Lovely," Uncle Bill agreed.

"Sometimes I feel like I'm living in a house full of exotic birds. Helen, Janet, Sophie. Beautiful, mysterious creatures."

"Frankly, I'm surprised Helen lets Sophie hang around as much as she does."

"It's funny you should say that, because as a matter of fact, Helen doesn't like it. Why do you suppose that is?"

"Well, Christ, John, look at her. The girl's a siren. She's Maggie the Kitten."

"What do you mean?"

"She's provocative as hell, that's what I mean. Coming around in those cute little outfits, all that bare young flesh on display, and then giving me these knowing looks like she can read every dirty thought in my head. I'm not a praying man, John, but I have begged the Lord not to leave me alone with that girl, not even for a minute. I would be too sorely tempted."

There was a silence.

"I must sound like an asshole," Uncle Bill said. "You've never thought of her that way, have you?"

"No." Dad's voice had a note of surprise in it, whether at Uncle Bill or himself I couldn't tell.

"Well, you're a better man than I am."

"It's not that, Bill, it's just—I guess I still think of her as a child. I mean, I knew she slept with Hector, but they were so young, and so devoted to each other, it just seemed very...innocent."

"Innocent," Uncle Bill repeated. "I don't know, John. She may be a tease, she might not be as willing as she comes on, but innocent?

No. Look again, pal. That girl is jailbait, pure and simple. I'm sure that's how Helen sees her."

"I don't know. This has been going on for a long time. Helen says she's a bad influence, but there has to be more to it than that. Janet's a very level-headed girl, she's not that easily influenced. I think Helen resents Sophie because Sophie's always been beyond her control. She can't stand that. Janet and I are pretty easy to keep in line, but Sophie's a wild card, she disrupts Helen's sense of order. And the fact that she's someone else's child…" He sighed. "Sometimes I think Helen closed up her heart a little more with each child we lost."

There was a brief silence, and then Uncle Bill said, "You've been with her a long time."

"Almost twenty years. We'll be married twenty years next spring. I've had an offer to do a book about El Yunque, the Puerto Rican National Rainforest. I was thinking I would take her there in February, kind of a second honeymoon."

"That sounds great," Uncle Bill said. "I would volunteer to stay with Janet if her friend didn't scare me so much."

"I appreciate that, but I think Janet will be fine. Besides, you've got your own home to tend to."

"Oh, that," Uncle Bill said. "Who knows, I may not even have a home come February. I might be beating on your door, begging Janet to take me in."

*

The next morning Sophie called to report on her success with Ray. She'd gone to two different parties before she made her entrance at the party where she knew he'd be, at his cousin Sylvia's house. He was in the kitchen playing cards with a bunch of his track buddies, including Hector. Sophie leaned over the back of Ray's chair, nibbled his ear, and asked him if he wanted to dance. She wished she could have seen the look on Hector's face as she led Ray out of the room, but strategy prevented her from turning around.

On the dance floor, Ray pressed her close to him and whispered in her ear that all the guys were talking about her.

"But they don't have to tell me," he said, "because I already know." He told her that he'd thought of her often since the night of his party. He regretted that their time together had been so brief; there were so many more things he wanted to do with her. He knew what she liked, he reminded her, and he promised that he would satisfy her completely or die in the attempt.

She remembered how, the first time, Ray's incessant whispering had repulsed her, but now she found it arousing, his breath hot in her ear, the scent of his body tantalizing. By the time the dance was over she was drunk with desire, and by the time they got to his car she couldn't wait for him to drive anywhere but took him in the back seat right there where the car was parked on the street, not caring that people coming and going from the party could see them. After that he took her to the place where he and Charlene used to park, and he did all the things he'd promised he would do.

I stood in the kitchen listening to this with the telephone pressed tightly against my ear to prevent Sophie's voice from carrying to my family, my parents and Uncle Bill, who were lingering at the breakfast table. I wondered what Dad would think of his innocent little sweetheart if he could hear her now.

There was another party tonight, she told me, and she and Ray were going together. She hoped Hector would be there.

"Is that why you're doing all this?" I asked. "To get back at Hector?"

I saw Dad glance up from his paper.

"I'm just having fun," Sophie said. "If I can get back at Hector in the process, well, that's just the icing on the cake."

*

"It's none of my business, I know," Dad said, "but I thought I heard you say that Sophie was getting back at Hector."

"She's going out with his best friend."

"Ouch," said Uncle Bill. "She knows how to hurt a guy."

"But wasn't it she who broke up with Hector?" Dad asked.

"Yes," I said, and then, because some explanation seemed to be in order, I added, "He was with another girl."

"Not *her* best friend, I hope," said Uncle Bill. "Wouldn't that be you?"

"Actually, it was his best friend's girlfriend."

Uncle Bill shook his head. "Can't tell the players without a scorecard. Is this the best friend who now has Sophie?"

142

"Ray," I said. "Ray was going out with Charlene, and Hector was going out with Sophie, but then one night at a party at Ray's house, Hector and Charlene were together, and that was all right with Ray, but it wasn't all right with Sophie—"

"Why was it all right with Ray?" Dad asked.

Uncle Bill smacked him on the arm. "Because that leaves Sophie for Ray," he said. "Come on, John, use your head. Ray's no dummy, am I right, princess?"

I nodded. "So Sophie broke up with Hector, but Ray and Charlene stayed together, only now they've had a big fight and I guess they broke up, and now Sophie's going out with Ray."

"Well, Ray certainly played his cards right," said Uncle Bill.

"But you don't think Sophie really likes Ray," Dad said. "You think she's using him to get back at Hector."

"She says she's just having fun," I said. "I know she doesn't like Ray the way she liked Hector. I don't think she really likes any of the guys she goes out with, not the way she liked Hector."

"And she doesn't think Hector was punished enough just by losing her?" Dad said.

"This is the icing on the cake," I said.

*

Sophie spent about a week with Ray, a week of fairly constant screwing, day and night, taking breaks only when they needed to eat or when Sophie insisted they get dressed and go to a party. Ray claimed he didn't really want to go to parties, but in fact, Sophie told me, the very act of getting dressed was a form of foreplay for them, because the moment they got their clothes on they began to anticipate taking them off again. Besides, although Ray would never admit it, the sight of Sophie dancing and flirting with other guys inflamed his desire for her. Her own debauchery was fueled by drugs and alcohol, and by flaunting herself in front of Hector, and so she and Ray always ended up leaving the party early, with a renewed appetite for each other. She was continually astonished that Ray's body could give her so much pleasure, when Ray himself could not.

Eventually she became restless, and finally one night she left the party with another guy. Ray claimed to be hurt, but he appeared to recover quickly. Within a few days he was back together with Charlene, while Sophie continued to try one guy after another.

Chapter 13

On the first day of school Brian and I were eating in the cafeteria when Sophie came and sat down with us.

"Hey, bufflehead." She wriggled up close to me on the bench and plucked a piece of pineapple out of my fruit cup. She sampled our lunches and decided that Brian's fries needed more ketchup. She had gone to get some when Walter joined us.

He had spent the summer as a bellhop at his uncle's resort in Bar Harbor. Part way through the summer I'd received a postcard from him, a picture of the inn overlooking the sea. The message he wrote said, "Get me out of this cartoon—I've got to get home!"

We started to trade information about our respective summers, and when Sophie returned with her ketchup he only glanced at her and kept on talking. He didn't acknowledge her until finally she said, "Yes, Walter, I've missed you, too."

"I guess I don't have to ask how you spent *your* summer," he said coldly. "I've been reading about it on the bathroom walls. You're getting great reviews, you must be proud of yourself."

From the way Brian blushed, I knew he'd read them, too.

"We've only been in school for three hours," Walter said, "and already there are half a dozen testimonials on the men's room walls. That would be one every half hour. Is that the rate you've been doing them at?"

"Do you always believe what you read on the bathroom walls?" she asked.

"All right, then, *you* tell me: what have you been doing all summer, Sophie?"

"I read a lot of books," she said. "I went to the beach a lot. I went to a lot of parties, and I fucked a lot of guys. Is that all right with you?"

"I can't believe this," he said. "I've seen you for five fuckin' minutes and I'm sick of you already. I'll see you guys later. I've lost my fuckin' appetite."

Sophie watched him stalk out of the cafeteria. She pulled his abandoned tray toward her and took a carrot stick. "What's his problem?"

Brian cleared his throat. "I hope you're not overly dependent on your psychic abilities, Sophie, because sometimes they seem a little slow to kick in."

"What do you mean?"

He leaned across the table and stage whispered, "I think he likes you."

"I make him sick, didn't you hear him?"

"There are none so blind," he said, "as those who will not see."

"A rolling stone gathers no moss," she replied.

They looked at me.

I shrugged. "Good fences make good neighbors."

*

As soon as we were alone, I asked Brian, "What do they say?"

"Who?"

"On the bathroom walls," I said. "What do they say about Sophie?"

"Janet, you don't want to know."

"Yes, I do."

"Well, then, you'll have to ask someone else, because I won't repeat it."

"Walter will tell me."

"Fine, then, ask Walter, if you want to know so bad."

"Well, don't get mad," I said. "Is there some reason why I shouldn't know?"

"Only that it's disgusting, and if you knew you'd be embarrassed to be friends with her."

"Why? What does it say?"

He shook his head. "I can't talk about this."

*

"Walter, that stuff on the bathroom wall—"

"Don't get me started," he said. "Sometimes I just want to slap her."

"I want to know what it says."

"No, you don't."

"Yes, I do. Is somebody going to tell me, or am I going to have to go in there and read it myself?"

"Okay, basically it says she's a hot fuck, okay? I don't want to go into any more detail than that, because it would make you sick."

"Well, let me ask you this: does it make you embarrassed to be her friend?"

"Embarrassed? To know that every guy in school knows who's doing what between her legs? Yeah, I'd say it's a little embarrassing. To know that she's giving it away to every pig who wants it? That's more than embarrassing, Janet, that hurts."

"Why don't you tell her that?"

"Because she doesn't care."

"I think she cares more than she lets on," I said.

"Well, either way, I'm wasting my time."

"You love her, don't you?"

"God help me," he said. "I'm a moron."

*

It was the first big party of the year and everyone was there. After a certain point there were very few people who were still sober, and Brian and I ended up in a lengthy conversation with one of them, our foreign exchange student Karin.

She was struggling with the language and with the culture, and her host sister had insensitively let on that Karin was something of a disappointment to the family. They had thought it would be fun to host a student, an assumption based on having met last year's student, a warm, bubbly girl from Argentina who had never seen snow before and who was charmingly and gratifyingly delighted by it.

Karin was from Finland.

We had been deep in conversation for a while when I felt a tug at my sleeve. It was Walter, and he was more than a little intoxicated.

"Did you see that?" he asked.

"Did I see what?"

"Did you see who tonight's lucky winner is? Can you fuckin' believe it?"

"Walter, what are you talking about?"

He leaned closer to me and I could smell the alcohol on his breath. "Sophie just left with Peter Van Dyke."

Peter Van Dyke was a pompous creep who was running for student council on a platform that included eliminating the free lunch program, as he considered it to be a serious drain on the nation's resources. He was a prig and a bore. He was also Alison Glickman's boyfriend.

"You're kidding," I said.

He fumbled with his fingers and finally gave me a peace sign.

"Scout's honor," he said. "And here I was trying to get up the nerve—Hey! Look who's here, the guy who started it all."

He lurched away from me and headed for the other side of the room.

"Hey, Hector!" he shouted. "Nice work, buddy. You did a nice fuckin' job on her."

"On who?" said Hector.

"On Sophie, you asshole, who the fuck do you think I'm talking about? You pimped her out to your friend Ray, and now she's a regular slut."

"I've got news for you," Hector said. "She was always a slut. Ask anybody, man, she loves it."

It took three guys to pull Walter off of Hector, and by the time they managed to do it Hector's nose was broken and the party's hostess was freaking out about the blood stains on the rug.

*

"I can't believe you did that," Sophie said to Walter the following Monday. "Violence doesn't solve anything."

"It made *me* feel better," Walter said, "although I'd like to have broken his whole fuckin' face. No, don't give me that look, Sophie, you didn't hear the way he was talking about you."

"What difference does it make?" she said. "Why do you care what he says? Why do you care what any of them say?"

He looked up at the sky and took a thoughtful drag of his cigarette. "Maybe what bothers me is the way you keep giving them so much to talk about."

She crossed her arms and lifted her chin. "I see," she said coldly. "This is all *my* fault. So, are you going to break *my* nose, too?"

"Don't tempt me," he said. "And speaking of I-can't-believe-you-did-that, what about you and Peter Van Dyke?"

148

"Oh, Sophie," I said, "how could you?"

"That was an act of mercy," she said. "That poor guy needed it bad."

"You're just a regular Florence Nightingale, aren't you?" Walter said. "Sophie, don't you care, even a little bit, what people think of you? Do you *want* people talking about you like you're trash?"

"I just want everybody to mind their own business," she said, "and that includes you."

"It's none of my business, when I have to listen to some prick like Hector talking about you? When I have to see the details of your sex life inscribed on every wall of every bathroom in the building?"

"Don't read them," she said.

"Some of them are illustrated." He flicked away his cigarette and ran his hand through his hair in a gesture of exasperation. "What do you want from me? You want me to just keep taking it?"

"Okay." She nodded as if they'd reached some sort of agreement, and then she turned and walked away.

Walter watched her go.

"You see, Janet? She doesn't care. I can't take it any more, I've just got to stop hanging around with her."

But a week later he was sitting in the cafeteria with her when Brian and I met her for lunch, and she was making him laugh as she described her latest adventures.

Over the weekend, she and Gina Gleason had hitchhiked to Boston to go to an Aerosmith concert. Along the way they scored some acid, which was exactly what they needed to ensure maximum enjoyment of the concert, and afterward, they crashed with Gina's cousin, who was a student at MIT and had a lab in his basement where he and his roommates manufactured speed. Gina and Sophie were treated to samples, and then Sophie paired off with Gina's cousin, and Gina went with one of the roommates, and nobody slept all night long. The next day everyone took some more speed, and they piled in the car for a road trip, and they drove Sophie and Gina home.

"Can someone explain this to me?" I asked. "If I tried to hitchhike to Boston—never mind the rest of it—if I tried to hitchhike anywhere, I'd end up dead in a ditch with my mother standing over me saying, 'I told you so.' But Sophie can hitchhike to Boston, take all kinds of drugs, have sex with a guy she barely knows, and she has a great time and gets home in one piece. Why is that?"

"Because you would never do those things," Sophie said. "They just don't come naturally to you."

"Do you really want to do those things?" Brian asked me.

"Well…not really," I said. "I don't know. Sometimes I think I'd like a little excitement in my life."

"Thanks a lot," he said.

"You want to know what protects Sophie?" Walter said. "Seriously? It's her own insanity. People spend two minutes with her and they can tell she's crazier than they are. Nobody wants to fuck with someone who's crazier than they are."

*

The next time I was scheduled to have lunch with Sophie, Brian told me that we were expected at a meeting of the orchestra committee.

"Today at lunch," he said.

"But I'm having lunch with Sophie."

"Bring her with you," he said. "This is the only time we can all be there."

The orchestra committee consisted of Bob Chandler, Vicky Dearborn, Victor Sorrento, Brian, and me. We were supposed to be deciding on the program for the spring concert, and we had already wasted two meetings arguing with Victor, who wanted only Wagner.

Victor was the concert master. He was a talented violinist, but he was also a pain in the ass, conceited and condescending. He thought he was sophisticated because he had supposedly lost his virginity to a college woman, a nineteen-year-old counselor at the summer camp where he worked as a junior counselor. He never missed an opportunity to mention that he preferred older women, and when we got sick of listening to him we deliberately offended him by calling him Junior. Junior Counselor, as if it were his name.

"This is Sophie," I said, and she gave the committee her most winning smile.

"I know who she *is*," Victor said, glancing at her disdainfully. "Why is she *here*?"

"You'll have to forgive him," Vicky said. "He's kind of an asshole."

"Charmed, I'm sure," Sophie said.

"Do you know anything about music?" Victor asked her.

"I know what I like." She sprinkled salt on my fries.

"And what do you *like*?" he asked in his most patronizing tone.

"Cat Stevens," she said. "He's my favorite."

He sniffed. "I'm talking about *real* music. Do you know any classical music?"

She considered this as she licked ketchup off her fingers. "I've always liked Mozart."

He rolled his eyes. "*Anybody* can like Mozart."

For a moment we seemed suspended in the cafeteria, the clamor of voices and dishes faded away and an absolute silence enveloped our table, and then, beside me, a low giggle bubbled up from Sophie's throat, a sweet sound, so soft it was almost inaudible. I had to look at her to see if I was imagining it. She was hiding her mouth behind her hand, but her eyes were dancing.

"Whose music do *you* like?" she asked Victor.

"Wagner, of course. He's the only true genius."

"Really? That's interesting," she said, "because I was just reading that men who like Wagner are, like, twelve times more likely to have premature ejaculations. Is that true?"

Vicky laughed.

Victor blinked uncertainly, then mustered his bravado and said, "Bullshit."

"No, really," she said. "I read it in one of Daddy's medical journals. They did a study of people in marriage therapy, and they interviewed all these men who couldn't satisfy their wives, and the one thing they all had in common was that they all loved German opera. Weird, huh? Janet, I showed you that article, didn't I?"

"Yes," I said. "Johns Hopkins, wasn't it?"

"Yes, I think it was."

Victor crossed his arms over his chest.

"I've heard about you," he said. "You're quite the little bitch, aren't you?"

Sophie shrugged. "*Anybody* can be a bitch."

"And a slut, too, I've heard." He narrowed his eyes and leered at her. "I usually prefer older women, but I bet I could teach you a thing or two."

"I bet you couldn't," she replied evenly, "but we'll never know."

"Too bad," he said. "You don't know what you're missing."

Vicky tapped her spoon on her glass. "Okay, Junior, let's get down to business."

*

Two weeks later Vicky's parents went away and she threw a small party, mostly people from the orchestra, but a few other people, too. She asked me to bring Sophie.

"I like her," she said.

There was wine and beer at the party, but it was pretty tame compared to what Sophie was used to. Since there was no hard liquor, and no drugs except a joint that she herself had brought, she entertained herself by flirting with a few of the guys. Victor Sorrento was clearly interested, but in the end she set her sights on Bob Chandler's younger brother Todd.

Todd was a scrawny, timid freshman who knew Sophie by reputation and was obviously intimidated by her. Every time she made eye contact with him he fairly trembled with fear. This seemed to amuse her, and she circled him for a while, teasing, until finally I saw her pressed up against his side, whispering something in his ear.

"I'll be right back," I heard him say, and he came over to Brian and me and confided that Sophie had just invited him upstairs.

"She's making fun of me, right? If I said I'd go with her, she'd just laugh at me, right?"

I said, "No, I don't think so."

He looked stricken, as if the humiliation of being ridiculed by Sophie was less frightening than the alternative, the possibility that she might actually take him upstairs and do things to him, unspeakable things from which he might never recover, if he even survived the night.

"I don't think she's kidding," Brian said, "but maybe you should stay away from her anyway."

152

"Maybe I'll try a beer," Todd said, and he headed for the kitchen.

We didn't see him again, and didn't miss him, until Bob announced that he was supposed to have his brother home by eleven but couldn't find him.

Victor spoke up. "He's upstairs with Janet's slutty little friend."

"How about that?" Vicky said. "I guess Todd likes older women, too."

Bob sighed. "I guess I have to go get him." He set his face into a look of determination, like a soldier volunteering for a mission, and he marched up the stairs.

He returned a few minutes later, alone and defeated. Todd was locked in the master bedroom with Sophie, and his only response to Bob's reminder of his curfew was a muffled, "Go away."

It was another fifteen or twenty minutes before Todd stumbled down the stairs with a hickey on his neck and a dopey smile on his face.

"I think I'm in love," he said.

"Oh, shit," Bob said. "How much did you drink?"

"Just that one beer," Todd said. "I'm not drunk, I'm in love."

"And you're going to come home late, looking like that? You dumbass, now we'll both be grounded."

"I don't care," Todd said. "They can do whatever they want to me. They could kill me right now, and I'd die happy."

"I could kill you right now, and I'd be happy. Let's go."

"Thank you, Vicky!" Todd shouted as Bob dragged him out the door. "I had a great time at your party!"

Several other people left at the same time, and I remarked to Brian that we should probably gather up Sophie and go, but Vicky insisted that we stay. We sat down and became engrossed in a discussion about the spring concert, and then the stereo went quiet between songs and we became aware of Sophie's voice screaming curses from the upstairs bathroom.

Vicky got there first. She threw open the door and stopped short, causing Brian and me to collide with her like Keystone Kops.

"It looks like someone's having a crisis," she said.

There was Victor, sprawled in the bathtub, his legs hanging over the side, his arms covering his head as Sophie beat him with a toilet plunger. The front of her blouse was torn open, exposing her breasts, and she had blood on her mouth, but she seemed oblivious to everything except the task of beating Victor.

"*I* decide!" she screamed. "Not you!" She was swinging the plunger as if it were an ax.

Brian grabbed her around the waist, and I tried to wrest the plunger from her grip, but she wouldn't let go. She looked at me without recognition, and her eyes were so full of rage that for a second I thought she was going to turn her attack on me. I shouted her name several times as we struggled for the plunger, and finally Brian pulled her off balance and she let go. She aimed a kick at Victor's legs, but Brian dragged her out of reach. Still struggling, she spit at Victor. She shook herself, trying to break free of Brian's grasp, but he held on, and finally she regained her footing and stood still.

She glared at Victor. "If you ever touch me again, I'll kill you," she hissed.

Victor pulled himself shakily to his feet. There were smears of blood on his shirt.

"You *are* a crazy bitch."

"You don't know the half of it," she said. "Try me, asshole."

Vicky wrung out a washcloth and wiped Sophie's mouth. "You're bleeding," she said. "What happened?" Almost as an afterthought she pulled the front of Sophie's blouse together to cover her.

"I'm not bleeding, he is," Sophie said. "He tried to rape me."

"That crazy cunt bit me," Victor said. "I'm going to need a tetanus shot." He held out his hand to show where she had broken the skin.

"Serves you right," Vicky said. "There's some peroxide in the medicine cabinet." She turned back to Sophie and said, "Come on, honey, you need a drink."

She ushered Sophie downstairs, Brian and I following. Victor was left alone to tend to his wounds.

Vicky broke out a bottle of whiskey from her father's liquor cabinet and poured some in a glass for Sophie.

"What happened?" she asked.

Sophie huddled up on the couch next to me. She was shaking so badly that I had to light her cigarette for her.

She had gone to the bathroom, she said, and when she opened the door to leave, Victor forced his way in and locked the door. He pushed her up against the door and shoved his tongue into her mouth.

"It was so gross, I almost puked," she said.

She pushed him away and managed to unlock the door, but before she could get out he was on her again. He put one hand over her mouth and tore into her shirt with the other hand, and that's when she bit him. Then she slapped him, kicked him in the balls, and pushed him into the bathtub. She grabbed the plunger and hit him with it, and then she just kept on hitting him.

"I don't know what happened to me," she said. "One minute I just wanted to get away from him, and the next minute I wanted to kill him."

"You were just defending yourself," I said.

"You don't understand, Janet, I wanted to *kill* him."

"It would have been a fitting end for him," Vicky observed. "Beaten to death with a toilet plunger. It would make a nice obituary."

"I'm not a violent person," Sophie said.

"I never thought you were," I said, but I had seen the look in her eyes as she attacked Victor, and I wondered if her mother had looked the same way when she took an ax to the piano, and a fire poker to the rest of the house.

Victor was lucky, I thought.

Sophie looked at me sharply, and I saw that she had read my thoughts. I gave her an apologetic shrug, but she had already turned away and was tossing back the rest of her drink. She closed her eyes and shuddered.

"I have to go home now." She handed the empty glass to Vicky. "Thanks for the drink. I hope I didn't ruin your party."

"Are you kidding?" Vicky said. "Seeing Victor Sorrento get pummeled with a toilet plunger has been one of the high points of my entire life so far. I'm just sorry about what happened to you."

"I'm okay now."

"Honey, you were great. He'll think twice before he messes with you again. And if it's any consolation, Todd Chandler's in love with you."

"Who's that?" Sophie asked.

Vicky frowned in confusion.

"Sophie," I said, "that's the guy you went upstairs with."

"Oh," she said. "He was cute."

In the car on the way home, Sophie lounged in the back seat, one bare foot resting on the top of my seat, nudging the side of my head in time to the radio.

Brian glanced at her in the rearview mirror. "Did you really not know that kid's name?" he asked her.

"I'm pretty sure he told me," she said. "I just forgot."

"You probably shouldn't be playing around with him," he said. "He's just a kid."

"Not any more," she crowed.

"He says he's in love with you," I told her. "I think he means it."

"I know. He asked if he could be my boyfriend."

I pushed her foot away and turned around to look at her. "What did you tell him?"

She blew some smoke rings. "I told him he can be *one* of my boyfriends."

"He's just a kid," Brian repeated. "Everyone's going to laugh at him."

There was a chilly silence, and then Sophie said, "Maybe he doesn't care if people laugh."

"He cares," Brian said. "He's just a kid, Sophie, leave him alone. What do you want him for anyway?"

"I like him."

"You didn't even know his name."

"So? I would like him even if he didn't have a name."

"Sophie," I said, "you're going to break Todd's heart. What if he's serious about you? Are you going to be serious about him?"

"Maybe."

"I doubt it," I said.

"You think people would laugh at him if he was going out with me?"

"I don't know, but I think he would end up getting hurt."

"Not like Victor," she said.

"No, but still—"

Brian made an abrupt stop in front of her house. "This is where you get off," he said.

He didn't even wait for her to get in the house before he drove away, and we went to our usual parking spot, where we proceeded to have a fight.

"I don't see why you want to hang around with someone like that," he said. "Doesn't it bother you that people think of her as Janet's slutty friend?"

"That's just Victor."

"It's not just Victor," he said. "If she wants to act like that, let her do it with her own friends. With our friends she should try to act a little more decent."

"Vicky likes her."

"Good, then let Vicky be her friend."

He turned his head toward his side window, and I noticed he had a clear view of the darkness surrounding us. The car windows weren't steamed, I realized, and I remembered what we came here for. We were supposed to be making out.

"What's wrong with you?" I asked.

He kept his face turned away. "Do you know what people ask me, Janet? They ask me if you're as horny as she is."

"What?"

"They ask me if you've learned stuff from her, and if the two of you are queer together."

"Who? Who asks you things like that?"

"Guys."

"Well, that's just sickening."

"Yes, it is. That's what I'm trying to tell you. They're not just talking about her, they're talking about you, too."

My stomach turned.

"Wow," I said. "I didn't know I was popular enough for anyone to care who I hang around with."

"You're not taking this seriously."

"Well, what do you want me to do, Brian? You want me to dump her because of some stupid things some guys are saying?"

The question hung in the air, and his silence confirmed that this was exactly what he wanted.

"Forget it," I said. "She's my best friend. I'd never dump her for you or anyone else."

"She's screwed up, Janet."

I didn't try to deny it. "Well, what about the people who are asking all these sick questions? Aren't they a little screwed up, too?"

He looked at me for a minute.

"She would have hit you, Janet. You know that, don't you?"

I didn't answer.

"She was completely mental, Janet, didn't you see her? Victor's lucky there weren't any razor blades laying around."

"Victor got what he deserved, Brian. If somebody tried to do that to me, I'd go mental, too."

"Okay, maybe. But Victor wouldn't do that to you, because you're not giving it away to every guy in school. Victor just wanted his share."

Victor just wanted his share. How much of Sophie, I wondered, was Victor's share?

"Does everybody—all these guys—do they all think they have a share?"

"Yes," he said. "That's what I'm trying to tell you."

"What are you going to do with *your* share?"

"What? No, not *me*, I'm not—"

"Is that why we're fighting, so you can break up with me and be free to get your share?"

"No, Janet, no, that's not what I want."

"You want to get laid."

"Of course, I'll admit it, and I'll admit that it's frustrating sometimes to have to keep waiting, but I don't want to be with anybody but you."

"Then why aren't we making out right now?"

He looked puzzled for a minute.

"You're right," he said, and we didn't talk any more that night.

*

The next thing we knew, Sophie was going out with Todd Chandler.

"You've got to be kidding," I said, but she was serious. She stopped going to parties and sleeping around, and at first, people did laugh, but as the weeks went by and Sophie stayed with him, the laughter turned into a grudging respect, and Todd became known as the Miracle Boy.

158

As unlikely a couple as they were, they seemed to be good for each other. After Sophie singled him out, other girls were suddenly interested in Todd, and the boost in his popularity gave him a self-confidence he had previously lacked.

For her part, Sophie was calmer, less inclined to party, and her grades improved, because Todd went home with her after school every day, and he always insisted that they finish their homework before they went to bed.

"I don't believe it," I said. "He makes you do your homework first?"

"Isn't that *cute*?" she said. "He's so cute, and guess what: he wants to take me home to meet his parents. That means he likes me, right?"

"Of course he likes you."

"That's what normal people do, right? When they like you, they take you home to meet their parents?"

"Sure," I said, "but since when have you cared what normal people do?"

Her eyes avoided mine and she shrugged in an obvious attempt to appear casual. "I just thought I'd try it."

"Good luck," I said.

*

Bob Chandler told me that his mother took one look at Sophie and decided Todd was too young to be going steady. She waited until Sophie went home, and then she explained to Todd that there were girls you got serious about and girls you didn't, and part of her job as a parent was to keep Todd from confusing the two.

Todd appealed to his brother to stick up for Sophie, but Bob agreed with their mother. He didn't blame Todd for wanting to get laid, he told me, but his advice was to start dating some nice girls, too.

"Sophie's nice," I said.

"Come on, Janet, you know what I mean."

So Todd explained to Sophie that he wasn't allowed to go steady, and that in order to continue seeing her, he would have to date other girls as well, and then he continued to do his homework at Sophie's after school, and on Friday and Saturday nights he left her on her own while he took other girls bowling, or to the movies, or out for pizza. He took to dropping off his dates a little early so he'd have time before curfew to stop by Sophie's and relieve whatever tension had built up over the evening.

"Sophie," I said, "if you're going for normal, this isn't it."

"But this is romantic," she said. "He only goes out with those girls to fool his mother, so she won't know that secretly, he's going steady with me."

"I'm not sure that's true, Sophie."

"What do you mean?"

"I hate to tell you this, but Saturday night I saw him at the movies, and he was making out with Stacy DeFoe."

She frowned. "Are you sure it was him?"

"I saw them, Sophie. Brian saw them, too. Honey, I don't think he's dating her just to fool his mother."

"You think he likes her?"

"It sure looked that way. They made out through the whole movie, and I saw her tucking her shirt back in as they were leaving."

She fumbled for a cigarette.

"I'm sorry," I said. "I just thought you should know."

*

She asked Todd about Stacy DeFoe, and he admitted that he might be falling in love with her. He hadn't meant for it to happen, but there it was.

"Besides," he said, "I already told you, I'm not allowed to go steady."

"Right," she said. "So, can I just ask what's so great about Stacy DeFoe?"

"She drives me wild," he said, "the way she keeps me guessing. I never know how far I'm going to get, so it's a real thrill if I get past first base."

"I see. You don't get that kind of thrill from me."

He shrugged. "I guess you're just too easy."

*

After that, Sophie stopped bringing Todd home after school, and started going out again on Friday and Saturday nights.

160

She also stopped doing her homework.

Chapter 14

"I already made moussaka," she said. "It was the only thing I got credit for."

We were sitting at her kitchen table with a pile of cookbooks in front of us, trying to find something Sophie could cook. She was flunking home ec, and her last chance for a passing grade for the term was to plan a balanced meal, which she would then prepare and serve to the class.

"How about spaghetti?" I suggested.

"I did that for the midterm," she said. "I was supposed to use roasted red peppers but I used crushed red pepper instead. Everybody's mouth got burned."

"Maybe breakfast," I said. "You can cut a grapefruit in half, can't you? Scramble some eggs?"

"I can make toast," she said confidently.

Dr. Prescott bustled into the room, doing up his tie. He was small and trim, with a tidily clipped beard and soft-looking hands. He stopped and peered at us for a moment, as if trying to determine which of us was his daughter. His eyes were the exact same blue as Sophie's.

"Did you drive Nancy's car last night?" he asked her.

A tiny smile flitted across her mouth. "Who's Nancy?"

"You know who Nancy is. She was here last night, and she thinks somebody drove her car."

"If she doesn't want people driving her car, she shouldn't leave it laying around," Sophie said. "Maybe she should park it at her own house."

He pointed one manicured finger at her. "Stop it," he said. "You'll push me too far, and you know what will happen."

She rolled her eyes at me. We both knew what would happen. Dr. Prescott would request literature from several Catholic girls' schools, and Sophie would intercept the mail and destroy the brochures, and he would forget about them until the next time one of his girlfriends complained about her.

"I don't know why you like that one, anyway, Daddy. She fakes her orgasms."

"Mind your own business," he said. "I bet Janet doesn't talk to her parents like that, do you, Janet?"

"Janet's father isn't sleeping with Nancy," Sophie said, "and her mother couldn't fake an orgasm if she tried."

He frowned at his watch. "I have to go," he said. "Don't stay out too late."

"Daddy, I'm not even out."

"Stay in, then," he advised her, "and stay out of trouble."

*

I'd often wondered what it would be like to have the kind of freedom Sophie had, her house to herself most of the time, no one watching her and telling her what to do. I got a taste of it during February vacation, when my parents went to Puerto Rico. I was allowed to stay home alone, my mother having given me a list of neighbors and relatives to call in case of an emergency.

"No parties," she instructed me. "No boys. If you do anything you're not supposed to, I'll find out. And I don't want Sophie here, either."

"But, Mom—"

"Tell her, John."

"Your mother doesn't want Sophie here while we're gone." He emphasized "your mother" just enough to let me know he disagreed with her.

"Okay, Mom," I said.

"People will be watching you, Janet. Your Aunt Louise will be stopping by to check on you."

They left early Saturday morning, and by Monday Sophie had moved in with me. I figured she was the lesser of two evils; I made her sleep in my room with me to alleviate the temptation of having Brian sleep in my room with me.

We ordered pizza and Chinese food delivered. I cooked pancakes for her, she made moussaka for me. She read my cards. I played the piano for her. She taught me how to smoke dope. We got stoned and made fudge, then we got more stoned and ate it all, and then we smoked more to relieve our stomach aches.

On Thursday night, after Sophie's shift at the soup kitchen, we went to a party, where she hooked up with Charlie Cunningham, one of the few guys she's been with more than once. In fact, she'd been

with him so many times that Walter had started calling him Charlie
Cunnilingus.

"Don't wait up," Sophie told me as I left the party with Brian.

Brian brought me home and I invited him in. We didn't go
upstairs, and we didn't go all the way, but on the living room couch we
were more daring than we'd ever been before, indulging in what Ann
Landers would have called heavy petting, the result of which was our
first experience with mutual gratification.

Sophie wasn't home yet when I went to bed, and I never heard
her come in, but the next morning I awoke to the sound of Aunt Louise
screaming my name. She had stopped by to check on me and found
Sophie sleeping naked on the couch, with Charlie Cunningham, also
naked, sleeping on top of her.

By the time I got downstairs Charlie was gone, and Sophie was
buckling up her overalls.

"I got you in trouble," she said, and she followed me into the
kitchen, where Aunt Louise was pacing furiously.

"When your mother finds out—" she began. "She trusted you,
Janet, and you let this go on in her house? This will break her heart."

"She didn't know," Sophie said. "She was asleep when I got
here, she didn't even know I was here."

Aunt Louise stopped pacing and looked hard at Sophie. "Do
you expect me to believe that you just wandered into this house
without Janet's knowledge or approval?"

Sophie shrugged. "Stranger things have happened."

"Well, I wouldn't know about that, and I don't think I'd care to
know. And right now, young lady, I'd say it's time for you to go
home."

Sophie shrugged again and went to retrieve her boots and coat.
Instead of going out the front door she paraded back through the
kitchen, looking like a Hollywood starlet in her mother's mink jacket,
a cigarette in her hand. She blew me a kiss and made her exit.

Aunt Louise shook her head. "I guess I'm going to have to stay
here until your folks get home, to keep you out of trouble. If you have
any plans for the weekend, you'd better cancel them."

So my freedom was gone, and the rest of my vacation would be
spent under house arrest.

"But I didn't do anything," I protested, because as far as she
knew, I didn't.

164

"We'll just wait and see what your mother has to say."

*

The first thing Mom said was, "What a horrible trip." She sat down at the kitchen table and kicked off her shoes. Dad came in behind her, carrying their luggage.

"Welcome home," Aunt Louise said.

"Hello, Louise," said Dad. "Is everything all right?"

"Yes," said Mom, "what are you doing here?"

"Oh, we're fine. Tell us about your trip."

"It's a beautiful country," Dad said. "I've got some great pictures."

"The weather was lousy," said Mom.

"Helen, I thought you understood," he said in the tone of someone who's had this conversation before. "That's why it's called a *rain*forest."

"Did you see a Puerto Rican parrot?" I asked.

"If he hadn't, he'd still be out in the jungle looking for one," Mom said.

*

My mother hit the roof when she found out about Sophie.

"Didn't you tell her she wasn't supposed to be here?"

"Yes." I didn't mention that she'd been staying with me all week.

"So this was a complete surprise to you."

"Yes," I lied.

"Your Aunt Louise didn't think you seemed all that surprised."

Dad asked, "How long has Sophie been going out with this boy?"

"All winter." Another half truth.

"Funny you've never mentioned him before," Mom said.

I couldn't think of an answer for that.

"You're grounded," Mom said. "Two weeks."

"But, Mom, I didn't even know she was here."

She raised her eyebrows. "You want to make it three weeks?"

"No, but—"

"Enough," she said. "Go to your room. I want to talk to your father."

*

If February vacation ended badly, April vacation was a disaster from the beginning.

A few days before vacation started, Mom announced that she and I would be going to her mother's for the week.

"What?" I said. "Why?"

"Gram wants to see you."

"No, she doesn't," I said.

"Helen, what's this about?"

"I need some time away, John. I need to think."

"And you need to take Janet with you?"

"Yes," she said. "I want you to do some thinking, too."

He was quiet for a minute, studying her, and then he said, "I see."

"Do you?"

"I don't," I said. "What does this have to do with me? This is my vacation, and I was planning—"

"This has everything to do with you," Mom said. "This is about the future of this family. You're coming with me, Janet, and I don't want to hear another word about it."

"Dad?" I appealed to my father, but I could see in his face that he wasn't going to fight her.

"It seems to me that if your mother feels this strongly, Janet, then we really have no choice."

"Oh, you have choices," she said. "You have choices to make, John, and it's high time you made them."

*

Then it was the end of the school day on Good Friday. April vacation had officially begun, and Sophie was rummaging through her purse, ridding it of everything related to school plus whatever trash she came across. The bottom of her locker was littered with school papers, gum wrappers, broken cigarettes and chewed up pencils.

"Let's go," I urged her. We were meeting Brian and Walter at Whiffle's Sandwich Shop for what Walter called my Going Away Pity Party.

"I have to get rid of this shit," Sophie said. "It will fuck up my vacation karma."

I leaned against the wall of lockers. "You want to talk about bad vacation karma? This is going to be the worst vacation of my life, and afterwards my parents will probably get divorced. I can't believe she's doing this. I can't believe she's making me go."

"It sucks," Sophie agreed, "but sometimes you just have to do stuff."

"That's easy for you to say," I snapped. "When have *you* ever had to do anything?"

She looked up from her bag. "I have to wear shoes."

"Yeah, well, you won't be wearing shoes this week. You'll probably go out every night, won't you?"

"*Every* night," she said. "I'm going to parties, and I'm going to dance, and—"

"I know, shut up," I said. "You'll be making out every night, and I won't even see Brian for a whole week."

"Write him some hot love letters," she suggested.

"I don't want to write him *letters*." Her lack of sympathy was irritating.

She kicked at the pile of debris that threatened to spill from her locker. "Well, Janet, if all you're going to do is complain, then of course you're going to have a shitty vacation."

"Thanks a lot, Sophie. That's real helpful, considering this is all because of you anyway."

"Because of *me*?"

I rolled my eyes in exasperation. "What do you think they're fighting about?"

She shook her head stupidly.

"They're fighting about *you*. They're always fighting about you, because you're always hanging around, and you know what? I'm sick of you. I'm sick of getting into trouble for all the stupid things you do. I'm sick of sticking up for you all the time. Why don't you stop trying to be part of my family, Sophie, because you're not, and you never will be."

Her eyes flared. "You think I don't know that? You think I don't know the difference between your family and mine? You're the one who always wanted to pretend, Janet, and you're the one who forgot that it was just pretend. I never forgot, not for one minute."

She slammed her locker. "You want your family all to yourself? Fine, you keep it. I don't need it."

She threw her bag over her shoulder and walked away.

"Fine," I called after her. "We'll all be happier without you."

*

After a thoroughly miserable week at my grandmother's, I was ready to take back every stupid thing I'd said to Sophie, but she didn't give me a chance. When I called her house she didn't answer. When I passed her in the hall at school she looked the other way. When I looked for her in her usual haunts, she was nowhere to be found. After a few days of being unable to talk to her, I left a note in her locker. She didn't respond.

"Maybe she's busy," Brian said.

"That's not it. This is the same thing she did to Hector, remember? She just cut him out, no argument, no discussion, nothing, she was just done with him."

"You're not Hector, you're her best friend, and frankly, not to be mean, but I don't see that she has a whole lot of other friends to fall back on. She'll come around."

"What if she doesn't?"

"I don't know, Janet. I guess if she would end your friendship over one stupid argument, maybe she wasn't that great a friend to begin with. Maybe you should just let her go."

But I couldn't. I thought about her all the time. I was constantly alert to catch a glimpse of her at school, to see who she was with, but usually when I saw her she was alone.

During the evenings I would wonder at odd moments what she was doing, whether she was partying, or reading, or screwing someone, or sitting in her room in the dark, holding Sid and listening to her Cat Stevens albums. I wondered if she thought of me at all. I concentrated on sending psychic messages to her. "Call me," I would think, over and over, but she didn't.

168

As the days passed and she continued to ignore me, I went through a cycle of emotions, not a roller coaster but a Ferris wheel, at the height of which I felt a kind of communion with her, a confidence that our friendship was indestructible and that our sisterhood would transcend this misunderstanding. At the lowest point I felt a physical ache, a heartsickness at the thought of losing her. In between I alternated between pitying her for her sad and lonely life, and hating her for blowing off eleven years of friendship as if it meant nothing to her.

Moreover, I found that I had been wrong to think my family would be happier without her. We weren't. Mom and Dad were rarely in the same room together, and when they were, they spoke in the formal and very civil tones they used when they didn't really want to speak to each other at all. Dad found excuses to leave the house several nights a week, and when he was home, he was in his study with the door shut. Mom was edgy and irritable. I didn't know what they were fighting about, but it couldn't be Sophie. She was gone, and none of us ever mentioned her name, except once I asked Dad if he still saw her at the soup kitchen.

"Of course," he said. "Why wouldn't I?"

"No reason," I said. "I just wondered." I wanted to ask how she was, but I didn't have the heart to tell him that Sophie and I weren't speaking.

This went on for several weeks, and then one day I found a note in my locker. It said:

> dear janet,
> i miss you so much. i'm dying to talk to you but i can't. some things are unspeakable.
> i really want to be friends again but there are things i have to figure out first. please don't ask me to explain right now. just don't forget me.
> love always,
> sophie

"That's clear as mud," Brian said.

"Do yourself a favor," Walter said. "Forget about her. Take this opportunity to dump her, save yourself the aggravation."

"But what's she talking about, Walter? What's going on that she can't talk to me about?"

He widened his eyes and dropped his voice dramatically to imitate Sophie's whisper. "It's *unspeakable*."

"Come on, Walter."

"All I know is that she's seeing someone, and he's married."

"*Married?* How old is he?"

"Forty, forty-five, something like that. Old enough to be her father."

"And she's...*dating* him?"

"She's screwing him, Janet. I'm sure they don't have time for much else, what with his having to sneak away from the wife and kids."

My stomach turned. "Who is he?"

Walter shrugged. "Some poor bastard who doesn't know what he's getting into. She won't say who. Oh, it's all very mysterious and dramatic. She'll have to tell you about it sooner or later, Janet, if only because she needs a bigger audience."

And sure enough, a few days later I got another note from her, asking me to meet her after school at Whiffle's. She was dying to talk to me.

We split an order of fries, and she explained why she'd been avoiding me.

"It's just that I never thought I'd have to keep a secret from you, and I didn't know if I could do it."

"You couldn't," I said. "Walter told me. Sophie, are you out of your mind? A married man?"

"I can't help it," she said. "I love him."

"But he has a wife."

"She left him."

"They have kids?"

"Yes," she whispered.

"Who is he?" I asked.

"Janet, I can't tell you. I wish I could, I wish I could tell you everything, but I can't."

"Well, why don't you tell me how this happened? And don't say, 'It just happened.' I want details."

It was the day after Easter, she said, and she was walking home from the library, and it was raining. Her books were getting wet, her

170

hair was frizzing up, and she was bummed out about the fight we'd had. She was miserable, and then he came along and offered her a ride home. She took the ride, but she didn't want to go home, so he invited her to his house for dinner.

"And you went?" I said. "You didn't think there was anything strange about a grown man inviting you to his house?"

"He was just being nice," she said.

So they went to his house, and she took a shower and put on his daughter's bathrobe, and he cooked dinner and she set the table, and afterwards she washed and he dried.

"Sounds cozy," I said.

It was *nice*, she insisted. They were just hanging out, talking, and they were having a good time but there was nothing romantic about it.

"It was like hanging out with you," she said.

After dinner they sat on the couch together, and somehow the conversation turned serious. She wouldn't say what it was about, but it upset her and she started to cry. He took her in his arms and held her— "Just to be nice," she said. "He didn't mean anything by it." But he was warm, and he smelled good, and he was so comforting and he said such sweet things to her that suddenly she realized she was somewhere she had seldom been before: in the arms of someone who truly cared for her. So she stopped crying and kissed him.

At first he protested, but she climbed onto his lap and persisted. He tried to resist, but his will was no match for Sophie's, and she had already made up her mind. When he began to respond to her kisses, she pressed her advantage, as it were, by shifting in his lap and loosening the belt on his daughter's bathrobe.

"We can't be together this way," he said.

On the contrary, she said, this was the only way they *could* be together, and this might be their only chance.

And so they made love on the couch, and when they were finished, it was her turn to hold him while he cried. His tears drenched her hair and her face, and she thought how unfortunate it was that they hadn't both cried at the same time, because the mingling of their tears would have made powerful magic, but as it turned out, she said, there was plenty of mingling of other bodily fluids, and she collected enough pubic hairs to cast a spell that would bind the two of them together for the rest of their lives.

"It can never be broken," she told me, "as long as we're both still alive."

Eventually he recovered from his fit of remorse, and they kissed some more, and then he carried her upstairs to his bed and kept her there for the better part of a week.

"You mean his and his wife's bed," I said.

Well, yes, she said, but his wife wasn't there, was she, or none of this would have happened. "She left him, remember?"

"I wonder why."

"She doesn't love him the way I do."

"So, are you saying it's his wife's fault that he's cheating on her?"

"It's nobody's fault, Janet. It was meant to be."

And she went on at some length about Fate, and Destiny, and True Love.

"You said you weren't going to let anybody love you," I reminded her.

"Because I couldn't be sure," she said. "I didn't want to get used again."

"A lot of people would say that a man in his forties who's sleeping with a teenage girl is using her, Sophie."

"A lot of people would be wrong. He loves me."

"You're sure about that?"

She *knew*. Had I not been listening? She had already said it was True Love. She *knew*. And she knew what Walter thought, but this was not Just Sex, although she had to admit the sex was great, because this was no eager, inexperienced high school boy fumbling around seeking his own pleasure. This was a man who knew his way around, a mature man who did things that few high school boys had the patience or the imagination to do. The bliss they found together was better than any drug she'd ever done, and she was not about to allow the conventions of marriage, or the law, or even common sense to interfere with the happiness she'd found. It was hers, she deserved it, she'd waited her whole life for it, and the rest of the world could go to hell.

*

"It's like trying to reason with a moth, isn't it?" said Walter, and I had to agree. But although I talked to her about the sin of adultery, and the crime of statutory rape, although I made some attempts to discourage Sophie's affair, I have to admit that for the most part I was a willing confidante, because the truth is, I loved hearing about it. I was fascinated by her foray into this world of secret passion and illicit love. Adultery was for adults, and it was exciting to be in on the kind of story I knew my mother's bridge club would die for.

"He whispers in my ear," she told me. "He says, 'Oh, Sophie, what have you *done* to me?'" She shivered. "It thrills me."

It thrilled *me*, just hearing about it, and there was plenty more where that came from. There were vicarious thrills to be had on an almost daily basis as the drama of Sophie and her lover unfolded. His wife returned to him, believing he had learned whatever lesson she'd been trying to teach him, but by then he was addicted to Sophie and he could not quit, and so there were the desperate arrangements of assignations, the rapture of their unions, the agony of their separations, the torment of having to act casual when they met by chance in public. And above all, there was Sophie's constant fear that each meeting would be their last, because while she had complete confidence in his love for her, she doubted his ability to sustain their relationship, given the constraints of his family.

She had no intention of breaking up his home, she assured me. She knew he couldn't leave his family and she didn't want him to. She was willing to share, she could go on sharing forever, but she could see that this arrangement was taking its toll on him, because no matter what Walter and I thought, he wasn't a liar; he didn't like to lie, and he wasn't very good at it, and consequently he had to shut down all communications with his wife and he had to be cautious with the kids. It unnerved him, on top of which he happened to be a decent Christian man who believed adultery was a sin, and the more he indulged, the more heavily his guilt weighed upon him, until Sophie advised us that if we should see a man of a certain age walking around town with his hand over his heart like the Reverend Dimmesdale, then we would know who her lover was. He couldn't go on like this much longer, and although she was prepared to demonstrate her panache when the time came—her French class was reading Cyrano—she was in a constant state of anxiety, waiting for the ax to fall.

But it appeared to me that it was precisely this fear of Sophie's that made her so irresistible to him. Every time he called her she expected him to say it was over, and every time she made love with him it was as if for the last time. She was deeply and sincerely grateful for every moment she could be with him, and she was determined to wring the most out of every second in his arms, and so she loved him with passion and desperation, willing to spend her last breath, and willing to go through it all over again two days later, or whenever he could next get away. Who could resist being loved like that?

Walter saw it differently. In his view, Sophie's lover had unwittingly chased a rabbit into a minefield and was now trapped, paralyzed with fear, frightened by the extremity of Sophie's devotion and terrified of what she might do if he left her.

"He's got a tiger by the tail," he said. "So to speak."

Still, however much Sophie disrupted her lover's life, he could not seem to get enough of her. They were together often. Sometimes, she said, they made love with such exquisite tenderness that it moved her to tears, other times they romped playfully, like puppies. But more and more, it seemed, they went at each other savagely, fiercely, like wild animals. She had unleashed a lust in him that could only be sated by repeated couplings of increasing intensity, until it seemed it would never be sated at all. Love bites began to appear up and down her neck, and the perfect pale skin of her inner arms was marred by handprints. The word "manhandled" came to mind when I saw these bruises, and I pictured Sophie's lover as a large and muscular man with a lot of body hair and brute strength, a man who held her not in his arms, but in his hands, twisting her small frame like a Gumby doll as he wrung his pleasure from her. There was something primal about the way he marked her as his own; at times I imagined I could smell him on her.

The boys at school felt jealous and neglected, and the few who hadn't had her yet felt cheated. There was a lot of speculation about the identity of the mystery man, and for once there was no information available on the walls of the men's room.

Some people said it was Mr. Salinger, who was the football coach, and who was known to have affairs with students, but he usually went for cheerleaders, and the fact that he saw value in team sports and competition and the wearing of uniforms pretty much guaranteed that Sophie would never be interested in him.

There were rumors that it was Mr. Scott, who had been her freshman English teacher. This was meant to be a joke, because Mr.

Scott was fat and bald, but I actually considered him a viable candidate because I knew Sophie admired his mind. I remembered how she got a little crush on him after he mentioned the Tao Te Ching in class one day—that's the kind of thing that could turn her on.

There was Mr. Fisher, the vice principal, who was called Fishface despite the fact that he was actually a good-looking man, in a very conventional way. He didn't strike me as Sophie's type, but God knows he'd certainly seen her in his office enough to have developed a relationship with her.

Mr. Leighton, one of the janitors, had been seen deep in conversation with her, and so he was a suspect, as was Miss Hannigan, aka Pokerface, the school librarian, who was generally believed to be a lesbian. Someone saw her laugh at something Sophie said, and everyone knew Pokerface never laughed, so there must be something going on. This possibility was hotly debated, as some people believed that Sophie would try anything, while others maintained that the one thing Sophie wanted most in the world was the thing Pokerface lacked.

It was suggested that the Miracle Girl had sold her soul, and that the demon who came to collect it had made her his sex slave. And there were those who thought it more likely that Sophie had called forth the Devil himself, and that *she* had enslaved *him*. Walter began referring to Sophie's lover as Lucifer, but his true identity remained a mystery.

"Gina Gleason thinks it's Walter," Sophie told us.

"Oh, great," he said. "There goes my reputation."

"I should have told her she was right," Sophie said. "We could start some rumors of our own." She pointed to a fresh hickey. "Oh, this? Walter did this. Oh, that? Walter got a little carried away."

"I like the sound of that," he said. "Would I get to make out with you in the halls?"

"Sure." Sophie giggled.

"And would I get to feel you up, just to make it more believable?"

She laughed. "Wouldn't it be fun? Let's do it."

He shook his head. "Sophie, if you tell people we're sleeping together, I'll tell them you took some bad acid and you've been tripping ever since."

"Oh, come on, Walter, what do you care?"

"I've staked my reputation on not sleeping with you. It's what makes me unique."

"But this would make sense," she said. "People would believe that if I was only going to be with one guy, it would be you. See? You still get to be unique."

Walter looked at me.

"It makes perfect sense to me," I said.

"It makes sense," he repeated.

"Yes," Sophie said.

"So I guess that's why you're not doing it, because it would make sense to be carrying on this torrid affair with someone your own age, someone you've known and loved since childhood."

She looked puzzled. "I don't know what you're talking about."

"That's because you're a moron."

"You think I should be with you? For real?"

He sighed. "Never mind. It was a bad idea."

"I drive you crazy."

He nodded in agreement. "I know. Forget it."

She turned to me. "He's just goofing, right?"

I shrugged. "I don't know, Sophie, maybe he's felt this way since kindergarten."

"Yes," Walter said. "Ever since you bit Mrs. Weed. I knew right then that you were the girl for me."

Sophie laughed. She nudged him affectionately and said, "Now who's a moron?"

"Touché," he said.

*

Walter and I assumed that Sophie's lover exaggerated in his dismal accounts of his marital relations, and we never knew how much he actually told her and how much she just *knew*, but if even half of what she told us was true, his sex life prior to Sophie had been bleak.

His wife had been his first and only lover, and she was no fun. He had expected intimacy to be a joyous thing, but his wife had no such expectation, and from the beginning she had been stingy and unresponsive. Her range of acceptable positions was limited to one, and she discouraged him from attempting or even suggesting anything that might give her pleasure. Pleasure, she believed, was for swinish men and indecent women. Sex was for procreation, and now that she was beyond childbearing she had no use for it and rarely tolerated it, and so she lay beneath him, grim and impatient, and she never made a sound except to say, "Stop that," or, "Hurry up." In addition, even though birth control was no longer an issue, she insisted on condoms because she didn't want to have to clean up his mess.

Sophie, on the other hand, liked it messy, and she claimed she would, and sometimes practically did, bathe herself in it—an unwelcome image that would later haunt my dreams. She would try any position, she rolled and heaved and bounced shamelessly, she moaned and sighed and giggled and cooed and squeaked, and there was even one time when she thought she heard herself singing. She valued imagination and spontaneity, and she encouraged these qualities in her lover, as she did in all her lovers. One of her admirers would later tell me that making love with Sophie was like a Grateful Dead concert—one long strange trip with lots of weird improvisational interludes.

"I went to a Dead concert once," I said. "It was like going to the circus."

"Yeah," he said. "That, too."

So the question of her lover's sexual gratification with Sophie was never in doubt. What we tried repeatedly to explain to her was that this was not the same thing as love.

"'Making love' is just an expression," Walter said. "Lovemaking and love are not that closely connected in the male mind."

"I know that," she said. "That's in my mind, too. I know the difference."

"He might love *being with* you," I said, quoting my mother, "but that doesn't mean he loves *you*."

"You think I can't tell?" she said. "I haven't had a lot of people love me, you know. It kind of stands out from my other experiences."

"You thought Hector loved you," Walter reminded her.

"That was when I didn't know any better," she said. "I've learned a lot since then."

"Sure, you've been around the block a few times," he said. "You may be older and wiser and all, but you're still a fuckin' head case and I don't think you know what you're doing."

"I'm liberating his spirit," she said.

Walter laughed. "Yeah, I bet you're doing wonders for his spirit. Who do you think you are, Martin Luther King? You been to the top of the mountain, have you?"

"Honey," I said, "I'm sure you've been good for him, but he's just too old for you. He can't be serious about you."

"What do you talk about?" Walter asked. "*Do* you talk, or is it all just you purring?"

"We talk about you, Walter, and what a colossal asshole you are."

"Hey, if you're going to talk about your boyfriend all the time, you're going to hear what I think. And I think he's a fuckin' creep, and I think you're a fuckin' moron. What do you think, Janet?"

They both looked at me.

"I think he's too old for you, Sophie. And I think going out with a married man is a bad idea. And to tell you the truth, I think he's kind of creepy, too."

"No, you don't," she said. "You like him."

I got a strange feeling when she said that, the sensation of some kind of pressure on my diaphragm, as if my heart had sunk and lodged itself there. He was someone I knew, someone I spoke to, possibly on a regular basis. Someone I thought was nice and perfectly ordinary. I liked him.

I had preferred to think that I would dislike him on sight, instinctively, that he would be conspicuous and recognizable, someone with a crazed gleam in his eyes, someone furtive, or perhaps someone Humbert-like, charming and cultured, using his suave European manners to mask his perversions.

"Who is it?" I begged her to tell me. "Sophie, please, I'll never tell a soul, I swear, but you have to tell me. I can't go around looking at every man I know and wondering if it's him. It's driving me crazy."

But she wouldn't tell me, and I did go around looking at every man I knew in a different light—my teachers, my dentist, my mailman, the guy behind the counter at Whiffle's, my friends' fathers, my father's friends. If one of them was ravishing Sophie to his evil heart's content, shouldn't there be some sign of it? Which one was doing it, and how many more of them would if they could?

*

"Jesus Christ, I wish she'd shut up," Walter said. "You shouldn't let her go on and on about him, Janet, it just encourages her."

But I had my own reasons, aside from the vicarious thrills. Brian and I had been together for a year now, and he was getting impatient. I wanted to take that final step, but I was nervous. I knew several girls who had done it, and some of them hadn't liked it at all. Others said it got better after the first time. None of them displayed the enthusiasm for it that Sophie did, nor were they willing to discuss technique with her candor.

She described some of the things she did that made it so difficult for her lover to tear himself away, including her willingness to perform an act that his wife claimed only a French whore would do.

"That's disgusting," I said, but she just shrugged.

"Don't knock it till you've tried it," she said. "Besides, if you're trying to hold on to your virginity, you could get by for at least another year with no complaints from Brian."

"Eeew, I'm not going to do that. I don't know," I said, "the whole sex thing just seems so…icky."

"You think too much," she said. "I don't know why you want to be a virgin anyway. Just do it, Janet. Just Zen out, just go with it."

When I didn't respond, her brow furrowed in concern. "Janet, don't you want to? I mean, aren't you dying to?"

"I—" I felt myself blush. I felt childish—stupid and immature. "I do want to, but—I don't know, it scares me."

"Oh, honey," she said. "Brian's not going to hurt you. He'll be really sweet to you, it'll be nice."

"You think so?"

"God, yes, Janet. Brian loves you, don't you know that?"

"I guess. But what if I get pregnant?"

"Why would you do that?"

"Well, I wouldn't do it on purpose, Sophie."

"Do you want me to go to the clinic with you? You could, you know, take precautions."

"Okay," I said. "That would be good."

It was ideal, really. I could tell Brian that I was making an appointment, and on the one hand we'd be making progress, while on the other hand it would buy me some time.

"What else?" Sophie said. "What else are you worried about, besides getting pregnant?"

"Stupid things," I admitted. "Like, what if he doesn't like me naked? What if we do it and I think it's gross? What if *he* thinks it's gross? What if I'm too embarrassed to talk to him afterward?"

"What if you like it? What if you can't get enough? What if you start flunking all your classes because you can't stop doing it long enough to get your homework done?"

"Don't make fun of me, Sophie."

"Okay, listen. First of all, I can absolutely, one hundred percent guarantee you, he *will* like you naked, okay? You can stop worrying about that. Brian's never done it before either, has he?"

"No."

"Then he's not going to know any more than you do. You can learn together. Think of it this way, Janet: it's like learning a new instrument. You already know the music, you just have to practice the instrument until you get the sound you want, right? You wouldn't be scared of a new instrument, would you? You'd pick it right up and start right in. You'd take it right out of its case, and you'd hold it, and touch it, and maybe lick the reed a few times—"

"Okay, Sophie."

"—practice your fingering—"

"Okay, yes, I get it, Sophie."

"Good." She nodded once, with finality. "Then there's nothing to worry about."

"So you think I should do it?"

"You know me, Janet, I think everyone should do it. And I think when you really want to, you will. And Brian will wait for you, because he loves you and he knows you're worth waiting for. It will be fine, Janet, don't worry."

But I did worry, and I envied Sophie's confidence, her optimism, her perpetual certainty that everything would turn out fine.

180

Chapter 15

On the first of June Sophie stuffed a note in my locker instructing me to get a library pass for my fifth period study hall and she would meet me at my locker. She had something important to tell me.

At the beginning of fifth period she appeared, breathless and agitated, and she dragged me around the corner into the back of the auditorium and up a short set of stairs into the projection booth. It was dark, and the air was dry, smelling of dust and evaporated sweat. I knew Sophie had screwed Alan Berube in this room last fall, every day during the week he was showing Julius Caesar to the freshman English classes. The distraction of Sophie's company in the booth caused him to show the second reel of the movie three times to the same class, and he and Sophie would have been busted but for the fact that no one in the class appeared to notice.

Now she pulled me down on the floor in a corner of the booth so we sat huddled side by side in the darkness.

"What's going on?" I asked.

"I'm pregnant."

"Oh, my God, oh, shit, Sophie, how could you let this happen? You said you *knew*, you said you always knew when it wasn't safe."

She nodded, watching my face.

"You knew?" I said. "You knew it wasn't safe and you did it anyway? Are you out of your mind? You can't do this."

"It's already done." She said this as if she were talking about a spell she had cast. She slid her arm under mine and took my hand. She rested her head against my shoulder and sighed contentedly, and suddenly I felt weighted down with dread as I realized that she was happy about this. She *was* out of her mind. She was pregnant and she was insane, and I was alone in this.

"How far along are you?" I asked.

"Three days."

"Three *days*? How can you know after only three days?"

"Because, Janet, I *know*."

I shook my head in amazement. "How could you let this happen?"

"It was meant to be."

"No," I said, "you did this. You think this is great, don't you?"

"I want it."

"What about him? Does he want it?"

She hesitated. "He loves babies."

"Sophie, lots of people love babies, but that doesn't mean they want to have them out of wedlock with their teenage girlfriends. What do you think he's going to say when you tell him?"

"He's not going to say anything, because I'm not going to tell him."

"Well, don't you think he's going to find out? He's not blind, is he?"

"No," she said, "but he's going to break up with me, and then he won't see me again."

"Sophie, you live next door to Mildred Farnsworth. If you have a baby, everyone in town's going to know about it."

"But they won't know whose it is. I'll be just like Hester Prynne, I won't tell anybody."

"But he'll know, won't he?"

"Yes," she said, "but I'll tell him it's not his, and then he won't have to feel responsible."

I shook my head again. Walter was right, I thought, it's like trying to reason with a moth.

"Have you told Walter?" I asked.

"No, and you can't tell him, either. You can't tell anybody, Janet, promise me you won't."

"Okay, but people are going to find out."

"Not yet," she said. "Right now, it's just ours."

We sat still. I tried to picture Sophie with a baby. I imagined her throwing away all the little booties that people gave her. I pictured her with her baby on her lap, reading to it, playing Cat Stevens to put it to sleep, feeding it moussaka. For some reason I remembered Sophie at the age of five, sitting at our table for the first time, telling my mother that she ate raisins.

"Sophie, why don't you come home with me after school? You can stay for dinner. You haven't been to my house in ages."

"Oh, Janet, I don't know—"

"Come on," I said. "My mother doesn't talk to me except to boss me around, and Dad, well, if he's home, I know he'd love to see you."

She still seemed uncertain, but she said, "Okay."

182

*

"Look who's here," I said.

"Sophie, how nice to see you." Mom almost sounded sincere.

"She's staying for dinner, is that okay?"

"Of course."

"Where's Dad?"

"He's in the study."

I grabbed Sophie's hand and dragged her through the kitchen.

"Dad, look who's here."

He looked up from his desk, and his eyes widened. He stood up quickly, as if he might come over and greet her, but he didn't, he just stood awkwardly behind his desk. He looked guilty, as if we'd caught him doing something, but when I glanced at his desktop, I didn't see anything incriminating.

"Sophie," he said, "this is such a nice surprise."

"How are you, John?" She was squeezing my hand.

"I'm fine, honey, how are you?"

"I'm great." She squeezed harder. "I'm in love."

"Are you?" He sank back into his chair. "How marvelous."

I pulled her toward the door. "We'll see you at dinner, Dad."

We ran up to my room and shut the door.

"Sophie, you shouldn't have told him that. Now he'll want to know all about your boyfriend."

She shrugged. "He didn't ask."

"No, but he will. And then my mother will hear about it, and she'll ask even more questions."

"You worry too much. Hey, do you want me to read your cards?"

"Oh, I'd love it."

She took out the cards and handed them to me. While I was shuffling, she took out her stash box and began to roll a joint.

"Sophie, what are you doing? You can't smoke that here."

"Just a couple hits, Janet, so I can read better."

"Sophie—"

"Just shuffle the cards, bufflehead. Don't worry about it."

She sat cross-legged on the floor under the window and smoked part of the joint. She offered it to me, but I refused.

"Oh, man," she said after she'd laid out some cards. "Look at this shit. There's conflict all around you. Resentment, hostility, people who want to hurt each other. It's not directed at you, but it's bumming you out because you're caught in the middle. You feel trapped, you don't know how to get out."

"That's true," I said.

She tossed down a few more cards. "It's your parents. Things are really bad. Your mother's really bitter about all those babies she lost. That's why she's so mean. She doesn't appreciate what she has because she can only think about what she's lost. She wants to give you good advice, she wants to do what's best for you, but what *she* thinks is best and what *you* think is best are two different things."

"That's her, all right. What about Dad, what's going on with him?"

She flipped some more cards. One of them pictured a giant heart, suspended in a stormy sky and pierced by three swords.

"Oh, Janet," she gasped, "look at that."

"That doesn't look good."

"Oh, Janet, he's in so much pain. He's tried so hard to be a good husband, and a good father—that's all he ever wanted—" Her voice broke. She put her hand to her own heart; there were tears in her eyes. "He's so sad."

"Those were his babies, too," I pointed out.

She took another hit off the joint. "He thinks with his heart, that's why he's so nice. Your mother thinks with her head, she's more practical. They don't understand each other, they're on completely different wavelengths."

"So what should I do?"

"There's nothing you *can* do, this is all between the two of them. They both love you but they want different things for you."

Again she flipped some cards. "Oh, look at this, Janet, this is you. You're very strong, this is a very powerful card. You get your strength from your father. You and John always think of Helen as the strong one, but the two of you have a different kind of strength. She's stubborn, and she can be very forceful, but you have more endurance."

"So I can outlast her?"

She nodded. "In the meantime, just nod your head and say, 'Okay, Mom,' and then do whatever you want."

"I can do that. Okay, what about Brian?"

184

"Ooooh, this looks good. He's very reliable, Janet, you can trust him completely. You have a well-balanced relationship, and it's very solid. It's really good, and it's about to get even better."

She looked up from the cards. "You're going to do it with him, aren't you?"

I couldn't suppress a smile. "If that's what the cards say, then it must be true. We're just waiting for the right time and place."

"You can use my room," she said. "I'll clean it up for you."

"Thanks. I'll think about it. What else do the cards say?"

She turned over the next card—the Moon. The smile fell from her face and her eyes grew large. She looked at the next card and sucked in her breath. The High Priestess.

"What is it?" I asked.

"This is so freaky."

Her hands were trembling as she relit the joint. She took several deep drags, and I found myself holding my breath along with her. When she finally exhaled, she threw down two more cards and shook her head, apparently in disbelief.

"What do they say, Sophie?"

"They say that someone you trust is keeping secrets from you."

"Brian?"

"No," she said, "not Brian." She studied the cards. "Maybe you already know."

"Know what? I don't know anything. What is it?"

"People are hiding things from you, but maybe you already know, subconsciously." She turned the full intensity of her blue eyes on me. "Have you had any strange dreams lately?"

"No, I—I don't remember any."

"Pay attention," she said. "You might see it in a dream."

"See what, Sophie? What should I be looking for?"

A knock at the door startled me. Dad stuck his head in the room to announce that dinner was ready.

"What's that smell?" he asked. "Are you girls burning something?"

Sophie held up the joint.

He glanced over his shoulder, then came into the room and shut the door behind him. "Sophie, are you smoking marijuana in my house?"

"Just a little," she said. "I was reading Janet's cards."

"Janet, are you smoking it, too?"

"No, Dad."

"She doesn't smoke," Sophie told him. "It was just me."

"Janet," he said, "why don't you go downstairs to dinner? Sophie and I need to talk."

Dad didn't get mad very often, but right now he was mad at Sophie, and I could tell she knew it. Her face reddened and she was gathering up her tarot cards with elaborate care to avoid looking at him.

I moved toward the door, reluctant to leave her. "But she's still staying for dinner, right, Dad?"

He looked at me as if he didn't know what I was talking about.

"She has to eat, Dad."

He nodded. "She can stay for dinner, but then she'll have to go home. Tell your mother we'll be down in a minute."

As I closed the door behind me, I heard Dad say, "How dare you?" I had never heard him sound so angry, and it scared me, so much that I fled down the stairs without waiting to hear more. I would never have been able to withstand that kind of anger from him, and I didn't know if Sophie could either, despite her greater experience in pissing people off. In her estimation there were very few people whose opinion of her mattered, and Dad was probably at the top of the list.

But when they came into the kitchen a few minutes later, it was Dad who seemed disconcerted. Sophie was fine. She flashed a cheerful smile at my mother as she slipped into her seat at the table, and in spite of everything I was glad she was there. She brought an enthusiasm to our meal that none of us had seen for a long time.

"So, Sophie," Mom said, "are you staying out of trouble?"

Sophie laughed. "I wish I could say yes, but I'd be lying."

Mom frowned. She peered at Sophie for a minute, and then she reached out and lifted Sophie's hair off her neck, exposing a large hickey just below her ear.

"Oh, Sophie," she said in dismay, "that's so vulgar."

"I know," Sophie said lightly, "but he can't help it." She leaned toward Mom and said in a confidential tone, "Sometimes he just can't keep his mouth off of me."

"No one wants to hear that," snapped Mom, and she might have said more, but she was interrupted by the clatter of Dad's fork as it bounced off his plate and landed on the floor. As he bent to pick it up I saw that he was blushing violently. Poor Dad, I thought, he doesn't know the half of it.

Mom said, "Boys don't respect a girl who's too easy."

"Why not?" Sophie sounded genuinely curious.

"Because a boy figures that if you're easy for him, you're easy for everyone."

Sophie turned to Dad. "Is that true, John? Is that what boys think?"

"I don't know what boys think." His voice was cold, and he didn't look up from polishing his fork with his napkin. He was still angry with her.

"You know how stupid boys are," I said to her. "That's how they think. That's why girls play hard to get."

"Are you playing hard to get with Brian?" she asked.

"No," I said. "I *am* hard to get."

She laughed. "That's true." She chewed thoughtfully, and then she said, "Do buffleheads mate for life?"

This was addressed to Dad, but he didn't answer.

"The point is," Mom said to Sophie, "you don't want boys to think you're a slut."

Sophie rolled her eyes. "Now you tell me."

After dinner, I washed and Sophie dried, and I asked her what Dad had said to her.

"He said that I should have listened to you when you told me not to do it, and he said I was lucky it was him and not Helen who caught me, and I can't come back for six months. And he told me that pot kills my brain cells and messes up my hormones."

"Six months is December," I said. "You can't come back until December?"

"Yeah. Sorry, I guess I shouldn't have done it."

"I *told* you." I sighed. "I've never seen him so mad. I suppose he's going to tell Mom."

"After I'm gone," she said. "She's going to yell at you, huh?"

"Are you kidding? She'll be yelling for a week. Thanks a lot."

"I know, I said I was sorry. Look at it this way, Janet, she might seem mad, but this is going to make her happier than she's been in a long time. She always said I was trouble, and now she gets to be right. She's going to be real happy with your father, too, you watch. They're going to start getting along better."

"You think so?"

"I *know*, okay?"

"But what about all that stuff in the cards, about how they're on different wavelengths, and there's all that anger and resentment? What about that?"

She was drying the silverware, and she turned away from me to sort it into the drawer. "Janet, do you remember when you told me that I was the only thing your parents ever fought about?"

"That wasn't true, Sophie, I shouldn't have said that."

"It *was* true. I just saw that when I was reading your cards."

"But you were gone," I said. "You haven't been around for a long time, and they still aren't getting along."

"That's because I was never really gone."

"What do you mean?"

She turned back to face me, and she looked inexplicably sad. "Wait and see," she said.

What I saw was that my mother was pleased with this turn of events. She was almost gleeful in her outrage over Sophie's behavior, and she didn't yell at all, although she did lecture me several times about Sophie's insolence and her trashy behavior. Having a friend with such bad judgment was a reflection on my own judgment, she told me. Sophie was obviously a drug addict and a tramp who didn't care about her reputation, and I should be aware that being seen with her would diminish my own reputation.

"People judge you by the company you keep," she said.

"If that's true, then wouldn't you have a higher opinion of Sophie because she hangs around with me?"

"Don't be smart, Janet. She's a trashy girl and it does you no good to be her friend."

But it did Mom good, because stories about drug addicts and tramps were valuable currency on the gossip exchange. I knew that Sophie was a topic of conversation at Mom's bridge club the following Wednesday, because she came home and reported that Mildred Farnsworth had been forced to buy heavy draperies for all the rooms on the west side of her house to prevent her husband from being disturbed by the sight of Sophie dancing naked in her room at night.

She looked expectantly at Dad as she said this, waiting for his response.

"I'd be disturbed, too," was all he said.

188

Sophie had advised me to pay attention to my dreams, and I tried, but they were elusive.

One night I dreamed I was in a house that was very familiar to me, even though I did not recognize it and couldn't say when I'd ever been there before. I was going from room to room, looking for something, and I opened a door and saw Sophie with her lover. They didn't notice me, and I knew, the way you know in dreams, that no one else in the house knew they were here. They were hiding from everyone, and no one had missed them.

They were standing naked in front of the window, silhouetted by moonlight. He was tall, and her arms were reaching up to pull him to her. Her curls were falling down her back as she tipped her face toward him, her neck stretched and her mouth open, like a baby bird demanding to be fed. Her lover was bending over her, and although I couldn't see his face, I knew that his mouth was open to meet hers. Despite their nudity and the apparent urgency of Sophie's demand, the impression they made was not one of lovers, but of parent and child, a father bird feeding his offspring.

I closed the door and moved on to other rooms, where I saw other things, and when I woke up I had no idea what I'd been hunting for, and only a vague recollection of the other people and events I'd seen, but I retained this image of Sophie seeking sustenance from her lover.

If this was the dream Sophie told me to watch for, it was a big disappointment. The cards said that a trusted friend was keeping a secret from me, and the dream indicated that it was Sophie.

But I already knew that.

*

The Monday after she read my cards, Sophie was absent from school, and on Tuesday she was absent again. On Wednesday she showed up, red-eyed and wrecked, wrapped in the same tablecloth shawl she'd worn a year ago when she broke up with Hector.

At lunchtime Walter and I found her sitting halfway up a tree at the edge of the woods.

"If you're going to jump," Walter said, "you should go a little higher."

"Sophie," I said, "come down from there and tell me what happened."

She didn't move.

"Come on, Sophie."

"Come on," Walter said. "I'm rolling up a big fat joint just for you."

She threw the shawl down and then flipped herself over a limb, dismounting as if from a piece of gym equipment.

"Looks like your panache is holding up," Walter said.

"No." She retrieved the shawl and wrapped it around her again. "I cried. I tried not to, but I couldn't help it."

"What happened?" I asked.

They had been together, she said. They had made love, and everything was fine, it was wonderful, and afterwards, she was spooned in his arms, sleepy and contented, feeling his heartbeat against her back, and she remarked that maybe this was what God saved her for all those years ago.

"And he just freaked out," she told us. "He got up out of bed and he kept saying, 'This? This? You think God saved you for this? For *this*?' He said it like it was a bad thing."

Walter and I exchanged a look.

Sophie's lover told her he was quite sure that God didn't save her to be someone's little concubine. What they were doing was wrong, and it was entirely his fault. He was wrong to have taken advantage of her in the first place, and wrong to have allowed himself to continue. It was unforgivable.

"And I said, 'In the eyes of God, nothing is unforgivable.'"

"You said that?" I was surprised, and a little annoyed. "Sophie, you don't even believe that."

"Just because I don't believe it doesn't mean it isn't true. Besides, whatever he thinks he's done—" She shook her head. "I've seen unforgivable, Janet, and this doesn't even come close."

"So," Walter prompted, "get to the part where he made you cry."

"That was at the end," she said. "I was good right up until the end. I gave him my ring." She held out her hand to show us that her grandmother's ring was gone.

190

At first he would not accept it, she told us, but finally he did, on one condition: that Sophie would come back to reclaim it when she fell in love again. She didn't believe that would ever happen, but he assured her it would, and he was going to be waiting for the day when she would come to him and say that she'd met the man she was going to marry. He wanted to see her happy.

"He means happy with someone else," she said. "How could I be?" Tears splashed on her cheeks, and she wiped them away with her shawl.

But this wasn't the part where she cried that night, she said. He told her he would always love her, nothing would ever change that, and he would never forget how wonderful it had been to be with her, but they could never be together again. It was over.

They kissed one last time, and even though she was dying inside, even though she knew she would ache for him forever, she remembered Cyrano, and she did not cry.

And then, just before he left her, he reached out and touched her face, and she had a psychic flash. She felt what he had been feeling, and she nearly staggered under the weight of it. Guilt, shame, remorse, self-loathing—this was what Sophie's love had brought him to, and she found that she could bear her own misery, but she couldn't bear his, and she broke down. She threw herself into his arms and wept.

"It was awful," she told us. "I finally pulled myself together, but just barely, and just until he was gone. Then I cried until I puked."

I wanted to ask if she had told him about the baby, but it was still a secret from Walter, and I already knew the answer anyway.

"So that's the end of old Lucifer," Walter said. "I suppose it would be too much to hope that we've *learned* something from this experience."

Sophie took a deep hit off the joint and exhaled slowly.

"Love is a terrible thing," she said.

"Shit," Walter said, "I could have told you that."

*

Saturday night I came home from my date with Brian to find Dad sitting in the dark in front of the TV.

He never watched TV.

"What are you doing, Dad?"

"Nothing," he said. "There's a Sherlock Holmes movie on."

"Which one?"

He shook his head vaguely. "I don't know."

The light from the television screen cast shadows on his face, making him appear gaunt and hollow. I sat on the couch with him and began to watch the movie.

"Oh, it's Basil Rathbone," I said. "I love him. Is this the one about the music boxes?"

"I have no idea."

He must have seen the concern on my face, because he roused himself and said, "I'm sorry, Janet, I guess I haven't really been paying attention."

The phone rang, and I ran to the kitchen to get it, thinking it might be Brian.

It was Walter.

"Hey, Janet, I'm over at Sophie's. Can you come over here?"

"I don't know, it's kind of late. What's going on?"

"I just brought her home from a party at Steve Blanchard's house, and she's completely fucked up."

"Steve Blanchard's?" Steve Blanchard was a senior and a football player, and he thought he was God's gift to the school. He didn't usually mingle with underclassmen, but maybe he was feeling magnanimous, allowing the peons to adore him before he graduated next week.

Or maybe Sophie and Walter crashed the party.

"Oh, Jesus," Walter said. "There she goes, she's puking again." He raised his voice and shouted at her. "Good! I'm glad you're sick. It serves you right, you fuckin' nympho!"

"Walter—" I said.

"I swear to God, Janet, if I could find that gun I'd kill her myself. You hear that, Sophie?" he yelled. "I would fuckin' kill you right now! No more fuckin' miracles, you'd be dead!"

"Walter, listen," I said, "I'll be there in twenty minutes."

"You're an angel of mercy," he said. "I'm sorry I can't come pick you up, but I can't leave her here alone, and I sure as hell can't take her anywhere."

"It's okay. Just don't kill her, okay?"

"I'm not making any fuckin' promises," he said, and he hung up.

I went back to the living room. "Dad, that was Walter. He's over at Sophie's house. She's sick. I told him I'd come over, okay?"

"Is she all right? What's wrong with her?"

"I don't think it's too serious. She's just throwing up. He just needs help getting her to bed and all."

He peered at me, a look so penetrating that I might have actually squirmed, convinced that he could see the thoughts in my head, the possible reasons why Sophie might be throwing up.

"I don't want you walking at this hour," he said. "I'll drive you."

"Thanks, Dad."

"Just take good care of her, Janet, and call me if you need anything."

*

I found the two of them sitting opposite each other in the kitchen, both with their feet propped up on the table, his clad in dirty white socks, hers bare, of course. They were eating Popsicles, their lips and tongues painted a garish raspberry color.

"Feeling better?" I asked. I kicked my shoes off and helped myself to a Popsicle.

"I'm fine." Sophie waved her Popsicle to dismiss the idea that she had ever been sick, and I saw that she was still drunk.

"Oh, yes, she's fine," Walter said. "Nothing like a good purge to restore that feeling of well-being."

"I was never as drunk as he thought I was," she told me.

"Oh, that's good to know," he said. "It's a great comfort to me to know that you were in complete control of yourself. What would you have done if you'd been *drunk*, I wonder?"

"Fuck you, Walter."

"What happened?" I asked.

"I left her alone for half an hour," he said, "I swear, no more than half an hour, and I come back and she's playing strip poker with the fuckin' football team."

"It was four guys," she said, "and I was winning."

"It was four big stupid drunken jocks," Walter said, "and believe me, you would have attracted a bigger crowd than that before it was over." He turned to me and counted on his fingers. "Steve Blanchard—it's his party, so he gets the first piece, right?—Mark Stanhope, Paul Daigle, and Bruce McAllister."

"Bruce the Moose? Sophie, what were you thinking?"

"I was thinking it was a free country."

"You never told me how you were planning to do them," Walter said. "All at once, or just one or two at a time?"

"Fuck you, Walter."

"So what happened?" I asked.

"He made me leave," Sophie said.

"I had to drag her out of there," he said, "and I almost got my fuckin' ass kicked in the process."

Sophie giggled. "He told them that he promised my father he'd have me home by midnight."

"That's sweet," I said. "Sophie what you've got here is a knight in shining armor."

"What I've got here is a royal pain in the ass," she said.

"Apparently Sophie doesn't grasp the concept that a young woman who consumes numerous shots of vodka and then strips in front of the football team is asking for trouble."

"They weren't going to hurt me," she said.

"No, of course not. I beg your pardon, I forgot you were the fuckin' Miracle Girl. Nothing could possibly happen to *you*. Those guys probably would have turned into big lovable teddy bears the minute they got your clothes off."

"What were you thinking?" I asked again.

She shrugged. "I just wanted to see what would happen. I thought it might be fun."

Walter waved his arm with a flourish. "There you have it, ladies and gentlemen: Experiments in Fun with Sophie Prescott. Join us next week when Sophie takes on a band of Hell's Angels and learns to play Russian roulette."

"Fuck you, Walter. It's none of your business, anyway."

He dropped his feet to the floor and leaned forward, glaring across the table at her. "If it's none of my business, then what the *fuck* am I doing here?"

"I don't know," she said, glaring back. "Why don't you leave?"

"Hey," I said, "is this what I came over here for? To watch you fight?"

She looked at me, and it was not a friendly look. "I don't know what you came over here for."

"Hey, she came over here to keep me from beating the shit out of you," Walter said. "Show a little appreciation, you fuckin' ingrate."

She gave him a condescending smile. "Is that what you want to do to me, Walter? Beat me up?"

"Right at this moment? Yes."

"All right, then." She stood up, lost her balance, and sat down again.

"Fuck it," she said. "I'm going to bed. Anyone want to come with me? Come on, Walter, I missed my chance to get laid tonight. You owe me. Come on, hey, you can do it to me hard, Walter, get all your aggression out."

"Shut up. I wouldn't touch a filthy slut like you."

She stared at him for a moment, then she stood up and peeled off her shirt. She wasn't wearing a bra.

Walter turned his head, refused to look at her.

"You're not man enough, are you?" she sneered.

"Stop it, Sophie," I said. "Just go to bed."

She looked back and forth between us. "Fuck you both." She tossed her shirt on the table and made her exit.

When she was upstairs, Walter pounded his fist on the table.

"That fuckin' bitch! Damn her!"

"She's drunk," I said.

He took a deep breath and leaned back in his chair, pressing the heels of his hands into his eyes as if to eradicate any lingering image of her. "I should have fuckin' left her there. I should have let them have her."

"No, Walter, don't even think that."

"Why not? It's what she wants. So what if she didn't do it tonight? She'll do it tomorrow night, or next week. There's a whole summer's worth of parties coming up, and I can't follow her around every waking minute trying to save her from herself. This is it for me, Janet. Count me out."

"You mean that? You're just giving up on her?"

"Yeah," he said. "As rewarding as it's been, I've had enough. She can do whatever the fuck she wants. I don't care any more."

"She's just upset," I said. "Maybe when she gets over this guy—"

"No," he said, "don't give me the deep-down-she-really-loves-you story, Janet, I can't take it any more." He helped himself to one of her cigarettes. "Listen," he said, "I didn't just happen to be at Steve Blanchard's party tonight."

"I wondered about that."

"I knew she was upset about Lucifer, and I figured she wouldn't want to be alone, so I asked her if she wanted to do something, and she told me to meet her at this party. So I go to fuckin' Steve Blanchard's house, and as soon as I get there she drags me down the hall to this room, and I'm thinking okay, she wants to spark one up, that's cool, we're partying, we'll smoke some weed. But that wasn't what she wanted."

He took a drag off his cigarette, and for a moment I caught a glimpse of him as an adult, maybe fifteen years from now. I could see where the lines would etch themselves at the corners of his mouth and eyes. I could see where his hairline would recede. He won't like that, I thought, but I could see that he was actually going to be a fine looking man.

"So she drags me into this room," he continued, "a den, I guess, or some kind of family room. I don't know, it was dark. And she pushes me up against the door and starts kissing me, and I mean, these weren't just friendly little kisses, Janet. And she's saying all this stuff to me, about how I'm such a great guy, and I'm the only one who really loves her, and I'm thinking, yes, thank God, she's finally realized this, this is exactly what I've been waiting for. And I said, 'Let's go, Sophie, let's get out of here right now,' but she wouldn't leave. She wanted me to fuck her in Steve Blanchard's den. Doesn't that seem strange to you?"

"I guess."

"Does it seem, maybe, even a little *sick*?"

I shrugged. "She's never been very particular about *where*, Walter."

"Well, she's never been very particular about *who*, either, and I got the feeling I was just some guy at a party, maybe the easiest target. I think she would have done me tonight and got around to the football team some other time. Maybe even later tonight, who knows?"

"So, what did you do?"

196

"I told her I thought we should just party for a while and maybe try again later. You see how graciously she offered me a second chance. I can't take it any more, Janet, she's driving me nuts."

"But what about the things she said to you, Walter, about what a great guy you are?"

"That was just bullshit, Janet."

"I don't think so. I don't think she's ever had to tell lies to get laid."

"You don't know what she might do, Janet, and I'm not hanging around to find out."

He stood and stretched. "Put your shoes on, bufflehead. I'll take you home."

In the car I asked myself what I had expected to happen. Did I think Walter would wait around until Sophie was done with her sexual adventures—whenever that might be—and then marry her, stay with her and cheerfully raise Lucifer's child as his own? Walter didn't even know she was pregnant. Surely it was better for him to remove himself now, before her life got more complicated than it already was.

*

The next day Sophie called and asked me to meet her at the duck pond. When I arrived she was scattering the last of her bread crumbs on the water. We sat down on the ground and she lit a cigarette.

"I called Walter this morning," she said. "He told me not to call him any more."

I nodded. "I know."

"You know? Did he tell you he was mad at me? Is it because I was playing cards with those guys?"

"There's a lot more to it than that, Sophie. Why were you so mean to him?"

"*I* was mean? Is that what he told you?"

"I was *there*, remember? You told him he wasn't man enough to go to bed with you. You don't think that's a mean thing to say?"

She looked away.

"Sophie, what happened?"

She hugged her knees. "He turned me down."

"He said you wanted to do it in Steve Blanchard's den."

197

"No one's ever turned me down." A spark of anger flashed in her eyes. "You and Brian, you're always saying, 'Oh, Walter likes you so much, he really wants to be with you.' Well, guess what, Janet, he doesn't."

"He said he thought it was a strange place to do it. He said he asked you to leave with him. Why didn't you?"

"I didn't really want to be alone with him."

"But…what do you mean?"

"I wanted to be with him," she said, "but I can't be *with* him. I'm still in love with somebody else."

"So, you just wanted him for sex."

"No, I—I wanted to be with *him*, Janet, but he turned me down, and now he won't even talk to me, and everything's all fucked up."

"Maybe it's you, Sophie. I'm not saying this to be mean, but maybe *you're* fucked up."

I saw that flash in her eyes again, but I went on. "Look, you want Walter to love you, but you don't want to have to love him back because you're all hung up on some middle-aged man who can't be with you because he's married, and even if he wasn't, he's too old for you anyway. That's fucked up, Sophie."

She opened her mouth to speak, but I wasn't finished.

"And I'll tell you what's even more fucked up: you can't deal with Walter, but you can take your clothes off in front of a house full of football players, and what exactly did you think was going to happen? Did you really want to fuck all those guys?"

She shrugged and looked away.

"I want to know," I said. "Is that what you wanted?"

"It seemed like a good idea at the time."

"So, that's a yes?"

"Yes," she whispered.

Almost before I realized what I was doing, I reached out and smacked her on the arm. "What the hell is wrong with you?"

"Ow, shit, Janet, why are you being so mean to me?"

"Because I'm sick of you. You only ever think about yourself, and what *you* want, and you don't care about anybody else."

"Like who?"

"Like Walter. Like *me*. I have to lie to my parents, I have to keep secrets from Walter, I have to worry about you hitchhiking and taking drugs and sleeping with strange men, and now I have to worry

198

about your baby, too, and I'll tell you right now, Sophie, I am not going to babysit every night so you can go out and fuck around."

A couple of ducks quacked. They sounded cranky, and for one disorienting moment I thought they were mimicking me. Sophie appeared to be studying her toes.

"And don't think you can bring them home every night," I said. "Not with a child in the house. You hate it when your father does that."

She glanced at me to see if I was through.

"This is all because I didn't sleep with Walter?" she said.

I sighed. "Sophie, don't you want to feel like you belong to someone?"

"I already do."

"To who? Mr. Married Man who doesn't want to see you any more? That's not real, Sophie, I'm talking about something real. You're throwing your whole life away for someone who was just playing with you."

She glared at me. "You think you're so smart," she hissed. "You think you know what's real? You don't know anything, Janet."

"I know better than to sleep with a married man. I know enough not to get pregnant when I'm only sixteen."

"Of course," she said. "Your life is perfect, isn't it? You have perfect parents and a perfect boyfriend, and you have perfect plans to go to a perfect school and get a perfect job, and then you'll get married and have a perfect marriage, and perfect children, and your whole life will just go on being perfect. It's too bad all your friends can't be as perfect as you."

"You're missing the point, Sophie—"

"You think I should have an abortion."

It was true. I hadn't been sure of my position on abortion until Sophie became pregnant, and although it seemed like a horrible solution, it seemed like the most sensible one, and maybe even the most merciful.

"I think you should consider it," I said. "Or maybe give it up for adoption."

"Leave it at the orphanage?"

"It wouldn't have to be like that."

"I can't, Janet, I couldn't stand it."

"See? This is exactly what I'm talking about. *You* want this baby. You're not thinking about what the father wants, you're not thinking about what's best for the baby, you just want what you want."

"It's all I have, Janet. It's all I'll ever have."

I shook my head. "I don't know, Sophie, I wish—" But I didn't know what to wish for. I didn't know where to begin.

"You wish you didn't have a friend like me," she said.

"I wish you weren't so stubborn. I wish you were a little less selfish."

"Why is it that everybody who loves me wishes they didn't?"

"You're not easy," I said.

"Do you think I'm more trouble than I'm worth?"

"I wouldn't say that," I said. "You're worth a lot. But you sure are a lot of damn trouble."

*

That night as we were finishing our Sunday dinner, Dad said, "Janet, your mother and I need to talk to you."

I tried to recall anything I might have done lately, anything they might have found out about.

"It's about Sophie," he said.

Right away, I could think of about thirty things Sophie had done. I shut my mouth firmly, determined not to tell them anything they didn't already know.

"You went to Sophie's last night because she was sick," Dad said, "and that was fine, you had my permission. But in the future, we'd rather you didn't."

I looked at my mother and she gave one brief, smug nod.

"Why not?" I asked.

"There's no supervision," Mom said.

"And, to be honest with you," Dad said, "we're a little concerned about some of Sophie's behavior. We don't want you to become involved in a situation you're not prepared to handle."

"Like what?"

Mom took over. "Like a drug overdose, or some kind of freakout. Don't roll your eyes at me, young lady, you don't know what people on drugs might do. Look at her mother."

200

"Oh, come on," I said. "You don't really believe Sophie's going to start shooting people, do you?"

Dad said, "Well, that's an extreme example. But, honey, you know her better than anyone. Can you imagine a situation where her behavior might get out of control?"

"Maybe," I said grudgingly. "But if that happened, then shouldn't she have her friends there to help her?"

"God damn it!" Mom pounded the table with both fists, rattling the dishes. "We're not talking about helping Sophie. You and your father may want to go on being Samaritans forever, but I'm sick of it. This family has given that girl plenty of help over the years, and frankly, I don't see that it's done her any good, and I don't appreciate her repaying it by exposing my daughter to sex and drugs. Enough. She can't come here, you can't go there, and I don't want you going out with her."

"That's not fair," I said. "Do you think Sophie's the only kid in school who's into sex and drugs? Do you think that when I'm out with her, I do the same things she does?"

"She's a bad influence," Mom said.

"But I haven't done anything. Are you punishing me for what Sophie does?"

"Honey, we're not punishing you," Dad said.

"Are you punishing Sophie?"

"No," he said. "That's certainly not my intention."

"But, Dad, you don't know. Her boyfriend just dumped her, and Walter just dumped her, and she's—" I stopped myself. I wasn't supposed to be talking about this. "She'll be all alone," I said.

He turned his face away from me.

Mom said, "Maybe there's a good reason why everyone is dumping her, Janet, did you ever think of that?"

"What's she ever done to you, Mom? Why do you hate her so much?"

"I don't *hate* her, Janet, but I won't have you running wild with her, or going off in the middle of the night to take care of her because she's been drinking and using drugs."

"I'm her friend, Mom."

"And how is she a friend to you?"

I shrugged. "She just is. I can talk to her. She understands me."

"Janet, she's nothing but trouble, and I don't want you hanging around with her."

My father would not look at me. I couldn't remember a time when he could not look me in the eye.

"And you agree with that, Dad? You want me to stop seeing Sophie because she's a bad influence?"

"She's a troubled girl," he said.

"And you want me to dump her," I persisted, "because she's troubled?"

"That's not it, Janet, I can't—She's beyond my reach now, there's nothing I can do for her. God knows. I can only protect you, sweetheart, that's my job. I have limitations, Janet, can't you understand that?"

"No." Tears of frustration sprang to my eyes. "You said you'd never turn her away."

"Believe me, I never wanted to."

"Then I don't understand at all."

There was a brief silence, which my mother broke with a brisk, "Well, dear, all you really need to understand is that you can't see her any more." She stood up and started collecting our plates. "I'll take care of the dishes tonight, and you may make one phone call to Sophie to explain the situation to her."

*

Mom was washing and Dad was drying, and I felt like a prisoner being allowed my one phone call under their supervision.

"My parents don't want me to see you any more." It made me sick to say it, and when she didn't respond, I thought I'd have to say it again. "Sophie? Did you hear what I said?"

"Both of them?" she asked. "Or just her?"

"Both."

Another silence. Dad threw his dish towel on the counter and went into his study, slamming the door behind him.

Sophie said, "But we can still talk on the phone?"

"No, I'm just supposed to tell you."

"Are they listening to you?"

"Yes."

"All right," she said. "I'll leave you a note in your locker."

"Okay. I'm really sorry about this, Sophie."

"I know," she said. "It's not your fault. We'll figure something out, we'll see each other." She hesitated. "I mean, if you want to."

"Of course I do."

"All right, then. I'll be seeing you, bufflehead."

"Okay. Goodbye, Sophie."

I hung up. I turned around and saw Mom watching me, her soapy hands on her hips.

"She didn't even ask why, did she?"

"No," I said, realizing that this was true.

"You see, Janet, even *she* knows."

*

I knocked once and didn't wait for an answer. I entered Dad's study and found him sitting with his elbows propped on the desk, his forehead resting on his clasped hands.

I said, "I hope you're praying for forgiveness for what you just did to me and Sophie."

"As a matter of fact, I am."

"Dad, how could you? She's my best friend. What am I supposed to do without her?"

"You have other friends."

"My other friends aren't Sophie, Dad, you know that. What's wrong with you?"

"Honey, listen to me. I am no happier about this than you are, but I'm in a very bad position here. This is the way it is, Janet. Your mother and I have made a decision, and you'll just have to accept that. In a couple of years you'll be an adult and you can see anyone you choose, but for now you'll just have to spend time with your other friends."

"And who is Sophie going to be spending her time with, Dad? Have you thought about that? Without me and Walter, do you know who her best friend will be? Gina Gleason, the girl she buys her drugs from. How could you do that to her?"

He sighed heavily and looked at me with weary eyes. "Janet, if I had to choose between the two of you, which one would I choose?"

"Why would you ever have to choose?"

"Suppose I did. Suppose we were in a boat, and it capsized, and I could only save one of you. Which one would it be?"

"The one who can't swim," I said. "The one who forgot her life jacket."

He shook his head. "I know this is hard on you, Janet, I know it doesn't seem fair. You'll never know how sorry I am. But you'll just have to trust me, sweetheart, there are things you couldn't possibly understand."

"What things?"

"Believe me, honey, if I could change this situation, I would. But, God help me, I can't. I don't expect you to understand and I don't expect to be forgiven, but I have to stand with your mother on this, Janet, and I won't change my mind. There's no point in arguing about it."

"I'm not trying to argue, Dad, I just want to know what's going on. Is Mom going to divorce you if you don't get rid of Sophie?"

"No one's said anything about divorce."

"But you'll get along better," I said. "What did you do, make some kind of a deal?"

"It's not that simple, Janet."

But to me it was exactly that simple. Sophie was being traded again.

*

My parents couldn't stop us from seeing each other at school, but it was almost summer vacation, and we would need to find a means of communication to arrange our meetings.

I was training as a shelver at the library, and my supervisor made a point of telling me that she'd had problems in the past with employees' friends visiting them in the workplace. I told Sophie that I could meet her during my breaks, and she said that was fine but we would also need a place to leave notes, and she suggested that we use a library book, a book called The Bad Popes.

"That sounds like the name of a band," I said, but no, she said, it was a book, and she knew right where it was in the 200s, and she knew for a fact that it had not circulated for several years, which was a shame, really, she said, because it was quite an interesting book.

204

Chapter 16

It was the 4th of July, 1976—the town was planning a big bicentennial fireworks display. Brian's family was going to spend the night at his cousin's house on Belgrade Lake. I told my parents that Brian would bring me home after the fireworks, which was true, and he told his parents that he would join them at the lake after he dropped me off, which was also true. What we didn't tell them was that we had no intention of going to the fireworks. We were going to take advantage of the vacancy at Brian's house to consummate our relationship.

I had left a note for Sophie, and she wrote back saying that she was going to a party with Gina Gleason on the Fourth, but she would meet me in the treehouse afterwards so I could tell her all about it. She wished me luck and offered a few words of advice: Relax. Zen out.

I took a bath and shaved my legs, and I put on my apple-scented perfume. I didn't usually wear it in the summer because it attracted bees, but it was Brian's favorite, and we wouldn't be outdoors, we would be in Brian's house. In Brian's room. Alone.

It was a muggy night, but I made Brain close his bedroom door and lock it.

"They're not coming home," he said.

"But they could. What if they forgot something?"

"If they forgot something, they would call and tell me to bring it."

"But they wouldn't call," I said, "because they think you're at the fireworks."

"The fireworks might be cancelled," he said. "It's going to rain."

"So, if the phone rings, are you going to answer it?"

"No," he said. "I've got better things to do."

*

There was a moment of discomfort, and a fleeting moment of panic when I thought it wasn't going to fit, but then suddenly it did, and everything was all right. Brian was as gentle as he could be, considering his excitement, and it was somehow exactly yet not at all what I expected. The room was filled with the smell of apples as the perfume burned off my body, but as hot and sticky as the whole thing was, I found I didn't mind, because I learned that what my friends had told me was true: no matter how nice the first time was, the second time was better.

*

The drive home had a surreal quality to it. The streets and houses looked the same, but something was different. *I* was different. I was one of the initiated, I was one of those people who would eat breakfast and go to work and go about my normal life savoring this secret knowledge of the sublime. My mother claimed that eventually your hormones calmed down and sex assumed its proper stature—that of No Big Deal—but I was finding it hard to believe that people who had done it didn't spend every waking minute thinking about it.

It was just a little after ten, but my parents were already in bed. In case they were still awake, I made deliberately casual noises, closing the door, turning on the TV in the living room, just to establish that I was home. Once they knew I was in, they would sleep soundly, and I could easily slip out the back door later on to meet Sophie.

I took a shower and watched the last half hour of The Music Man, which was playing on the Boston movie channel. I ate a bowl of ice cream. I was killing time. I hoped Sophie wouldn't stay out too late because I was dying to talk to her.

The rain had held off, but now I heard thunder, and I decided to go up to the treehouse before the rain started. I considered taking a flashlight from the utility drawer, but I decided I would prefer to talk in the dark.

When I climbed through the hole in the floor of the treehouse, I was surprised to find Sophie already there. I could just make out her presence near the front door.

"Oh, I'm so glad you're here," I said, but she didn't respond. I moved closer to her and found that she was slumped against the front wall, her knees raised, her arms across her stomach. I thought she must be sleeping. Shit, I thought, she's wasted. I felt a streak of anger; tonight, of all nights, she could have stayed alert.

"Hey, bufflehead." I poked her shoulder, and she slid sideways, and then a flash of lightning illuminated her, and I jumped, recoiling so violently that I almost fell out the front door.

206

Her eyes were open but unseeing, two dark hollows in a pale, lifeless face. Fighting panic, I leaned closer to her and discerned that she was breathing. Okay, I thought, she's not dead, but she didn't look far from it.

I shook her gently.

"Sophie, what's wrong? What is it?"

She moved her lips but I couldn't make out any words. The rain had started, and it was splattering on the roof and on the leaves around us.

"Sophie, look at me. What's wrong?"

"I'm thirsty," she croaked. A spasm shook her, and she clutched her belly and moaned.

"Is it the baby?" I asked.

She nodded. "I need some water."

"Sophie, you have to go to the hospital."

"No, I just need some water. Please, Janet, I'll die if you don't give me some water."

I didn't want to leave her, but I was afraid she *was* going to die right in front of me.

"I'll be right back," I said. "Sophie, don't—Just—I'll be right back, okay?"

"You'll bring me some water?"

"Yes, I'm just going to run into the house and get you some water. I'll bring it right back."

"Hurry," she said.

I had every intention of hurrying. As I scrambled down the tree I heard my father's voice saying, "a situation you're not prepared to handle." This is it, I thought, and I ran to the house, slipping and skidding on the wet grass, into the house and up the stairs, and then I was pounding on my parents' door, calling for Dad.

He threw the door open, saying, "What, Janet, what is it?"

"Sophie," I panted. "In the treehouse. She's sick."

Mom came out behind him, pulling her robe on over her nightgown.

"In the treehouse?" she said. "I thought I told you—"

"Mom, I think she's dying. She's just laying there, she can't move, and she's barely even breathing."

"What's wrong with her?"

It took only a split second to decide to lie. "I don't know. She's just really sick, Mom, she needs a doctor."

"John, get the ladder," she said.

I ran down to the kitchen and, with shaking hands, filled a cup with tap water. The wind had picked up and it was raining harder, and by the time I got back to the tree my clothes were plastered to my body. Mom was standing at the foot of the tree, and as I passed her, she shouted, "What's that?"

"Water," I yelled back. "She's thirsty."

"If she's in shock she shouldn't have water."

"She says she's thirsty."

"Give her a couple of sips, that's all. She shouldn't be drinking anything."

I climbed up the tree. Sophie was pretty much as I'd left her, but she had dragged herself to the front door and was reaching her hand out to catch the rain. She eagerly took the cup from me and started gulping down water, and I had to wrest it away from her.

"Just a little," I said. "You're not supposed to drink anything. Dad's bringing the ladder, we're going to get you out of here."

"Run quickly," she said deliriously. "Run and get The Old Man With The Ladder. Tell him your brother has fallen into the well."

"Oh, Sophie," I whispered, "please don't die."

And then, just as I was about to fall apart, Mom was there, asking Sophie where it hurt, taking her pulse, taking charge. She instructed me to go get the car and park it by the back door of the house.

"Sophie, are you pregnant?" she asked, and I froze for a second on my way down the tree but I didn't hear Sophie's answer.

I moved the car, and from across the yard, above the wind and the rain, I could hear Sophie's howls of pain as Dad carried her down from the tree. She gave one final shriek as he climbed into the back seat with her, and then she went limp.

"She's unconscious," he said. "I can still feel her pulse, but it's faint."

"I think her appendix burst," Mom said. "She told me the pain started on her right side. Janet, how long was she up there?"

"I don't know. I found her there just before I came and got you." I turned around and saw Dad bending over her, his lips moving and his hands making signs of the cross. He was giving her last rites. I felt my panic rising again. "Is she going to die?"

Mom didn't respond right away, and Dad continued to murmur in Latin. He had told me that Extreme Unction was for the faithful, for those who wanted one last chance to put themselves in God's hands and accept His will. That he was saying it now indicated that he had reached the end of his prayers and was acknowledging that God would do what He wanted.

I was not ready for that.

I remembered what Sophie had told me about the Magician, about making things happen through the force of one's will. I closed my eyes and willed Sophie's heart to keep beating. I heard the rhythmic pulse of the windshield wipers, and I set my own heart to that pace and willed it to beat strong enough for both of us. I concentrated on pouring my life and my breath into Sophie's body. I would keep her alive.

"Dad," I said, "hold her against your chest, let her hear your heart."

"I don't know, Janet," said Mom. "She's already used up one miracle, she can't have too many more coming to her."

She doesn't need another miracle, I thought. She has me, and I won't let her die.

*

Mom dropped us off at the emergency room door, and Sophie was taken from us in a flurry of white coats and stethoscopes. They were already wheeling her away when Dr. Prescott appeared and said, "What is it?"

"We think it's her appendix," Dad said.

"No, it isn't," I said. "She's having a miscarriage."

If Dr. Prescott was surprised, he didn't show it. He maintained his professional demeanor as he questioned me about Sophie's pregnancy and her symptoms, and then he said something I didn't understand and he rushed down the hall. I turned to my father to ask if he'd understood Dr. Prescott's words, but just then a nurse stepped up to him and said, "Sir, are you all right?"

His face was completely white, and he was swaying slightly as if he might pass out. I saw for the first time that his tee shirt was soaked not just with rain, but also with blood. His gym shorts were darkly stained where Sophie had been on his lap.

"Oh, my God, Dad."

He looked down at himself and a strangled sound came out of him, something between a cry and a whimper. He touched the front of his shirt with both hands, and he continued to stare at his clothes as the nurse led him to a row of blue plastic chairs and seated him.

"Are you hurt?" she asked.

"No." He sounded dazed. "This is her blood."

The nurse seemed relieved that he didn't require medical attention. "Okay, then, you just stay right here and we'll let you know when we hear anything." Her shoes squeaked on the tile floor as she walked away.

Dad closed his eyes and crossed himself.

"Dad," I said, "did you understand what Dr. Prescott said?"

"Ectopic pregnancy."

Yes, those were the words, but I didn't know what they meant. "I've never heard of that."

"It's what happens when the egg is embedded in the fallopian tube. The fetus grows in the tube and ruptures it."

"But she'll be okay, won't she? I mean, if they know what's wrong, they can fix it, right?"

He shook his head. "There's no guarantee, Janet. It's a very serious thing. It can be fatal. If you hadn't found her—" His voice broke. He pulled me close to him and held me, stroking my wet hair. "Janet, what happened?"

"She was supposed to go to a party, and then we were going to meet in the treehouse, but when I got there—" All at once the events of the night caught up to me, and I leaned into Dad and cried.

"It's okay, honey." He kissed the top of my head. "You're a good girl."

I cried harder, confused, not knowing what he meant. Good because I had recognized a serious situation, good because I came to him for help? Did he think it was good that I had disobeyed him by agreeing to meet Sophie in the first place? Would he still think I was good if he knew what I was meeting her for? Maybe he was just grateful that I was not in Sophie's situation, that he was not sitting in the emergency room waiting to hear if his own daughter would live or die. Maybe he didn't really think I was good at all, but merely good enough.

*

My mother joined us. She had gone home to get dressed, and she had brought dry clothes for my father and me.

"It wasn't her appendix," Dad told her. "It was an ectopic pregnancy."

"She told me she wasn't pregnant," Mom said.

"She isn't any more, is she?" I asked.

"No," she said. "Did you know about this?"

I nodded.

"And you didn't say anything?"

"I told Dr. Prescott."

She was not pleased, but she just glanced toward the desk and said, "Have you heard anything?"

"No," I said.

"Go change your clothes," she said. "We're going to have a long talk when we get home, young lady."

Ordinarily these words would have paralyzed me with dread, but tonight they had no effect, maybe because home seemed so far away.

*

Dad went to give blood, and Mom and I went to the nursery to look at the babies.

"Everyone thinks they're so cute," I said, "but some of them aren't, really."

"They're not dolls, Janet. They're a lot of responsibility."

"I know that, Mom."

She shook her head. "What was she thinking?"

"She wanted it."

"Do you think she's capable of caring for a child?"

"No. Maybe. I don't know, Mom, I mean, I know it's not an ideal situation, but least she would have loved it. She would have done better than *her* mother."

"Well, that's not saying much, is it, dear? She's young, Janet. If she keeps on using drugs and alcohol for the next ten or twenty years, she could end up exactly like her mother. Do you think her mother should have been having children?"

This seemed like a trick question. I couldn't say yes because Mrs. Prescott was clearly an unfit mother, but if I said no I would be saying that Sophie should never have been born.

"I'm glad she had Sophie," I said.

"And yet," said Mom, "I can't help thinking that maybe she shouldn't have."

*

After nearly four hours of surgery Sophie was moved to recovery, but we were warned that her condition was still critical.

"Can we see her?" Dad asked.

"Just a peek," the nurse said.

By now it was the middle of the night, and if the rest of the hospital was relatively quiet, there was an absolute hush in the recovery room, as if we had entered a place of prayer. Sophie was covered with a white blanket, laid out like a sacrifice. A nurse bent over her, wiping her face with a cloth, washing off what looked like a white crust around her eyes.

"What's that?" I asked.

"That's salt from her tears," the nurse said.

"Is she in pain?" Dad asked.

"She's being medicated for the pain, but she's been through a severe trauma. It's not uncommon for a trauma like this to reduce the patient to an infantile state."

At that moment Dr. Prescott came into the room. He conferred quietly with the nurse, who, it suddenly occurred to me, was small and blonde and might have been one of his girlfriends. She patted him on the shoulder and retreated from the room.

Dr. Prescott picked up Sophie's chart and studied it before turning his attention to us.

"She did well to survive the surgery," he said, "but she's not out of the woods yet." He launched into a lengthy explanation of ectopic pregnancy and peritonitis, and he told us that Sophie had lost one of her ovaries, and he sounded calm and professional, as if we were the patient's family and he merely the doctor on duty. Finally he said, "Thank God you people were there. If you hadn't found her when you did, we would have lost her. We almost *did* lose her." His voice broke and he began to cry.

Mom raised her eyebrows.

He covered his face with his hands. "My little girl," he sobbed.

Mom rolled her eyes, and I could tell she was already thinking about how she would describe this scene to her bridge club.

I looked at Dad, and he was crying, too, but quietly.

Then Dr. Prescott took a deep breath and appeared to recover from his fit of emotion.

"She'll be all right," he said. "She's a tough kid, she's strong."

"Bullshit," Mom said.

"*Helen*," Dad said, but she waved him off.

"Are you blind?" she said. "Look at her. Does she *look* tough? Does she look *strong*? She's a child, for God's sake."

"I think we'd better go," said Dad.

"Do you wonder how this happened, Ted? Because I'd like to know. Where were you when she was out until all hours of the night? Where were you when she was drinking herself sick, and taking drugs, and letting herself be used by God knows who?"

Dad took my mother by the arm and ushered her toward the door.

"We're going home now," he said, and then he turned to Dr. Prescott and said, "I'm very sorry. We'll look in on her tomorrow."

"It's been a long night," Dr. Prescott said. "I'm sure we're all a bit overwrought."

"Overwrought, my ass," Mom said, but by then we were out in the hall.

"For God's sake, Helen, the man nearly lost his child tonight."

"That man lost his child a long time ago, John, and you know it as well as I do."

"Now is not the time." Dad put his arm around me. "How are you doing, sweetheart?"

I felt tired and stupid with fatigue. "I'm okay. I just want her to be all right."

"She will be, honey, thanks to you. You saved her life, Janet, you're a hero."

"Well, before we go handing out medals," Mom said, "there are a few things we need to talk about."

*

When we got home, Mom sat at the kitchen table and indicated with her eyes that I should take my seat.

"I'll make breakfast," Dad said.

My mother looked at me for a long time, and I fidgeted under her gaze, wondering where she would begin. She made me wait until she had a cup of coffee in front of her.

"What were you and Sophie doing in the treehouse?" she asked.

"We were just going to talk."

"After you were forbidden to see her?"

"Just to *talk*, Mom."

"When it was forbidden."

I watched the cream swirl in a dizzying pattern as she stirred her coffee.

"I suppose you think you don't need parents any more," she said. "You think you know better than we do, that you don't have to obey us."

"That's not it, Mom."

"You want to be like Sophie and have no rules to follow and no parents who care, is that it?"

"No, Mom—"

"Well, look where she is right now, Janet, because this is what comes of her pot-smoking, free-love, no-rules way of life. Not so much fun *now*, is it?"

Dad set a glass of orange juice in front of me, and I took it gratefully.

"You knew she was pregnant?" Mom said.

"Yes."

"How long have you known?"

"Since the first week," I said. "Since that last time she was here."

"The night she was smoking pot in your room," she said in her let-me-get-this-straight tone. "She was pregnant."

"Yes."

214

Dad turned to look at me. "She knew then?"

"She told me that day at school. That's why I wanted her to eat with us."

"And when were you going to tell us?" Mom asked.

"As soon as Sophie said I could."

"And what about the baby's father?" she asked. "Did he know?"

"No. She wasn't going to tell him."

"She thought she could keep it a secret?"

"She was going to tell him it wasn't his."

For a minute there was only the sound of bacon hissing and spitting in the pan. Then Mom asked, "Why on earth would she do that?"

"She didn't want to mess up his life," I said. "She knew he was going to break up with her, because—" I hesitated, not sure how to put it. "He was sort of with somebody else already."

"He had already found a new girlfriend?"

"No, I mean, he sort of already had a girlfriend to begin with."

"So she was sleeping with someone else's boyfriend." Mom closed her eyes and shook her head. "Why doesn't that surprise me? Janet, you can't trust a girl like that. How do you know she's not sleeping with *your* boyfriend?"

"She wouldn't, Mom. Besides, Brian doesn't like Sophie, he likes me."

"I don't think *liking* has anything to do with it, Janet."

"Mom—"

"So, did anyone else know she was pregnant, besides you?"

"No, I don't think so."

"And how exactly did the two of you think you were going to handle this situation?"

"That's a good question," Dad said. He turned from the stove and regarded me with grave curiosity. "What were you going to do?"

I shrugged. "She'd already decided she was going to keep it."

"Good God," Mom said. "Can you imagine?"

We were all quiet—all of us, perhaps, imagining. Then Dad asked me to set the table, and he scrambled some eggs and made some toast, and we sat down to eat.

"So," I ventured, "can I visit Sophie in the hospital?"

"Why bother to ask?" Mom said. "You're going to do what you want anyway."

She was being sarcastic, but I felt a shift in the balance of power. I had been right to go to Sophie, right to disobey my parents. I *was* going to do what I wanted, and with that acknowledgement I saw the limits of what my parents could do if they didn't like it, and I lost all fear of them.

*

It was odd to go to bed when the sun was coming up, odd to wake up in the afternoon and realize that in less than twenty-four hours, everything had changed. I wasn't a virgin any more, and Sophie wasn't pregnant, and in a strange way, I felt as if my life had finally begun. Up to now my days had been an endless cycle of school and homework, work and piano practice, but now the routine had been broken. Today was different from yesterday, and there was no telling what might happen tomorrow.

Sophie had been moved to the intensive care unit, and I was allowed to visit her but warned not to expect much coherence from her.

Her skin had a deathly pallor and her hair was pale and lifeless, and she blended into the white sheets so completely that only the blue of her hospital gown distinguished her presence in the bed. She was lying on her back, one arm resting on a pillow on her stomach, the other arm stretched alongside her body with a concoction of tubes and needles protruding from it, and she looked so ghostly that I had the impression this elaborate tether was the only thing that kept her from floating away, that without it she might levitate toward the ceiling and disappear.

"Sophie?"

She opened her eyes but didn't look at me. I stepped closer into her line of vision, clutching the bag of magazines and Twizzlers I had brought her, and I saw that her eyes were clouded and unfocused. I said her name again, and she turned her head toward me and blinked slowly. A few moments later I saw a flicker of recognition.

"How are you feeling?" I asked.

She licked her lips and worked her mouth, but the words were lost until her voice picked up momentum.

216

"—good drugs," was all I heard, and her lips curved into a thin, twisted smile.

She waved her hand vaguely toward the side of the bed, lifting a feeble forefinger, and I found the button that raised the head of the bed to an incline. I put the magazines on the bedside table and admired her one flower arrangement.

"From Daddy," she said.

"Oh, my God, Sophie, you should have seen him last night," I said, and I told her how her father had wept at her bedside.

She rolled her eyes, much as my mother had done.

"No, really, Sophie, he was very upset. You almost died, you know."

She shrugged and looked away. "I wish I had."

"What are you saying? Don't talk like that."

"I'm being punished," she said. "I've been a bad person."

"You're not a bad person," I said. "This just wasn't meant to be, that's all. Look at my parents, this happened to them lots of times. They thought they were meant to have a big family, but they weren't."

"Oh, God," she moaned, "I'm just like your mother."

"No, Sophie, you're missing the point. This baby, it wouldn't have been born no matter what. You thought it was meant to be, but it just wasn't."

A large nurse trundled into the room and checked Sophie's apparatus. "How are you feeling, cupcake?" She spoke in a loud voice, as if Sophie's ears were as weak as the rest of her.

"I'm still alive," Sophie said.

"Well, you can thank your lucky stars for that, dearie. It was a close call." She stuck a thermometer in Sophie's mouth and took her pulse. "It would have been a shame, too, a sweet little girl like you. It would have broken your father's heart. Everybody knows how hard Dr. Prescott works to take care of his precious little girl."

Sophie cocked a skeptical eyebrow in my direction.

"You sure would make a pretty little angel, though, wouldn't you? You must be something special, honey, to tempt God. He almost took you before your time." She took the thermometer and squinted at it, then lumbered to the foot of the bed and wrote on Sophie's chart.

"Your temperature's normal, sweetie, you're going to be fine. You rest now. You want to have roses in your cheeks when Daddy comes to visit." As she left she said to me, "Don't stay too long. She needs to rest up and get her strength back, the poor little thing."

"God knows," I told Sophie, "I don't want to do anything to delay the roses returning to your cheeks."

"Daddy works so hard," she said.

"Precious."

We giggled, and she said, "Ow, Janet, don't make me laugh. It hurts."

"You must be something special," I said. "Walter will love that, you tempting God."

And then we stopped giggling and looked at each other, remembering where things stood with Walter.

"I'll call him," I said. "He should know you're here. He'll want to see you."

She said, "You can call him, but I don't think he wants to see me, unless it's just to tell me what a moron I am."

"And here you are, a captive audience. He won't pass up an opportunity like this." I looked over my shoulder to make sure we were alone. "Sophie, is there anyone else I should call?"

She looked at me quizzically. It was a pointed enough question, but it took a minute to penetrate the haze of drugs. Finally she shook her head.

"No," she said. "Nice try, though."

"If you say so."

"Janet, what about your parents? Are they mad?"

"They're pretty upset," I said. "Well, you know them. Dad stood there and cried right along with your father, and Mom's having conniptions because there was something going on that she didn't know about. They were pretty shook up."

She closed her eyes and said nothing.

"I'm going to go now," I said. "Is there anything you want from your house?"

Her eyes flew open. "Sid," she said. "Will you feed him?"

"Sure."

"And will you use my bed? You and Brian?"

I laughed. I hadn't expected her to remember. In fact, except for a pleasant ache in my thighs, I'd almost forgotten myself.

"Really," she said. "I want you to."

She held her hand out to me, and I took it.

218

"It was nice, wasn't it?" she said.

"Yes, very nice."

She nodded and gave me a sleepy smile. "Use my room. Don't worry about Daddy, but watch out for Mrs. Farnsworth."

I was about to leave when my father came in carrying a dozen red roses. He was overcompensating, I thought, trying to make up for the fact that he'd abandoned her. Of course he wouldn't realize that Sophie would prefer to have roses from her lover, that it might even be depressing to receive flowers from someone as innocuous as Dad.

He went to set the roses on the wide windowsill, but she instructed him to move her father's flowers to the window and to put his on the nightstand beside her. When he was done arranging the flowers he stood and looked at her for a long time.

"Sweetheart, I'm so sorry," he said, and he pulled a chair up beside her bed and took her hand.

"That's twice God has saved you," he said.

"I think He's mad at me," she said.

"No, Sophie, he's not mad at *you*. You're going to be fine, sweetheart, that's the most important thing, that you're alive and you're going to be fine."

She gazed at him with her drugged eyes.

"It would have been a beautiful baby," she said. "I would have loved it."

"I know, sweetheart." He moved her hand to his heart and pressed it against him. "I'm so sorry. You should never have had to go through this."

She whispered, "I'd be a good mother."

He glanced at me, and then he leaned closer to her and said, "I know you would, honey, but you don't have to. You don't have to prove anything."

She closed her eyes. "I'll prove it," she said. "I'll be good."

He kissed her hand and laid it gently on the bed beside her.

"You *are* good," he said, but I think she was already asleep.

*

When I called Walter to tell him Sophie was in the hospital, he immediately assumed that she'd attempted suicide.

219

I explained what an ectopic pregnancy was. I described the way I'd found her in the treehouse, the rush to the hospital, the brush with death, and when I was finished, he said, "*His* baby?"

"Yes."

"And you want me to feel sorry for her, because she can't have her lover's love child?"

"She almost died, Walter. I think if she died and you weren't speaking to her, you'd feel bad."

"As opposed to feeling bad when she's alive and I *am* speaking to her," he said. "I can't win, can I?"

I gave him directions to her room in the hospital. "Wait till you see her, Walter, it will break your heart."

"Great," he said. "That's exactly what I need."

*

Brian and I went to Sophie's house every day. We made love in her bed, quietly, guiltily at first, and then with greater abandon. Brian would say that it was just that we were becoming more comfortable with each other, more comfortable with the act itself, or maybe more confident in the privacy that Sophie's room afforded us, but I believe it was more than that. Something happened to me in Sophie's room. I felt a psychic connection with her, as if the entire room, and particularly the bed, had been infused with her spirit, and making love opened me up to it. At times I lost my inhibitions and my sense of self so completely that I imagined I had become Sophie, expending her passion for her lover on Brian, who reaped the benefits, although he wouldn't have wanted to think that Sophie had anything to do with it.

We left food out for Sid but he didn't eat it, and after the first day he didn't even come around to see us. I thought he must be despondent over Sophie's absence, and after several days without seeing him I began to worry that he had run away.

One day we were coming in just as Dr. Prescott was leaving for work, and I mentioned to him that Sid seemed to be missing.

He was rifling his pockets, looking for his something. "The cat?" he said. "I got rid of it."

"You got rid of it?" I echoed.

"She's not coming home, and I can't take care of a cat."

He found his keys and left. It didn't seem to occur to him that there was no reason for us to stay in his house if there was no cat to feed.

"What do you think he did with it?" Brian asked.

"I don't know. What does he mean, she's not coming home?"

"Maybe he's getting rid of her, too."

*

I went to see her later that day, and I noticed that on the nightstand beside my father's flowers was a small blue vase holding a single pink rose. I looked closer and saw that the vase was actually a bong, and the card was addressed to Sister Morphine.

"Let me guess," I said. "Uncle Bill?"

"No, it's from Walter. He was here this morning."

"What did he say?"

"He said he was glad I hadn't tried to kill myself, and if I ever feel like I want to, I should call him and he'll do it for me."

"So you're friends again?"

She shrugged.

"Sophie, have you talked to your father?"

She leaned back against her pillow and sighed. "I'm getting out the day after tomorrow, and I'm going to Nana's for the rest of the summer, and then I have to go to a Catholic girls' school in New Hampshire."

"You're kidding."

"I'm going away, Janet, just like my mother."

"*Are* you going?"

She nodded.

"Just like that? Aren't you even going to put up a fight?"

"It doesn't matter any more, Janet. I don't care where I go."

I looked into her eyes and I saw that she really didn't care. It unnerved me. I was looking for defiance, I expected civil disobedience and passive resistance, but she was looking at me with the same zombie-like gaze I had seen in the treehouse. Passive, but not at all resistant. It's the drugs, I thought, but having an explanation for it didn't make it any less disturbing.

"They're still giving you drugs, right?"

"Maybe I should get away from him," she said, and I knew she wasn't referring to her father. "Maybe we just shouldn't be near each other. It will be easier for everybody if I just go away."

"But what about me? And Walter?"

"You, too. Think about it, Janet. Even if I could stay here, which I can't—Daddy's probably having the locks changed right now—your parents don't want you hanging around with me, it would just be one giant hassle for you. And Walter will be about a hundred times happier without me, you know that. And Daddy already gave Sid away."

I had been visiting her every day, sometimes several times a day, and this was the first time I had seen her cry. It started as two or three tears at the mention of her cat, and it quickly became a deluge. She was shaking and heaving as she tried to catch a breath between sobs, and I moved closer and took her in my arms. She seemed incredibly small, and she felt warm and damp against my neck, like a baby when it falls asleep on your shoulder. I remembered her telling me about her last night with her lover, how she had wept in his arms, and I wondered if he had realized, finally, how wrong he had been, how self-deluded, to have ever imagined she was anything but a child.

I twisted my fingers through her curls and murmured every bland reassurance I could think of, and eventually she quieted. She pulled away and reached for the tissues. She blew her nose, and then made a useless attempt to blot my shirt.

"It's okay," I said. "It doesn't matter. Sophie, I wish you weren't going."

"I have to." She sniffled. "I have to start a new life. I have to be good."

"So you're going to get thee to a nunnery? I just can't picture it. What are you going to do, become a good little Catholic girl? Confess your sins and say your prayers and do penance for the next two years?"

"I was too happy."

"And you don't think you've suffered enough? You've lost your baby, you've lost your lover, you've lost one of your damn ovaries. You've lost your cat. You almost lost your life, Sophie, isn't that enough?"

She shook her head. "I made him suffer, too, Janet, and you know what the worst part is? I would do it again."

222

"Maybe he deserves to suffer. Does he know you're here? Has he even come to see you?"

"Yes."

"He has? Because I've been here a lot, Sophie, and I haven't seen him."

She didn't say anything.

"Is he sorry for what he did to you? He didn't even bring you flowers, did he?"

She closed her eyes and turned her head away. "Janet, why are you being so mean?"

"Because it makes me mad, and it should make you mad, too. He used you, Sophie, he got exactly what he wanted from you, and now he's back home with his family like nothing ever happened, and look where *you* are. You've lost everything, and you can't even *go* home."

"It's not his fault, Janet."

"And you're still sticking up for him, and that makes me *really* mad." I was so agitated I had to get up and pace. "He's a creep, and he's ruined your life, and he's got you so twisted around that you can't even see it. Where's your pride, Sophie? How come you could walk away from Hector, and from all those other guys, and you can't see how this asshole has fucked you over?"

She shook her head. "You're wrong, Janet. He loved me. He still loves me."

"He *never* loved you, Sophie, how could you be so stupid? You, of all people, how could you be so blind?"

"Me?" she said. "You think *I'm* blind?" She crossed her arms over her chest and settled herself back against her pillow. She took a deep breath and appeared to be making a conscious effort to remain calm. She spoke in a determinedly quiet voice. "I'm going to tell you something, Janet, and this is something that I *know*, okay? He may be back with his family, but he's not going to forget me. We're bound together for life. He's going to remember me every day for the rest of his life, and every time it's going to hurt like hell. You think he's over this? Janet, he'll never get over this. Never."

"I hope you're right. I hope he suffers for the rest of his life, and then I hope he dies and burns in hell."

She shook her head sadly and looked away from me. Her eye fell on the arrangements of flowers on the nightstand, and she plucked out one of the red roses and gave it to me.

"Will you write to me?"

My heart melted, and I hugged her tearfully. "Sophie, I'm going to miss you so much. Of course I'll write."

She brushed my hair away from my ear and whispered, "I'm going to be gone for a long time, Janet. Promise you'll always be my friend, no matter what."

I promised.

Chapter 17

She wrote me letters from school at least once a week, about the nuns, about her classes, about the other girls in her school. There were some bad girls, she reported, and she was staying away from them. In fact, she was keeping her distance from all the girls, because she was trying to start her new life, and it was easier, she said, if people didn't know you.

"I pray to the Holy Mother," she wrote. "I pray all the time to be good, to stop thinking about him and to let him be happy with his family, but it's not working, because secretly, in my heart, I'm praying to be with him again. You can't fool God."

Later she wrote that she had confessed her sinful desires and done her penance, but it was not enough. She was practicing self-denial, trying to get her body under control. She was fasting, continuing her prayers after grace was said and the other girls were eating. She allowed herself no pleasure, and certainly no sexual gratification. When she felt those indecent urges, she smacked herself with a hairbrush and prayed harder.

It was hard to know how to respond to this, especially since Brian and I were indulging in carnal delights at every opportunity, having discovered an unused dressing room over the stage in the auditorium. The old Sophie would have been happy for me, and proud of me for finding a place even she hadn't known about, but I wasn't sure how much I could tell this new Sophie without imposing my sins upon her.

My mother never asked about her. She referred to Sophie rarely, and only in the past tense. Sometimes when Mom wasn't around, Dad would make an earnest inquiry, but I spared him the details and gave him only the good news—she was drug-free, she was chaste, she was trying to be good. I knew he would rather be told the truth, and at times I longed to confide in him, but I knew it would only worry him, and I was worried enough for both of us.

Her letters were getting longer and less coherent, and she rambled on for pages about her own wickedness and her battle with the evil that inhabited her. She alluded to sacrifices and offerings she had made. She had burned her tarot cards. She was eating nothing but the Eucharist in an effort to purify her body; she was down to 92 pounds.

She was beating herself regularly. Did I know that Saint Augustine believed that miracles could be performed not only by God but also by the devil, and did it not seem likely, in retrospect, that she had been saved not by God, to do His work, but by Satan, to do his?

Before I had a chance to refute this, she wrote again. Her theory had been confirmed. Her confessor, Father Donovan, was a kind and understanding old man, kinder than she deserved, and his voice in the confessional reminded her of my father, which she took as a sign that he would help her find forgiveness.

Father Donovan suspected that the uncleanliness she felt was caused by some aspect of her sin that she was holding back. She had confessed the nature of her sins, he pointed out, but not the details, and perhaps what she needed to do was to think long and hard, and to account for every time she had ever given in to temptation. It was a daunting task, he knew, but it was the only way to purge her soul. She need not do it all in one session, the important thing was to take her time, to tell him everything she remembered and to leave nothing out.

And so she told him all the evil thoughts she'd had. She told him how she practiced witchcraft, how she used it against her enemies. She told him about the drugs and alcohol. She told him that she was lustful, that she had fornicated with a lot of boys, and with a married man.

"How many boys?" he asked.

She had no idea. Too many to count.

"God's been counting," he told her. "God knows how many, and He wants you to account for every one."

So she began with Hector, and she quickly realized, as Father Donovan began to question her, what a long and shameful process this was going to be, because, she reported, "When he said details, he meant *details*," and at this rate, she figured, it would take weeks of daily confessions to recount the sins she'd committed with Hector, and then she would still have to confront the rest of them, if she could even remember them all.

But she would try, she said, because it did help. Every session was like a tiny flame illuminating the vast darkness of her sin, giving her a sense of how far she had to go, of how much suffering she would have to endure before she could begin to hope for redemption.

And then one day, as she was describing a particularly sinful night she'd spent with Hector, she realized with horror that, on the other side of the screen, Father Donovan was masturbating.

She was struck speechless.

"Go on," he said. His voice was husky.

"Father, I shouldn't—"

"Go on, child, confess your sins."

And so she did, and the shame burned her from the inside out, and what else could she be but an instrument of the devil, when even her appeals for forgiveness could incite a priest to sin?

*

She later found out that, had she been friendlier with the other girls, they would have warned her about Father Donovan, but as it was, she endured these humiliating confessions for weeks.

She removed the mirror from her room, and she learned to bathe and dress herself with her eyes closed, so as not to look upon her own flesh. She now weighed 86 pounds, and in addition to starving and beating herself, she decided to stop sleeping. She had to, she said, otherwise she would continue to meet her lover in her dreams.

On the third night of her sleeplessness, she was on her knees in her room, praying deliriously, when, just before dawn, her door opened and someone entered her room. At first she thought she was having a vision, but even in her deranged state she realized the unlikelihood of the Blessed Virgin appearing in a red miniskirt and a black leather jacket, and she recognized her visitor as a girl from her class, Lisa Venuti, who was obviously sneaking in from a night out. Lisa shut the door, put a finger to her lips, and crawled under Sophie's bed.

A moment later the door opened again, and Sister Mary Elizabeth turned on the overhead light.

"Sophie, what are you doing?" Her bulk filled the doorway.

"I'm praying, Sister."

"Were you just out in the hall?"

"I—I might have gone to the bathroom, Sister."

"You might have?"

"I probably did."

Sister Mary Elizabeth put her hands on her hips and squinted at Sophie, and that's when Sophie realized that the nun wasn't in her habit. She had hair, straight and blonde and cropped just below her ears, and she wore a faded blue bathrobe that matched her faded blue eyes, which were peering at Sophie without the benefit of the John Lennon glasses she usually wore.

"Sophie, what have you done to your hair?"

Sophie reached up to touch her hair, and then she remembered what she had done earlier that night. "I cut it off as a sacrifice to the Lord Jesus Christ, Sister."

She saw Sister Mary Elizabeth's frown, and she was suddenly embarrassed to have made such a paltry offering.

"Have you been praying all night, Sophie?"

"Yes, Sister."

"Well, I'm sure the Lord appreciates it, but it *is* a school night. Perhaps you should try and get some sleep."

"Yes, Sister."

Sister Mary Elizabeth turned out the light and was about to shut the door when she stopped and said, "I'd like to see you after class tomorrow."

"Yes, Sister."

When Sister Mary Elizabeth was gone, Lisa crawled out from under the bed and threw herself on top of it. She fumbled in her purse, produced a pack of cigarettes, and lit one, blowing a plume of smoke into Sophie's face.

"Were you really praying," she asked, "or were you just thinking up more smut for Father Come-again?"

Sophie stared at her, and Lisa laughed.

"Everybody knows," she said, and Sophie's poor sleep-deprived mind could not fathom how everyone could know what a depraved slut she'd been when she had never said a word to anyone but her confessor.

It must show, she thought. Obviously she wasn't beating herself hard enough.

"Everybody knows he's a perv," Lisa said. "He gets off on hot teenage sex. Do you tell him the truth, or do you make stuff up?"

Sophie's mind was reeling. "What do *you* do?"

Lisa made an unsuccessful attempt to blow smoke rings. "I memorize letters from Penthouse," she said. "He really likes it when

228

there's two girls. If you want to get him off fast, tell him you licked another girl's clit."

"I never have," Sophie said.

Lisa shrugged. "Suit yourself. You got an ashtray?"

"There's a seashell on the desk." Sophie tried to get up, but she couldn't summon the strength, and she collapsed into a sitting position.

Lisa got up and helped herself to the seashell.

"What are you always praying for?" she asked. "Are you sick?"

Sophie shook her head.

"You *look* sick," Lisa informed her. "You look like you just got out of a death camp. Tina Grimaldi says she's seen lots of girls like you, bucking for sainthood."

The idea that she, of all people, could ever aspire to sainthood was so absurd that Sophie had to laugh, and once she started laughing, she found she couldn't stop. She laughed until she thought she would die, and when, finally, she stopped, she found that every breath she took make her feel cleansed, pure and lighter than air. She felt wonderful.

She said, "God, I needed that."

Lisa was watching her with raised eyebrows. "Are you all right?"

"Hell, yes. In fact, I haven't felt this good since the last time I got laid." She laughed some more, and this time Lisa laughed with her.

"You know what?" Lisa said. "I think I could fix your hair."

"Okay. I think I could teach you how to blow smoke rings."

"You want a cigarette?"

"I'd love one," Sophie said, and at that moment, she told me, she knew she was herself again. But she didn't get a chance to savor the feeling, because after a few puffs she felt dizzy, and then she passed out on the floor.

*

She woke up in the infirmary, and Sister Mary Elizabeth was sitting in a chair beside her. She had her glasses on now, and her pale blue eyes snapped through them.

"This is exactly what I wanted to talk to you about," she said without preliminaries, and she proceeded to lecture Sophie on the wrong-headedness of young girls who thought they could induce visions, or rapture, or what-have-you, by depriving their bodies of sustenance and driving themselves half mad with suffering. Ridiculous, she said, a senseless waste.

"Is this how the Lord wants to see you? Lying flat on your back and wasting away to nothing? Does this serve Him? You're an intelligent girl, Sophie, and you're throwing away the gifts He gave you. Well, I won't stand for it. You will stop this nonsense immediately, do you understand me?"

Sophie smiled. "Yes, Sister."

"Don't 'yes, Sister' me." She pointed her pudgy finger at Sophie. "I don't know what you've done, and I don't want to know. You may be the most wretched sinner that ever walked the earth—I doubt it, but you could be—it doesn't matter. The way to redeem yourself, child, is not to wallow in your misery. Acts of kindness, compassion for those less fortunate than yourself, devotion to a Christian life, that's what you can offer to God. Not you *hair*, or your tortured flesh. He's probably seen enough of that sort of thing, don't you think?"

"Yes, Sister."

"All right, then. You eat, and you sleep, and when you get up out of that bed, I want to see a healthy young woman ready to concentrate on her studies and put her talents to good use. Can you do that?"

"Yes, Sister. Thank you, Sister."

Sister Mary Elizabeth heaved herself out of her chair. There was something endearing, Sophie said, about the way she was muttering to herself as she waddled toward the door.

Penguins, Sophie thought as she drifted back to sleep.

*

After that, she began to join Lisa on her excursions into town. They hung out at a pool hall, where they picked up sailors. She wrote me about their adventures—threesomes, foursomes, "all kinds of parties," she said—but then one night someone mistook them for prostitutes and gave them a hundred dollars. Sophie wanted to give it back—it didn't seem fair for him to pay when no one else did, and anyway he had already paid for the room and the booze and all that cocaine—but Lisa said she knew where they could get some Thai weed, and that was fair, wasn't it, if he treated them to a little gift after the good time they had shown him? And that was okay, Sophie said, but after that Lisa wanted to charge every time, and Sophie couldn't go along with that.

"I may be a slut," she wrote, "but I'm not a whore."

So she and Lisa went their separate ways, and consequently Lisa was not present the night Sophie went to a motel with three sailors and overdosed on Quaaludes and Jack Daniel's.

When they could not wake her up in the morning, the sailors panicked and left her there for the hapless chambermaid to find. The ambulance attendants found her school uniform on the floor and the sisters were contacted. (Sophie had come to enjoy wearing her uniform. I'd be amazed, she told me, how many men were turned on by it.) The sisters called Dr. Prescott, who called me, partly to inform me of her condition, but mostly, I think, for my reassurance that her overdose had not been deliberate.

"She's not unhappy, is she?" he asked me.

I tried to keep the details from my parents, but one of Dr. Prescott's girlfriends blabbed it around the hospital, and Mom heard it all from her friend Vivian Talbot, every detail, including the fact that one of the sailors was black. Mom couldn't wait to repeat the story to Dad, even though it clearly broke his heart to hear it.

I approached him in his study that night as he was working on a sketch, and I asked if he wanted to go with me the next day to visit her.

A pained look crossed his face. "I can't," he said. "I'm sorry. Please give her my love, for what it's worth."

"It would be worth more in person, wouldn't it?"

"I'm not sure that's true." He tossed down his pencil. "Janet, this was very sudden, wasn't it? I mean, she was doing well, wasn't she? What happened to make her go and do a thing like this?"

"She wasn't doing well, Dad." I threw myself down on the couch. I put a pillow under my head and crossed my ankles, pretending I was in analysis. "She's been losing her mind since last spring, ever since she started seeing that guy."

"What guy?"

"The one who got her pregnant and then dumped her. The one who used her and then forgot about her." I remembered Sophie telling

231

me that her lover would never forget. "Well, maybe he hasn't forgotten, but he ignores her, so he's as good as forgotten. For all practical purposes."

"I see."

"And she's over there practically killing herself trying to get over him." I told him about the sacrifices and the praying, the fasting, the sleeplessness, the hairbrush.

"Janet, you never told me this."

"I know."

"Honey, I *asked* you how she was, and you said she was fine."

"Yeah, well, maybe if you had kept in touch with her yourself, you would have known that she *wasn't* fine."

"You couldn't tell me?"

"What for?" I sat up and looked at him. "What would you have done, Dad, said a few extra prayers for her?"

He stared at me blankly. He didn't answer me, because he had no answer.

"See, Dad? You're no better than he is. In fact, you may even be worse. He used her for a little while, but you spent years convincing her that she could trust you, and then the minute she got into real trouble, you dumped her."

"I suppose you're right."

I waited for him to say more, but he didn't.

"So?" I prompted.

He shook his head.

"I'm not saying it just to be *right*, Dad. What are you going to do? I mean, you can sit here and say how much you care, but that doesn't do her any good, does it?"

"I'm not sure it ever did her any good, Janet. You can love a person for the wrong reasons, and nothing good can come of it. I'm afraid that's what I've done."

"No," I said, "that's Mom talking. That's why you won't go, because Mom doesn't want you to."

"I wish it were that simple."

"I don't know what you mean."

He said nothing.

"Forget it." I got up to leave. "I'm sorry I asked."

"But, Janet," he said, "this overdose—you're sure it was an accident?"

232

"If I said it was intentional, would you go and see her?"

"I just want to know."

"I'm pretty sure it was an accident," I said, "but I'll tell her you asked. Don't worry, Dad, I'll be sure to tell her how much you care."

*

"I shouldn't have had that last shot," she told me. She had lain in the hospital in a coma for twelve hours, and when she woke up, her official story was that she had no recollection of being in any motel room. She hated to disappoint that nice police detective, but she could not identify any of the men she had been with. She didn't know how she got to the motel, she had no idea who gave her the drugs, she didn't remember anybody taking her clothes off. The last thing she remembered, she claimed, was sitting in her room doing a translation for her Latin class.

"There's no point in lying," I told her. "They already caught the guys, they already know what happened."

"Well, then, I shouldn't have to answer a lot of questions, should I?"

"Sophie, you have to stop doing this. What's with all the sailors, anyway? I thought you didn't like uniforms."

"I like it when they take them off."

I told her that Dad sent his love. "For what it's worth," I added.

"Oh, God, Janet, you didn't tell him what happened, did you?"

"*I* didn't, but Mom did. She heard about it from somebody at the hospital."

She closed her eyes and sighed.

I wanted to cheer her up, and I tried to think of good things to tell her. Uncle Bill and Becky Oatmeal broke up, I told her, Uncle Bill was living in Maine again.

She nodded her approval, but she still wouldn't look at me, and I made some lame attempts to engage her in conversation about Uncle Bill, and about people from school, but her mind was elsewhere.

I gave up. "Sophie, what's wrong?"

She shook her head and didn't answer.

I said, "It's him, isn't it? Your married man. You're not over him yet."

She brushed tears from her eyes. "Sometimes I hate him."

"Why shouldn't you hate him? He ruined your life."

"I've tried everything, Janet. I can't forget him, and it's my own fault. I cast that spell, I bound us together for life."

"You'll find someone else."

"No, I won't, and it wouldn't matter even if I did. It can't be undone, not even by me. Not by anybody."

"God could undo it," I said.

"He could, but He won't."

She said this with chilling finality, and I understood that all her prayers and confessions and sacrifices had been in vain. She had begged God to release her from this obsession, and He had refused. She had lost all hope.

"Tell me the truth," I said. "Were you trying to die?"

"I wasn't trying to, but I wouldn't care if I did."

I later asked Dad if there was such a thing as suicide by indifference, and he said that there was.

While I was there, Sister Mary Elizabeth came to visit. She looked exactly as Sophie had described her, like a big blue-eyed penguin in wire-framed glasses. She introduced herself to me and then turned her attention to Sophie.

"How did this happen, dear?"

Sophie widened her eyes in an obvious attempt to convey innocence. "I don't know, Sister. I don't remember anything."

The nun gave her a stern, skeptical look. "We can't seem to find a happy medium, can we, between sainthood and sinfulness?"

"I guess I just don't know how to be good," Sophie said.

"Nonsense, dear. All you have to do is obey His commandments, and stay in your room at night. You can do that, can't you?"

"I can try, Sister."

"Sophie, I'm here to tell you that you'll have to do more than try. If you want to come back to school, you'll have to make a serious commitment. You'll have to decide that you want to be pure and chaste. That means no drugs, no alcohol, no cigarettes, and no sexual activity of any kind. Is that what you want?"

Sophie looked at me. I shrugged.

"Think it over, dear. You'll be getting out of here tomorrow, and you can come back to school as long as you understand that any infraction of the rules will result in your being dismissed. Do you understand that, dear?"

"Yes, Sister."

"All right, then. You think about it and let me know what you decide." Sister Mary Elizabeth patted Sophie's hand. "Sophie, it's never too late to change. I hope you'll come back to us. You know the Lord rejoices when a lost lamb returns to the fold."

When Sister Mary Elizabeth was gone, I asked Sophie what she was going to do.

"I don't have much choice," she said. "I already asked Daddy if I could come home, and he said no."

*

So she went back to school, but two weeks later she was caught smoking dope on the fire escape, and she was expelled.

"Expelled, but not excommunicated," she said, and her father sent her to another Catholic girls' school in Rhode Island, where she lasted about six weeks before she was caught in bed with another student.

"She was a great kisser," Sophie told me.

"Did she get kicked out, too?"

"No. The dildo was hers, but I was the one wearing it, and I was already on probation."

By now she was seventeen, and she decided to quit school altogether. Dr. Prescott set her up in an apartment in Portland, and she lied about her age and got a job in a tavern on the waterfront, where she had all the booze and sailors she could ever want. She seemed content.

Chapter 18

I heard from her less frequently. She was busy. She worked her way up from dishwasher to waitress to bartender. She met a lot of men, and they liked to take her places—to dinner, to concerts, to Caribbean islands. They took her skiing, and sailing. One guy took her skydiving, and for a while it looked like she might fall in love with him. He outlasted his competitors by several months, but when he started talking about moving in together, she got scared and broke it off. Afterwards, whenever his name came up, she got wistful, and I would urge her to call him, but as far as I know, she never did.

She refused all invitations to come home, and on those rare occasions when I could convince her to come to town for a day, she would not come to my house. I attributed this to the memories of her last night there—the night she lost her baby—and to my mother's hostility, and so I usually agreed to see her in Portland. During our senior year, Brian and I spent several weekends at Sophie's house, sometimes when she was home and sometimes while she was away. "Playing house," my mother would have called it. We were still borrowing Sophie's bed.

Walter started dating Vanessa St. Pierre, the girl he would eventually marry. She was a nice girl and she treated him well. I saw him around, and we talked occasionally, but he had lost interest in Sophie, and we didn't have much else in common.

And the truth is that although I saw her every few weeks, she seemed far removed from the concerns of my life, and when I wasn't with her I didn't think about her much. I was busy with school, with rehearsals and performances, with college applications, with dances and proms, and finally with graduation.

I was accepted at the Boston Conservatory of Music. Brian was going to Berkeley. We decided to break up before leaving for school—it seemed silly to consider ourselves together when we would be three thousand miles apart, and we agreed that we didn't want to hold each other back as we embarked on our college adventures. We also told each other that our breakup wasn't really official—neither of us was looking for anyone new and we didn't really expect that anything would happen to change our feelings for each other.

I intended to stay faithful, and I hoped that Brian would, too, although I had to admit that Berkeley made me nervous. I imagined a campus full of girls like Sophie, braless, free-spirited flower children who were passionate in their idealism and liberal in their sexuality. Brian claimed he had no interest in such girls, but I wondered what would happen when he was surrounded by them, so far from home. I was sure he would be tempted.

I was equally sure that I would *not* be tempted, and so it came as a complete surprise to me when I was the one who fell in love, with a man I met the day I moved into my dorm. His name was Eric, and he was my roommate Pam's older brother. I didn't fall in love with him on sight, although I did notice that he had a nice smile. Pam and I became close, and she invited me to many Sunday dinners at her parents' house in nearby Methuen. Eric was living there while he finished his master's degree at Boston College—he was becoming a therapist—and I began to look forward to his mother's dry pot roast and stringy chicken. It was worth a bad meal once a week to bask in that smile.

"I think he likes you," Pam said.

"Really?" I'm sure I was blushing. "He doesn't think I'm too young for him?"

"It's only six years, and I'm sure he can see that you're mature for your age. Would you go out with him?"

"God, yes."

I told myself it wasn't really dating, that technically I wasn't cheating on Brian because we weren't a couple any more, and besides, I reasoned, it wasn't like Eric and I were sleeping together. We went to dinner and to the movies, and we talked. He was working at a shelter for runaway teens, and he talked about the kids he met, about their tragic lives and their dangerous behavior, and I told him about Sophie. I kept telling myself that I would stop; I felt guilty exploiting her personal history to hold Eric's attention, but he seemed fascinated, and my own life just wasn't that interesting.

Eventually we did sleep together, and when he finished school he took a job in Boston, and he and Pam and I shared an apartment. My parents disapproved, his disapproved only slightly less, but we didn't care. We were happy.

*

I wanted Eric and Sophie to meet, and I suggested that we go to Portland and take her out to dinner.

"Wouldn't you rather have her here?" he asked, and I explained that I didn't like to encourage her to drive, because she didn't actually have a license.

"I thought she had a car," he said.

"She has a friend who runs a car dealership. There's an ugly little Toyota that she likes, and he keeps it on the lot for her. She can use it whenever she wants."

"That seems unnecessarily complicated."

I shrugged. "That's Sophie."

*

We ended up getting Vietnamese takeout and eating it on the floor of Sophie's living room. She had a kitchen table but no chairs. In fact she had no furniture to speak of—a rocking chair, a stereo, a mattress on the floor of her bedroom, and a few bookcases.

We talked about books for a while, and then Eric dropped out of the conversation, choosing to watch and listen as Sophie chatted excitedly about an upcoming trip to Amsterdam with one of her boyfriends.

"I heard they have penguins there," she said, "and when you go to the zoo, the penguins are walking around, because they don't keep them in cages. They let them wander around free, so you could be standing at the monkey cage, and a penguin might come up beside you and stand there looking at the monkeys with you."

I laughed. "Who told you that?"

"I don't remember," she said. "I might have dreamed it. But I hope it's true."

"Why don't they let the monkeys run free?" Eric asked.

"Because monkeys throw their feces at people," she said. "They're not polite like penguins."

"So, who's this guy?" I asked.

"He's just a guy," she said. "He's nice."

"Is it serious?"

"No." She would not allow that, she said. She tried not to let any relationship progress to the no-fun-any-more stage.

"How long does that usually take?" Eric asked.

She shrugged. "A few months, more or less. It depends on the guy."

"So, how do you know when it's time?"

She gave him a pointed look. "When they start asking too many questions."

"What kind of questions?" I asked.

"Oh, you know. They ask about your old boyfriends, or they ask about your family. Sometimes they ask about my scar. Why do they need to know all that?"

"It's called getting to know you," Eric said.

"Well, I've got a better idea," she said. "It's called minding your own business."

"You have to let them get to know you," I said.

"I'm fun," she said. "That's all they need to know."

"Do you have a lot of female friends?" Eric asked.

She narrowed her eyes in suspicion. "Are you analyzing me?"

He smiled. "Not without a court order. I'm just wondering if your female friends are allowed to know you better."

"Nobody knows me better than Janet," she said, which didn't really answer the question, a fact I knew would not escape his notice.

"But Janet has known you forever," he said, "so that makes it easier, doesn't it? You only have to tell her the fun stuff. She already knows the rest."

She blinked as if in confusion. "That's all there *is*, is fun stuff." Her tone conveyed a certain finality, a warning not to pursue her across this particular boundary.

I saw Eric take this in, and I saw him decide to push just a little further. Part of me wanted to stop him, but another part of me wanted to see how far he could get.

"So, in other words," he said, "the answer is no, no one is allowed to really know you, no one is allowed to get too close. No one is allowed past the so-called fun stuff."

She went very still, and I saw a flash of something in her eyes before she steadied her gaze at him and said, "Why is it that some people only think they know you if they know all the bad stuff?"

"Why is it," he countered, "that some people think if they ignore the bad stuff, it will go away?"

She turned to me. "I don't think I like him. He asks too many questions. Does he do that to you?"

I nodded. "I don't mind, though. I usually think they're good questions."

Eric said, "Janet doesn't mind because she's not trying to hide anything."

She snorted in contempt. "What do you think I have to hide from *you*?"

He shrugged. "It's not what you hide from me that matters. It's what you hide from yourself."

Her eyes went ice cold. "I suppose it's one of the hazards of your profession, that you can't stand to see anyone happy. You must hate to think there are people who don't need your help."

He held up his hands in surrender. "I apologize. Forgive me for mistaking your happiness for something else."

"Janet," she said, "don't I seem happy to you?"

"You're going to Amsterdam," I said. "What could be happier than that?"

She smiled. "I'm going to see penguins."

*

In the car on the way home, Eric said, "I'm sorry, I guess she doesn't like me."

"You'll grow on her," I said. "She's not used to being challenged that way. Walter used to do it, but I never could."

"Why not?"

"Because when I think of all the things that have happened to her...I don't know if I would have been able to handle it. So I always figured, however she wants to deal with it, that's okay with me. If she says she's happy, that's fine with me."

"But don't you think she's confusing fun with happiness? Don't you think there's something a little desperate about all this fun she's having?"

I shrugged. "All I know is that she's not beating herself any more. She's not having sex with three or four people at once, she's not laying in the hospital in a coma. That's good enough for me, Eric, I'm just glad she's alive, and why shouldn't she have fun if she wants to?"

He drove in silence for a few minutes, and then he said, "So what's your definition of fun, Janet? Casual sex? Drugs and alcohol? Prostituting yourself for a trip to Amsterdam?"

240

"She's always wanted to go to Amsterdam."

"And you don't care that she's sleeping with someone to get there?"

"She would have slept with him anyway, Eric, she's not doing it for a trip to Europe."

"She's doing it for fun," he said.

"I don't see anything wrong with that."

"She's happy."

"Sure, why not?"

"Right," he said. "And she's going to see penguins in Amsterdam."

*

I was visiting my parents one weekend when Uncle Bill stopped by for lunch.

"I just delivered a dining room set up the coast," he said.

After he and Becky Oatmeal broke up, he had gone back to work for the cabinetmaker in Portland. In his free time he designed and built his own furniture, using a rented barn as a workshop. He sold some pieces to a wealthy couple who had a summer home on Prout's Neck, and they told their friends, and eventually he was able to quit his day job.

"Hey, I ran into our mutual friend," he said. "I went out with some friends in Portland, and who do I see tending bar but your friend Petunia. Man, she hasn't changed."

"How is she?" Dad asked.

"Wild and crazy as ever," said Uncle Bill.

"I hope you're not sleeping with her," Mom said.

I almost choked on my sandwich. "Mom—"

"I can answer that," Uncle Bill said. "I can ease your mind. I did not sleep with her, but I did take her up on her offer to go out back and smoke some weed. She told me horror stories about Catholic school."

"She got kicked out," Mom said. "Two different schools, did she tell you that?"

"Yeah, she mentioned that. She told me about the priest who jerked off during confession."

"Oh, my God," Mom said. "That's just like her to say a sick thing like that. That's disgusting."

"Is it true?" Dad asked.

"Yes," I said. "She told me about it."

"How awful," Dad said.

Uncle Bill shook his head. "Makes you wonder, though, doesn't it? What do you think she was confessing?"

"I can guess that it involved sailors," Mom said.

"This was before the sailors," I told her. "This was when she was trying to be good."

Mom scoffed. "*That* didn't last long, did it?"

"Sailors?" Uncle Bill said.

"One of them black. I guess she didn't tell you about *that*," Mom said, and Dad got up and left the room as my mother repeated the story of Sophie's overdose, the motel and the three sailors.

"Oh, my," Uncle Bill said. "I'm sorry to hear that. That's too much of a good thing, isn't it?"

"What good thing are you referring to, Bill?" asked Mom.

"Take your pick. I mean, fun is fun, but that's just excessive." He looked at me. "Does she do that kind of thing often?"

"Not any more," I said. "Not like that, but she's still not exactly a normal person."

"She'll never be a normal person," Mom said.

Uncle Bill rapped his knuckles on the table. "Knock on wood."

*

At the beginning of my senior year, I found out I was pregnant. Eric wanted to come with me when I broke the news to my parents, but I declined. They might be upset, and I didn't want Eric trying to counsel them.

I sat Mom and Dad down in the living room and told them, "Eric and I are getting married."

"Yes, dear, we know," Mom said. "After you graduate."

"Well, actually, it looks like it's going to be sooner than that."

"Oh, Janet." My mother had never sounded so disappointed in me.

"Oh," Dad said, catching on. "Oh, you're—Are you—?"

"Yes, Dad. Due March 27th."

242

"March 27th," he repeated. "Imagine that."

"Is that during midterms?" Mom asked. "How will you take your exams?"

"Helen, we're going to be grandparents."

"Yes, John, but first we've got to get her married."

"Eric must be thrilled," he said. "Are you excited?"

"Yes," I said, although I wasn't sure excited was the right word. Most of the time when I was with Eric, I felt like an adult, but this scared me. It was one thing to play house, it was quite another to take on the roles of Mommy and Daddy. I remembered how certain Sophie had been at sixteen, believing she could take care of her baby, and I wished I had her confidence.

My mother immediately began plans for the wedding. She would alter her own dress to fit me—"*I* wasn't pregnant," she said—and she would make a dress for the maid of honor.

"I assume you'll want to ask Pam."

"Actually, I might ask Sophie."

She frowned. "I think Pam would be a more appropriate choice. After all, she's family. I'm sure her parents are expecting you to ask her."

"I'll think about it," I said.

"Well, don't think too long. We've got to fit her for a dress."

*

I met Sophie at the Seaman's Club for lunch. She was late, but I was seated at a window with a view of the water, and I didn't mind. I was idly twirling my water glass on the linen tablecloth and gazing out to sea, remembering a time when I was a child and a wave knocked me over and sent me tumbling, rolling in somersaults until I couldn't tell up from down. It was fun; I didn't know enough to be scared until the ride was over, until my head broke through the water and I heard the panic in my mother's voice as she screamed my name. I thought about the baby in my womb and imagined that while I worried and fretted over it, it was floating around helplessly. Helplessly, but without fear.

"Janet!"

I looked up as Sophie swooped down on me in a cloud of perfume and kissed my cheek, and then she stepped back and threw off her mother's mink. The host scrambled to assist her as if he believed she would throw her coat on the floor and kick it under the table. I laughed, thinking maybe she'd been here before and done exactly that.

She sat down and reached across the table for my hand.

"Oh, Janet, you're going to have a little girl."

So much for surprising her with the news.

"A girl?" I said. "Are you sure?"

"Who do you think you're talking to, bufflehead? I *know*. She's going to be beautiful, too, and smart."

She recommended the clam chowder and told me that the secret ingredient was nutmeg, a fact she had learned while she was sleeping with the chef. She ooohed over my engagement ring and asked about the wedding plans.

"That's what I wanted to talk to you about," I said. "It's going to be small. I'll probably have just one attendant."

She cocked her head.

"I always assumed it would be you," I said. "I mean, I always wanted it to be you—"

"But you want to ask Pam instead."

"It's not that I really *want* to—"

"But it would make the families happy."

I sighed. "I don't know what to do."

"You worry too much," she said. "It's fine if you want to ask her. I'm sure she'd be better at it, anyway."

"I don't think she'd be *better* at it—"

"It involves responsibilities, right? Throwing showers for all your aunts and shit like that? Getting fitted for a dress and all?"

"My mother's making the dress."

"Well, there you go, Janet, doesn't that settle it?" She leaned back in her chair and raised her open hands to show me how simple it all was.

"I just—"

"What are you going to do, Janet? Stick me in a room with your mother and her tape measure, and all those pins and needles? No, thanks. Make it easy on yourself, honey, it'll be fine. Eric will be happy, his parents will be happy, your parents, Pam, everybody."

"My mother," I said. "Not Dad so much. He's staying neutral, but I think secretly he's rooting for you."

She looked down at her lap, and for a second I thought she'd dropped something.

"He'll understand," she said. "*I* understand. Really, it's okay."

"But you'll be there, right? Even if you're not the maid of honor?"

"Oh, I'll *be* there." She smiled. "I won't be wearing any dress your mother made, either."

*

I saw Sophie as I walked down the aisle, and I tugged on Dad's arm and nodded toward her. He fell a half beat behind in our march, and no wonder, I thought. Sophie looked like a million bucks in a strapless blue sequined sheath. Her blonde curls were cut short, making her look both younger and more sophisticated, like Shirley Temple posing for Calvin Klein. And as if the dress were not costume enough, she was also wearing elbow length satin gloves, dyed to match. Only Dad's hand on my arm kept me from accelerating down the aisle to where I could see what she had on for shoes.

She winked at me, and I almost laughed out loud, because at that moment it seemed we were thinking the same thought: we were playing grownup. It was as if the entire wedding had been staged for the two of us, so we could fulfill our childhood games. I was the princess about to marry my true love, and Sophie was my fairy godmother, twinkling on the sidelines, blessing us with her presence.

*

"Sophie," Mom said at the reception, "what lovely shoes."

They were the same blue as her dress and her gloves, with four-inch stiletto heels, and she obviously hadn't had much practice walking in them. She teetered and swayed as she approached us, and she latched onto Dad's arm to steady herself, pressing up against his side and clinging as if to a life raft.

"We all look beautiful, don't we?" she said. "We smell nice, too."

"It's wonderful to see you," Dad said, and indeed, he seemed unable to take his eyes off her, as if she'd risen from the dead. Another miracle.

"You're not married yet, are you, dear?" Mom asked.

"Hell, no," Sophie said. "I mean, I'm sure Janet and Eric will be happy and all, but that's a rare thing, isn't it? I don't really know too many happily married people."

"Maybe it's the company you keep, dear."

Sophie laughed. "That's funny, I never thought of that. I guess it's an occupational hazard, meeting so many unhappily married men."

"Well, and who knows, dear? Maybe some of them *were* happily married, before they met you."

"Where's Bill?" Sophie said. "I need a drink."

*

A while later I said, "Sophie, you haven't danced with Dad yet."

She shrugged. "He hasn't asked me."

"Well, ask *him*." I aimed her toward him and gave her a little shove. "Go on. This is a slow one, he can handle this."

She seemed about to say something, but then she set her mouth as if she were about to undertake a grim mission, and she marched resolutely toward my father.

I watched them move onto the dance floor. She lifted her arms, reaching for his shoulders, and her face was tipped up to look at him, and he was reaching for her, bending over her, talking to her, and I was reminded of something, something I could almost but not quite remember. And then Uncle Bill swept me onto the dance floor and made me laugh, and when I next saw Dad and Sophie she was leaning into him, one side of her face pressed against his chest, her eyes closed, and now I remembered how he always kept her on his left side when he was reading to us, because his heartbeat calmed her down.

"I think Sophie's asleep," I said to Uncle Bill, and he turned to look.

"Either that or she's passed out," he said. "She's not drunk, is she?"

"No, I don't think so."

But when the dance was over, Sophie went directly to the bar. She exchanged a few words with the bartender, and then she tossed back two shots, one right after the other.

"Maybe she should keep dancing," Uncle Bill said, and I watched as he led her away from the bar and onto the dance floor.

246

They were playing a fast one now, and she kicked off her shoes and danced.

*

I was on my way to the ladies' room when I found Uncle Bill standing in front of the elevator with the photographer.

"What are you doing?" I asked.

"Oh, *there's* our princess." He threw his arm around me and kissed the top of my head. "Take our picture," he said, and the photographer obliged.

"Why are you hanging around the elevator, Uncle Bill?"

"I'm expecting someone." He glanced toward the reception room. "What's Helen doing?"

"She's busy circulating," I said. "What's going on?"

Suddenly there was a yelp that echoed up and down the elevator shaft.

"What's that?" I asked.

Uncle Bill laughed. "That would be your friend Maggie May. The elevator's stopped, what, maybe a floor up from here?" He consulted the photographer, who nodded in agreement.

"Is she all right?" I asked.

"Oh, I think so."

From the elevator came a surprised sounding, "Oh!" It was definitely Sophie.

"Oh, no," I said. "In the elevator?"

"Don't tell your mother," said Uncle Bill, "but I just had to borrow your photographer. When that door opens, I want the image preserved."

"Who is she with?"

"Not me," he said. "You can bear witness to that."

Again Sophie cried out, and a male voice groaned in counterpoint.

"I have to go to the bathroom," I said.

"You're going to miss the grand finale."

"That's okay," I said. "I'll see the pictures."

*

It was a tricky business, going to the bathroom in my wedding gown, and I was gone for a while, but when I came back, I found I had not missed the grand finale after all. The photographer was sitting on the floor smoking a cigarette, and Uncle Bill was standing with his hand on the shoulder of a bellhop, a slack-jawed youth who seemed entranced by the increasingly urgent duet that was now emanating from the elevator shaft.

"My mother's going to have a fit," I said.

The voices launched into a crescendo, and finally there was a release and a resolution, followed by a coda of deep shuddering sighs. On the ground floor, we all let out our breath. The photographer took his position and prepared his camera. There was a long minute of silence before the elevator hummed into motion, and then the door opened and Sophie stepped out, a little flushed, a little unsteady on her heels, but otherwise looking remarkably dignified.

The flash went off, and she teetered backwards for a moment, and then she saw us all standing around, and she laughed. The photographer snapped another picture.

"My goodness," Sophie said, laying one gloved hand demurely on her chest. "I thought we were going to be trapped in there all night. Did you come to rescue us?"

"Yes, dear," said Uncle Bill. "You sounded distressed."

"Well, who wouldn't be?" she said, and she headed for the ladies' room without a backward glance.

Her paramour, if that's the word I want, turned out to be Eric's cousin Ben, who emerged from the elevator looking completely dazed, like the sole survivor of a train wreck. Uncle Bill stepped forward and shook his hand, and the photographer took another picture.

"Soldier, let me buy you a drink," Uncle Bill said, and he led Ben back to the reception. The photographer went with them. The bellhop and I looked at each other for a minute, but there seemed to be nothing to say, and at the same instant we both turned and went our separate ways, he toward the front desk, and I to the ladies' room.

*

The ladies' room proper was preceded by a kind of ladies' lounge, a plush pink room with floral armchairs and a mirror and countertop that ran the length of one wall to form a long dressing table.

Sophie was perched on the edge of the counter smoking a cigarette.

"This is a great wedding," she said.

"And I was worried that you weren't having a good time."

"It was the shoes," she said. "Isn't that funny? I had taken them off to dance, and he wanted me to put them back on. That's what he wanted, Janet, was the shoes. He thinks I'm a stiletto-wearing bimbo."

"And so you are."

"And so I am, for today. You're not mad, are you?"

I arranged my dress so I could sit down, and I kicked off my own modest two-inch heels and put my feet up on the counter. I felt comfortable for the first time all day.

"I'm not *mad*," I said, "but Jesus Christ, Sophie, you're in a hotel, couldn't you have gone to a room?"

"He has a room," she said. "His family's staying here."

"Well, so, why didn't you go there?"

"We were going to. We were on our way there, but I thought this would be more fun." She blew some smoke rings. "Sometimes it's better if you don't get too comfortable."

"You like to able to make a quick getaway."

"Careful, Janet. You've only been married a few hours and you're already starting to sound like him."

"I like his perspective."

"Yeah, well, be careful what you wish for. Sometimes it's better not to know why people do the things they do."

"It's always better to know," I said.

"Except when it isn't."

I watched her crush her cigarette in the ashtray, and I remembered how, at parties, I could always tell which butts in the ashtray were hers because they were so thoroughly mangled, even the filters bent up and crippled, looking somehow more used than other people's.

"So," she said, "is this the happiest day of your life, or what?"

"Yeah, so far I think it is." I laughed. "You know what made me happy, Sophie? Seeing you standing there in the church in that dress."

She preened. "You like it? My hairdresser picked it out. I hope Helen noticed that I had the gloves and the shoes dyed to match."

"There's not a doubt in my mind that she noticed. She's going to want to know about those pictures, you know."

"Tell her to ask Bill. Let him explain it."

The door opened and Pam came in.

"There you are," she said to me. "Your mother's looking for you."

"What now?" I asked. "More pictures?"

"More pictures, more circulating," Sophie said. "More dancing, more smooching with the groom. Back to work, bufflehead."

Chapter 19

Sophie was right, it was a girl. We named her Samantha. My professors allowed me to reschedule some of my work so that I could graduate, and then Eric and I moved to Maine, where he found a job in a private hospital not far from my parents, who were thrilled to have their grandchild so close by.

Especially Dad. When I saw him with Samantha, I realized I couldn't remember the last time I had seen him happy. Now he talked all the time about when I was a baby, about when Sophie and I were little girls, and I thought maybe that's what he'd missed for so long, was having children around.

By the time Samantha was four, I was anxious for her to start school so I could find a teaching job, but then I discovered I was pregnant again, and the job would have to wait.

I was exactly five months along on a Tuesday morning in April, and I thought I knew what to expect. That's what I remember most, is feeling comfortable, feeling that while my life was not exactly as I'd planned it, it had a certain logic to it, and an element of predictability. I was putting a load of laundry in the dryer when my mother called and told me that my father was dead.

He was getting a cup of coffee in the faculty lounge when he suddenly dropped his cup, put his hand to his heart, and collapsed. The other teachers who were there said they believed he was dead before he hit the floor, and they emphasized that it was quick and seemed relatively painless. He never made a sound, they said. They initiated CPR, and they called an ambulance, but he was already gone. The hospital pronounced him DOA at 10:57 a.m., dead of a heart attack at the age of 52.

When I got to my mother's house, she was sitting at the kitchen table staring at the plastic bag into which the hospital staff had put Dad's personal belongings—his clothes, his wallet, his watch, his wedding ring.

"It didn't seem real to me," she said. "It didn't seem real until they handed me this."

I made coffee, not knowing what else to do.

"Eric's going to pick up Samantha from nursery school," I said. "Have you called anybody?"

"I called Louise," she said. "She'll call the rest of the family."

"I have to call Sophie," I said.

She looked at me blankly, and I saw that it would never have occurred to her that Sophie should be called.

There was no answer at Sophie's house, so I called information to get the number of the bar where she worked. She picked it up on the first ring.

"Janet?" she said, and I burst into tears.

"Oh, God," she said. "It was his heart, wasn't it?"

"Yes," I said. "Sophie, he's gone."

"Where are you?"

"I'm at my mother's."

"I'll be there," she said. "I'm leaving right now."

It was a relief to know she was coming. She was the only other person, I thought, who knew Dad as I knew him, who shared the same memories of him. She had never felt more like a sister to me.

She flung herself into my arms and we wept together, and then she hugged Samantha. Eric had explained the situation to Sam, and I don't know how much she understood, but she was sufficiently in awe of the grief surrounding her to adopt an appropriately solemn attitude.

Sophie did not hug my mother, nor did Mom make any move toward her. They looked at each other for a long moment, but neither of them spoke.

Sophie sat at the table with us, and we repeated the facts as we knew them.

"I know exactly when it happened," she said. "I heard him say my name. He was thinking of us, all of us."

We sat quietly for a minute, and Samantha saw her chance to join the conversation. "Aunt Sophie, Grampy's gone to heaven."

"I know, honey."

"Grammy says that God needed him there."

Sophie nodded. "I guess God needs the best people He can get."

"What for?"

"Maybe He's got too many birds," Sophie said. "Maybe He needed someone to help Him feed all those birds."

Sam's face brightened. "Is that what he's doing, Grammy? Is he feeding all those birds?"

"If they've got birds, he's feeding them," Mom said. She sighed. "Janet, we've got to get to the funeral home."

252

"Can I stay here with Samantha?" Sophie asked.

Eric said, "That would be nice, because I'd like to go with Janet and Helen."

"Thank you," I said. "Sam, you don't mind staying with Aunt Sophie, do you?"

"Is she going to keep crying?" Sam asked.

"Well, she might, honey, she's very sad."

"That's okay," Sam said. "I'll sing to her."

*

So Sophie stayed with Samantha while Eric and I accompanied my mother to Moriarty's Funeral Home, where Mr. Moriarty showed us an overwhelming array of caskets. As he walked us through the display, he murmured in his cultivated voice about tailored satin linings and brass tone accessories.

"Well, it hardly matters, does it?" said Mom.

Copper, bronze, stainless steel to resist the elements. Hand rubbed oak with a French provincial finish. Dove gray velvet in a Viennese fold design. Birch, ash, cherry, mahogany finish with brush bronze accents and rounded cornices.

"Talk it over," he urged us. "Take your time."

Mom looked bewildered. "Do you have a preference?" she asked me.

I pointed. "That one has the nicest pillow."

"We'll take it," she said.

*

When we got home we found Sophie and Samantha in Dad's study, sitting on the floor looking through a pile of his drawings.

"Look, Mom," Sam said. "There's us."

She held up a pastel done from a photograph he had taken last Easter. We were in the back yard, wearing our Easter dresses, and Sam had given me her Easter basket to hold while she held onto the birdbath with both hands and lifted herself to peer over the edge. She had actually been quite peeved to find no birds bathing, but the camera had caught her just before that, at the moment of anticipation.

"Aunt Sophie said I could keep this one."

"I think you probably can," I said, "but we should check with Grammy first."

"I'll ask her," Sam said, and she trotted off with her picture to find my mother.

"He did it for you," Sophie said. "He was going to give it to you for Mother's Day."

"I'm sure it's fine. I just want Mom to feel like she's giving it, and not like we're taking it."

"Suit yourself," she said. "Bill called. He'll be here tonight. I told him I'm staying at Daddy's, and there's plenty of room if anybody else wants to stay there."

She reached for her purse and produced a silver flask. "Does anyone else need a drink?"

"I do." I sat on the floor beside her and accepted the flask. It was Southern Comfort, and I shuddered as I swallowed it.

"None for me, thanks," Eric said, but he joined us on the floor. "That's a nice flask, though."

"It was my mother's," she told him, and then she turned to me. "So, how was it?"

"It was like a bad dream." I told her about the casket selection and the numerous other decisions that had to be made. "I've never seen Mom at a loss before. She seemed so...helpless."

"I'd like to have seen that," Sophie murmured, and Eric cocked his head and studied her.

"I noticed you didn't speak to her," he said.

"Nothing to say." She took another drink.

"Not even, 'Sorry for your loss'?"

Sophie looked at him blankly, then turned her attention to her purse, fishing for a cigarette. "Did you also notice, observant as you are, that she didn't speak to me, either?"

"I did," he said. "Still, it's customary to offer condolences to the bereaved."

"*I'm* bereaved," she said. "I'm bereaved, too."

"That's true," I said. "Dad and Sophie used to be good friends."

"Used to be," Eric repeated. "Until—?" He turned to Sophie and waited.

I had already told him the whole story of Sophie and my family, but this was one of those counseling things he did, asking

254

someone for their version of events even though he already knew what happened. To Eric there were never just two sides to a story, there were as many sides as there were people involved.

"We weren't allowed," Sophie said. "We weren't supposed to see each other, and so I wasn't allowed to see Janet."

"Don't you have that backwards?" I said. "You weren't allowed to see *me*, and so you couldn't see him."

She shook her head. "That's how it was supposed to look. She did want to keep me away from you, but she wanted to keep me away from him even more."

"Why?" Eric asked.

"Ask *her*," Sophie said. "She's the one who makes the rules."

"I'm asking you," he said. "Why do you think she wanted to keep you away from John?"

"Because he was only supposed to have one daughter. She only gave him one child so that's all he was supposed to love." She lowered her voice to a whisper. "But he loved me anyway." She covered her face with her hands and bent forward, emitting a low wail that came from deeper and deeper inside her until she was heaving with sobs.

My own eyes began to leak again, and I wondered how long it would take to get used to this grief. I knew I would learn to live with it, because that's what people do. What choice do we have? I just wondered how long it would take for it to settle into my life, and what shape it would take.

I rubbed Sophie's back, feeling the knobs of her spine through her tee shirt.

"He did love you," I told her. "Even Mom couldn't stop that. He always asked about you." I didn't mention that he also worried about her, and prayed for her.

I hadn't seen Eric get up, but now he sat down again and placed a box of tissues in front of me. That was another counseling thing—he always knew where the closest box of tissues was.

I pried loose one of Sophie's hands and stuffed a handful of tissues into it, and I took some more for myself.

She said something, but it was muffled.

"What, honey? What did you say?"

"I've missed him so much already," she wailed.

I was a little taken aback, and I didn't know how to respond. She had never indicated to me that she particularly missed my father, and if she did, why didn't she come and see him? Nothing prevented her except my mother's objections, which had never meant anything to her before.

I looked at Eric, unsure what to say.

"Sophie," he said gently, "when was the last time you saw him?"

"I saw him at the hospital when Samantha was born."

That was four years ago.

"And when was the last time before that?"

"At your wedding."

Eric glanced at me. "So, you saw him on family occasions?"

She shook her head. "Just those two times I saw him since— since I went away. Except in my dreams. Sometimes I see him in my dreams."

She took a ragged breath and reached for the flask. She upended it, pouring the contents down her throat, then she staggered to her feet and said "I have to go."

"Sophie, don't go," I said.

"I have to. I have to go home and cry."

"I'll take you home," Eric said.

""No, I can get there all right."

"I'd be glad to do it," he said.

"I'm not going anywhere with you," she said. "You ask too many questions."

We walked her to the front door. Samantha heard our voices and came running from upstairs.

"I want to kiss Aunt Sophie good night," she said.

My mother appeared at the top of the stairs and stood with her arms crossed.

"Did you find what you were looking for, Sophie?"

Sophie looked up at her. "Pardon?"

"Samantha said you were looking for something. I just wondered if you found it."

"Don't worry about me," Sophie said. "I'm fine. I'll see you all tomorrow."

And she was gone.

"Sam," I said, "what was Aunt Sophie looking for?"

"I don't know," she said. "She was looking in Grampy's desk."

I looked up the stairs at Mom.

"I don't want her left alone in this house again," she said, and she went to her room and slammed the door.

*

That night Eric and I made love four times. I had never experienced such a furious and desperate need; I couldn't stop. Between bouts I asked for his professional opinion.

"Is this sick?"

"It's a form of self-medication," he said, "an altered state of consciousness. It's a perfectly normal response to your situation, and it's much better for you than drugs or alcohol." He smiled. "Better for me, too. I wouldn't worry about it, Janet, it's not like you're driven to do this every night of your life."

Not like Sophie, I thought. Is this what she's after, every night, this oblivion, this annihilation? My God, I thought, every night?

"If I needed to do this every night, I'd need more than one man, wouldn't I?"

He nibbled on my ear. "Are you thinking about it?"

"I'm thinking about Sophie. I never understood why she needed so many men, but now it kind of makes sense."

"She's an interesting case," he said, "but let's not think about her right now."

*

The next two days seemed endless, and I remember them now only as a blur of tears and condolences. I was overwhelmed by the number of people who showed up for visiting hours at the funeral home—teachers, students, former students, bird watchers, people who worked with him at the soup kitchen and people who regularly took meals there. Fellow parishioners from the church, tellers from the bank, administrators from the orphanage, Mrs. Palmer from the library and Mrs. Galos from the blood bank, and it seemed that every one of them had a story to tell me of some kindness he had done, and every one of them made me cry.

Friends and neighbors filled my mother's kitchen with casseroles, pies, hams, turkeys, cakes, brownies, and lasagna. My mother's sisters Louise and Cathy stayed at Mom's house, along with my grandmother and Aunt Louise's husband Phil. Aunt Mary and her husband Bob stayed with Eric and me, as did Uncle Rudy, who wasn't really my uncle but liked to pretend he was—he was Dad's agent. Various other aunts, uncles, and cousins stayed at a hotel. Only Uncle Bill took Sophie up on her offer to stay at her father's house, a decision my mother thoroughly disapproved of.

"Don't I have enough to deal with," she said, "without you humiliating the entire family by staying over there with that tramp? How do you think that looks, Bill?"

"I'm not worried about how it looks, Helen, and frankly, with all you have to deal with right now, I can't believe *you* have time to worry about how it looks."

Aunt Louise cleared her throat. "It doesn't look good, Bill."

Aunt Cathy concurred. "It looks like you're picking up a piece of tail on the way to your brother-in-law's funeral."

"I don't believe this," Uncle Bill said.

"You know what it looks like to me?" I spoke louder than I meant to, and they all turned to look at me. "It looks like Sophie opened up her home to anyone who needed a place to stay. Any one of you could have stayed there, and if you think Uncle Bill and Sophie need a chaperone, you can still go over there and supervise."

"Thank you, Janet," said Uncle Bill.

"As far as I'm concerned," Mom said, "they both need supervision."

"They're both adults," I said. "I think they can handle themselves."

Mom waved her hand dismissively. "You always stick up for her."

"And you always put her down. Can't you give her credit, just once, for doing something good?"

"I've never seen that girl do anything that didn't serve her own interests more than anyone else's. She's always been a selfish little bitch, and you and your father just couldn't see it. She manipulated him and she manipulates you, and I want to know when in God's name I will ever be free of her."

Uncle Bill winked at me. "And here I was thinking of asking her to marry me."

"That's not funny," Mom said.

"Yes, it is. Admit it, Helen, the only reason you don't like her is because she doesn't follow your rules. You want everyone around you begging for your approval all the time. Well, some of us don't need it. Some of us are perfectly fine without it."

"Some people don't care about being decent human beings," Mom said. "All they care about is smoking pot and sleeping around and having a good time. You were a bad influence on these children."

"No, he wasn't," I said. "I don't smoke pot and sleep around."

"But you don't see anything wrong with it."

I shrugged. "They're not hurting anyone. I love Uncle Bill the way he is, and I love Sophie the way she is."

Aunt Louise clucked. "Well, of course, we all love Uncle Bill."

"It's just that some of us don't like him very much," said Uncle Bill, and when his sisters protested, he said, "No, that's okay, Uncle Bill doesn't mind. He's just going to take his badass self over to Sophie's and get stoned. Who knows? He might even get lucky."

Mom said, "Bill, don't you dare sleep with that girl."

"I've got no intention of sleeping with her," he said, "but, hey, ain't nobody's business if I do."

*

On the day of the funeral I found I had no more tears to shed. Eric said it was a sign that I had exhausted my grief, but I thought it was the other way around—my grief had exhausted me.

I sat numb and detached throughout the service, and my mind wandered. The chorus from the high school where Dad taught stood up in their red blazers and sang He Watching Over Israel, from the Mendelssohn oratorio Elijah. It's a beautiful and consoling piece— "Shouldst thou, walking in grief, languish, He will quicken thee"—but it was too intricate to have been learned just for the occasion, and I concluded that they must have started rehearsing it some time ago, never knowing that it would come in handy if someone died.

I barely listened to Father McGovern's eulogy. He had been my father's friend and confessor, and as he enumerated Dad's fine qualities and good deeds, it occurred to me to wonder what my father could possibly have had to confess. I also wondered how many masses Father McGovern had said in his lifetime, and whether this one would stand out for him. And I wondered why it was that when Father

McGovern put on his ritual clothing and lit candles and burned incense and chanted over his altar, he was performing a sacred rite, whereas when Sophie did it, she was a witch, although as far as I knew, she never did anything as ghoulish as turning wine into blood and drinking it.

Behind me, Sophie was sitting with Uncle Bill. If my own supply of tears had run dry, hers appeared to be endless. Throughout the service I could hear her sniffling and weeping. At the cemetery she leaned on Uncle Bill's arm and sobbed. At the house afterward, she climbed up into the treehouse and cried herself to sleep.

"I don't know," Uncle Bill said. "Maybe I should have given her a Valium or something. She's taking it hard."

"She needs this," Eric said. "It may seem like she's overreacting, considering how distant her relationship with John had become, but I would guess that this is the most genuine emotion she's expressed in a long time. All those old issues are coming to the surface."

Uncle Bill raised one eyebrow. "Which issues are those, college boy?"

"The ones she's been avoiding all her life," Eric said evenly.

Uncle Bill scratched his beard thoughtfully. "What do you think, princess? Do you think she's overreacting?"

"No," I said. "I think she's just realized that she should have come to see him. All those years, she could have seen him whenever she wanted, but she didn't, and now it's too late." And then my tears came back, not for my own grief, but for Sophie's, because her grief was complicated by regrets.

I left Eric and Uncle Bill and climbed up into the treehouse to sit with her until she woke up.

Chapter 20

The second child, the one my father would never see, was a boy. I wanted to name him John. Eric didn't think children should have to live up to a revered family member's name, but since I was the one whose father had passed on, and I was the one bearing the labor pains, I decreed that he would be named John Jeremy, and we would call him Jeremy.

By the time he was three, Jeremy seemed intent on devoting his life to his sister. He followed her around like a lovesick puppy, wanting to do whatever she did, to eat whatever she ate, to wear whatever she wore.

I asked Eric, "Do you think he's confused about whether he's a boy or a girl?"

"He'll outgrow it," he said.

*

Sam was seven now, and I had promised that during her Christmas vacation we would go to Portland to visit her two favorite places—the Maine Mall and Aunt Sophie's.

Sophie lived on the third floor of a huge Victorian on the West End. She had more furniture than before, but still not enough to fill the rooms. She had high ceilings and tall windows, and in the summer, she said, when the trees surrounding the house were in full leaf, she felt like she was back in the treehouse.

We followed Jeremy as he toddled from room to room, and when we reached the bedroom, I gasped in surprise. Where before she had always slept on a mattress on the floor, she now had a bed, and not just any bed but a solid looking polished oak structure with an elaborate design of tree branches and birds carved into the headboard.

"Sophie, this is beautiful. Where did you get it?"

"It's my Christmas present," she said. "This guy I'm seeing, he built it for me."

"He must be crazy about you."

"Or just plain crazy," she said. "Here, try it," and she picked up Jeremy and tossed him onto the bed. Samantha scrambled up beside him, and the two of them began rolling and tumbling around.

"You guys, don't bounce on Aunt Sophie's new bed."

"Bounce all you want," Sophie said. "This bed was built for bouncing."

"Oh, great. Wait till they go to Grammy's and tell her that Aunt Sophie has a bed built for bouncing."

"That's nothing," Sophie said. "Wait till she finds out who built it."

"Who?"

She tilted her head and looked at me, as if considering whether or not to tell me.

"One of your boyfriends," I prompted.

"Actually, I'm only seeing one guy."

"Really? Sophie, that's great. Who is he?"

She pulled me into the living room and sat me down on the couch.

"He said he always wanted to make his own bed and lie in it." She laughed. "It's Bill."

I blinked stupidly, not knowing who she was talking about, and then it clicked.

"My Uncle Bill?"

She smiled and nodded, and she even blushed a little.

"You're sleeping with Uncle Bill?"

"Every chance I get."

"Seriously? You and Uncle Bill? Since when?"

"It was off and on for a while. Now it's on all the time."

"Sophie, why didn't you tell me?"

"I didn't think you'd like it if I was just fooling around with him."

"*Are* you just fooling around?"

"No."

I waited for her to say more, but she didn't.

"You and Uncle Bill," I said. "How did this happen?"

"He was coming into the bar sometimes with his friends, and he was just always so much fun. You know how he is. He'd call me Trixie, he'd tell people that he knew me from some other town, that I was his ex-wife, that I owed him money, all kinds of shit. Never anything true."

She laughed. "He told people that I grew up in the circus, and my father was the knife thrower and I was his target, and I grew up riding elephants. He'd tell all these stories, and then he'd come back a few months later and pretend he didn't know me, and he'd ask people about me, and then he'd just sit back and listen to all the rumors he'd started. I don't know, I just started feeling like I was being stupid, wasting my time with all these other guys. So one night I just asked him to bring me home." She bit her lip. "Are you mad at me?"

"I don't know," I said. "It's just so weird."

"You have no idea," she said.

"Aunt Sophie," Samantha called, and she dashed breathlessly into the room. "Aunt Sophie, can I try on your sparkly dress?"

"Are you going through Aunt Sophie's closets?" I asked. To Sophie I said, "Are they going to find anything they shouldn't?"

"I don't keep my drugs in there," she said. "It's okay, honey, you can try on anything you want. Jeremy, too."

"You're going to let them play dress up with your clothes?"

"Why not? *I* play dress up with my clothes. That's what they're for."

"They'll get into your underwear," I warned her. "They love to wear mine, and I'm sure yours is sexier."

"I play dress up with that, too."

"So," I said, "you and Uncle Bill. Is it serious? Do you love him?"

"Janet, I love him so much it scares me. He makes me feel so good."

"I'm sure," I said. "Spare me the details, though, okay?"

"No, I mean he makes me feel like *I'm* good. He makes me feel like a real person."

"What did you feel like before?"

She smacked my arm. "Don't start talking like Eric. *You* know what I mean."

"My mother's going to freak out. Oh, my God, Sophie, if you marry him you'll be her sister-in-law. You'll be *my* Aunt Sophie. Now, *that* I could not get used to. Are you going to marry him?"

She shook her head. "I'm not going to get married. He knows that."

I thought of something. "Hey, Sophie, does this mean you're finally going to get your ring back? Are you going to tell Lucifer that you're in love with somebody else so you can get your grandmother's ring back?"

She stared at me as if I were making a bad joke. "No, Janet, I can't."

"Why not? Are you afraid to see him? Are you afraid you might fall in love with him again?"

"It's not that, it's just—"

"This is better, right? Isn't this better, Sophie, than some creepy guy who's cheating on his wife? Don't you love Uncle Bill more?"

She seemed to struggle with this. "It's not a question of *more*, it's just—"

"Come on, Sophie, this has to be better."

"Well," she conceded, "it's nice to make love with someone who doesn't hate himself afterwards."

Samantha and Jeremy came into the room to model their outfits. Sam was wearing the blue sequined dress that Sophie had worn to my wedding, with the matching shoes and a black feather boa. Over his own underwear, Jeremy had on a lacy red bra and panty set, with the matching garter belt draped around his neck in imitation of his sister's boa.

"Look, Mommy," he said, "it's pretty."

"Lovely," I said. "Stunning."

"Oh, you look so beautiful," Sophie gushed. "I think those clothes look better on you than they do on me."

"I want to try on the purple thing," Sam said, and she scuffed back into the bedroom in her high heels, Jeremy following her.

"He loves lingerie," I said.

"And Eric doesn't mind?"

"He says he's not worried about it. My mother is absolutely appalled, but Eric says he's just doing what Samantha does, and just because he's cross-dressing at three doesn't mean he'll be cross-dressing at thirteen. I say even if he is, there are worse things he could be than a transvestite. But Mom's worried that his life will be hard."

"Transvestites have a hard time finding shoes," Sophie said. "*That's* probably what she's worried about."

*

A few days later Uncle Bill was in town, and he stopped by to have lunch with us.

264

"Sam," I said, "tell Uncle Bill where we went the other day."

"We went to the mall," she said, "and we had lunch at Friendly's, and we went to Aunt Sophie's house and I got to try on the sparkly dress."

"Wow," he said, "is there anything you *didn't* do?"

"Tell him about Aunt Sophie's new bed," I said.

"Aunt Sophie got a new bed for Christmas and it's got birds on it and me and Jeremy got to bounce on it because Aunt Sophie says that's what it's for."

Uncle Bill laughed. "Aunt Sophie's a lot of fun, isn't she?"

Sam nodded enthusiastically. "And she's got pretty underwear, too."

"Well, yeah." Uncle Bill gave me a sheepish glance. "There's that, too."

"That bed is beautiful," I said. "Why didn't you tell me?"

"I could hardly believe it myself," he said. "I'm still not convinced it's real."

"It sounds pretty serious to me," I said. "How long have you been seeing her?"

"It's hard to say. We were dancing around each other for so long."

"But now it's serious."

"Oh, hush, princess, we don't use that word. That word freaks her out. The pretense is that this is a casual thing."

"Why should there be any pretense?" I asked.

"Janet," he said, as if he were exercising great patience with me, "who makes the rules in Sophie's world?"

"Sophie does."

"Exactly. And if Sophie doesn't want it to be serious, then it's going to be casual, no matter how serious it gets. Am I right?"

I considered this. "But if it's always casual, then how do you know when it's serious? Doesn't it get confusing?"

"Only when you try to make sense of it."

"But she loves you," I said. "She told me so."

Samantha had wandered into the other room, and I glanced around to make sure she was out of earshot.

"So tell me," I said. "Tell me how you got together."

"I don't know if I should," he said. "You might not appreciate it."

"I'm dying to know. She said she asked you to take her home one night."

He looked surprised. "Yes, but that wasn't the first time."

"It wasn't?"

"The night before John's funeral," he said, "we spent the night together."

"The night before—Uncle Bill, that was over three years ago. You've been seeing each other all this time and nobody told me?"

"No, princess, we didn't see each other again for a long time after that. I didn't expect to see her again. I thought it was just a situational thing. She was very emotional, of course, we both were. You understand, we meant no disrespect. It just seemed like the thing to do at the time."

"You were comforting each other." I remembered how my own libido had raged in the days following my father's death. "It's a form of self-medication."

"Exactly. That's what it was. And I don't flatter myself, princess, the fact is, this was a case of Uncle Bill being in the right place at the right time. I was just a substitute for someone else who couldn't be there."

"What do you mean? Did she tell you that?"

"Not in so many words," he said. "She called me by another man's name."

"You're kidding."

He shook his head. "Well, like I said, she was very emotional. I'm sure she didn't even know she'd done it, but that's why I wasn't expecting to see her again. I wasn't the one she wanted."

"Who was it?" I asked. "What name did she call you?"

"That's not the point, Janet, the point is—"

"Uncle Bill, you know I love her dearly, but you shouldn't let her use you if she's hung up on someone else."

"I'm not complaining, princess. The point is, whoever he is, he's gone. He's out of the picture. She's with me now."

"I hope so. I mean, I know she loves you, but I know how she can be. I hope she's not going to break your heart."

"Ah, princess," he said, "she's been doing that for years."

*

266

Sophie moved in with Uncle Bill, and when my mother heard about it, she called me, outraged.

"He's making a fool of himself, living with a young girl like that," she said.

"Mom, she's thirty years old."

"I suppose you approve of this."

"It doesn't matter whether I approve or not, but actually, I think they're perfect for each other."

"They deserve each other," she said. "That's not the same thing."

But Uncle Bill was happier than I'd ever seen him, and Sophie seemed settled in a way I would never have thought possible. They both still smoked dope, but she didn't do any other drugs, and she rarely drank any more, although she never attended any of my family's gatherings without her flask, God bless her, and she never failed to offer it to me. More often than not, I accepted. We would huddle together in a corner, or sneak into the bathroom to share a drink and giggle over the absurdity of finding ourselves here, still together, still hiding from the grownups.

My aunts were constantly demanding to know when Uncle Bill intended to marry her.

"She won't have me," he'd say, and when they looked to Sophie for an explanation, she just shrugged and said, "Why buy the cow?"

"Don't you want to have children?" Aunt Louise asked.

"We try all the time," Uncle Bill said, "but we just haven't been blessed yet."

"Maybe you could change your luck if you had your union blessed first," said Aunt Cathy.

"*Are* you trying?" I asked Sophie privately.

She shrugged. "It's not going to happen. He likes to pretend it will, but I think we both know it's pretty unlikely, considering I've only got one ovary, and he's smoked so much dope that his sperm count is probably in the negative numbers."

"You could adopt."

She shrugged again. "There's a woman who comes into the bar sometimes, she works for the Department of Human Services. She was telling me that they need people to do emergency foster care. You know, like when they have to take a kid out of their home very suddenly, and they need a place to put them for a few days."

"Sounds like serious stuff," I said. "What kind of problems do these kids have?"

She gave me a reproachful look. "The same kind of problems *I* had, Janet. I had to leave my house twice, remember? If I couldn't stay with you, where would I have gone?"

"I don't know," I said. "One of these emergency places?"

"If they have to stay with strangers, they could do worse than me and Bill, don't you think?"

"I guess," I said. "I mean, of course. But you'd have to stop smoking dope, wouldn't you? And I imagine you'd have to tone down the sex a little."

"Yes," she said, "but that's the beauty of it. It's just for a few days."

*

One night when Eric was out of town at a conference, I took the kids to Uncle Bill and Sophie's for dinner. Sophie made moussaka.

Alone in the kitchen with her, I said, "So, I guess you've forgiven him for going to Vietnam."

Her expression indicated surprise that I would make such an assumption.

"Have you?" I asked.

She shrugged and then shook her head. "He still has nightmares sometimes, Janet. It's been more than twenty years. I don't understand how he could have done that to himself, to put himself in such a fucked up situation."

I thought of some of the situations she had put herself in, but I decided to let it pass.

"So, what do you guys do?" I asked. "Do you hang out with his friends?"

"Sometimes. Mostly they're cool, but some of them don't like me very much. Some of the women. They have this friend they wanted Bill to go out with, and they're not too happy that he picked me instead of her. You know, Someone His Own Age. They think I'm just some little squeaky toy that he plays with, and they think I want him for his money."

"That's pretty funny."

268

"It would be, except that it's kind of sad. They don't like him as much as they used to. They think he's shallow. He told them that he's known me for twenty years, and they said, 'So why does she like you now, all of a sudden?' and he said, 'It's not sudden, it took twenty years.' But they don't understand. They think it's just sex."

"They're jealous," I said.

"Maybe, but it doesn't matter. He knows I love him."

"You really do?"

"Yes," she said. "Isn't it funny how things happen sometimes?"

We went into the living room, where Uncle Bill was playing his guitar for the kids. He winked at Samantha and launched into a silly tune, kind of a rag. He sang:

"I've got me a sweet little honey bee
She's cute as a bug and her name is Sophie
Oh, Sophie
Will you marry me?"

Sam squealed. Sophie rolled her eyes in a see-what-I-have-to-put-up-with kind of way.

"Aunt Sophie, are you going to marry Uncle Bill?"

"No, honey, Uncle Bill's just goofing."

Sam frowned. "But why don't you?"

"Because." Sophie took Sam onto her lap and cuddled her. "We're happy the way we are, aren't we?"

Sam nodded.

"Happy as clams," Uncle Bill said, and he resumed his song:

"They say there are other fish in the sea
But this little guppy is the one for me
Oh, Sophie
Come on and marry me."

"If you got married, I could be your flower girl," Sam said.

"Samantha," I said, "no one's going to get married just so you can be a flower girl."

"It's a good enough reason for *me*," Uncle Bill said, "but what can I do, pumpkin? Aunt Sophie doesn't want to get married."

"Well, did you buy her a ring?" Sam asked.

Uncle Bill slapped his forehead. "Oh, man, I knew I was forgetting something."

"You *have* to buy her a ring," Sam said. She took Sophie's hand and examined her fingers. "Aunt Sophie, don't you want a ring?"

"I only ever wore one ring," Sophie told her, "but that was years ago."

"Oh, yeah, I remember," Uncle Bill said. "Your grandmother gave you a ring, didn't she? How come you never wear it, kitten?"

She nuzzled Samantha's neck. "I don't have it any more."

I said, "You never got it back, did you? That's a shame."

"Where is it?" Sam asked.

"It's lost," Sophie said.

"Is that what he told you?" I said. "Are you sure he didn't give it to some other girl?"

"Who?" Sam said. "Uncle Bill?"

"No, honey." Sophie addressed herself to Sam, avoiding Uncle Bill's eyes. "I gave it to someone else. Before I fell in love with Bill."

"You loved somebody else?" Sam looked stunned.

"Yes," Sophie whispered.

"Who?" Sam whispered back, obviously thrilled.

Sophie ran her fingers through Sam's hair. "It was a long time ago," she said. "Turn around, honey, and let me braid your hair."

Sam turned around obediently. "But aren't you going to tell me who?"

"I can't tell," Sophie said. "It was a secret love."

She concentrated on French braiding Sam's hair, and if she knew that Uncle Bill was watching her, she didn't let on. He strummed his guitar again.

"She's my honey, she's my kitten, she's my little sweet pea
And if she ever left I'd be in misery
Oh, Sophie
Why don't you marry me?"

Chapter 21

After five years as a widow, my mother decided to sell her house and move into something smaller, and she recruited me to empty my father's study.

"Take what you want and throw the rest away," she instructed me.

I put it off for a while. His study was the one room in the house where I could still feel his presence, and it broke my heart to think of dismantling it. Finally Mom informed me that she was going to her sister Cathy's for a week at New Year's, and if there was anything in Dad's study when she got home, she would throw it all into the back yard and set fire to it.

"Okay, okay," I said, and then I had the idea that I would ask Sophie to help me. We would be like sisters again, living together in my parents' house, reliving our memories of Dad while sorting through his field guides, his drawings and paintings, his pens and brushes and paraphernalia.

Sophie eagerly agreed to help me, but she had to work over the weekend and couldn't come until Sunday.

"But we've got all week, right?" she said. "We've got plenty of time, so don't start without me, okay?"

But I figured she would mostly be interested in his books and drawings, and on Saturday afternoon I decided it wouldn't hurt to take a look at his files. Uncle Rudy had sorted through them at the time of Dad's death, extracting contracts and other things of a legal or business nature, and all that was left were his notes and personal papers—ideas for illustrations, bits of research from certain projects, dozens of scraps of paper covered with sketches and labeled with Dad's square, precise handwriting. Most of it was easily disposed of, but then I came across a folder of personal correspondence, letters from Uncle Bill, written while he was in Vietnam.

I read a few of them—they were different from the letters Uncle Bill had written me, which were cheerful and conversational. To Dad, Uncle Bill had written more candidly about the details of his work and his feelings of despair. I recalled the time he spent with us after his return from Vietnam, and I understood now that he had been depressed, and that he had been carrying his sadness with him for a long time.

"He doesn't ask a lot of questions," Sophie once said in praise of him, and I understood her to mean that he didn't pry into the painful areas of her past. It occurred to me now that maybe one of the things that kept Uncle Bill and Sophie together was the respect they had for each other's private sorrows. They were good to each other, and as I gathered up Uncle Bill's letters, I was glad they were together, glad they gave each other some comfort.

At the moment I was thinking this, I came across an envelope that was different from the others. It was not a letter, it was a small manila envelope, the end folded over several times and worn soft at the creases, as if it had been opened and closed many times. It was wrinkled and pocked with the imprint of something small and circular, like a button, but with more weight to it, like a coin. I dumped the contents into my hand, and my heart stopped for a moment when I recognized what I was holding.

It was Sophie's ring.

*

It's been said that a truth once known can never be unknown, it can only be denied. God knows I tried. I told myself there was a logical explanation for this, and then I put my mind through some strenuous calisthenics trying to imagine what it could be. I invented implausible scenarios and tried to believe them, and at the same time I tried to forget the things Sophie had told me about her lover, details that came rushing back to me with sickening clarity.

Tomorrow she would be here. She would come into my parents' house pretending to be my friend, pretending that we shared the same memories of Dad. For half our lives she had been pretending. How was that possible?

And what about my father? It suddenly seemed that all my memories of him were false. If my father was the man who bedded Sophie, then I had not known him at all, and what was I doing here? What would I want to keep to remind me of him? Sitting at his desk, I could see the Audubon print that Sophie and I had given him for Christmas one year—the magpies. We were ten, and the price seemed like a fortune to us, but we were in complete agreement that no other gift would do, and we sacrificed our gifts to each other to come up with the money for it. He loved it. I didn't want to dispose of it, but I didn't really want it around, either, any more than I wanted the framed photograph on his desk, the picture of me and Sophie at age eight, smiling and waving to him from our new treehouse.

*

I called Walter.

"I hope I'm not interrupting anything," I said, "but I need to ask you a question."

"You have my undivided attention," he said. "Ask away."

"Did you ever find out who Lucifer was?"

"No. Did you?"

"I think I just did, but I don't know if I can believe it. Walter, I just found Sophie's ring in my father's study."

I gave him a minute to let it sink in.

"Holy fuckin' shit," he said. "Are you sure?"

"I'm looking right at it. It's hers. It was in with some letters from Uncle Bill."

"Could your uncle have sent it to him?"

"No, Walter, if it was Uncle Bill she would have told me. In fact, I think if it were *anybody* else, she would have told me."

"Shit, Janet, this is bad. I knew she was a fuckin' slut, but I didn't know she'd do something like this. You must want to rip her face off."

"I just can't believe it. How could this be true?"

"I believe it," he said. "I'm sorry, Janet, but now that you've said it, I can't believe I didn't see it before. I can absolutely see the twisted Sophie logic of it. She's fucked up, you know that, right? She's never been in her right mind."

"What about Dad?" I said. "What was he thinking?"

"She probably raped him, Janet. She probably whipped up one of her little potions and slipped it into his coffee. She's insane. The poor guy probably never knew what hit him."

"She's coming here tomorrow," I told him. "She's supposed to help me clean out his study."

"Well, if you want to kill her and bury her in the back yard, I'll swear you were with me all day. Not that it wouldn't be justifiable homicide, but if you want an alibi, I'm here for you."

*

I spent a sleepless night, plagued by images of Sophie and my father making love. I was appalled to remember the eagerness with which she shared the details of her affair, and even more appalled to remember the eagerness with which I heard them. It had seemed so romantic at the time, that a man would need her so desperately and crave her so intensely that he would defy the law and risk his family, his career, and the eternal damnation of his soul.

But that man was my father, and I was part of what he was gambling with.

And I remembered the other side of it, too, the times I had wondered what kind of a monster would take advantage of a girl like Sophie. A vile and lecherous man, a disgusting old ogre who consumed the flesh of young girls to satisfy his unnatural desires.

Was *that* man my father?

*

I was sitting at his desk the next morning, ready to face her, but Sophie, of course, was late. I thought of calling Eric, but I wanted to get through this first.

She burst into the room, bringing a shock of cold air with her. She moved briskly, tossing a bag of doughnuts onto the desk in front of me, tossing her coat on the couch, pushing up the sleeves of what Uncle Bill called her Smurf sweater, a cobalt blue cable knit with a thick turtleneck collar that did, in fact, give her the disarming appearance of a pixie-ish cartoon character. She surveyed the room quickly, then she plopped down on the couch and lit a joint.

"I was thinking," she said, "that you might want to give some of his pictures to the library and some to the orphanage. Don't you think he'd like that?"

"I guess you would know."

She caught my tone and looked up sharply. I held up her ring and watched her face register shock and dismay. The tip of her tongue darted out and she licked her lips, and she took another hit off the joint, stalling for time.

Finally she said, "Where was it?"

"It was in the file cabinet with Uncle Bill's letters."

274

"You weren't supposed to find it."

"You weren't supposed to sleep with my father, Sophie, how could you?"

"I loved him," she whispered. "Don't you remember how much I loved him?"

"He was *my father*."

"I know." She sighed. "You were so lucky."

It seemed like an odd thing to say, under the circumstances. "I don't feel lucky," I told her. "I feel stupid, I feel betrayed. I feel like that guy in your tarot deck who's laying on the ground with all those swords sticking out of his back."

She nodded. "The ten of swords. You feel like everything is ruined."

"It *is* ruined. You ruined it."

"I feel like The Tower," she said. "One big bolt of lightning, and everything comes crashing down." She said this to me as if nothing had changed, as if I still cared what she felt like, as if we were just two best-friends-since-childhood sitting around eating doughnuts and talking about tarot cards.

"All those years, you lied to me, both of you. How could you do that?"

"I wanted to tell you, Janet. You were worried about me, remember? You thought I was with some horrible man."

"I wish you had been," I told her. "I'd rather you had been with someone who raped and killed you."

She looked at me searchingly, as if to determine whether I meant what I said, and she saw that I did. She let herself fall back into the couch cushions, and she lay still for a minute, just her eyes moving around the room until they came to rest on the Audubon print.

"I was going to ask you for something," she said absently. "One of his field guides, or a picture, maybe. Something I could keep, you know? Something I wouldn't have to hide."

"Keep this," I said, and I hurled her ring at her. It bounced off her shoulder and landed on the couch beside her. She picked it up and put it on, spreading her fingers as if to admire it.

She said, "Everything would have been fine if I had found this the night he died. You would never have known, and you would have kept on being my friend."

"God, you're so stupid. Everything would have been fine if you'd kept your hands off him in the first place, did you ever think of that?"

"What do you want, Janet? Do you want me to say I'm sorry? God, don't you know how sorry I am? Don't you think I was sorry already, even without you finding out about it? I put him through hell, Janet, don't you think I'm sorry for that?"

"What about me?" I asked. "Are you sorry for what you did to me?"

"Yes," she whispered.

She was looking directly into my eyes, and I could see the depth of her sorrow. I remembered her sitting on the floor of this room after my father's death, crying, heart-wrenching sobs that threatened to turn her inside out, and then I saw her at sixteen in her hospital bed, crying for her lost baby.

His baby.

"You know what?" I said. "It doesn't even matter how sorry you are, because sorry isn't enough. I'll never forgive you for this, Sophie."

She closed her eyes and turned her head away. She seemed to slump deeper into the couch.

"What about Uncle Bill?" I asked. "Does he know?"

She shook her head.

"Who's going to tell him, you or me?"

"No, Janet—"

"I'll tell him," I said. "I can't trust you."

"Janet—"

"He should know what kind of person he's with," I said. "It's better for him to know the truth."

She brushed tears from her eyes. "Do you really believe that?" she asked. "Or do you just want Bill to hate me as much as you do?"

"You don't deserve him."

"I never thought I did. Will it make you happy if he doesn't love me any more?"

I didn't answer, but she knew: yes, that would make me happy.

She pushed herself upright and began to gather her things.

"Wait a minute," I said. "Is there anything else I should know about?"

She blinked. "How much more do you want to know?"

276

"I mean, is there anything else I need to get rid of before my mother comes home? Love letters, photographs, anything like that?"

"No," she said. "There were some drawings, but I found them."

"Drawings?"

"I posed for him."

I closed my eyes and rode out a wave of nausea.

"Some of them are beautiful," she said. "You should see them."

"You're a sick person," I told her. "Get out of here, and don't ever come back."

She sat still for another minute, and then she took a deep breath and stood up. Without another word, she picked up her coat and walked out, leaving all the doors open behind her.

*

I called Uncle Bill and told him everything. He didn't seem all that surprised.

"Did you know about this?" I asked.

"No, not really. There was a time when I kind of wondered."

"You knew, and you didn't say anything? When? When did you know?"

"I didn't know," he said. "I figured whatever happened, *if* something happened, it was between the two of them, and I figured it was best to leave it that way."

"That was his baby," I said. "She was going to have his baby."

"Shit," was all he said.

"So what are you going to do, Uncle Bill?"

"I don't know, Janet. I'll talk to her, I guess."

"You can't stay with her."

"I'll talk to her," he repeated. "I'll let you know."

"I don't want to see her again. I mean it, Uncle Bill. You're welcome at my house any time, but I don't want to see her, ever, anywhere."

"I'll get back to you," he said.

*

I finally called Eric. I broke down on the phone, and he coached me through my hysteria and managed to extract from me a relatively coherent account of the situation.

"Don't do anything," he said. "Don't go anywhere. I'll ask Pam to take the kids, and I'll be there as soon as I can."

He did his best to comfort me, holding me while I cried, and making grilled cheese sandwiches for me when I thought I couldn't possibly eat. He sent me into the living room to play the piano while he finished cleaning the study, and when there was nothing left but a few boxes and the furniture, he sent me to stay with Pam and the kids while he and Uncle Bill hauled it away.

"I put the boxes in our attic," he told me. "You can go through them when you're ready."

"I'll never be ready."

"Well, maybe the kids—"

"Eric, do we have to keep it?"

"I could give it to Bill and Sophie."

"No."

"Then let's just leave it in the attic, Janet. You won't always feel this way, honey, you might be glad to have some of his things someday."

But I couldn't imagine when that day would be. Most days I couldn't stop crying. I felt forever drained and exhausted, but I dreaded going to sleep, because while I was awake I could fight off the images, but in my dreams I was helpless against them. In my dreams, I saw my father kneeling before Sophie in a semblance of worship, caressing her thighs beneath the plaid skirt of her Catholic school uniform.

I was a mute priest, trapped in a confessional with Sophie's voice all around me, describing the sins of passion she'd committed with her lover.

I was Sophie, and I was having sex with my father.

"I think you're going to want to talk to someone," Eric said.

I couldn't make love any more, because whatever we tried to do, in my mind I pictured Sophie and my father.

"Janet, please, you've got to talk to someone. I'll come with you, if you want, but honey, please, you can't go on like this."

"*I* need counseling?" I said. "Of all the people involved in this mess, you think *I* need counseling?"

"Honey, listen, I've counseled a lot of families, and I can tell you, the first one who comes in for help is never the sickest one. In fact, it's usually the sanest one, the one who's trying to cope. It's also, by the way, the one who has the best chance of succeeding in therapy."

"Why can't *you* help me?"

"I can, honey, up to a point, but I can see where this is going. If your father wasn't the man you thought he was, then that throws all of your beliefs into question, doesn't it?"

"God, yes."

"And the next logical step is for you to question all the decisions you've made based on those beliefs, up to and including your choice of a husband. I'm too invested in the outcome to be objective, Janet, but I can give you some names of people who can help."

"I'm not ready for that."

"Well, let me know when you are. And please, God, let it be soon."

*

"I've given this a lot of thought," Uncle Bill said on the phone, "and I've decided it's none of my business."

"Uncle Bill, she fucked my father. You can't just ignore that, can you?"

"I'm convinced it was a love affair," he said. "An affair of the heart."

"And you think that makes it right?"

"Nothing can make it *right*, princess. I think the most we can hope for is a little understanding."

"Oh, please. Do me a favor, okay? Don't talk to me about understanding, or forgiveness. You sound like my father."

"I know you don't mean that as a compliment, but I'm going to take it as one, anyway. He might have made a mistake in a moment of weakness, Janet , but that doesn't change the fact that he was one of the most truly Christian people I ever met."

"And what he did with Sophie, was that charity? How can you stand it, Uncle Bill? Doesn't it make you sick to be with her?"

"Not at all," he said. "But I'll tell you what still makes me a little queasy whenever I think about it. Do you remember when she came to your house that summer we built the treehouse? After her mother tried to kill her?"

"Uncle Bill—"

"You talked about her all summer, you said she was your sister. And then I met her, and first thing, she says, 'Are you Janet's, too?' And I could see in those big blue eyes that she already knew the answer. Anything that was any good was Janet's."

"That's not true—"

"You had everything, princess. The loving and attentive father, the cool uncle—if I may say so—the mother who actually *played* the piano, instead of hacking it into kindling in a fit of rage. You had everything, and what did she have? She had a cat."

"She had *me*," I said. "Are you forgetting that? Where would she have been without me?"

Through the phone I could hear him scratching his beard. "That's a good point. Look, no one blames you for being angry—"

"I'm not angry," I told him. "I'm perfectly calm. I just don't ever want to see her again."

"Well, that could get kind of tricky, what with the family and all."

"Uncle Bill, I'm asking you to keep her away from me."

"I hope you're not asking me to choose, princess."

I understood what he was telling me, that if he had to choose, he would choose Sophie. Suddenly, bizarrely, I wished I had a cigarette.

"What about John?" he said. "Are you mad at him?"

"Don't," I said. "I can't even think about him."

"Well, when you do, princess, just keep in mind that the human heart is a dark and mysterious place. It takes a brave soul to explore the depths of it."

"Is that how you see this? As an act of courage? I wonder if you'd feel the same way if you weren't fucking her yourself."

"Janet—"

"I suppose it makes sense that you'd have to rationalize the whole thing somehow, in order to go on fucking her. What is it about her, Uncle Bill? Is she really that good?"

"Maybe you're right," he said. "Maybe I am rationalizing, and if that's the case, then I guess I'm not the person to help you. I think it was a sad thing, and I'm sorry for everyone involved, but I can't hold it against her, Janet, not some misguided thing she did when she was sixteen."

"Misguided? How about sick and perverted? Uncle Bill, he was practically her father."

"But he *wasn't* her father, and I believe if you think about it, you'll realize that that particular point was hammered home pretty hard by your mother, and sometime in the future, let's explore *her* role in all of this, shall we? For now let's just say we're talking about two decent people who made a mistake and lived to regret it."

"I don't know," I said. "I don't know anything any more."

"Well, I don't know much, but I know a decent Christian when I see one. I haven't come across that many. You do what you want, princess, but Uncle Bill isn't going to be casting any stones."

*

At Easter, the family was invited to Aunt Louise's house for dinner.

I called Uncle Bill. "Is she going to be there?"

"I don't know," he said. "She's invited, but I don't know if she's made up her mind yet. Would you like to speak to her about it?"

"No, I would not. Maybe you could just tell her that I'd hate to have to explain to the entire family why I won't stay in the same room with her."

But she showed up anyway. I tried to ignore her, but it killed me to see my children running to greet her, climbing on her lap and kissing her, chattering and dancing around her excitedly like a couple of chipmunks. I allowed myself to take a small, mean satisfaction in the fact that those children were mine, that she could fuck Uncle Bill until hell froze over, but she would never have any children of her own.

I was passing through the dining room some time after dinner when I saw her standing alone by the china cabinet. At first she tried to hide what was in her hand, but then she saw it was me, and she raised her flask in a toast and took a shot.

"He wanted me to come," she said. "I told him it was a bad idea." She took another shot and offered the flask to me.

I declined.

"What am I supposed to do?" she said. "I can't spend the rest of my life hiding from you."

"I don't see why not."

"Janet, I can't change what happened. I can apologize for the rest of my life, and I will, if you want me to, but it won't change what happened."

"Stay away from me," I said, "And stay away from my children. And don't get any ideas about my husband, either."

I turned to go.

"If we were really sisters," she said, "you couldn't just dump me."

I turned back. "Jesus Christ, Sophie, if we were really sisters, I hope to hell we wouldn't be in this situation."

She raised her flask again and gave me a wry smile.

"See?" she said. "It could be worse."

*

Samantha asked, "How come we never go to Aunt Sophie's any more?"

"It's grownup stuff," I told her, but my mother wasn't so easily evaded.

"She went after your husband, didn't she?" she asked me on the phone, and I had to let her believe it, because I couldn't tell her the truth.

"I really don't want to talk about it, Mom."

"I knew it. Didn't I always say you couldn't trust that girl? Well, now you know. It's just as well. Remember what your father used to say, Janet, it's always better to know the truth. I wonder if Bill knows."

"I have to go, Mom."

"Well, somebody ought to tell him, although it probably wouldn't even bother him, he's such a great believer in free love. I wouldn't be surprised if he encourages it. Do you think they have one of those open relationships?"

"I really have to go, Mom, I'm not feeling very well."

*

282

I lost weight, and my clothes hung on me, clownishly large. Eric moved the full-length mirror without telling me, and when I stumbled across it, my reflection caught me off guard. I looked like a scarecrow. My hair was dry and brittle, my face was gaunt, my clothes looked empty. Oh, my God, I thought, I look like Becky Oatmeal, and that's when I decided it had to stop.

"I'm ready," I said to Eric. "Please, tell me what to do, I'll do it."

"I'll give you some names," he said. "Talk to one of them, or talk to all of them. Don't be afraid to shop around until you find the one you're comfortable with. The whole point is to find someone you can talk to."

The first one gave me the creeps. During our first and only meeting, she asked about my family, and I saw the way her eyes lit up when I said my father was dead. She looked almost gleeful in anticipation of the issues I might have with my dead father. I knew exactly what she was thinking: that this was a case of anorexia caused by repressed memories of sexual abuse, and that she, in all her healing wisdom, would be the one to release those memories and set me free. I decided right then that I was not going to tell this woman what my father had done. I wouldn't give her the satisfaction.

I got lucky with the next one; I had a good feeling the moment I met her. Her name was Deidre, and she was a large woman, round and soft and completely feminine. She had billows of dark, radiant curls, her clothing was loose and vibrantly colored, she wore big gold hoops in her ears and lots of bracelets on her arms, and when she extended her hand to greet me, I noticed that the red polish on her elegant fingernails was a perfect match for her lipstick. Her designer perfume smelled heavenly. She invited me to sit in a blue velvet armchair that was as large and comfortable as she was.

I think it was her gypsy-like appearance that prompted me to ask if she could read cards.

"Would it help if I did?"

I shrugged. "Probably not."

"What *would* help?" she asked.

"I don't know. I guess I just need somebody to talk to."

"Okay, then, let's talk." She gave me an encouraging smile. "You start."

Chapter 22

And so I began my therapy.

There was a lot to sort through, and after talking for a while I began to feel that Sophie was not my biggest problem. Sophie, after all, was just Sophie, and while her betrayal had come as a shock, it was not, upon reflection, all that surprising. She had always believed in free love, and if she had been extreme in her practice of it, that was not uncharacteristic. I was hurt and I was angry, but I wasn't mystified.

My father, on the other hand, had completely blown my mind. Every time I tried to reconcile the gentle, deeply principled man I had known with the crazed, reckless lover who left his hand prints all over Sophie, my brain short circuited and shut down, so that for many weeks, whenever Deidre questioned me about my father, I insisted that I knew nothing about him.

"What you need," she said, "is a new picture."

My image of my father had been shattered, she said, and her job was to help me pick up the pieces and determine which ones to keep and which to discard.

"I never knew your father," she said, "so I'll be building my picture from scratch. I'll help you, and you'll help me."

I protested. "But my picture was all wrong."

"Maybe not as wrong as you think. Maybe you just need some adjustments. A different perspective, some changes in proportion here and there."

"You make it sound so manageable."

"Well, no doubt it's easier said than done, but let's get to it. So, tell me this: do you think there were others?"

"Other what?"

"Other girls," she said. "Other women."

"Oh, my God, do you think so?" I had never considered the possibility, and it sent me reeling.

"I'm just working on my picture," she said. "I'm trying to get a sense of whether this was part of a pattern."

I considered this. "No, I'm pretty sure it wasn't."

"You think this was an isolated incident."

"I'm pretty sure." I stroked the nap on the arm of the blue velvet chair. "Uncle Bill thinks it was an affair of the heart."

"What do you think?"

"I don't know."

*

In a dream, I saw Sophie standing in my parents' bedroom. The bed had been stripped, and she was holding the bundle of sheets in her arms. She held it out to me, but I was reluctant to accept it.

"It's yours," she said, and then I saw that it wasn't a bundle of sheets, it was a baby. Sophie was smiling as she placed it in my arms.

"This is your sister," she said.

*

I heard from my mother that Uncle Bill and Sophie were taking a trip to Canada.

"A honeymoon, he calls it. Of course, they aren't bothering to get married first."

"Maybe they won't come back," I said to Eric. "Maybe they'll like it there and they'll decide to stay."

"Would that solve your problem?"

"It would help," I said. "Do you think this honeymoon thing is a desperate attempt to salvage a failing relationship?"

He gave me a sympathetic pat on the shoulder.

"We can hope," he said.

*

It was a great relief to know that Sophie was gone. I hadn't realized how tense I had been until the tension was gone, and I realized that although she had not tried to contact me, I had been living with the constant fear that she might, that at any moment, I would hear the phone ring, or the doorbell, and she would be there, talking to me, drawing me into the maze of her Sophie logic, convincing me that we were still friends.

"But at one time you *were* friends," Deidre said.

"Maybe not," I said. "Maybe she only ever came to my house because we fed her. Maybe she was only after my father the whole time."

"Have you ever asked her?"

"No."

"Well, we could speculate," she said, "or you could just ask her."

"No, I'm not speaking to her."

She nodded. "That's a choice you've made."

This sounded familiar. I remembered Eric telling me that the hardest part of counseling was not so much helping people to make new choices as it was getting them to acknowledge the choices they'd already made.

"You think I should talk to her?"

"That's entirely up to you," she said, "and I suppose it depends on whether you're satisfied with speculation and conjecture."

"What if I am?"

"It's up to you," she repeated, and when I didn't reply, she said, "Are you looking for the truth, or are you looking for a story you can tell yourself?"

"I can only take the truth in small doses," I said.

"Fair enough."

"I could talk to her," I said, "but how do I know she won't lie to me?"

"You don't," she said.

"Well, anyway, she's gone to Canada."

"She'll most likely be back."

"I'll think about it."

*

Her phone didn't even ring before she answered it. She sounded happily surprised.

"Janet? You're calling to talk to *me*?"

"Yeah, well, don't get too excited. This isn't a friendly call. I just want you to answer a question."

"Okay," she said, "hold on." She left the phone, and I heard her shooing Uncle Bill out of the room. She came back and said, "Janet, I've been dying to talk to you."

Her tone was too familiar. We're not friends, I reminded myself, and I twisted the telephone cord around my wrist, imagining I was wrapping it around Sophie's neck. I pictured the bruises it would leave.

"Just answer me," I said. "When did you decide you wanted him?"

She answered without hesitation, as if she had anticipated the question. "Right then," she said. "Right when it happened. I told you about that, Janet, I told you everything about that night."

"Not quite everything," I said, and she didn't reply. "So, all that time before, when we were supposedly friends, were you just trying to get to him?"

"Oh, my God, Janet, is that what you think?"

"It's not like you never used anybody," I pointed out.

"And you think I was using you? All this time we've been friends, you think I was faking it? Janet, you know me better than that. You were the only real friend I ever had."

"Yeah, well, you weren't thinking about that when you were wearing my bathrobe, sitting on my father's lap, doing whatever it was you did to him."

"You weren't supposed to find out," she said, "but I thought if you did, you would understand. I thought you might even be happy for us."

"Happy." The word seemed meaningless, I could make no sense of it in the context of my father's downfall.

"Janet," she said, "let me ask *you* something. Have you ever thought about what it must have been like to be married to your mother?"

"Married is married."

"And lonely is lonely. I just wanted to make him happy, Janet, don't you think he deserved that?"

"A cheap affair with a teenage slut? I would have thought he deserved better than that."

"Shit," she said, "have you been talking to Walter? I didn't sleep with John because I was a cheap teenage slut. You know better, bufflehead."

"No, I don't. I don't know anything."

"You know," she insisted. "You know that I loved him, and deep in your heart, you know he loved me, too. And I hope you also know that he gave me up because he loved you more."

287

I didn't want to hear this. I had a sudden memory of Dad, looking up miserably from his desk and saying, "Which one of you would I choose?" And I remembered how angry I had been to think that he was sacrificing Sophie for no other reason than to please my mother.

On the other end of the phone, Sophie said, "Do you want me to say I'm sorry again?"

I hung up.

*

I reported this conversation to Deidre.

"She said she loved him. She said he deserved to be happy."

"And was he happy? When you think back to the time of this affair, would you say that it made him happy?"

"Well, I assume it did. Why else would he do it?"

"Why, indeed? So, did he wake up singing every morning? Would you say he seemed particularly happy at this time?"

"Not really." I described my father as I remembered him from those days: absent, withdrawn, perpetually distracted. "Maybe he was only happy when he was with her."

"Maybe." She paused to scribble something on her pad. "Or maybe he wasn't happy at all."

Suddenly I felt very tired. "I give up," I said. "I could think about this for a million years and it will never make sense to me."

Deidre sat back and regarded me. I couldn't tell whether this was one of those silences in which she was waiting for me to say more, or one of those in which she was preparing to say something herself. I hoped it was one of the latter.

She said, "One of the biggest mistakes we make with our loved ones is to assume that they know what they're doing. We forget to consider that they might sometimes be as confused and irrational as we are ourselves."

"I can't think about this any more."

"Then we'll let it go for now. Let's change the subject."

I had nothing to say.

"I have an idea," she said. She opened her desk drawer and plucked something out of it. "I've been looking at these. I was hoping you would tell me what you know about them." She handed me a deck of tarot cards.

I hadn't seen them for years, and I wasn't sure I would remember anything about them. I flipped through them, but nothing looked familiar until I came to The Moon.

"I remember getting this one," I said. "I think it has to do with secrets, or mysteries. Things that are unknown. Or things that aren't what they seem." I laughed a little. "I guess *that* was accurate."

I set it aside and kept looking. I stopped at The Tower and showed it to Deidre.

"This is Sophie," I said. "A disaster, a catastrophe. Also completely accurate."

The next card I recognized was the Strength card, the one Sophie had designated as mine. I tried to remember what she'd said about it—something about endurance, a different kind of strength from my mother's, a strength I got from my father.

"I don't know if this one's true," I said. "Can I keep this one for a while and think about it?"

"Sure."

I was almost all the way through the deck, and nothing else looked familiar, and then suddenly I was looking at the three of swords, and I gasped.

"Oh, my God, I know exactly what this is."

I showed it to her, the enormous heart pierced by three swords, suspended in a stormy sky.

She raised her eyebrows.

"This is my father's heart," I told her. I felt a sudden stab at my own heart, a pain so acute it brought tears to my eyes. I had a sense of what it must be like to be able to read the cards; I didn't see the picture so much as I felt it, and I knew the anguish it evoked was not mine, but my father's. And it was also clear to me that the three swords were my mother, Sophie, and me, all three of us tearing into his heart to stake our claims. "You wanted a picture of him, here it is."

Deidre took the card and studied it.

"It doesn't look very happy, does it?" she said.

"I remember when this card came up, Sophie was very upset about it. She said he was in pain, but I didn't see it. I thought—I knew it was no picnic, living with Mom. I lived with her, too. I didn't think he was any unhappier than I was."

"And what do you think now?"

"It wasn't just Mom. It was Sophie, too, and me. He was being torn in three different directions. I always thought of us as Mom on one side, and me and Dad and Sophie on the other, but it must not have seemed like that to him. It must have seemed like him against the three of us. Not *against* us, exactly, but all of us wanting different things from him. I had no idea."

"Well," she said. "Now you know."

Chapter 23

For several years I was able to avoid Sophie almost completely. We spent a lot of holidays with Eric's family, and on more that one occasion when we visited my family, Uncle Bill and Sophie failed to appear because they were called upon at the last minute to take in foster children.

My mother had sold her house and moved in with her mother, who was getting forgetful and could no longer be trusted to take care of herself. Gram didn't like to travel—it was too confusing for her, she was likely to forget where she was—and so all the family gatherings were held at her house.

"I want you there for Christmas this year," Mom said. "Your grandmother isn't getting any younger."

"Are Uncle Bill and Sophie going to be there?"

"I'm expecting them, and I'm also expecting you. Whatever happened between Eric and Sophie, it's over now, right? Put it aside for one day, Janet, this might be Gram's last Christmas."

"Mom, nothing happened between Eric and Sophie."

"Whatever you say, dear."

A few days before Christmas Uncle Bill called my mother and told her that he and Sophie would be there, and they would be bringing two children with them.

I was in the kitchen when they arrived, Sophie carrying a baby and Uncle Bill carrying a dark-haired little girl in a blue parka. They looked like a real family, I thought. If you saw them on the street, you'd never guess the truth about them.

"Merry Christmas," said Uncle Bill. "This is Lacey, and that's her sister Nicole."

He put Lacey down and took her jacket off, and she gazed around the room with solemn eyes.

"What a pretty red dress you're wearing," Aunt Louise said to her.

"I got it for Christmas," Lacey said softly, and then she put her thumb in her mouth and did not speak again.

"Aunt Sophie, is that your baby?" Jeremy was seven and didn't quite understand why Uncle Bill and Aunt Sophie sometimes had children and sometimes didn't.

"We're just taking care of her," Sophie said, and she crouched down so Jeremy could see the baby.

"We were very good this year," said Uncle Bill. "We got two little girls for Christmas."

At eleven, Samantha was planning a career as a babysitter, and she hovered around Lacey, trying to coax a word or a smile.

"Do you want to see the Christmas tree?" she asked.

Lacey looked uncertainly at Sophie, who nodded encouragement.

"Of course," Uncle Bill said. "We love Christmas trees, don't we, Lacey? We can't get enough of them. Where is it? Show us your Christmas tree."

Samantha took Lacey's hand and led her away. Uncle Bill went with them. Jeremy kissed Sophie and the baby and took off after them.

"You look good holding that baby," Aunt Cathy said to Sophie. "How old is she?"

"Ten months."

"She's adorable," said Aunt Louise. "May I?"

And so the baby was passed around and bounced and tickled and cooed over—she was remarkably good-natured—and nobody asked the question they were dying to ask, which was how Sophie came to be in possession of her, and why. They understood what emergency foster care was, and they approved of it in the abstract, but they were suspicious of children who had been traumatized, as if their bad luck might be contagious, and they thought there was something freakish about people who could allow children to come and go so freely through their home.

"Don't you get attached to them?" Aunt Cathy asked.

"Just while they're here," Sophie said. "But you always have to let children go eventually, don't you?"

"Not while they're still children," Mom said.

"And so many of them," clucked Aunt Cathy. "It must break your heart every time."

"Sophie doesn't have a heart," I said meanly. "She gave it away, back in high school."

There was an awkward moment of silence, and then Sophie said, "I'm going to look at the Christmas tree," and she left the room. My aunts pursed their lips and turned their attention back to the baby.

*

When dinner was over and the dishes were done, my aunts settled at the kitchen table to play cards. Uncle Bill joined them, while the rest of my uncles unbuckled their belts and nodded off in front of the TV. Eric and I were solicited to hang around the kitchen, to watch Uncle Bill so he wouldn't cheat.

At one point there was a lull in the conversation, a rare moment of quiet, and I heard Samantha's voice coming from the dining room. I went to the doorway and peeked in.

At first I saw only Sophie. She had pulled a chair away from the table and was sitting with the baby on her lap, rocking gently from side to side. And then I saw that underneath the table, Samantha was sitting cross-legged on the floor, reading to Lacey and Jeremy. Lacey's thumb was in her mouth and her wide eyes scanned the pictures as she listened to the story of Tikki-Tikki-Tembo.

The words were familiar, of course, but I hadn't realized until this moment that I must have read the story to Samantha exactly as my father had read it to us, because I recognized his cadence and his inflections in Samantha's reading. She had reached the point in the story where little Chang, in an effort to save his brother, runs breathlessly to The Old Man With The Ladder, only to find him babbling about some drug-induced vision he's had. At this point, Sophie's voice joined Samantha's, and in unison they rendered a perfect imitation of the piteous desperation with which Dad had always delivered Chang's next line.

"'Please, Old Man With The Ladder, please help my brother out of the cold well.'"

I thought my presence was undetected, but suddenly Sophie lifted her head and looked directly at me. Her eyes were filled with tears. She stood up and walked past me into the kitchen, where she pressed the baby into Uncle Bill's arms. She stuck her feet into his boots by the back door and let herself out. My mother and her sisters exchanged looks but no one commented. Eric was leaning against the counter watching me, his eyebrows raised as if to ask what I had done, or what I was going to do.

I got my coat and went after her. I found her sitting behind the wheel of Uncle Bill's car, her face buried in her hands, sobbing. I got in on the passenger's side and sat without speaking, just waiting, thinking about nothing in particular. I didn't know why she was

293

crying, and I wasn't even curious. I felt completely detached, as if I had walked in on the final act of a play I knew nothing about.

She didn't have the keys to turn on the car or the heat, and it was cold. I rubbed my hands together, thinking about Tikki-Tikki-Tembo, all alone and freezing at the bottom of the well, waiting for his brother to bring help. He was the first and honored son, and he must have known that his brother was sometimes jealous. He must have wondered what was taking Chang so long; he must have wondered if his brother would ever come back for him at all.

As Sophie continued to sob, I found myself staring at the lock on the glove compartment, and it occurred to me that I had never known anyone who actually locked their glove compartment. I reached out and tested it, and sure enough, it was unlocked. There were no tissues, but there were a few flimsy fast food napkins, and I handed them to her. There was also a mangled pack of cigarettes and a lighter, and I set those on the dashboard.

When she finally stopped crying, Sophie blew her nose and reached for the cigarettes. She cracked the window and smoked in silence, the cold air exaggerating her plumes of smoke.

"Where's your flask?" I asked.

"I didn't bring it."

"What happened to those kids?"

She sighed. "Their father came home early, caught his wife in bed with one of his friends, and shot them both. Lacey took the baby and ran into the woods to hide. In the snow, in her pajamas and her bare feet."

I felt my throat close up. "A girl after your own heart."

"She's six, Janet." She wiped fresh tears from her eyes. "She's six years old, and her mother's dead, and her father's going to jail, and her sister will never remember any of this. It's all on her."

"What will happen to her?"

She shook her head, as if she couldn't bear to think about it.

I said, "You want to keep this one, don't you?"

"Yes."

"Have you talked to Uncle Bill about it?"

"Not yet," she said, "but you know how he is. If it were up to him, we'd keep them all. The more the merrier."

"It will change your life," I warned her.

She had composed herself, and she looked at me steadily. "Maybe my life needs a change."

"Maybe."

She said, "I miss you, Janet. Do you ever miss me?"

I didn't answer. I wasn't feeling mean enough to deny it, but I wasn't about to admit it, either, not even to myself.

I watched her put out her cigarette in the ashtray. She hadn't worn her coat, and she was shivering in the cold.

I said, "I'm stuck with you, aren't I?"

I meant this as a simple observation of fact rather than a complaint, but she got defensive.

"I know what you want, Janet. You want me to give up Bill and go away, just disappear from your life. I can't do that. I'm sorry, I know I'm being selfish, but I can't help it."

"I know."

She was shivering violently now, her shoulders hunched as she hugged herself for warmth.

"You should go back inside," I told her.

"I just wish I knew how much longer you're going to stay mad at me."

"You're the psychic, you tell me."

She sighed. She opened the car door and gave it a half-hearted push, but she made no move to get out. She appeared to be gathering her strength, and for a moment I saw exactly what she was facing: a houseful of my relatives, most of whom considered her, at best, superfluous, and at worst an intruder; Samantha and Jeremy, who adored her and who were counting on her to fix whatever was wrong between us; myself, who for the past few years had been determined to see her suffer; Uncle Bill, for whose sake she endured the rest of us, and two motherless children with no one else to cling to.

I took pity on her. I said, "I'm not as mad as I was, or at least, I'm not mad so much of the time. It comes and goes."

She nodded. "I guess it will take as long as it takes."

"I think we might be okay for now, as long as we don't try to talk about Dad. I'm not ready for that."

She nodded again. Her teeth were chattering.

"Let's go in," I said, and we got out of the car and headed for the house, Sophie clomping along in Uncle Bill's boots. I took off my coat and draped it over her shoulders.

She gave me a shy smile, and then she kissed the tips of her fingers and pressed them against my cheek. Her fingers were cold, and yet they left an impression of warmth on my skin. I was reminded of a day when Eric and I were walking through Harvard Square and all of the pigeons suddenly took flight in one great rustle of wings. One of them flew so close to me that the tip of its wing brushed my neck. Eric and I had just recently become lovers, and he made a big display of chivalrous concern for me, but the truth was that I was not at all disturbed by it. In fact, it felt lovely, like a gift, beautiful and unexpected, soft and somehow intimate, the kind of touch that you continue to feel for a long time afterward.

It felt like a blessing.

Printed in the United States
98656LV00006BA/109-144/A